The Bricks that Built the Houses

Bloomsbury USA
An imprint of Bloomsbury Publishing Plc

1385 Broadway
New York
NY 10018
USA

50 Bedford Square
London
WC1B 3DP
UK

www.bloomsbury.com

BLOOMSBURY and the Diana logo are trademarks of Bloomsbury Publishing Plc

First published in Great Britain 2016
First U.S. edition 2016

ISBN: HB: 978-1-62040-901-5
ePub: 978-1-62040-902-2

Library of Congress Cataloging-in-Publication Data has been applied for.

2 4 6 8 10 9 7 5 3 1

Typeset by Integra Software Services Pvt. Ltd.
Printed and bound in the U.S.A. by Berryville Graphics Inc., Berryville, Virginia

The Bricks that Built the Houses

Kate Tempest

BLOOMSBURY
NEW YORK • LONDON • OXFORD • NEW DELHI • SYDNEY

For my family, both blood and otherwise

For Dan Carey

For India Banks

And for south-east London

They told me that the night and day were all that I could see;
They told me that I had five senses to inclose me up;
And they inclosed my infinite brain into a narrow circle,
And sunk my heart into the abyss, a red round globe hot burning.

William Blake, 'Visions of the Daughters of Albion'

LEAVING

It gets into your bones. You don't even realise it, until you're driving through it, watching all the things you've always known and leaving them behind.

They're driving past the streets, the shops, the corners where they made themselves. Every ghost is out there, staring. Bad skin and sunken eyes, grinning madly at them from the past.

It's in their bones. Bread and booze and concrete. The beauty of it. All the tiny moments blazing. Preachers, parents, workers. Empty-eyed romantics going nowhere. Street lights and traffic and bodies to bury and babies to make. A job. Just a job.

People are killing for gods again. Money is killing us all. They live under a loneliness so total it has become the fabric of their friendships. Their days are spent staring at things. They exist in the mass and feel part of the picture. They trust nothing but trends. The most that they can hope for is a night out smashed to pieces, sloppy-faced from booze and drugs that hate them in the morning.

But here they are, leaving the stress and shit food and endless misunderstandings. Leaving. The jobcentre, the classroom, the pub, the gym, the car park, the flat, the filth, the TV, the constant swiping of newsfeeds, the hoover, the toothbrush, the laptop bag, the expensive hair product that makes you feel better inside, the queue for the cash machine, the cinema, the bowling alley, the phone shop, the guilt, the absolute nothingness that never stops chasing, the pain of seeing a person grow into a shadow. The people's faces twisting into grimaces again, losing all their insides in the gutters, clutching lovers till the breath is faint and love is dead, wet cement and spray paint, the kids are watching porn and drinking Monster. Watch the city fall and rise again through mist and bleeding hands. Keep holding on to power-ballad karaoke hits. Chase your talent. Corner it, lock it in a cage, give the key to someone rich and tell yourself you're staying brave. Tip your chair back, stare into the eyes of someone hateful that you'll take home anyway. Tell the world you're staying faithful. Nothing's for you but it's all for sale, give until your strength is frail and when it's at its weakest, burden it with hurt and secrets. It's all around you screaming paradise until there's nothing left to feel. Suck it up, gob it, double-drop it. Pin it deep into your vein and try for ever to get off it. Now close your eyes and stop it.

But it never stops.

THEY LEAVE TOWN IN a fourth-hand Ford Cortina. It's night and the city is full of itself. There is thunder in the sky. The kind of clouds that make you bow your head.

They are heading for the motorway. Leon is driving. His shirt damp with sweat, his arms sore at the wrists from gripping the wheel. He sits low down in the driver's seat but the top of his head still kisses the roof of the car. Leon is muscular, built like a fighting dog. Six foot two and light on his feet. His movements are liquid-slick. His face is screwed up with worry as he turns left down the roads he's always known and pushes the tired engine up Blackheath Hill, towards the A2 roundabout, weaving between the clattering suction of the heavy-goods lorries.

Harry's in the back, one arm stretched across the top of the seats, drumming her fingers, shifting her weight. She is small and getting smaller every second. Her little body hunched in the back of the car, her limbs splayed like the arms of a broken umbrella, jittering. She clutches the brown suitcase that rests on her lap; she grips the handle so tight its stitches are imprinted on her palm. Fear knots her shoulders and they spike together at her back like folded wings. Becky's in the front, her legs are crossed tightly, her elbows are tucked into her hips, she's biting her thumbnail. Her body is taut as a trip wire. Her features are soft and generous like the faces carved in stone on temples. Nose pierced with a shining stud. A mouth that turns up at the corners. Tall and straight-backed with a commanding presence. Her dark eyes stare at the dark road while the dark car shakes on its wheels. Becky watches the wing mirrors, noticing every movement, every fierce headlight. Harry watches the cars behind. Leon keeps his eyes on the road; if someone is coming after them, there isn't much they can do but keep going.

The car slows at a red light and Becky sees TVs blazing brightly through the windows of some flats. One man's adjusting a younger man's collar. Sorting the edges out, smiling proudly. *What am I going to do about the rent? Work?* Her thoughts are wringing their hands and pulling their hair. Kaleidoscopic slides, repeating. Pete's face, fuming. The hotel room where he set her up. She holds on to her knees. Harry is watching from the back seat. She sits forwards and reaches and finds Becky's hand and holds it. Becky looks at her lap. Her fingers look so much rounder and wider than Harry's. Her skin is tough and calloused from work. Her fingernails are bitten right down; the remnants of some bright blue varnish cling to two nails on her left hand and one on her right. She notices how soft Harry's skin is. The backs of her hands are intricately lined. Becky strokes them, squeezes Harry's fingertips. Investigating all the routes, from nail to knuckle to wrist, until her thoughts slow down.

The suitcase full of money sits fat and happy as a baby. Harry can't stop glancing down at it. Noticing its shape. Nobody has spoken in a full ten minutes. The silence is loud and getting louder.

Eventually, Leon's voice limps from his chest and staggers out of his mouth. 'Out of town? Or what? Out the country?' He hunches over the wheel, nobody answers, the seconds pulse as they pass. 'It's a mess,' he says ruefully.

Harry thinks hard, breathing carefully. 'How serious are your uncles, Becky?'

Becky sees them in her mind's eye, smiling and blood-covered. She speaks calmly, without ceremony. 'Depends what you done.' Her words smash through the floor of the car, rip the undercarriage into pieces and leave their feet exposed, skimming hot tarmac.

In the moments just before they ran off, she'd found her uncle Ron leaning down into Harry's face outside the pub and he'd looked so sinister; his snarling mouth, his finger stabbing out his words, his eyes weirdly gleeful. She'd seen his face twisted up like that once before. He'd been in the caff, out the back by the store room, and she'd only popped in to get the phone charger she'd left in the corner socket. She'd unlocked the door and walked over, and as she bent to unplug the charger, she saw her uncle through the open doorway, with a boy she didn't know who must have been about seventeen. Uncle Ron was gripping the boy by the shoulders and speaking sharply into his face. Becky couldn't hear the words, but she saw how scared the boy was; she watched her uncle take him by the throat and squeeze; she saw the colour draining from the boy's face: white then red, then darker, purple. She wondered if he was going to die. She was paralysed by the thought for a moment, fascinated by it and afraid, about to jump up and shout and stop it happening when her uncle let the kid go. The kid spluttered, rubbed his Adam's apple, tears in his eyes, and half staggered, half sprinted out the back door while her uncle walked out of eyeshot and she sat there hunched up by the power socket under the corner table, terrified, not sure what it was she had seen.

She tries to send the memory back to where it lived when it was still forgotten, but its echoes reverberate inside her skull.

'Think they know you're with us?' Leon asks Becky.

'Pete might work it out,' she says, and Pete's name hangs in the air like a shot bird, about to fall out of the sky, then, true enough, plummets softly into their laps, and sits there, warm and bleeding.

Pete.

'What a little cunt,' says Leon, with affection.

The car returns to silence. Each alone with their panic rising, falling, rising higher. The tension clogs their mouths. Becky turns in her seat to look at Harry. Her face is lit by passing street lights.

'We'll be OK.' Becky smiles and all the streets in Harry's heart are on fire, all the windows in all the houses smash at the same time. A tidal wave charges in and puts the fires out and the water floods the houses and comes pouring through the broken windows, carrying debris on its waves. Becky turns back to the window, stares at the brief white lights of the shops they pass. Seen then gone. Seen then gone. Brutal blazing flashes like someone shouting swear words in your face.

The road behind is darker than the road in front and the street is warped with memories. The routine, the working, the practising patience, the sitting with people and not saying anything. Auditions and stage lights, the pull of her muscles. Her face staring back from the lenses. The make-up and powders. The nausea like an endless empty corridor inside, hands on her knees, deep breathing backstage. Doing her hair and waiting for buses and clearing the tables. The ring of applause. The endless exhaustion. She can see it all, out on the street, getting smaller as they drive away. She opens the window and smells the storm coming up from the tarmac and spouts a gasp of laughter.

The roads are getting broader, the houses are getting bigger, fewer chicken shops now, more gastro pubs. Their city is loosening its hold. They're turning onto the motorway. On the radio, Billy Bragg is singing 'A New England'.

I

MARSHALL LAW

a year before

It's coming on for half ten and Becky is on the wrong side of the river; a part of town full of professional creatives with dreams of simpler living – radical, secret aspirations for cottages and nuclear families.

Hundreds of bodies move around each other in the upstairs room of a fashionable bar. Everybody's talking about themselves. *I'm doing this*, says everyone. *It's going great. And have you heard about this that I do, and this other thing as well, have you heard about that?* Questioning postures and emphatic responses. The air is heavy with cocaine sweat, hidden fragility and the prospect of good PR.

Becky is twenty-six years old but feels like she's on her last legs. She's leaning against the bar; all around her are monsters and slimeballs and showgirls, shouting and screaming to prove they exist. Her shoulders are squared, pulled backwards. She looks confrontational but she doesn't mean to. This is just how she stands. She is gifted with the kind of upright posture and ease in her own limbs that results in a love of movement, a fluidity of physicality that makes dancing her most primal joy. She is dark-browed, sarcastic and occasionally mean-spirited. A knife amongst all this flesh. The kind of woman who starts chaos in strangers all day.

She leans heavily, her elbow aches. Beside her in the busy room, a girl called Aisha is looking around for important people. Aisha is rich with confidence. The brutal, unnerving confidence of a twenty-one-year-old. She has, for some reason, attached herself to Becky and they have been standing together for the last half an hour. They've danced together twice before, but Becky is surprised that Aisha has stopped so long to hang out with her. She makes Becky feel old.

Becky smiles as brightly as she can for the faces that dip as they pass. Her head has been pounding for days now. A deep, sharp pound that began in the left temple and has been clawing its way across the entire circumference of her skull.

She entertains fantasies of natural disaster. Sees the people moving in the bar as if they're the remnants of a dying age. A live camera-feed of some hideous alien invasion. She stares at the faces, desperate to ascertain the flicker of a human, but all she can see are props.

On Becky's other side, an older woman is speaking to a younger man. He is morose and listening begrudgingly, dressed in the rent-a-personality uniform of obscure-band T-shirt, faded jeans and I-play-guitar leather boots. 'I *love* your songs, sweetheart,' the woman tells him. She is tall, emphasises every word with a flounce of her hands, her hair spins upwards like a coned shell and she is expensively dressed in black. 'But they're too *short*. If I was you, I'd slap a guitar solo on the end and repeat the chorus to fade.' The man looks unsure but his eyes shine as he allows himself to be persuaded. '*No one* is doing guitar solos these days,' she tells him as he runs his ringed fingers through his hair in what seems to Becky a practised gesture. Becky wonders whether she is witnessing the birth of a star. The woman traces her hand across his cheek and then jabs him in the shoulder. 'Get me ten tracks of that sort of thing and I'll get you in a room with some shit-hot A and Rs, and you'll see what happens next, OK?'

Tonight is the video launch for the Cool New Band With The Retro Feel's new single. It coincides with the launch of the lead singer's new Fashion Stroke Art range. The band are ignoring each other on different sides of the room. Their managers are giggling into each other's nostrils in the toilets.

Across the back wall of the venue, three large screens hang end to end, playing the video on a constant loop. Becky watches the screens absent-mindedly, cringing at the face she's making, the pouts you have to pull to get seen. It feels like she's watching someone else's body moving. She can see all the years she spent working on her dancing, loitering amongst the fashionistas and superbloggers. They are either skin and bone or too fat to move, drunker than everyone else, punching each other in the face with shaking hands. There was so much more she used to dream of.

'He's amazing, isn't he?' Aisha is dressed in vibrant colours. She is slender and tall and her mouth makes up two-thirds of her face. She has at least three different outfits on. Her features are striking and everything about her body is impressive. 'You're so lucky that you got to work with him,' Aisha gushes. Her voice moves up and down like a sound effect in a children's TV show signifying surprise.

'Yeah. I know. I feel, like, super blown away.' Becky finds herself mimicking Aisha's vernacular. She can see her future: the hype, the push, the rise, the braying bitterness of her peers, the mounting pressure, the slow decline, the inevitable agony of being replaced by someone more malleable, with younger cartilage and better boobs.

'What was he like?' Aisha dangles her straw in her mouth. Becky feels flirted at, a welling pound mounts in her throat.

The shoot with Marshall Law had been a nightmare. He was late to every session, and when eventually he did arrive, he spent the whole time on his phone posting photographs of himself to various online identity generators. Becky ended up having to choreograph 80 per cent of the routine because nobody knew what was going on and there was a film crew who needed something to film, even though she knew she would never be credited for the work.

'Yeah. He was really exciting,' Becky says. Dying inside. 'Really cool and exciting.' Becky has learned that, once a director is a big deal, any ideas that occur in rooms that he's in, even if they don't spring from the director's imagination, are somehow understood as being his by osmosis. Even if he didn't create the work, he 'curated' it.

'He's got such a particular style.' Aisha sighs.

Becky nods her agreement. 'Yeah. He has.' To bad-mouth him now would only make her seem bitter, and she wouldn't be listened to, and it's not worth the breath.

Becky trained at the London Contemporary Dance School. She graduated with a first-class degree six years before. Out of a class of twenty-five graduates, only four dancers got jobs and, despite finishing top of her class, Becky wasn't one of them. She tried for a year to find work but had no luck. It was hard not to be crushed by the constant judgement.

One of Becky's oldest friends was the music producer Sasha, who got lucky with some dated dubstep, all dramatic top-line vocals and shit predictable drops. It was a huge hit. Sasha asked her to dance in the video. Marshall Law was to direct it. The record label were unsure at first, but Becky rose to the challenge. Relieved to have found work, even if it wasn't the kind of work she wanted.

The video got upwards of a million views in its first two weeks online. Becky found herself with more work coming in, but all of it was commercial. She took one job after another, and the years melted. And so here she was. Bound to Marshall, bound to sexing it up behind piss-poor rappers in obvious dance routines.

'I've been asking my agent to get me on one of his shoots for AGES now, my God, you wouldn't believe . . .' Aisha laments and Becky feels her stomach weaken.

'You've got an agent?' she asks, trying to play it cool but feeling the power dynamic shift irreversibly.

Aisha glows. 'Yeah. Sure. You know Glenda Marlowe, right? She signed me up, after that thing last month, you know, at the Opera House.'

Becky's liver pulses. Blood rises in her cheeks. 'And has she been getting you work?'

'Yeah, tons. Mainly, erm, film. It's cool.' They nod at each other. Becky feels small and stumpy and unrepresented. 'She's here,' Aisha says. Pointing. Becky's smile is becoming increasingly difficult to maintain. 'She doesn't really do, like, unsolicited, you know . . .'

'Yeah, sure,' Becky agrees gravely. 'Sure.' Already so old and her body so sore from the years of despising it.

'But she's just there, I can introduce you. You never know?' Aisha tips her head to the side, twirls her straw with her tongue.

'Yeah? You could do that?'

Aisha leans across Becky's body slowly to tap her agent on the arm. Becky sees that it's the woman in black she'd been hatefully eavesdropping on.

'Glenda?' Aisha whispers. Their bodies press together and Becky feels like a pervert.

'Yes, peach?' Glenda extricates herself from the musician she had been talking to and stands before Becky now, legs parted, rocking back on her heels.

'This is Becky. She's a dancer.'

'Of course she is,' Glenda says. Fake smile, monotone.

'From the video. She's worked with Marshall.' Glenda nods at the name-drop, a little more interested.

'Hi!' Becky says. 'Lovely to meet you.' Becky goes in to kiss Glenda's cheeks, but Glenda is kissing the air around Becky's face. Becky leans in too far, and ends up planting a kiss on Glenda's neck. Embarrassed, Becky shrivels. Glenda remains blank as a page.

'Becky's looking for representation,' Aisha explains.

Glenda looks her over. 'Are you?' she says.

Becky turns her head to the side to show her profile, pushes her hand into her hip, shoulders-back tits-out wet-mouth stomach-in. 'Yeah, I think so. Things are busy, but they could be busier.'

'And where are you hoping to get to, eventually?' Glenda flattens her eyes like a striking snake.

'I'd like to do some more videos, work my way up to, eventually, a full tour with a bigger artist.'

Glenda raises her eyebrows. 'OK,' she says.

'I'd also really like to do some contemporary work, I'd love to join a company.' Glenda clears her throat, a flicker of annoyance flashes in her eyes. 'And, like, my thing is, that I want to choreograph my own pieces. I'd like to make a good living freelancing as an independent dancer who makes and performs her own work.' Her toes clench.

Glenda gazes over her head at the other people in the room. Aisha nods at nothing, mute and beautiful.

'Oh I *see*, you're an artist.' The sarcasm drips like wax from Glenda's sneering mouth. 'There's not much scope for working with an agent if you're planning on following that route,' she says, her tone patronising, her eyes bored.

Becky loses two feet in height. Looks up at the women from knee level.

Glenda's attention is caught by someone more important behind Becky's left shoulder. 'Do you want to meet Marshall?' Becky offers, trying not to seem needy. 'He's just over there.'

Glenda's smile is a wet, dark smudge. Like wine or blood, seeping outwards across her face. 'Sure,' she says. 'Let's tango.'

HARRY IS WALKING THROUGH the drizzle, watching drunk party boys in expensive clothes laughing like the camera's on them. The rain rushes through the gutters and the traffic clogs the roads. Sharp financial buildings rise like fangs in the city's screaming mouth. Harry's vision is blinkered by office blocks and advertising hoardings and high-rise new builds that make her keep her eyes low, skimming the passing bodies as girls throw their heads back and laugh horsily at nothing. She spits in the gutter and hates everybody. She sees a man on the corner she's walking towards, standing underneath the awning of a closed corner shop. A tall guy, wearing baggy jeans, limited-edition Air Force Ones, a massive parka. He's got thick, dirty hair underneath a cap with its peak tipped up almost vertical. He's selling balloons, talking loud.

'Who wants?' he's saying. 'Come on, you little terrors, come and have a go on one of these.'

Fuck's sake, Harry thinks. *It's Reggie.* A beacon in the wasteland.

'Reg!' Harry stops beside him. The rain is dripping thickly from the awning. 'You alright, Reg?'

Reggie looks at her, angry for a second to hear his real name used, and then his face bursts open into recognition. 'Harry! Fuckinell! What's going on, bruv? What ya sayin'?' Reggie throws his arms around Harry and pulls her into his chest, slapping her hard on the back.

Harry speaks into Reggie's armpit until he lets her go. 'Yeah, I'm alright, mate. You know. Same old thing.'

Reggie looks her over, holding her elbows. 'Fuckinell!! How long's it been?' He sings his words. Like always.

'Too long, mate. What you doing out here?'

'Selling nitrate, innit. Tell you what, though, I'm feeling a little wobbly to be totally honest with you, mate. I been selling acid all fucking month, I think some of it must have got through the palm of my hand or something. I'm getting fucking trails when I look at you.'

He holds Harry at arm's length and moves his head from side to side to check how his trails are doing. 'Definitely fucking something's going on, mate.' His eyes are wide as empty tunnels as he stares straight into Harry's face. He moves his heavy head slowly to either side, watching the trails as they blossom outwards. Harry moves her head with him.

'Where you staying now, you still with your mum?' she asks him.

Reggie stops moving his head and drops his arms. 'She passed away, God rest her soul.' He looks at the pavement, then at the sky. Holds his left hand over a ring he's wearing on his right index finger. Raises it to his lips and kisses it.

'I'm sorry to hear that, Reg.' Harry's voice is small and useless. She wishes there were more to say. They stand together quietly for a long moment.

'She was a fighter. That's for sure.'

'She was a lovely woman, your mum.' All over the street young men are screaming at each other and falling over. Harry feels her stomach twisting for her friend.

'I'm at my dad's now, ain't I, but he's ill. He's not well at all, mate. His ankles are all swollen bad, so I have to piggy-back him to the fucking toilet, sit with him while he shits so he don't fall off, clean him up after, pick him back up, take him back to the fucking . . . chair and that. Bed. Whatever.' Reggie nods. Clenches his jaw and raises his eyebrows. Sighs deeply and shrugs, palms stretched out, turned upwards.

'Fuckinell, Reggie.' Harry shakes her head sadly. With nothing else to do, she lights a cigarette, offers one to Reg, Reg takes one. Gets an almost full pack from his pocket and puts it away for later. Harry pretends not to notice.

'Can't even fucking . . .' He pauses, watches the trails. 'Keep a girlfriend, Harry.'

'Nothing new there then, mate.'

'I'm starting to think it must be my personal fucking hygiene.' He lifts up his arm, sniffs it deeply. 'I don't smell too bad do I, sis? You'd tell me, wouldn't you?' He moves towards Harry to get her face into his armpit.

Harry pushes him away. 'Fuck off!' she squeals. Backing away. Raising her fists. 'I ain't going nowhere near that fucking armpit.'

'Come on, Harry, help me out!' Reggie grabs hold of her by the shoulders and stuffs her face into his armpit. Harry wriggles free, Reggie grabs her again, laughing, arm raised, armpit out. Harry wrestles herself out of his hold and pretends to land a couple of digs in his belly. Reggie responds, folds over as if he's hurt. 'You killed me,' he says, bent double.

'Get up, you idiot,' Harry says, kicking him softly in the back of the leg.

They stand side by side again, smiling. Harry straightens her hair as best she can. When it's loose it hangs down to her shoulders and sticks out at the sides. It's corkscrew curly. She wears it pulled up at the back, but bits of it always wiggle free and spark off in different directions.

'Don't worry, babe, your hair looks lovely.'

'Fuck off, you prick,' Harry says, and she carries on sorting her hair out.

Reggie looks at the rain falling, speaks with a gravelly throat. 'She left me again, didn't she? I don't blame her. It's the hours. She wants me to stop going out all the time. But this is how I'm living, know what I mean?'

'Tell me about it, mate.' Harry wraps an arm around herself, dips her head towards her cigarette and sucks its smoke up, staring at her work shoes. Scuffed and bland and brown.

'You got a girlfriend, Harry?'

The neon sign above them, illuminated with the legend *Casablanca Mini Market*, begins to flicker. The low-level street roar seems to rise in Harry's ears for a moment. A motorbike revs its engine as it passes.

'Me? No,' she says, frowning. 'No.'

'Boyfriend then?'

'Keep dreaming, Reg.'

Reggie laughs. Stretches his back out, stretches his neck.

'Shit though, innit, eh? Not having one.'

Harry turns towards him, squinting a little.

'Well, you look alright, Reg. You look happy.'

'I'm always happy, mate, can't keep a good dog down. Can you?' He shouts at the street, 'CAN YOU?' The street ignores him. He laughs. 'Fuck 'em. What you doing up here anyway?'

'Ah just some work thing. Some do.'

'What is it you do again?' Reggie's weighty frame towers beside Harry. They look like a pair of unlikely cartoon friends, a bear and a mouse. The people surge past them in a babbling, viscous current.

'I'm in recruitment.'

'That's right. Recruitment. How's that going?'

'It's good, yeah. It's steady.' Traffic goes past blaring bass. They watch the rain fall. Harry smokes in sharp blasts.

'Look, Reg,' she says quietly, 'I'm really sorry to hear about your mum.'

'Don't worry about me, mate. I got her ring here.' Reggie's chin is scrawled with stubble, his long hair sticks to his forehead beneath his cap. He lifts the peak with one hand and pushes his hair back with the other, then readjusts it, tilting it so that it lifts at just the right angle, up towards the falling rain. He brings his hand up to eye level, palm towards the street. They look at the ring, dancing there in the grim blue night. 'I wear it now, she always told me to keep fighting and that.' The ring is chunky, made up of seven or eight gold plaits woven together, and it shines in the street light.

Harry sways with the force of her feelings, dwarfed by sudden grief, and the guilt of knowing life goes on. She reaches out and slaps Reggie on the back gently. She leaves her hand there for a moment before bringing it back to her side. 'How are the kids and that?' she asks breezily.

'No, they're good, yeah. Fit and healthy, pair of angels. They're with their mum.' Reggie grins and shows the gold in his teeth. As his smile widens Harry sees the wormy pink scar that cuts him cheek to neck as it fattens and elongates, before settling back into the shadows of his scrubby beard. She remembers the night it happened, feels herself pulled towards it.

'How old are they now?'

'Michael's seven and Rochelle's fourteen this May.'

'Fuckinell,' Harry whistles.

'Tell me about it.'

'Flies by.'

'That it does, Harry,' Reggie agrees sadly.

They stand and feel the time flying by them.

'Listen,' Reggie says, brightening up, 'you want any Mandy, any gear?'

'I'm OK, thanks, mate. I'm alright.' Harry straightens up. Puffs on her cigarette.

'Sure? I'll sort you out. You know I got the good stuff, innit?'

'I'm all good. Thanks though.'

Reggie kicks at the floor. 'Suit yourself.' The street is packed with people going to bars, leaving bars. Coming out of the station. Packed like a clogged artery. 'I'm telling you. Nitrate, mate. The kids love it. It's a fucking festival round here. Look at the state of it. Pissing it down with rain, look at this lot. It's a fucking dream round here. I'm out most nights doing this, get back to the old man later, make sure he's alright.'

As if on cue, a young guy walks up, gurning. 'How much the balloons, mate?'

'Fiver each or three for a tenner.'

'Wicked. I'll take six, please, mate.'

Reggie raises his eyebrows at Harry.

'Look Reg, I better get on.'

'Alright then, girl. Lovely to see you. Watch out for the chem trails. Don't drink the tap water.'

Harry nods. 'See you later, mate. Look after yourself now, won't you?' She smiles warmly as she turns her collar up and walks away. The rain gathers in the curls of her hair, the other hand cups her cigarette in the downpour.

She is wearing her work clothes. A dark navy suit that hangs strangely on Harry like all clothes do. Her white shirt is tucked in, her trousers hang a little too loose on her waist. Her skinny frame cuts through the crowded street and her coat billows in the wind of passing buses. She pulls it around her and does up the buttons. She looks sharp. She moves in confident strides. Feet fast, she takes long steps. She is all London: cocksure, alert to danger, charming, and it flows through her. Reggie's face repeats on all the strangers she passes and her eyes prickle and she blinks hard. She sees a homeless woman sat with her head on her knees by the cash machine outside Tesco Express; her upturned hands are red with bulbous sores. The woman looks up as Harry slows her pace and Harry's hand goes to her pocket. They look at each other. Harry sees that the woman is much younger than she'd thought at first. A teenager. But her face is all cracked and lined. Scars and spots and dirt creep across her skin, but her eyes are strong and clear. There is no fear in them, Harry notices, just exhaustion.

'You alright?' Harry asks.

'Cold.' The woman's voice is quiet. 'Hungry.'

Harry looks up and down the street at life carrying on all around them, her heart kicking. 'How much you need for a hostel?'

'Twelve quid.' She shields her eyes from the rain. 'Spare me a fag, please?' the girl asks, nodding at the butt smoking in Harry's fingertips.

Harry gives her a cigarette and pushes a couple of £20 notes into her hand. 'Look, don't spend it on smack, alright?' The girl flinches a little. 'Get into a hostel for a night or two. Get some food. Will you do that?' Harry says desperately. The girl doesn't answer, just looks at the notes in her hand, and after a couple of heartbeats, Harry walks off, dizzy. Guilt unfurling inside her. Shaken by sadness. *If I could do more, I would.*

Her feet land lightly as she sways like a boxer down the road. Full of the swagger of knowing there's work to be done. The city's not going to get her like it got the others. She knows it. She nods at the thought. Ducking and weaving, she passes through the teeming crowds. She runs across the road, through the traffic, the rain falls against her face, music blares from bars and people shout to be heard as they walk side by side. She steps over puked-up kebab meat and dropped chips and bops on, invisible.

Harry enters a bar she's not been to before. She surveys the room, watches the people forcing a good time out of their tired, broken hearts. She feels someone looking at her, turns and sees Leon in the crowd, walking up some stairs at the back.

Leon is her best friend and her business partner. He watches everything; he can see the move before it's made, bristling in secret corners. The agreement is that Harry handles sales, Leon handles everything else. They never work apart. It's a good system. Both partners know their roles and respect each other's talents. For the most part, they love their jobs.

All these fucking people, doing all this fucking Charlie just to feign interest in what other people say.

A man roars in exaggerated jubilation. Harry flinches. She thinks about Reggie, standing out there on the street selling balloons to sixteen-year-olds. That homeless girl sitting on plastic bags in the rain.

She takes her coat off, a sharp navy trench coat, waterproof and well cut. A designer brand but creased and wrinkled, slicked with rain. She hands it to the smiling man in the cloakroom, along with her suit jacket. He gives her a ticket, she reads it: 111. *Of course*, she thinks. Although the number holds no relevance for her whatsoever.

She heads to the bathroom. As she walks in she is greeted by the usual double takes as the women washing their hands wonder whether she is male or female. It only lasts a moment, but it happens all the time. Harry is a boyish woman who swaggers when she walks. Her body is angular and she wears men's clothes. Her face is soft, a woman's face, but she sets it in a scowl when she's working. She smiles at the women; they look down at their hands or concentrate on their eyelashes in the mirror. Harry checks her clothes, stares at her face. Her pupils retract in the brightness of the bathroom light. *I don't answer to no one.* All the violence that she's seen whips her in the chest and throws her against the cubicle doors. That night when Reggie got his scar. The night Tony fell off the roof of that party and died in the street, all broken. The blood on her clothes after Leon had finished with the man who followed her out of the club. The violence is smashing its hands across her face. Her head is stuffed in the gap between the toilet and the cubicle wall and the violence is standing above her, drawing its hand back. *You're doing it,* she tells herself. *You're doing it, Harry.* She adjusts her collar, does up the top button. Smart as a tack.

A low heat draws them closer, it surges under the floorboards. It maps a route and pulls their feet across the party.

Becky, Aisha and the agent are heading to the corner of the room; the curtains are trimmed with gold. The lampshades are antique. The carpet is dark red. People paw the floor like bulls. Becky looks carefully into each face, remembering to smile. She is kissed on upturned cheeks by men she doesn't recognise.

'Hiya,' she says, flashing her teeth. 'How's things?'

Harry scans the floor for her clients; the affable fun-seekers who like to have more than they need. One big shot and three lesser specimens have requested her presence this evening. Plus, the aristocratic twins who dress in rags and take more drugs than customs. So it should be an earner. Seeing no one she knows, she walks the perimeter and lingers with a group of people who are standing in a circle around a talking man. She is handed a cocktail she doesn't understand, made with spirits she's never heard of, poured into a glass she's not sure how to hold, and she begins drinking it quickly, the ice hitting her teeth with each fast swig.

Becky keeps looking back over her shoulder at Glenda to nod and smile and then she stops, victorious, next to a group assembled breathlessly around a man dressed head to toe in yellow velour.

'Marshall Law,' Becky whispers proudly into Glenda's ear. Glenda eats her own body in ravenous chomps, vomits herself all over the floor at Marshall's feet and gazes up at the underside of his chin.

'Oh of course. I mean, of course.' Marshall nods deeply at no one in particular. 'I mean, I was in Indonesia and I saw him, just pulling a fishing boat up from the sea, bare feet, wet shorts, you know, very Mowgli, and I just thought wow, what *beauty*. Because he is, isn't he? I mean, it's not the photographs, is it? In this case at least, it's *him* that's so captivating. You know? So *real*!'

Becky's heart punches itself out of her chest and runs screaming through the room, smearing blood all over the walls. She looks down, bemused and studies the new hole in her chest. For years she has been smiling in all the right parties and standing neutral in audition rooms, listening attentively to directors like this one. She is sick of it. Her throat is sore and dry and there is a burrowing mole clawing soil in her head.

She looks around the group at the others in the circle. And her eyes jar on a woman opposite, caught like a socked foot on an upturned nail. Snagged. She looks away but finds that she is being drawn back to the woman. Some ancient thing that tugs and hurts and pleases Becky. She can't get her eyes back. They're staying put. The woman's sweet, and tough-looking. Dignified and scruffy, distant. Becky nurtures an endless soft spot for awkward queer women like this one. She notices her crooked teeth. Her springy hair. Her furrowed brow. All the parts are singing, separate lines that soar together, cheekbones high and delicate, hawky little nose, small bright eyes, set deep in her face, powerful. Something about her. Composed and definite like she knows herself. Her brow is creased in confusion. She's squinting like her vision's bad at Marshall.

Harry feels the prickle of attention, looks over, sees a woman she doesn't recognise watching her. Even just a glimpse is blinding. The woman shines so hard in Harry's eyes. She explodes out of herself like a fireball. Brighter and brighter. Electric and surging, her outline ripping the party like lightning, forking and searing and flashing, shining like sunlight on water reflecting back on itself and becoming heat. A fierceness about her. Shining so golden and yellow-hot, black fire, burning blue in her middle. A new sun blistering bright. Harry blinks, gathers her body parts up from the corners of the room and pieces them back together again. She raises her eyebrows in the direction of Marshall, heaving a pantomime sigh. Becky laughs behind her hand and doesn't look away. Harry's movements become rigid and strange. She looks at the floor for as long as she can, and then back up to see that the woman is still looking. She is standing there, tough and unimpressed. Dark complexion, rich soft skin. Harry sees it all, like sudden wounds opening in her chest. Burned entirely. She lifts her head and watches her out of the corners of her eyes and, as they look one another over, the low heat that brought them closer passes between them. Harry feels herself standing taller on her legs, her ears ringing, her eyes burning from the sudden brightness.

A sulky little man with flowers in his hair appears beside Becky and leads Marshall off across the room. Everyone in the circle follows behind like bridesmaids, entranced, including Aisha and the agent, until only Becky and Harry are left, stunned in the aftermath, staring around like it's the morning at a rave. Harry wants to reach for her hand and take it and see what happens. But there is no part of her that would actually allow her to do that, and so she drains her glass in a fast gulp and reaches for another from the smiling tray-bearer who appears beside her.

'Interesting man,' Becky says, following Marshall and his disciples with her eyes.

Harry watches the top of Marshall's head as he sashays across the room. 'I was interested,' she says, 'definitely.' Becky hears the familiar accent of home: south-east London's curving vowels and glottal stops. 'You in the band?'

'No, I'm a dancer. I was in the video.'

Harry is impressed. Looks at Becky with wide eyes. 'A dancer, yeah? What kind of stuff?'

'All kinds.' She brushes over it.

'You in a company or something?'

Becky looks at Harry strangely. 'No. Not at the moment. Just videos and telly stuff.'

'You enjoy it?' Harry watches her face. Some lonely distant thing behind the smile.

Becky nods. 'Yeah, it's really cool . . .' She heaves a deep sigh. One hand goes up to her hairline, strokes her forehead a couple of times and drops back down again. 'What about you?' Becky drinks, watches Harry over the top of her glass. 'You work with these lot then?'

They look around at all the cackling crotch-hungry monsters. Throwing their heads back.

'Yeah.' Harry nods. 'I'm in recruitment, I work with a couple of guys from the record label.'

'Lucky you.' Her sarcasm is well practised. It lives deep in the tissue of her language.

Harry also knows the code. 'Yes,' she says wearily, 'lucky me.'

A fat hand lands on Harry's shoulder and pulses there, leech-like. 'Harry!' a man says. 'Lovely to see you, sweetheart.'

Harry looks round. 'Julian,' she says, and an awkward silence descends on the three of them. Julian grins into it, begins to guide Harry away towards the corner of the room, Harry looks from Julian to Becky and digs her feet in, pulls him back. Stands her ground.

Julian, confused, smiles at Harry and lifts his hand. 'Harry?'

'It's OK,' Harry says, mouth dry. 'She's a friend.'

Becky feels pride swimming through her, pausing at the shallow end to shake its hair and flex its muscles.

Harry, allowing herself a rare departure from routine, looks briefly around her as she takes four chunky wraps from the pouch attached to the inside of her waistband and, in one subtle movement, presses them into the fat-handed man's palm. So swift it is almost invisible. They shake hands. Vigorous. Friendly. The cash in Julian's palm is transferred to Harry's pouch. The man sends his froggy eyes over Harry's body, and then over Becky's. Harry's heart is thumping hard as marching troops.

Becky watches the exchange like it's a piece of immersive theatre. Wondering what she is meant to be discerning from it.

'Friend of Harry's?' Julian asks her, his bloated face bobbing.

'Yeah,' Becky says, looking away from him.

'Lovely, just lovely. What a picture.' He grins. Flashbulb wink. He nods enthusiastically. Sniffing and swallowing and jerking his face around. His voice is a bellow. As if he has never known shyness. He roars. 'AND AND AND AND HOW ARE YOU, HARRY? HOW'S THINGS? YOU LOOK WELL, DON'T YOU? YOU LOOK VERY WELL.' He looks her up and down, sniffing loudly, huge darting eyes, lips moving faster than the words they're trying to say, brain pulsating almost visibly through his skull.

Harry smiles patiently at him, talks slowly. 'I'm fine, thanks, Julian. Getting by, you know. Getting on.'

'Oh that's great to hear, that's great.' He spits as he talks, brittle flecks explode from his Ss. 'OK, well. My drink's getting cold.' He forces two stabs of laughter out of his gullet and then waves, winks and staggers fatly away.

'Bye,' says Becky in a monotone, watching him walk off. She looks at Harry, who swallows nervously. Julian's back is bustling noisily towards the toilets.

Harry feels Becky's eyes on her, glances up, then away.

'Your name's Harry?' Becky asks her.

'Uh huh.' Sirens howl in Harry's ears. Why did she just do that? She looks around for Leon: no sign of him. She raises a hand to her temple, pushes her thumb in.

'As in, Harriet?'

'Nope.' Harry shakes her head, smiling at the woman, in spite of herself. 'As in Harry.'

'Fair enough.' Becky watches her closely, like a child with a caught beetle. 'You smoke, Harry?' she asks.

'Yep.' Harry holds the back of her neck, leans into her hand.

'Wanna go for one?'

They walk towards the smoking patio, out through the double doors at the back of the room. The air's cold. The city's twinkling all over the place. Becky lights a cigarette. Breathes in. Loves blowing smoke into cold night air. Takes another puff but it doesn't feel the same.

'You don't look like a drug dealer,' she says simply, a smile at the corner of her mouth.

Harry's eyes pop at the words. She rubs her jaw and laughs a quick breathy laugh. She leans in closer and speaks low, checking around her. She speaks nonchalantly. Acts natural, but her palms are damp and her legs are shaking. 'What do drug dealers look like?'

'You know what I mean.'

They sit close together on a concrete bench next to a large flowerpot. There's a tall heating lamp above them and every five or six minutes it turns itself off and then someone has to lean over them to press the switch again. Hardly a private place. Harry notices all the groups of people laughing loudly at each other; she can hear them talking, she wonders if they can hear her.

'Is it a tough job then? For a woman, I mean?'

Harry decides that they can't hear her. She feels judders of electricity in her face and hands.

'No more than any other job.' She looks at the end of her cigarette. 'No tougher than being a dancer.'

'How long you been doing it?' Harry screws her face up in discomfort. Becky pushes her leg. 'What?!' she says. 'I'm not the fuckin' police!'

Harry takes a puff, holds it in, blows it out. 'Ages,' she says. 'All my life, pretty much.'

'How'd you get into it?'

Harry taps her feet a few times, leans back. In all the years of showing up at parties like this, she has never locked eyes with a woman and sat down and discussed the ins and outs of her trade. Never. Not once. Usually, she turns up when she's needed, does what she has to do and then she leaves without speaking to anyone. Invited by clients, she walks in smiling, makes her trades and then it's off to the next one. Sometimes she stays longer, if the client is somebody she likes. But she never tells *strangers* what she does. Why did she just give Julian the chop like that, standing next to this woman? Her heart is swaying like a pendulum. She feels someone looking over. She lifts her eyes and finds Leon staring with his eyes narrowed. She waves him away with a shake of her head. He watches her, puzzled. She looks away from him pointedly, and when she looks back to where he was standing she sees with some relief that he's not there any more.

Becky looks at Harry, and thinks she has the physicality of someone who is desperate to escape themselves; she is constantly adjusting unruly strands of hair or pulling at her clothes and she is riddled with the haunted, shy defiance of a woman born with all the bits adding up to the wrong amount. Becky recognises this in her. Watches her with interest, thinks about what it must be like to be a dealer and so small. Wonders if it's dangerous. Imagines Harry running; she looks like she can run fast.

Harry feels a whirling pressure mounting between them. If she was smoother or more confident or male she might have the nerve to lean in and kiss this girl. But as it is she rubs her face with a clumsy hand and stretches her legs out and crosses them at the ankles. She never knows if girls are coming on to her or just being friendly. She never knows. She always feels creepy for assuming. She sweeps the patio again for

Leon or for a client wandering over, but seeing no one she recognises, she shifts on the bench and looks into Becky's face for as long as she can without going blind. Which is about a quarter of a second.

'I have a plan,' she says, 'that I'm working towards.'

Becky waits for more.

'Go on then,' Becky urges, waving her cigarette in the air like a conductor with her baton.

'Go on then, what?' Harry asks, laughing.

Becky rolls her eyes, looks away. 'You're no fun.'

'What's your name?' Harry asks her.

'Becky.'

'Becky.' Harry repeats it to herself. Logging it. Someone leans over and pushes the heater switch. They lean forwards together, ducking the arm that leans in, then backwards again. 'What about you? How long you been dancing?'

'Same, all my life.'

Harry finishes her cigarette, stubs it out carefully, places it on the floor, neatly, next to the leg of the bench. Becky flicks hers towards the corner of the patio; the little bulb blooms as it soars through the air. They sit in silence, listening to the party roaring.

'So, is it always parties like this?'

Harry sways on the bench, knocked by the confidence of this woman.

'I shouldn't even be talking to you,' she says quietly, looking away. 'I don't know you, do I? You could be CID. Or fucking . . . you could be working for anyone.' Harry holds her knees. Eyes darting.

'Yeah, but I'm not though,' Becky says. 'I'm obviously not.' Harry watches her closely. 'It's alright. Keep your hair on. You don't have to tell me anything. I was just trying to make conversation. I'll keep it to myself next time.' Becky looks away, at the people standing round. Her hair, almost black, has the remnants of a dyed redness running through it and when she moves, Harry sees the redness and is drawn towards it. She leans back, crosses her legs.

'Tell you what.' Harry's heart is rolling up its sleeves.

'What?'

'I'll tell you all about it.' She pauses, holds the moment, watches strands of Becky's hair ripple in the wind. 'But you have to tell me something first.'

'Like what?' Becky leans back on to her hands.

'Don't know. Something you don't tell people?'

'Fine,' she says simply.

'Yeah?'

'Why not?' She flicks her hair and glances around, keeps her eyes elsewhere as she talks. 'The dancing don't pay so well. It's not regular income and it's crazy hours. So . . .' She drinks. Harry watches her throat pulse as she swallows. 'I work as a masseuse.' The word lasts a long time in Becky's mouth. 'You know, a *masseuse*.' She shrugs. 'It's the same deal as your job really, no one knows. Except I don't have a massive chip on my shoulder about it like you seem to.'

It hits Harry like a thrown brick. Knocks the wind out of her for a moment and she hiccups as she draws smoke in. She plays it cool. 'No one knows?'

'Nope. Well, a couple people know, obviously. But mainly I keep it to myself. Less hassle that way.' Harry stares at her, eyebrows raised; Becky looks back, bold and unflinching. 'So don't worry. I can keep a secret.' Harry's blood starts pumping the other way round her body. 'Now you,' Becky says gently.

Harry looks up for Leon, sees no one, checks around her for the others on the patio and begins to speak softly, which pulls Becky closer towards her.

'Well. OK,' she says. 'OK.' She psychs herself up for it. 'So. I go round offices uptown, all, like . . . pre-arranged.' She measures her words as she speaks, her voice is low, slow and gradual. A soft lisp curls up from the ends of her words. Becky studies the body she sits beside. Legs apart, shoulders back, but still girlish, somehow. 'Fucking media firms, literary agencies – I got a *diary*. We have *meetings*. You believe it, Becky? Coz that's the truth of it.'

They have turned themselves towards each other, Harry's knees touch in the middle like two oars. She feels like she's at the crest of a ravine, tipping downwards. She breathes out through a weak smile.

'I mean, I get phone calls from secretaries of company directors. I go in, like, we have a coffee, talk about the weather, then, like, I give them a load of gear. Eleven thirty in the morning, right in the centre of town! And then on to the next one. I could probably start doing bank transfers, make it all legit. Register as a sole trader. Taxes too. Coz it's booming. It really fucking is. It's fucking *booming*!'

She pauses, stares into Becky's face.

'Meant to be a recession on, right? I never sold so much gear! I never sold so much fucking gear in my life!' Harry throws her hands up in disbelief. Lets them land gently in her lap. She checks around her. Lowers her voice. 'I'm unthreatening, aren't I, punctual. You know, *female*. So. No danger. They recommend me to their accountant mates, and then the accountant mates recommend me to their art-dealer mates, and then the art-dealer mates recommend me to their film-director mates. And that's how come I'm here.'

Becky plays with her earring, leaning in towards her new friend, focusing on her mouth as the words come out. Harry dries up.

'Can I have some then?' Becky asks.

'Have some what?'

'Go on,' she says.

'You want some gack?' Harry furrows her eyebrows.

'Yeah, go on. Is that alright? I'll buy it?'

'Buy it? No way.' Harry shakes her head, she lifts her shirt slyly and takes a wrap from a pouch in the waistband of her trousers. Becky glimpses the softness of her stomach, the sharp kiss of her hip bone, the stretch of her side as she reaches. She puts a decent gram into Becky's hand. Becky widens her eyes in thanks, opens it in her palm like a seasoned pro, takes a little bump out with the edge of her lighter. Sniffs it up.

Harry watches her. *Fucking hell*, she thinks. She'd only had a couple of those cocktails, hadn't she? What had she even been saying? Becky purses her lips in concentration, discreetly arranging another bump. She sniffs it, nonchalant. Arranges one for Harry. Nobody notices. Expertly done. Harry leans over, sniffs. *Kiss*. The slope of her neck. *All over. Kiss her all over*. The coke is nice. Sobers her up. She tilts her head back. Breathes in and out. Soon now, she'll be back to normal.

'I'm trying to raise enough capital to buy premises and start a business, you know what I mean?' Harry nods at the seriousness of the statement.

'What kind of business?'

'It'll be a restaurant and café and a bar, so that it pays for itself. But also it will be, like, a community centre. There'll be workshop space. You know, it'll be a place for people to go. To relax and hang out and learn things.' Her eyes skirt around as she talks, she bounces a little in her seat, sitting up straight, seeing it. 'We'd do classes there, for young people, get them cooking healthy food on a budget, and, like, cooking meals for OAPs' – she pulls her words out of the air with her fingers – 'and then, right? They'd all eat the meals together, young and old, build relationships back up in the community, that was my thinking, and you know, gigs, we'd have gigs there, and a recording studio too. It's . . .' Her batteries flicker and die. She winds down. 'I got a big plan.'

Becky starts laughing. 'That's why you're selling coke? To finance a community centre?'

Harry is embarrassed.

'What?' Her voice is small. 'What you laughing at?'

'No, not at you. Just. Funny.' Becky stops laughing, shakes her head. Looks around the balcony at the cool kids with their cool hair, all stardom and boredom, and then back at Harry, tiny frame bunched up like a scribble, gripping her hands together, furrowed brow, eyes like smashed diamonds. 'Good for you,' she says. 'Robin Hood.'

'Are you taking the piss?'

'What do you think?'

'I can't tell.'

'What will it be like?' she asks.

Harry leans forwards, sees it as she starts to describe it. 'Well, in my head . . . I think of it like a kind of 1940s New York type of place, I suppose, dance floor and a stage, loads of space and light and everything done up all nice, tables in front of the stage. Dunno, have you seen the movie *GoodFellas?*'

'No.'

'Well, I watched it a lot growing up. There's this bar one of the guys takes his girlfriend to in that film, and it's, like, I dunno. Maybe that's where this all started.'

'I never seen it.' Becky sniffs twice. Mind drifting.

Harry could float off the bench she feels that light. She uses her hands to punctuate every word that explodes out of her. 'I tell you what it is, right? I'm sick of the way that if you're from where we're from, you're not supposed to want nice atmosphere and good people and conversation. As if all we want is shit beer and silence, beans and chips and fucking scratch cards. Now, don't get me wrong. I do like scratch cards, and beans and chips, and silence, come to that, but my point is, I want to open up a place where couples would come, and families, and groups of mates, all different kinds of people. Do you know what I mean? A nice place that isn't some stupid posh eatery that charges twelve quid for a breakfast. A lovely place that makes people feel welcome. A space for people to meet. We're lonely. We're so lonely in this city. We need places to go, I think. I don't . . .' Harry breaks off, looks for Leon, but there's never any sign of him until he wants to be seen. She looks back to Becky, earnest, it's all coming out, *fuck it*. Good coke.

Even though Harry seems tough, Becky sees that she's gentle in her manner, and far too kind for the work she does. 'You've got to do it,' Becky tells her, watching her eyes.

Harry's face floods with gratitude. 'I really want to.'

They look out over the city. Someone reaches over them to push the heater switch again. They duck and straighten up. Harry looks behind them, back through the double doors, into the bar at someone else's dream. The attractive bar staff wishing they weren't there, everything dark and red and antique, but no soul in any of it. All of it just a clever idea dreamed up by some savvy bunch of business people, seeing a trend and throwing their money at it. Everything, from the drinks they serve to the colour on the toilet walls, all cleverly done to keep certain people out and get certain people in. It makes Harry sick to her stomach. The way London's changing. And not just this side of the river, either. It's changing down south. She hardly recognises it these days. It's heartbreaking. She lets her mind wander down its favourite path: *Harry's Place*. The detail of the tiles on the bathroom walls, the smiles of the barmen, the colour of the light against the cymbals on the stage, the singer swaying, eyes closed, meaning it. Really fucking meaning it. None of this soulless on-trend bullshit. None of these jumped-up little 1960s throwbacks thinking they're doing something groundbreaking because they got a blowjob in a dressing room once. No. Not at her place. She can see it. A couple at a table watching the singer with their skin tingling. An image of herself, older, smiling, leaning over the bar to embrace a friend. *Nice to see you, pal.* Full of colour and light and people, real people, eating well, and dancing and laughing with each other, and drinking and happy. Doing classes, learning languages, an allotment out the back for growing veg. *Harry's Place*.

'I've never told anyone that,' she says, reaching down to scratch her ankle, her words sticking together. 'Not really, not like that.' She hangs her head, looks through her pockets for something she can fiddle with. Finds her cigarette box. Starts flipping it over in her hand.

Back inside, the people around them are hysterical, bent double, breath coming out like air from punctured lilos. Everyone's beautiful and standing in groups or talking earnestly in couples or striking power poses. They move aside for a small, sharp-featured man, wilting beneath a thick forest of champagne glasses. His hair is blow-dried into a puff. Becky thinks to herself that he looks like a TV newswoman from the early 90s. His eyes are red at the edges and his toy waistcoat is too big for him. He offers them the champagne without making eye contact. They thank him and take two glasses each, but he doesn't acknowledge anything about the exchange, he just falls back into the crowd.

Becky spins her glass around in her hand, body turned towards Harry. 'I go to these weird business hotels on the outskirts of town in the middle of the night. Slough or fucking New Malden.'

'Erith.'

'Right.'

'Reading borders.'

Becky laughs. 'Exactly. Mostly it's just strange business travellers who work in printing or sales or something so boring they don't even know how to explain it, and they spend their lives in airports and hotels and boardrooms and haven't been touched in weeks, or months, or even fucking years. Haven't been *touched* by a human being in months. Or they feel so far away from their wives that it's easier for them to pay a stranger to touch them.' She pauses, turns her glass again, looks at Harry, 'So, I go, and I give them a massage. And I enjoy it too—'

Harry can't work it out. Troubled, she interrupts. 'But, wait though, what is it? I mean, like, what do you *do*?'

Becky thinks it over, fiddles with her earring. 'I touch them,' she says simply, 'with my body and my hands.' She looks at Harry, smiles a little. 'It can be really beautiful,' she says, shifting on the bench. 'And yeah, sometimes, like, if you get someone looking at you like you're a piece of meat, it's . . .' She screws her face up, frowns and shakes her head. Mimes the feeling of cringing. 'You know?' Harry nods that she's listening. 'It's pretty rare that the guy looks at you that way, but it does happen, if he's loaded or something usually, if it's like a really rich guy he acts like a prick, treats you like shit. But most guys are cool, they're very respectful.' She shrugs into the silence at the end of her words. Harry swallows champagne too fast; she's not used to it, and the bubbles burn her nose. 'I don't have a problem with it, but other people get all high and mighty about it, you know what people are like.'

'Yeah.' Harry's head is spinning. She's pissed. She tries to stop her body from swaying without her telling it to.

'It's honest work,' Becky says, watching Harry's face for a sneer. Seeing none, she continues. 'Obviously, I do it for the money. But also, I love it. And where I want to do less of *this* kind of work . . .' She indicates the room with a sweeping hand. Harry follows the gesture, takes in the pouting, fawning desperation. 'I couldn't even make that choice without the massage work to support me.' Harry listens earnestly. Hums that she gets it. 'But still, I don't tell anyone what I do.' Becky stares at her and Harry twitches in the beam of it. 'I've not told anyone actually, in ages. Just a couple of my mates know and that's it.' Harry nods, dumb as a cake, her heart beats like techno. 'And now you.' Becky's mouth twitches with the cocaine. She tilts her chin towards the ceiling as she talks. 'Sometimes it is a bit like it's all happening to a different person though. Still *you*, but just . . . different.'

'Like you got two lives. And which one's real? Which one's actually the life that you're living?' Harry's voice is rising, her eyes wide. Becky stares at her, not smiling, more peering into her face. Listening. 'It does my head in sometimes. You know what I mean?' Becky reaches out a definite hand and touches Harry's earlobe. She holds it, strokes it a couple of times, then takes her hand away just as abruptly, her attention caught by a man dressed in tight white denim who tiptoes past them clutching a mannequin to his chest; the mannequin has unblinking blue eyes painted onto it and it stares at them as it's carried past.

The music is loud, there are more people at the bar now and it's pushing them closer; behind them Marshall Law is throwing his head back, screaming.

'Darling!! If you've never fingered a schoolgirl at a train station you've never lived. Honestly. Their little lips, their little hot tongues. It's like they think you were born to please them. Little minxes. It's outrageous, darling, it really is, but I mean it, that's the next big thing, it is! Real schoolgirls, real train stations. Sixteen, of course. Picture it: rural, deserted train stations. Mud on her knees. Honestly, darling, so sensual, isn't it? Just thinking of it.'

Harry feels all yanged up. She's rushing, her throat's hard, she can't breathe fast enough. Inside her brain is hot and tense. It's been a while since she's gone near the stuff, and she can't work out quite how she managed to say so much to this woman. Her mind begins to glitch, the last bump wearing off, the shine dulling and the party revealed in all its boredom. She jerks her head round as two women come bustling through the crowd. Harry thinks they're going to walk past, but they stop right beside them.

'Becky! We're bored,' they sing out together. One is slight and giggly, straight shoulder-length hair, the same pale blonde as her skin. Her clothes are perfectly neat and tidy, she wears trousers that stop before her ankles and pastel-coloured Nike Air Max, the large hoops in her ears shine the same shine as her tooth enamel under the bright lights. Her companion is softer-faced, fuller in her body, taller too. She moves with a swing in her strut, self-assured and haunting because of it. Tight black trousers and a baggy black T-shirt. Gold-and-black Adidas Superstars. Gold rings kiss each knuckle. A gold cannabis leaf hangs on a chain around her neck and her ears are studded with gold Wu-Tang W earrings. Harry can feel them making their appraisal of her and she shrinks before their femininity and evident close friendship.

She touches the scar on her forehead, two small lines that cross and make a diamond on the left up by her hairline, from a swung bat when she was twelve. It tells her to stay focused, while all around her the bellowing pillow-soft faces smudge and shriek and wobble.

The smaller of the two is Charlotte, the deeper is Gloria. They seem to appear out of nowhere and they swing their arms around Becky's shoulders and talk at the same time. Charlotte is brimming with the kind of confidence that shy people get when they're drunk.

'This is shit now,' she says. 'Let's go?'

Gloria joins in. 'Yeah, I think it's time. Can we go?'

Becky turns from Harry and faces them, grinning warmly. 'Hi! Yeah, we can go. You two alright?'

'Yeah.' Charlotte leans towards Becky, delivers her words like a bird pecking crumbs off the floor. 'I'm well pissed and all these men are gay anyway. Or psychopaths. So . . .'

Gloria looks at Harry, sees her standing there, mournful with shyness, reeling from all her confessions.

'Hi,' Gloria says. Looking down at her.

'Alright?' Harry smiles at the two women, mouth dry.

'It was good to meet you.' Becky talks right into her face, eyes shining, with Charlotte hanging from her side.

Harry nods her agreement. Becky leans in and kisses Harry's cheek slowly, close to the mouth. Half her lips touch Becky's like it's no big deal. Harry's face is on fire, the flames are rising and obscuring her view. She tries to act natural.

'See you later then,' she says, keeping her tone as bubbly as she can, aware of the sphinx-like gaze of Gloria, wondering if somehow Gloria can see the flames that are engulfing her head.

'Yeah,' Becky says, looking back over her shoulder, already walking away. 'Bye, Harry . . .' and Harry's sure that was a wink she gave her. A dark flash of lips and winking eyes. She stands, stunned, watching until she loses them in the bodies. A slim wrist reaches out and grabs a wine bottle from the bar, sparkling bracelet flashing beneath the lighting, and then they're gone.

She breathes fast and shallow. Pats the flames down with quick hands. The embers crackle. She goes to touch the earlobe that Becky had touched, but finds that it's melted, only her earrings remain, two little hoops spinning round nothing. She looks up and sees that Leon is staring at her from the other side of the room, suddenly visible, shaking his head, smiling to himself. Harry straightens her shirt, meets Leon's eyes, sips her drink. *Right then*. Her legs feel miles away from the floor. The walls are closer every second. Each breath is a thrown dart that has to be wrenched from the board before she can throw again. She turns from the bar towards the tables in the corner and walks over to the man standing with his legs wide apart, shifting his weight backwards and forwards.

'Morris. Hello.' Harry speaks gently, businesslike. 'Good to see you again.'

'Harry! Glad you could make it.' Morris grins emptily down into Harry's face and places a large hand on the small of her back, holding her hip. 'Follow me.'

THE TRUTH

The flat Becky shares with Charlotte sits in a neat, friendly block behind Deptford High Street where everybody has plants on their windowsills and the communal gardens are bright with tulips and bluebells. Beyond the gardens though, out on the street, the colour pales dramatically. Everything is pigeon grey and flecked with spit stains and dried-up chewing gum.

Somewhere nearby two women scream at one another and their voices bounce along the empty roads. Overhead a freight train rattles the bones of the bridge, while down dark alleys and behind closed doors, adolescent affirmations are being punched out, one wet slap of bodily fluid at a time.

The girls clamber out of the cab. The rowing women are in full throttle now and no words are discernible in the shrieking waves. The road is strewn with picked-clean rib bones, and the faint smell of boozy piss mixes with the sweet rot of skunk smoke.

As the girls climb the steps, their voices ricochet off the concrete walls and flood the block with their presence, bringing the old man downstairs to his doorway to stare disapprovingly in their general direction.

In the front room a tiny yellow sofa squeezes itself along the back wall, a little square coffee table stands before it; along the opposite wall there are a couple of shelving units with a stereo on and some books and the telly. If there are any more than two people in the room, it feels like being held inside a mouth full of too many teeth.

They sit on the yellow sofa and listen to nineties R'n'B. They sniff the rest of Becky's gram and talk the same shit that they talk every time an evening ends this way.

Just before four, Becky heads to her room. She lies in her bed, brain like a sack of electric drills, all switched on and roaring. Harry keeps floating back into her mind: her funny stance, her too-long arms, the way she kept pulling her hair around and it kept springing back to being exactly where it was. Becky's mind is wild as a dark sea, foaming, tugging lost things down into its depths. Which one is the real one? The professional dancer who never complains? The south London girl sniffing gack in her flat? The obedient niece washing dishes in her uncle's caff? The erotic masseuse, lipsticked and high-heeled, crossing town with her money to make?

She could have brought her home with her.

No strings and flings, and one-night stands, she's not after any more than that. She prefers to keep things simple. She likes girls and she likes boys. If something is exciting, she lets it be exciting. But the minute people get too keen, she cuts them off. She can't handle any more than casual things. It gets too painful. You give too much, they take too much, they want too much, or not enough, and suddenly you find yourselves emptied out and open-handed, grabbing for some more.

She doesn't like to think of her mum, but it happens late at night when she's alone and chopped up like this, when she's rushing and caked and her defences are weak. The ever-repeating motif that she tries to escape, building momentum, the age-old crescendo. And then, through the dark and churning sea, looming up from the depths, she senses the bad thought approaching. She tries to escape it, swims hard against the current, but she's smashed back down and she can't get away, and she feels it approach, the lumbering, formless dread.

'Fuck off, Dad,' she says, and the words drop softly. Her voice is sticky in the darkness, throat raw from smoke. She allows herself to think of him for the first time in months, years maybe. She tries to remember his face. If she thinks hard enough, forces her brain back to remember an image, there is one that still lurks beneath her lungs somewhere. Her dad, young and smiling, curly-haired and handsome, big enough to fill a doorway, in the armchair in the front room of the flat they used to live in, smiling, maybe at her or maybe at her mother's camera.

She turns over in bed, agonising, squirming, fidgeting. Body so tired, but head so busy, head so sore and sharp and whirring.

She gets up, drags her doughy limbs to the shelf in the corner where she keeps her drugs box and digs around through the small chunks of hash and half-pills for the pack of diazepam. She takes one out and holds it in her mouth, finds a swig of water in a glass by the bed and waits to pass out.

In the space between the cocaine and the alcohol and the diazepam, her brain expands, floods her with the past.

BECKY'S MUM WAS A woman named Paula, pronounced like the Italian – Powler, and she had been a professional photographer. Her dad, John, pronounced like the Elton – John, had been a lecturer in politics at the University of London.

John Darke was a young and brilliant PhD student, working on a book that would, by all accounts, change the way we thought about politics in this country. His mother was a sitar player from Jaipur, his father a double bass player from Bromley. They had met in the summer of 1952, playing together as part of an orchestral exchange programme set up for young players by the London Symphony Orchestra.

John had grown up in Catford in the 1960s. The only mixed-race kid in his class. Skinny white boys in army-green balaclavas had thrown bags of dog shit through his mother's letterbox. They set fire to his school bag at the bus stop and pushed him in the playground.

When he was thirteen he won undying schoolyard respect by swinging his arm back and punching a bully out cold. Something changed in his guts after that. He stood over his attacker as he came round from the blow, watched him snivel on the ground like a blind pup, and he understood that to his surprise he felt no sense of victory. Only sadness. After that, John Darke could be relied upon to stand up for every young boy in the school. He became a hero. With his new-found respect, he built an alliance. Every suffering hurt him, not just his own. But he wanted the bullies to be a part of it too. He wanted all the kids in the school to stand together.

They caned him. They tensed their foreheads and ground their teeth. Their nostrils flared and the loose flesh around their necks fell around their collars as they drew back their arms. John Darke felt his anger rising and breathed into its redness. He didn't shed a tear or let a squeal out his mouth. His stoicism didn't go unnoticed. The next week they expelled him for bullying.

He was sent to a school for 'troubled' boys deemed 'educationally subnormal'. Apart from one – Jamie, a stuttering pyromaniac whose bones showed through his shirt – none of them were white. He saw how his friends would come in on Monday mornings, limping, cheeks swollen from the weekend encounters with truncheons or boots. Here he was, dumped at the bottom of the rung. He and his classmates were viewed as criminals. John rejected the idea that 'troubled' kids were to blame for their troubles. If young boys stole, or stabbed each other over debts, or felt compelled to arm themselves when they walked the streets, it was not even considered that it might be the fault of the social structures they lived under. Instead, it was always the fault of the boys themselves. *It's on* us, *the people at the bottom,* John realised, *to fix things for* ourselves, *even though it's us who suffer the decisions of the people at the top the most.*

His best friend at this time was a boy named Duane who was brighter than anyone John had ever met, he wrote rhyming verse and knew equations by heart. They played football, ate chips and sat at bus stops together. One day, Duane didn't show up. Months passed before John heard that Duane had been stopped and searched by police and had drugs planted on him. He was serving a lengthy sentence in a young offenders' institution in Surrey. That afternoon, on his way home, choking on the news, John was chased by three boys who spat at him and called him a 'dirty Paki'. They caught up with him at the junction where Lewisham High Street met Bromley Road and they knocked him to the floor. He was winded. He retched while they kicked his back and stomach. It wasn't until he vomited that they laughed and ran off. He lay on the street; it was five in the evening, still light, the road was busy enough. Not one person stopped to ask if he was OK. He lay there for ten, maybe fifteen minutes, getting his breath back, until eventually he picked his sore bones up and walked home, wiping the blood off his lips with the cuff of his school shirt.

His teachers conferred in the staff room about his increasingly militant temperament. They swilled lukewarm tea around their stinking gums and huffed into yellowing moustaches as they marked a black dot beside his name on their forms: *Potential Radical.*

On 13 August 1977 John Darke was twenty-three, a long time out of Park Hill School for Educationally Subnormal Boys. He stood with a group of young socialists on New Cross Road and faced the National Front, who were attempting to march from New Cross to Lewisham, home to one of the largest West Indian communities in London. The people of the borough and people from all over the city rallied together to stop the march. They became involved in clashes with the police in what would later be known as the Battle of Lewisham. The National Front were humiliated. People of all colours stood together. John saw white people standing alongside black and Asian people, he saw them go down in front of the bucking horses, he saw them take the brunt of the heavy shields, he saw them fighting, thousands of them, together, unified in standing against fascism and racism and the brutality of the police. In a strange, flickering moment, John found himself leaning against a shopfront briefly, wiping the sweat and the smoke from his eyes. He looked out at the scene, the streets and the people, arms linked, and he felt a hope surging through him; at last, he thought.

In that moment he vowed that he would dedicate his life to politics.

He grew into a man who was sure of his opinions but humble enough to listen carefully to his detractors and debate properly with his peers. He was an impressive speaker and a handsome man. His lectures attracted young people from outside the university. He could be found giving passionate talks in the back rooms of crowded pubs, or in cafés where he would stand on two chairs, one foot on each, and rock slightly as he spoke, or to crowds of young mothers in the usually deserted public libraries on winter afternoons. He was a champion of strong belief and positivity. He was out for something and it radiated from him and made him someone wonderful to be around.

He had his detractors. There seemed to him to be an abundance of miserable grey-faces whom he assumed had never known passion in their lives, who made it their business to hate everything about him. They were deeply suspicious. They discussed his sex life. They wrote articles for university magazines where they found fault with the tone of his voice, his beard and even the way he drank his coffee. They didn't like his popularity, or the fact that it didn't seem to be diminishing his ability to work. They were jealous of him, and his success made them uncomfortable because it reminded them of how often they had not followed their own dreams or cultivated principles worth sticking to. The universities were, it seemed to John, filled with stillness and loathing. He tried to shake it off, but it remained.

In the long months and years when John was working on the final draft of his book, *How We Can Take Power Without*

Power Taking Us, he was consumed with the project and unable to relax. His mind was so full of his ideas that his body began to spasm and fidget. He found himself rubbing his hands and nodding his head furiously when he was alone. His whole frame would shake violently and he would clench his teeth and have no choice but to go with it. He would fit like this silently in toilet cubicles at train stations for five straight minutes. Then he would gather himself, stretch his tensed-up mouth, shake his fingers like they were wet, smooth his clothes down and step back out into the chaos of the platform. Dazed.

One clear September night after a long summer of touring, and a hard week back at the university, he attended a concert given by a friend of his, the famous cellist Marco Abbadelli, and felt calmer than he had in months. Marco and John had spent many hours discussing life and the point of the artistic temperament. The meaning of beauty. The language of music. They had once made love and it had been something wonderful and honest, but it had only happened the once and it was never spoken of again. They had huge affection for each other, and whenever Marco was in London they enjoyed nothing more than meeting up and drinking until dawn.

Paula Shogovitch had fallen in love with the idea of capturing moments when she was five years old and playing in the garden of her grandparents' house. It was coming on for dusk and the lights were on inside. She was on her way back in, when she noticed through the window her two brothers, Ron and Rags, stealing sweeties from their grandma's cupboard. There was something so perfect in the poise of their bodies, strained, listening for footsteps, ready to run. Something so familiar in being the younger sister, looking on while the elder brothers did things that they imagined she couldn't understand. She began to look for moments like this. Moments that gave away so much. She started to find them everywhere. She learned to capture them. A couple fighting in a train carriage, a married woman walking with her grumpy husband, staring after a beautiful young man as he passed them at a crossing, a boy smiling in the middle of a fight, two women sneaking sips from a bottle at the theatre. There was an intimacy to Paula's photos. Something so careful about the way she captured London people. Whether she knew it or not, she was doing something that hadn't been done before. Photographs taken with so much love for their subjects that you felt like you were looking at pictures of relatives when you flicked through her images.

Paula was on the ascendancy. London was alive with beauty, talent, movement. And she was young and had a vision. She moved up in the world. Didn't have to give anyone a feel of her tits. Didn't have to pretend she was thick to appear unthreatening. She allowed herself to be herself, and people were charmed and impressed. And Paula Shogovitch had a job and her job was her calling and her calling was her love and her love was her job and she could pay her rent on time.

Paula's favourite subject was Marco Abbadelli. Arguably the best photograph she ever took was her iconic shot of Marco, naked at his cello. People have since tried to stage similar photos, but the reason her photo worked so well was that it was real. They had been together, and in the final moments of their passion Marco had seemed to be singing. As they pulled themselves apart and lay there, resting, Marco had carried on with the melody, softly, on the out breath. Paula had reached for her camera. She was fascinated by photographs of men taken in the moments after lovemaking. She had been playing with apertures when Marco, in a state of intent calm, got up and walked across the bare floorboards for his cello. He opened the case, and began to play, no time for a chair, half standing, half crouching. Framed perfectly by the window that hung slightly open and the curtains billowing ferociously around him. She took the photo. It made her a star.

In the winter of 1985, Marco Abbadelli came to the end of a long European tour that culminated in his biggest ever London show at the Royal Festival Hall. To celebrate he hosted a late dinner at El Gran Toro, his favourite restaurant, not far from the concert hall, and was joined by his manager and a few of his closest London friends. They were seated at a long table in a private room in the exclusive basement of the restaurant. The back wall was lined with wine casks and barrels of fine Spanish sherry. The waiters made a big show of dipping their heads and bringing tastes from each cask over to Marco, who beckoned them close and spoke to them softly and allowed them to touch his hands when they gave him the glasses.

Among Marco's friends that evening was the notable rock 'n' roll political writer, John Darke, and the famous young photographer, Paula Shogovitch.

The moment Paula saw John she felt her throat constrict; the blood flowed thicker through her veins. He felt it in his hair follicles and in the beds of his fingernails. Something about her hurt him all over. The air was heavy between them. They ate at separate ends of the table and avoided each other's eyes.

After the food had been eaten and the diners were drinking their coffee, Paula got up and moved her chair to the corner of the table, set it beside John's and sat down. They said nothing, made no eye contact. They sat side by side, almost touching, completely ignoring one another.

The coffees and cognacs were finished. The guests were sitting back in their chairs, slapping their thighs at Marco's anecdotes. Paula got up and, without even thinking, John followed her out of the dining room and into the Ladies. The air was thick with silence, which gave them both the feeling that the world had stopped for them. Bone white flowers dripped from red glass vases on plinths by floor-to-ceiling mirrors. Paintings of women in flamenco dresses fighting raging bulls hung by the hand dryers. John and Paula saw all of it and none of it. They undressed each other silently behind the locked door of a black cubicle and had their first sex in the toilets of El Gran Toro.

Paula and John were in love. They found each other's work inspiring, enjoyed each other's strangeness. They lived in a yellow-brick housing association block a few streets behind Lewisham Way. Their proud block was five storeys high, and looked out at three other identical blocks across a patchy green with a creaking see-saw and a couple of swings in the bottom corner. Their flat, number seventeen, had a little balcony where they planted honeysuckle and snapdragons and grew weed in big pots, and trained a climbing jasmine to tickle its way along the railings.

When John's book eventually came out, politics was on the turn. It was 1989 and Thatcher was in government. John felt that the world was in its death throes, and the hearts of the British people were being pushed to breaking point.

In the early spring of that year, Paula Shogovitch fell pregnant. At first, she was convinced that she would continue working through her pregnancy, and that having a baby did not necessarily mean she would have to put her camera down. John assured her that he would support her in whatever decisions she made, but as the pregnancy progressed, it became clear to Paula that John, whether he knew it or not, had no intention of making any sacrifices when it came to his schedule. She felt, in some gnawing part of her mind, that he viewed his work as a purpose, and her work as a hobby. She started saying no to the odd assignment, taking on less until the word got around, and as she grew heavier and more exhausted she stopped walking the streets hunting the hidden moments that she had made her name capturing. She felt too conspicuous for it now. She began to photograph her own body, at home, but found this uninspiring. A growing belly in a bedroom mirror didn't speak to her as loudly as a mounted policeman chasing two prepubescent football fans down a tiny alley, scarves wrapped around their heads, clutching fireworks.

It was a gradual process, learning what it meant to be a woman. Her boyfriend had no time really for her despondency. He tried to buoy her up, telling her that she was sure to get back to work when the baby arrived. 'You can take lots of pictures when the baby's born, when you push the pram around.' He didn't mean to condescend, but he had no grasp on what was slipping out of Paula's reach. She sat for hours with her swelling bump, resigning herself to a new life. She felt guilty for every stab of jealousy she felt in the face of his burgeoning career; she knew that he was trying to make the world a better place, and that he suffered for it terribly. But it made no difference when she was stuck at home that long, hot summer; uncomfortable and bored and lonely, while he was manic with his work, and drunk at night when he came home.

Winter laid her solemn hands across the city and stroked all the colours out of the sky. The pavement was wet and cold outside the maternity ward. She named her daughter Rebecca, after her favourite aunt, who had been a poet and a tennis player, and England's first female locksmith.

Paula held her baby in her arms and understood the meaning of life. Rebecca had John's serious oak-dark eyes, and

Paula could see her mother in the shape of Rebecca's mouth. She passed the baby to John who held her and stared down into her pudgy face, aware that he had found something he didn't know he lacked. The love was immediate and more profound than any he had known. In that moment, while Paula, exhausted from the birth, watched her boyfriend with their baby, she entertained a thousand quick-fire fantasies of how their lives might play out, the three of them, together. John, meanwhile, was watching his daughter's tiny hands, feeling only the urgency to keep pushing himself onwards in his work so that he could improve things for her. His fantasies were of political success and the building of a brighter future.

John's career was blossoming. His book was well received in the press, and wildly popular, selling tens of thousands of copies in its first months, which was a lot for a political science book. He was celebrated by those on the Left, ridiculed by those on the Right, and was sneered at by politicians who saw his approach as unorthodox and flash-in-the-pan. He was unmarried, living with his girlfriend and their baby. He was seen as a man with questionable morals. He was determined his success would be based on his ideas and his policies, and not on his personal life – or on the version of himself that he was expected to sell to the press – but that determination made him an easy target. He refused to fall in line or scrub up or blend in, he was vitriolic about Westminster. His message was clear: things have to change, we are in a state of emergency! He didn't want to be another baggy-mouthed puppet in the popularity contest, lined up against the wall before the press like it was execution day.

He kept going, touring the country in a beaten-up van, sleeping in the back on a half-frozen mattress in supermarket car parks. Driving through the night, guts ruined from motorway burgers and cheap, thick whisky. He was out to make a difference. He couldn't bear what was happening to the world. To his country. It was just a question of information, he was sure. People just had to know and that would be a start. Instead of smashing up the football stadiums, we could be smashing up the institutions that were keeping us in this misery. If people just *knew* that what was happening was not the only option, and even if it was, know that it wasn't *right*.

He was sick of seeing the people pitted against each other, black against white and north against south, and so many were dying and poor, beaten up, demonised and kept in a state of dejection. He couldn't rest, not for a moment. He could see so clearly what the government and the multinational corporations were doing: enslaving the country in the name of freedom and getting away with it. He was teaching the brightest students he'd ever taught; they were coming in droves to politics. It was a time of great upheaval and chance and chaos and pain.

He was going about things the only way he could trust. Grass roots. Driving all day to talk with a hundred hungry young men who couldn't find work, and then driving all night back to London to teach his classes in the morning. He went to the people, with no cameras, and no story to sell. He put himself in front of single mothers, office workers, immigrants and prisoners and talked and listened, and it gave them hope.

While John toured the country and passed out exhausted to snatch a few hours' fitful sleep on the floor of his university office, Paula and Becky lived in the flat and spent their days together. The weed didn't grow on the balcony now. They had to cut the precious plants down for fear of the press or arrest. There was a lot that Paula couldn't do any more; she couldn't gossip with her neighbours in her dressing gown, or go out dancing with her girlfriends. She couldn't sit topless in the sunshine on her balcony. Their lives were not their lives, they belonged to John's job and to the looming shadow of potential public disfavour.

But she could watch her daughter and feel the surge and peace of motherhood. She watched the fingers grow, the toes, the legs, the tiny eyelashes. *My baby is growing.* All things repeated this. *I have a child. She is a girl.* Paula would pick up her camera occasionally, turn it over in her hands, change the shutter speed, raise it to her eye and look through it, but each time, before she could decide on a shot, the baby would be hungry, or need her attention, and the camera would feel like an indulgence. The notion of 'making it' seemed so trivial. What was important was Becky being occupied, happy, warm.

Becky learning words. Becky painting. Becky's hunger, Becky's thirst, Becky sleeping well. The fury of her creative pursuits belonged to a different person. She often thought about it, intensely, while doing the endless cleaning up, washing of clothes, changing of nappies, cooking of food; did she miss it? She couldn't honestly say that she did.

John would come home at nights with a deep, furrowed brow. He seemed emptied of something. He barely noticed the things Paula would do. Little things in the home to make it feel brighter when he got back. He ate and he smiled and he touched her, but he wasn't there.

In 1992 John Darke was thirty-eight and had become a formidable force in public opinion. The negativity that he was lambasted with by the establishment only served to prove to his followers that he was committed to change. There were societies set up at the universities to discuss his ways of thinking, leagues of his followers gathered in pubs and cafés across the country and, as the local election loomed, he stood outside the shopping centre, without placards or leaflets, at a table, answering people's questions. The media hated him, the government hated him, but the people loved him and so he was dangerous. Dangerous John fought on. He expressed himself with the clarity of someone who was telling the truth. The general consensus was that John Darke was about to do something no one had ever seen done. And the feeling was everywhere.

At home, he was uncommunicative. He didn't sleep well at night and was often in bed long after Paula had fallen asleep and up long before she awoke. He showed no interest in cooking meals, or sitting with Paula and talking in the evenings. He was a crumpled shell, often collapsing in the hallway as soon as he came through the door. Paula would see him canvassing on the streets and answering questions for reporters, and it would shoot her through with jealousy that he could be so sparkly-eyed for them but he could barely raise a smile for her. A loneliness had fallen on him, the like of which he'd never known. Nothing could cure it, not his girlfriend, his daughter, not his friends, not his studies. It was only momentarily dispelled when he was giving his speeches. But they would leave him, in his private moments, more depleted than ever.

The Darke day, as it came to be known, fell on 22 February 1995. Becky was a little over five and was dancing all the time. Paula was sitting in a tap and jazz class with Becky at the leisure centre and her daughter was a marvel. Becky's teacher smiled over at Paula. Paula blushed and fiddled with the tops of her socks.

That evening John had promised to cook them all dinner. She was not prepared to lose him to his politics. As she watched Becky doing her steps she was sure things were going to get better. He was her man and he was her daughter's father, and she had resolved that that night they would talk. It wasn't enough to skirt over the fact that he wasn't himself and was losing them both.

As Becky counted the beats and pointed her toes, John Darke was in his study amending the opening of a speech he was to deliver the next day. He was just debating whether it was better to start with a friendly greeting or a damning statistic when he heard three knocks at the door. He opened it and saw the usual students gathered in crowds, waiting, as they had been doing these past few months, for an audience with him, but at the head of this crowd, staring stone-faced, three large policemen stood, legs parted, arms by their sides. Two of them wore uniform, one of them was clearly Special Branch, dressed as he was in a once smart trench coat and beaten-up shoes, his pursed lips opened beneath his weary moustache.

'Mr John Darke?'

They crucified him. Painted him a villain. He was drawn in the press as an alcoholic manic-depressive dope-fiend. A callous reprobate out for the country's young. Lurking in the classrooms of the university where he taught, poisoning minds and seducing bodies. Features were written by TV personalities calling him an insatiable sexual deviant. Columnists, gossip hounds and serious political journalists all had their piece to say on the matter, and it wasn't just in the right-wing papers. It became fashionable to hate John Darke. Damning him meant you absolved yourself. They discussed his homosexual leanings in the comments pages. They burned his reputation to the ground.

He was charged with having sexual intercourse with underage girls. Six counts of rape. He denied all the charges. For weeks there hadn't been a page that wasn't full of John Darke's suspect character and his deviant tendencies.

He had never shown interest in underage girls, but he had been a man who enjoyed sex immensely. Before these serious days he had often indulged in casual affairs, but since he'd met Paula all that had changed. Or had it? The jury could not forget that here was a man who, intent on power, was charging around the country like a rock star on tour, meeting young girls who found him impressive. Who could be sure? Were there not testimonies? Young, crying girls, fourteen and fifteen, weeping in courtrooms, while John sat, silent, dark-eyed, destroyed.

Paula stuck by her man as long as she could but he was so quiet and strained in the visits. And no smoke without fire and she couldn't bear to think that the man she loved most in the world, those hands that she'd held and adored, were the hands of a man who could do things like these. She swallowed her doubt, but the hook stuck in the flesh of her mouth, pulling her upwards, away from him. *This is a set-up*, he told her, and she nodded and told him she knew that it was. But if enough people believed in a lie, the truth didn't matter at all.

On 17 November 1995, John Darke was found guilty by a jury of his peers. Some maintained that the jury must have had their perspectives tinted by the hysteria in the papers, but these complaints died down after the complainants found themselves tarnished as paedophile apologists and conspirators.

Paula and Becky threw their clothes into bin bags and moved out of the flat. Paula held her child in one hand and dragged their bags with the other, and together they walked aimlessly into the night. Becky watched her mother dance in the paparazzi strobes.

Who could be sure if the accusations were true? Was he really a rapist of underage girls? Could he have done it? There were those who didn't believe in the conviction. Who carried on reading his papers and meeting in secret, trying to get mobilised. But the damage was done. They couldn't gather momentum against such a force. His followers were heartbroken, destroyed. They felt they had been shown by the ruling classes what happens to those who don't play by the rules. The fire went out of the movement. John Darke's followers became as shamed as their figurehead.

After three weeks, not knowing where else to turn, Paula and Becky moved in with Paula's eldest brother Ron and his wife Linda, and their son Ted, who was only a year or so younger than Becky. Ron and Linda lived in a three-bed maisonette in a quiet cul-de-sac away from the bustle of Lewisham Way, up towards Charlton. The house looked out on to a sloping communal green and if you stood on your tiptoes at the top of the hill you could see the river churning its way to Greenwich.

Becky's Auntie Linda was a tidy-framed lady with natural hair and skin the colour of fired clay. She dressed well and prided herself on her ability to find the only gem in a sprawling car-boot sale. Her heritage was Jamaican/Irish and she slipped between both accents when she was saying something important, but for the most part she spoke in the round vowels of south London. She was a straightforward woman, gentle-mannered. She could not tolerate stupidity and when she encountered it she called it by its name. She worried constantly about the state of things: she'd worry about the city, her family, her business, the weather, her husband's health. She had a habit of staring off into the middle distance and tutting slowly whenever anything happened, convinced of some prophecy that was becoming truer and truer every day; everything on the news, in the street, in the house, fed her sense of growing dread. But she maintained a mischievous sense of humour. She was Becky's favourite human being.

Ted was a goofy kid with little tight curls and dimples, and a sweet manner. As time passed, he became like a brother to Becky. He'd push her over and give her Chinese burns and lock her in cupboards.

Becky's Uncle Ron was short and round, and had a laugh like a broken engine, stuttering and guttural. He was south London Jewish and was proud of his heritage. He was a softy really, but in public he scowled and swaggered and cut his eyes at anyone he didn't like the look of. He wore what Linda picked out for him. His dark hair was long at the top and neat at the sides, swept back off his head in a little baggy quiff. He had a happy mouth full of teeth, ground down from cheap teenage speed and yellowing from sweets and fags, piercing bright blue eyes that shone when he thought hard, set deep in his face, and a brow that stood out like a headline. He walked with his arms linked behind his back, chest pushed out, greeting people he knew with a bow of the head.

Ron had met Linda in the early 1980s. He was a ska boy, and she was a DJ at the clubs he used to go to. The process was not without its dramas, but it all ended well; she got the boy, and he got the girl and he still felt gooey in her arms. He had tattoos on his wrists that Becky knew meant something but she never asked what, and a dark temper that would flare up suddenly when roused and hands big enough to break faces.

Ron and Linda ran a caff together called Giuseppe's on Lewisham High Street. There was a market there and lots of people and shops and noise. Becky liked going to Giuseppe's after school and sitting at the counter and drinking the milkshakes that Linda made especially for her.

Paula told Becky that her dad was in jail because the police were scared of him. Her family hid the papers from her in the first few weeks after John's arrest, and they were careful with the telly.

They never talked about it. Every time she tried, her mum got panicky and tore at her hair and tears came to her eyes, so Becky learned it was best to stop asking and soon the silence around her father's absence seemed too prevalent and painful to challenge.

In Becky's earliest memories, her mum was always strong and funny, beautiful and talented, no nonsense. Smoking fags out the window of Ron and Linda's house. Shouting at the telly when they sat and watched *EastEnders*. Holding Becky's hand while Becky learned to roller skate, walking round and round the field eating endless ice creams. Showing Becky photos of all the famous people she had shot; beautiful black-and-white moments from a time when Becky hadn't happened yet. Going out for tea and cake in town together, looking through the pages of high-end magazines at all the colours and the clothes. She remembered her mum taking her to dance class and staying when the other mothers left, sitting quietly and watching all the steps her daughter learned.

But Becky would hear her crying in the night. And when no one else was in, Paula would stand in the doorway of the room she shared with Becky, drunk, her eyes drooping and her voice shrill, and she'd start the same old monologue Becky had heard hundreds of times. 'I could have been a legend, you know. Before I met your father I was famous. I was destined for great things . . .'

The crying mum and the happy mum were like two different people, never in the same space at the same time, but both lived in Paula, and you never knew which one you'd get. Over time, Becky grew scared of getting home from school in case her mum was still in bed and drunk and crying. When she was like this, nobody was safe, she would surface in a silk dressing gown, make-up smudged and smoking fags and shouting foul abuse at people who weren't there, and at people who were.

It was a Saturday morning in the middle of December, Becky had just turned thirteen and Paula wanted them to go ice skating, like they used to, but Becky was embarrassed to be seen out with her mum, temperamental as Paula was; drunk, loud, and usually outrageously flirtatious with bewildered men. Becky was sitting in the front room watching the telly. Paula was leaning in the doorway.

Paula had suffered a crushing blow that morning. For the past three months she had been desperately trying to find contact details for her old workmates and commissioning editors, and had at last tracked down the mobile number of Katarina Raphael, once a photojournalist like her, but now the picture editor at British *Vogue*. Paula had counted Katarina as a friend some fifteen years before, but they hadn't spoken in over a decade, although Paula had been watching Katarina's progress from afar. Katarina's recent well-publicised promotion had fuelled Paula's latest attempt at stirring the ashes of her career. But Katarina had not remembered Paula. She had not remembered Paula's name, Paula's voice or Paula's photographs. She had told her that she was sorry, but Paula must have dialled the wrong number.

'I don't want to go ice skating.' Becky wouldn't look up from the TV; she was watching an American high-school sitcom.

'You used to love it.' Paula held on to the wall, watched her daughter staring at the screen.

'I'm happy just sitting here, Mum. I'm tired.'

'You just want to watch TV all day?'

'Yeah.' Becky shrugged. Annoyed at the interruption.

'We hardly see each other any more, Rebecca.' Paula walked over and stood in front of the TV. 'Let's go out.' Her words baggy from drink. 'Let's go look at the photos in the Portrait Gallery.'

Becky looked up at her mum, spoke firmly, her voice tired. 'I don't want to.'

Paula started pacing backwards and forwards in front of the TV. Shaking her head. Breathing heavily. She gritted her teeth behind her pursed lips.

'Can you let me just watch this, Mum? I like this programme.' Becky weaved from side to side, trying to see round her mum. Paula saw what Becky was doing and stood firmly in front of the screen, trying to catch her daughter's eye. Becky looked down at the carpet. 'It's only on once a week.'

'NO!' Paula shouted. She turned the TV off, and stood victoriously in front of it with her hands on her hips. She stared at Becky, eyes burning, but Becky didn't look up. Becky sat very still on the sofa and tried to count the individual strands that made up the carpet.

Paula walked towards her and leaned down into her face. 'Are you not even going to look at me, Becky?' she asked, her voice calm, but her movements jagged.

'Mum,' Becky moaned. 'Muuuum, please.' She turned her head away.

Paula raised an extended finger. Spoke at a dramatic volume. 'I gave my life up for you,' she began.

Becky rolled her eyes and sat back into the sofa, huffing in exaggerated boredom. 'Heard it all before,' she sang, covering her face with a cushion.

'Your Dad and you. I could have had a life of my own. But I gave everything up, and look where it's got me . . . You don't even talk to me any more. And *him*?' Her dressing gown billowed as she thrust her hands about, her underwear visible, the curtains open.

Becky heard him referred to and tears came to her eyes. She breathed them back without her mother seeing, and shrivelled inside to think of the neighbours. She watched Paula's face contort and squash and puff.

'Your precious fucking father.' Paula's hair was sticking out madly from her head; it was always wild before she tamed it with products and special brushes and rollers. Her skin was stretched and thin at the edges of her face, blue lines appearing beneath the surface.

Becky looked at her mother and saw a monster. She cowered down into the sofa, hoping she'd never end up looking like that. Paula stood, one hand on her hip, the other holding her head. Her dressing gown was open, her boob was hanging out of her night slip. Becky's stomach pushed itself out of her belly button and sprinted for the door. Ran down the street with no shoes on.

'You think he's better than *me*? Because, what? I take a drink now and then, to calm the nerves. Now and then?'

Becky breathed quietly.

'Can't you hear me?'

Becky stared at the corner of the cushion that she clutched to her chest. Promised herself she wouldn't cry. There was no use crying, it just made things worse.

'You wait here,' Paula said, raising a finger and pointing it hard at her daughter. 'Just wait here.'

She backed out of the room. Becky heard her running up to their bedroom and slamming the door and banging around up there. She heard the door being wrenched open, hitting the wall, and footsteps thumping down the stairs, skidding on the steps, and the door being smashed into. Then her mother, breathing ragged breaths, holding her hand against her mouth, eyes like open bottles, walked purposefully into the room. She handed her daughter an old newspaper.

'There you go,' she said. 'There's your fucking father.' Paula stared at Becky, spiteful, hurt. Wanting love. She waited for Becky to look at the newspaper. Becky didn't move. Paula waited for as long as her nerves could take, but seeing that Becky was not going to look, she slammed the paper down at her daughter's feet and left it spreadeagled on the floor before she turned and flounced out, back upstairs. Becky heard the door slam and the music start playing. *You don't have to say you love me . . .*

Becky fell towards the paper, slipped from the sofa and sat awkwardly hunched on the floor next to it. She crumpled her body together, her knees tucked up to her chest, and she read it, weeping till it hurt her face, cover to cover, twice over.

After that episode, Becky grew timid around her mother. She couldn't stop thinking about what she'd learned. She saw her dad everywhere. Every shop sign she noticed had *John's* written on it, every TV show was about dads and daughters. Every lesson in school was about people being punished for what they believed in. And then some girls in her year who she smoked fags with all started boasting about the older guys they were sleeping with, and Becky couldn't help but imagine the girls themselves. The ones he had apparently slept with. There had been six of them. What did they look like? They can't have looked much older than she looked. She had nightmares about it. She felt disgusted with herself for missing him. She sat in front of the computers in the library searching for his books, and finding all of them had been recalled. At lunchtimes she hid in the IT department, going online on the old school computers and soaking up all she could find. Every spare minute she had, she found herself back there, logging on and searching and then hating everything she'd just read and wishing she could forget it. She became withdrawn, she lost weight. She started skipping dance classes, punishing herself.

One afternoon, instead of going to her dance class, she was sitting alone on the wall of the playground in the park, watching a cold February rain falling. She stared at the sharp, slanting rain for three hours, getting drenched to the bone. She was laid up in bed with a fever for a week, lost in heated nightmares of monsters and jail cells and internet chat rooms and her dance teacher crying. It was then, sick in bed, feeling too bad to put the telly on or pick up a book, that she promised herself she wasn't going to let this get the better of her. She wasn't ever going to skip another dance class, and she wasn't going to search her dad's name on the internet, no matter how tempting it was, because it only made her feel shit. She decided she was going to focus on what she loved the most, and slowly she felt the yearning for her dad grow into dull, agonising indifference. She told herself she didn't have a father. She made herself forget him. She was going to be a dancer and get as far away from her parents as she could.

Paula couldn't bear the distance she had driven between herself and her daughter. But every time she tried to apologise, she saw herself from above and was consumed with self-loathing. She started attending a local church discussion group, one that advertised itself as being a good place for finding answers, and by the time Becky turned fourteen, Paula was a fully fledged born-again.

Suddenly her mother was always there, at her shoulder, needy and apologetic, wistful for the past and terrified of the present, and clinging on to Becky for everything she had. So Becky started doing what young teenagers do when the whole universe is made of insane adults: she stayed out of the house and she stopped going to school.

She started hanging out on the benches outside the shopping centre in Lewisham. There was a scrappy little patch of grass frequented by drunks that Becky liked because she could watch all the people getting on and off the trains. A few other kids hung out there too. The park backed onto a railway arch and behind that arch was a little estate. Kids that didn't go to school hung around skinning up under the arch or they sat on the benches waiting for something to happen that they could look at.

Becky was sitting on her usual bench; it was coming on midday and the sky was concrete. Two girls walked over. One was tiny and blonde, coughed constantly and moved like a little bird, jerking her head when she talked, hopping from foot to foot. The other was big and black-haired, her skin was gold as hazelnuts and her eyes were endless rings of amber, black and brown. She was sipping from a carton of strawberry Ribena and moved like a cat, slowly and purposefully, stretching herself out with each stride.

The bigger one looked at Becky for a moment, then sat down next to her on the bench. The smaller stayed standing at the end of the bench, looking around. Becky tensed up;

this looked like trouble. The bigger girl sipped from her Ribena. She blew bubbles into the carton. The smaller girl giggled. Becky didn't respond.

'I've seen you here a lot. Ain't you got nothing better to do?' the dark-haired one asked her, looking at the side of her face.

Becky didn't move, kept staring straight ahead at the hard grey mud beneath her school shoes. 'I ain't going nowhere. It's a free country.'

The Ribena girl laughed loudly, and rocked hard on the bench, backwards and forwards. Threw her head around. The other one smiled softly at Becky and coughed deeply into her hand, moving her weight from foot to foot.

Becky started to get hot, her cheeks were going red. 'What you laughing at?' She stared at the bigger girl, frowning, ready to get angry.

'Nothing.' The girl stopped laughing and it sounded like a vacuum cleaner being turned off at the mains. 'Relax.'

Becky didn't move. Stayed completely still. Hoped that they'd get bored and walk away.

'Where you live anyway?' the girl asked her, kicking an empty crisp packet and watching it blow away.

'Nowhere.'

'You don't live nowhere?' The bird-like one's voice was quiet and she had a slight lisp.

'Why you asking? Leave me alone.'

The cat-like one threw her head back again and started creasing up. 'You're funny,' she said. 'What's your name?'

Becky's hands gripped the edge of the bench. She sat on her thumbs, leaned forwards and straightened her arms.

'I'm Gloria,' the bigger girl said, 'and that's Charlotte, my friend, but I call her Chips. Why ain't you in school?'

'Why ain't *you* in school?' Becky turned towards the girls. Looked at them. Charlotte's face was covered in freckles, like a pear on the turn. Gloria had her hair done in lots of little bunches all over her head with colourful bands tying them in place. The strands that didn't fit into the bunches were gelled into intricate curls in front of her ears and at the nape of her neck. Becky was impressed.

'We don't like school,' Charlotte said. 'What music do you listen to?'

Becky looked at them both staring at her, flicked her hair out of her eyes. 'Garage and that,' she said.

The sun was bright through the sparse leaves of the bushes that lined the edge of the path. It shone in Becky's eyes. She squinted at the girls.

'We like garage too, don't we, Glory?' As she spoke, Charlotte sat down in the tiny space between Gloria's body and the end of the bench. She wiggled Gloria over with her bum and shoulder and leaned all the way forwards so she could see Becky. The point of her toes just about scraped the floor. 'What school do you go?' she asked her, blinking and freckly.

'St Saviour's, up the hill.' Becky pointed behind her to the road that led up to the school.

'Do you know a boy called Reece?' Gloria swung her feet. Scuffing the bottoms of her shoes. She had black Kickers on with baby-blue laces. Becky liked them a lot.

'Reece who?' she said.

'Reece McKenzie?' Gloria looked deadly serious as she said his name.

'Yeah, why?' she asked.

'I go out with him. He lives near me,' Gloria said, matter-of-fact.

'*I* don't like him.' Charlotte shook her head. 'Not one bit.'

'Did you hear anything about him recently, at school?' Gloria looked down at her Kickers, swinging.

'Anything like what?' Becky said.

'Someone told me he did something. I want to know if it's true.'

Becky looked at the floor for a long time. Didn't know what to say. Charlotte took out two cigarettes from her bag. It was a tiny Nike rucksack about as big as an A5 bit of paper with really long straps. The cigarettes came from the bottom of the bag and were battered and floppy. She straightened them out carefully. Offered one to her new friend.

'Twos me?' she said, giving the other to Gloria. Gloria tore half off, put it behind her ear and gave the other half back.

'You smoke weed?' she asked Becky. Becky nodded. But she'd only smoked it once before.

Gloria put her hand inside her top and got a little bud of skunk wrapped in a Rizla out of her bra. Becky pretended not to be interested but felt her heart racing. Charlotte gave Becky a lighter and she lit the cigarette and looked out at the shitty little park. She watched a young mother walking past, dragging a screaming son in one hand and carrying six bags of shopping in the other; her son was clutching an ice cream but somewhere along the way the top of it had fallen off, so it was just a dry cone. She watched them until they staggered out of view. She watched a boy on a bike doing wheelies past a group of four girls sitting on a wall who weren't looking at him. She watched a man in a suit on a bench by the bus stop, leaning down to offer his sandwich to two fat pigeons, while behind him a homeless man was passed out on the floor, next to a sign saying *HUNGRY. PLEASE HELP*. Everywhere she looked she saw her mother's photographs.

She thought about Reece McKenzie. He was horrible to her and all the girls in her year. He was always going through girls' bags and taking tampons out and covering them in ketchup and throwing them at people's heads.

'He gave Kirsty in Year Eight an eighth of skunk and then made her give him a blowjob,' she said solemnly.

'It's true then.' Gloria dried her lips with the back of her hand and held the bud between them softly. She straightened the Rizla out in her palms, stroking the creases out. Shaking her head.

'Don't know if it's true, it's just what I heard.' Becky fiddled with the cuff of her school shirt. Picked at the knees of her tights.

'He's dirty, Gloria. Forget about him.' Charlotte spat on the floor.

'He's a dickhead.' Gloria started to crumble the bud. For a moment, nobody moved. 'So what's your name then?' Gloria didn't look up from the Rizla.

'Becky.'

'Becky.' Gloria considered her. A brief stab of sunlight fell across her knees. 'Wanna be our friend, Becky?'

Charlotte nodded energetically, leaning forward so far Becky thought she might fall off the bench. She liked these two. She nodded.

'Yeah. OK.'

They went to under-eighteens garage raves, kissed boys and did pills for the first time. They had a big group of mates that they sat around drinking with, talking shit and committing petty crime. They were best mates and they looked out for each other. The other kids they knew were afraid of them and in love with them and gave them things because they didn't know what else they were supposed to do with the feelings that they had.

But no matter what else was going on, Becky kept going to her dance class. She went to hip hop and street sessions in the community centre with other girls from the area. She watched Michael Jackson's *Moonwalker* on video every night. She learned the steps for every song. Michael and the community-centre dance classes remained her biggest influence well into adulthood. As she grew older and became interested in contemporary dance, she came at it from this perspective, and it grounded her movements, kept everything deep and strong and low; nothing too upright or rigid.

Becky stayed at Gloria's or Charlotte's most nights. She couldn't stand the talk of heaven and forgiveness at home. Her absence just made her mother more intent on cornering her when the house was quiet and begging her to spend some time with her. Becky couldn't bear the careful worried eyes, followed by the mention of her father.

But then, when Becky turned fifteen, Paula moved away. Driven mad with passion for a God she could believe in. Paula joined a convent that prescribed a born-again programme of growing vegetables and prayer and sobriety and song, a refuge for the saved in the mountains of the American Midwest, and as she waved her goodbye at the airport, Becky breathed out.

Life went on. Ron and Linda took a bigger role in looking after her. Teddy and Becky laughed at the TV and beat each other up and stole each other's things. They were as close and as distant as any family. Becky had her own room for the first time in years.

At Christmas, on birthdays, or after something momentous had happened, Becky thought about her dad and where he was and what he might be doing. When it happened, she wrote him letters; long, complicated letters that never began or ended, just picked up with whatever it was that she wanted to tell him and went anywhere and everywhere. She wrote similar letters to her mum; occasionally she addressed them to both parents. She kept the letters in a shoebox in her wardrobe, and every few years, once the shoebox was heavy, she would take the letters out and read them to herself, sitting alone on her bedroom floor, allowing herself to cry. And then, after all the tears had come and gone, she'd take the letters up to the park in the night and set them on fire.

IN HER FLAT IN Deptford, Becky kicks her feet wildly. She moans half-words and turns herself about, twisting her bedcovers up in her fist. After one more shuddering kick her body stills and she enters a more peaceful dream; her brow is beaded with sweat, the blinds are rattling in the breeze.

LONELY DAZE

Eight comes too soon. Pete is ripped into consciousness, suddenly woken from a bad dream. He is on the sofa in the front room, his head is throbbing, his breathing is fast from the nightmare. He moans loudly and digs around down the back of the cushions for his phone. Finds it, checks the time, moans again. Then he gets up, holding his head, runs to the bathroom, splashes his face, brushes his teeth and tries not to retch. He's got an appointment at the jobcentre, and if he misses it they'll sanction him, and if they sanction him, he's fucked.

Becky turns the alarm off, stands up, rubs her face. A climbing tiredness behind her eyelids. Nauseous from booze, her nostril crusted white at the edge, she blows red chunks into a tissue, pushes a couple of painkillers out of their plastic sheet and swallows them calmly, before going to stand in the shower until she feels like a human.

Harry is standing, ghost-faced, at her front door waiting for Leon to find his keys. Smoking fast. Swallowing rapidly, twitching her nose. Clutching a newspaper.

'I reckon it was an inside job, I've said it before and I'll say it again. It's just too convenient, don't you think? They want us afraid so they can take our freedoms away. That's what it is, mate. That's what they're doing. It's all about control.'

Leon doesn't respond, finds his keys at last in the first pocket he looked in. Opens the door. 'There's a pack of Valium on the shelf in the bathroom,' he tells her.

Harry stands in the open doorway finishing her cigarette, shaking her head. 'Dark times, Leon. Dark fucking times, mate.'

'Night, Harry,' Leon says, heading up to bed. 'Get some kip. It's the morning.'

Pete is tall and long-limbed. He walks on his tiptoes with a precarious strut that makes him look like he can't keep up with himself and he's about to fall over. His hair is so thick it grows out instead of down so he keeps it shaved short. He finds jogging bottoms and climbs into them sleepily, staggering as he does it; he rubs his eyes to try and wake himself up and, yawning, pulls on a baggy white T-shirt with the insignia of his favourite sound system, 'Valve', graffed across the chest, from the glory days when he used to go raving and life hadn't slowed him down yet.

Becky waits for the bus to pull away, then crosses the road to Giuseppe's. The street is busy, full of things she has always known. Old women bullying fruit and veg men. Worksmart people with their heads in their phones, walking in time with each other to the station while the ancient drunks huddle on benches, earnest eyes all screwed up, shaking their dirty heads, fingers pointing.

'No,' they're saying, 'I never said that, I never. What I said was . . . No . . . I never.'

The furniture in Giuseppe's has seen better days, but it's cosy and the food is good. Becky walks in to the large open-plan room. The tables and chairs are separated by an aisle down the middle. At the end of this aisle is a large counter with sections for hot and cold food, and to one side of the counter is the till. On the other side is a tiny bar area, big enough for one person to stand behind, formed by a little wooden hatch that flaps down. There's a couple of optics and a beer tap. Behind the counter, in the two back corners, are the cooker and the fridge. Between them, stretching along the back wall, is the sink and the work surface.

The walls are light, the woodwork dark, the tablecloths are dark green with gold trim. On each table there is a bowl of salt, a little pepper mill and a candle in a beer bottle. Along the right-hand wall is a large blackboard with the menu written on it. Along the left wall, pride of place, is a large framed photograph of Giuseppe, his name emblazoned on a plaque. In the picture he's wearing his uniform, his thick dark hair is smartly combed back. His moustache is neat and not too long. His eyes turn up at the edges, set wide apart in his face, his cheeks and his temples are wrinkled with smile lines. A handsome man. His broad jaw, clean-shaven, tapers to a slight bulb at his chin. His eyes, deep and bright and full of good humour, look at something funny happening just behind you.

'Morning, Giuseppe,' Becky says as she turns the alarm off and opens the blinds, letting the light pour in.

Pete gets to the jobcentre. The security guard is tensing his muscles and staring at his reflection in the glass doors. It's packed. Fluorescent bulbs and crying babies and birthday cards pinned up on cork boards.

Pete sits down and watches an older guy – a few teeth missing, dirty face, long hair, scars mess his skin up like piss lines in a sandpit. He's got a cap on, can in his pocket. Mumbling to himself. Pete feels a faint terror. *Am I you?* He looks away, notices a young man, smartly dressed, keeping his voice quiet and trying not to rise to the job-search assistant who is talking to him like he is a thick child. The horrible fake patience they use. Pete prickles.

'That's all very well,' the job-search assistant is saying, 'but as you well know, the rules are the rules, I'm afraid. You should have let us know in good time if you had to go to hospital.'

Pete stares at the ceiling. His stomach whines and squelches strangely. He tries to ignore the self-important man with the

Jobcentre Plus name badge who's making peace with the fact he never had any friends at school by asserting his authority over anyone he possibly can. Reeling off platitudes and identikit slogans as if they were actually his thoughts. Memorised coping devices for difficult customers.

Pete looks down at his job-search form. The type of work he is looking for is printed in the appropriate box: *Library and Leisure Industries. Catering and Hospitality. Postal Work.*

'Hello, Peter, and how are we this morning?' Pete's vision is still throbbing and watery from the pills in the pub the night before and everything feels very far away. 'I hope we've got our forms all filled out nicely this week?'

She has a sensible haircut and a white blouse open three buttons down that reveals a neck all folded up like an accordion, and eczema shouting from behind the folds. She breathes and he can hear the protest song of her sinuses. She has glasses and pursed lips and disapproving mannerisms, and she obviously fucking loves her job. He offers an obedient nod and hates himself for it.

'Good,' she says. 'I have just had this in, actually, and you'll love this, because I see here that you've listed one of your areas of interest as "Catering and Hospitality", yes? Cooking? Well, a vacancy has just opened up at a kitchenware company for a demonstrator, a salesman? "People skills" it says here. You *are* good with people, aren't you? I can see we've ticked that on your skills sheet? Shall we have a closer look?'

Three years of university loiter at the edge of the frame, leather-jacketed, collars turned up, smoking rebelliously. *You guys ain't no good for me*. He listens to her suggestions and waits for it all to be over.

A woman stands at the counter with her crying child; he is thumping his mother's stomach with closed fists and demanding a jam doughnut.

'But, Jasper darling,' she says, 'you've already had a choccy muffin today, you can't possibly want a jammy doughnut already?'

She smiles thinly at Becky. Becky says nothing. Waits.

Jasper screams. 'But I WANT a jammy doughnut.'

His mum catches his wrists before he can hit her again and shudders a smile towards Becky. 'Now let's stop that, shall we?' she says to the kid. 'Let's just stop that this instant now, shall we?'

She's trying to keep her voice calm but it's wobbling.

'NOOOO!' Jasper screams, throwing himself to the floor.

She looks back to Becky. Raises her eyebrows. 'And a jam doughnut as well, please.'

Becky brings the order over to their table. 'Right,' she says. 'Here's your cappuccino, here's his babychino. Here's your fish finger sandwiches, crusts cut off for him, and here's your jam doughnut.'

The woman doesn't thank her. Doesn't even acknowledge her. 'Jasper,' she says, 'are we ready to eat our sandwich now?'

Becky walks back behind the counter to serve a man who's been waiting there for all of ten seconds. He is wearing a suit, carrying a laptop bag and keeps checking his watch and shuffling.

'How long is this going to take?' he asks. She looks at him. 'I mean, can you make it quick?'

She tells herself he doesn't mean to be rude. He's probably late for something important. He's stressed out about something. She imagines him trying to find a birthday present for a son he barely knows.

'Because I've got a very important meeting to get to, and I *am* in a hurry, so if we could . . . erm . . .' He checks his watch again. 'Chop chop?' he says.

Fuck you, she thinks. *Fuck. You.*

She can see the next twenty years playing out in the space between the counter and the flat and the casting calls and the auditions she can't get and the missed opportunities and the pie and mash and the pub and the injuries and her body in the mirror. Updating her profile page, happy in the photographs, smiling in her skintight sequins, diva week on *The X Factor*, shots for the road and lines and pills and arms around her friends as if it's fine, it's fine. But her muscles have a shelf life, and she is jealous of every struggling dancer in a company. Twenty years and she'll be here, cleaning up the café, still trying to prove to Auntie Linda that she can trust her with the seasoning. Twenty years of nothing changing but the rent. Maybe she just doesn't have what it takes. She forces herself to snap out of it, but her mother rages drunken through her mind as shooting pains bite down inside her, somewhere near the liver.

Pete heads out of the jobcentre. The security guard is still watching his reflection, making occasional menacing sweeps across the room with his bored, narrow eyes, wishing something would happen.

The little old guy with the bad teeth is outside having an argument with a shopkeeper, smoking and swigging from a can of black cider. Schoolgirls throw chicken bones at each other and scream in the road and don't move out of the way for cars. A few religious fundamentalists are shouting outside McDonald's, watched by a group of angry adolescent boys, while community support officers patrol the perimeters, looking for kids to save or report. Pete watches an elderly couple walk gently through the chaos arm in arm and feels easier.

He takes half a cigarette from the pack in his pocket, lights it, feels his stomach churn. He has one drag then throws it away. He steps into the café on the corner and closes the door behind him. There's a girl clearing plates. He watches her move across the room. Light blue jeans and a long black jumper. Her necklaces and earrings flash gold in his vision; she sways as she walks, like a lion in the sun. He waits for her to get back behind the counter, smiling politely when she meets his eye.

He is the first customer all day to shut the door behind him. Becky sends him her deepest gratitude.

'Hello,' she says. 'What can I get you?'

He puts his hands in his jacket pockets and turns to look at the blackboard. She watches his profile, the shape of his shoulders. He has hollow cheeks. He's wearing black jogging bottoms, a battered Fred Perry jacket, collar up. A black cap. His clothes hang off him like sails on a still day. His face is long and gaunt, bruised with stubble. Not a handsome man exactly. His eyes are deep and round and watery, like dolphin's eyes. He speaks slowly, working it out as he goes.

'Can I have a strong cup of coffee, with no milk, and a bacon and egg sandwich on brown bread, please?'

She nods. Time is slow as glass today. She watches the letters looping across the pad. *Bacon. Egg.* Looks back up at him.

'Where will you be sitting?'

'Over there.' He points. 'By the window.'

'OK, I'll bring it over,' she tells him.

'Cheers.' He smiles and the sun blasts the desolate landscape of his face, turns it film-set perfect.

She is surprised by the transformation. The smile fades though and his cheeks are hollowed and fretful again. His strange round eyes blink at her slowly. She waits for him to say something. He doesn't. He drops his head into the slouch of his shoulders. Unsteady on his legs like he's surprised at their length, he walks over to the table by the window. He has a book in his jacket pocket, it looks like it's trying to wriggle free. She hears it thud as it hits the table. He takes his cap off and rubs both hands over his face and head. He looks like he's been up all night, poor thing.

A queasy feeling runs its hands across Pete's stomach. He notices the candle in the beer bottle that sits in the middle of the table and he fingers the molten wax, traces its ridges. It always takes him a while to recover from the jobcentre. Everything about that room makes him want to spit and shout and kill people. He stretches his legs out underneath the table and checks Facebook on his phone. It tells him things he doesn't need to know about people he hasn't seen in years. He absorbs their aggressively worded opinions and quasi-political hate-speak. He sees a photograph of his ex-girlfriend with her new boyfriend smiling at a picnic and he realises, with a strange cascade of emptiness, that she is pregnant and wearing an engagement ring. The comments are jubilant. He reads every word before he forces himself to put his phone down.

A loneliness descends. He feels its familiar talons grabbing him violently out of his chair and hanging him, swinging, up by the ceiling.

Pete had his heart broken a year and a half before and he's still not managed to fix it. It sits there in his chest with its arms crossed, livid. He drops his head into the crook of his elbow and gazes sideways out the window. He feels old and boozesick and bored of himself. A torrent of coughs punches its way up from his lungs. He smothers them in his fist, leaves his hand glistening with yellow spit. He wipes his palm on a tissue and stuffs it in his pocket. His chest burns.

He looks up at the waitress. She is dizzying bright in his vision like sudden daylight in a darkened room and it gives him a terrifying kick in the guts. He swims towards her, teeth full of roses.

She glances over, catches him looking and she smiles her acknowledgement. It's all he needs. The smile is enough to transform the whole vomit-inducing rolling sea of nothingness. The prospect of sleeping with her thunders in the sky and rains heavily down against the windows. He prepares his most cavalier attitude, but notices with a jolt of shame that she isn't looking over any more.

Plates and forks and bread and ketchup. Endless tea-stained wash pots. Becky's spatula moves expertly over the griddled strips of swine. She pours the coffee, thick fuel steaming in white china, and moves, assured as always, to his table.

This morning she'd had the two builders who barked orders, ignored her and didn't say thank you. Then there was that couple that came in arguing. Shovelled eggs in a cloud of stress and fury and left in heavy silence. At least the men she massages look her in the eye. This man shut the door behind him. And he waited patiently for her to get back round the counter before ordering.

'There you go, love,' she says, putting the plate and the cup down gently. He sits up quickly from his slouch and rubs his hands with glee.

'Thank you,' he says, dripping gratitude. 'Looks lovely.' He reaches for the coffee cup. 'How's your day been?'

A shocked smile spreads its wings and soars across her cheeks. 'It's been alright,' she says happily. The stock answer. 'How's yours been?'

He rolls his eyes, heaves an exaggerated sigh. 'Oh you know. Not bad.'

She notices the book face-up on the table. It's simply bound, a pale yellow front cover. No graphic, just dark red lettering in bold type. She reads it in slow motion and then rereads in fast forward, fifteen times per second, her eyes stuttering on every letter. *How We Can Take Power Without Power Taking Us*. And across the top, as if it's no big deal: *John Darke*.

She doesn't know where to look. She hurries back to the counter, ducks clumsily into the store room, spinning. She leans her forehead against the wall, her throat dry, her breath paper.

The little bell above the door rings and she grows busy with a sudden flurry of customers, but even as she serves them she is aware of him at all times. She sees him take his last chew, wipe his mouth and sit in quiet contemplation for a long moment, tonguing the shreds in his teeth. He checks his cup and drains the last swigs, holding it in the air as he swills them round his mouth. Everything is happening in half-time. She sees him stand and lope towards her out of the corner of her eye. Her body is a frequency. A low rumble without shape. The world is slow and she feels sick.

'Can I settle up?' He stands, swaying slightly, in front of the picture of Giuseppe.

'Yep,' she says. Her voice leaps strangely out of her mouth. She flattens it, speaks low now, measured. Fixes her eyes on a point in the middle distance. 'Three ninety, please.' He digs around in his pocket for a fiver. Hands it over. Stares dumbly at the salads on the counter while she jangles through the till.

'There you go.' She hands him his change.

He puts it away slowly and stands there for too long wondering what to say. He's sure that she's been giving him the eye.

The pressure in her head is unbearable. She thinks she's going to faint or die or something. She wants to rip her skin off and reveal herself, all blood and sinew and pulsing fag-stained lungs and poor exhausted heart. John Darke. John Darke. John Darke. John Darke. Her fingernails repeat it. Her eyelashes repeat it. She clears her throat.

'See you later then.' She keeps her voice level, her tone calm and friendly.

'See you later,' he says over his shoulder as he shuts the door behind him.

She watches him through the window as he walks off down the high street.

Alone at the end of her shift, Becky sits with a beer at the table opposite Giuseppe's photo. She stares at him. There's definitely something in his posture that reminds her of her mother. She presses the cold beer bottle against her brow, drags it over her nose and mouth.

'What's it all about, Giuseppe?' Her voice is a stranger in the empty room. Terrified of its own shape.

She comes from a long line of people who fought like dogs for everything they had. Who pushed themselves onwards to impossible places.

Her dad gave his life for the words in that book. Now he's ticking days off in some lonely cell. She wonders if he's still alive. She's sure she would have felt it if he wasn't.

Images flicker across the room, still fragments of prison doors, pale blue lunch rooms, barbed wire crouched menacingly on the tops of high walls, white sunlight in a brick yard, the windows barely slits, a man's arms pushed through, dangling, just enough room to let his wrists feel the breeze. Inherited images from the internet. She hates him so much she can't bear it.

Her mum had the impossible dream of being a photographer on her own terms. She never saw it through but she was close. She got so close.

She owes it to them both to not just stagger blindly but to choose the route and walk it.

The muscles in her face are tense and she rubs her jaw and temples. It burns through her. Conviction so heavy it hurts in her throat. When she dances, it needs to be everything she's ever needed to say. She's got so lost in arse-licking, posing and pushing for roles, playing it cool behind vulnerable pop stars. The girls she dances with are all really sweet and they all get on great, say they're a family until the job's over, but then, they'd trample her bones to get to her part. It needs to be truer. It needs to be bolder and as heavy as this feeling in her throat and in her empty guts. It needs to kick her face open and flood her skull with light. She wants to make a piece of work for a company to dance that will terrify an audience and smash them back to feeling. But how? She can't even get seen in auditions. She hangs around the studio after class, chatting to the dancers about phrases that she's thinking of, running certain things again. Talking to the teachers. The dancers there are tired and their eyes are dark and their skin is bad and their feet are sore and broken, but they have a steel in them that Becky lacks. A sure, smiling steel that they got from sticking with it. Not like the girls she works with, who have glossy hair and sexy lips and satiated, peaceful eyes.

She wants to join a company. Really be a part of something. Dance beneath the guidance of a choreographer that she respects. Push herself before it's too late. For every member of her family who ever lived and died.

She used to vomit every meal. The enamel on her back teeth has been eroded from the stomach acid. It was all about control, she realises now. Her body was what haunted her. The ghosts of both her parents were inside it, somehow more than her, and less than her, and everybody staring at it. Dance teachers pinched her arms, and she would squeeze handfuls of herself, standing shell-shocked in the shower, staring at the bits she hated. This body. It was all she had. She needed it to work for her. Starved and gorged. The toilet doors. It was so sad and lonely there. But hers. All hers.

She would be more than the sum of her parts.

She swigs at her beer and two thin jets of foam drip down her chin. She lets them course towards her neck, swallowing in fast, hard gulps until the bottle's dry.

GIUSEPPE WAS UNCLE RON's father. His real name was actually Louis but, for a while, everyone called him Giuseppe.

In 1939, Louis was a young man living in Manchester, the son of two poor Jewish immigrants. His father had sickened and died, leaving Louis, his mother and his seven brothers and sisters to fend for themselves. His younger sisters would have to go to the synagogue at least once a week to beg for food. Louis was training to be a tailor. He was a charismatic, well-liked young man and was working hard to learn his trade.

When war broke out, Louis had just asked his girlfriend Joyce to marry him, but Joyce's mother refused. 'He has the look of a man who will never come back!' she fretted, clapping her hands dramatically to her brow as she worried the washing.

'My youngest daughter, and she wants to make a widow of herself before she's even seventeen?' So Joyce told Louis to make sure he came back home and, if he did, she'd marry him. He promised that he would, and off he went to war.

He was on the beaches at Dunkirk. They died and were killed and they died and were killed and the sand turned putrid with men's insides. Blood and shit and sweat, the rancid stench of war. He was commanded to stay where he was and hold the fort while the rest of the battalion went for help. He was left with twenty-nine others, and they dug in as fiercely as they could, but the company never came back for them. He would often say later that he learned more about life in those couple of hours than he'd ever learned before or since. Seven of the thirty men were killed, and the twenty-three that stayed breathing were captured. Including himself.

In the coming days, more than 200,000 British troops would be evacuated from the bloodied beach, but Louis would not be among them.

Louis's best friend in the regiment was a tall, lopsided, skinny man named Joseph. His hair was black as onyx and his smile wrapped itself around anyone who saw it. His constant laugh sounded like he'd swallowed a siren, and he was never still, he moved like a bouncing ball, no matter what he was doing. Everyone called him Giuseppe because he was in love with an Italian girl and was prone to outbursts of song in struggling Italian late at night when he was drunk and out of his mind with missing her.

When Louis was left on the beach, Giuseppe was one of the other twenty-nine men who were with him. They had been through a lot together in the short time they'd been friends, and as Giuseppe approached his final moment, shot through the stomach and bleeding all over the sand, Louis crouched beside him and whispered into his dying ears, 'You're walking along with all the people you love, it's a sunny day. You're somewhere you haven't been for a while, it's beautiful, the trees are swaying, your family are all there, your girl's there too, holding your hand. Everybody's smiling and happy and the sky is blue blue blue. You've got a picnic, all your favourite food, nice cold bottles of beer. Your girl's giving you a nice kiss. The sun's warm on the top of your head. It's a lovely day, it really is.'

As the Germans came to round up the prisoners, Louis had to think fast. He knew Hitler was killing the Jews. He didn't know the extent of what was happening in the camps, but he'd heard enough to know he didn't want the Germans to find out who he was. He kissed Giuseppe's forehead and swapped identity discs. He left Louis Shogovitch dead on the beach, and joined the other prisoners as Joseph Jones, 'Giuseppe' to his friends.

They were stripped of their arms and lined up in single file, and they began the march to the prisoner of war camp. This sorry line of captured men, haggard and gun-struck, was headed and tailed by clean-shaven German soldiers, who marched with their guns and their dogs and their dignity. As well as the soldiers at the head and the tail of the line, there were two soldiers who patrolled the length of the line constantly, each holding a fearsome German Shepherd. They walked either side of the POWs, one on the right, the other on the left, starting from opposite ends, so that one began at the head of the line, the other at the tail, and they crossed in the middle.

The ground was even as the prisoners walked, each one thinking, or not thinking, staring at the back of the head of the man in front. They entered a forest. It was thick and the trees smelt fresh and clean after the stench of battle. The air became softer, light tangling in the leaves, trickling down through branches that clasped other branches like praying hands.

Louis studied the soldiers that passed him on his right and on his left. He noticed that they walked in step, and that each time they marched the length of the line, it took them exactly the same amount of time to reach the end, turn round and walk back.

When he was passed, he counted the seconds until he was passed again. The gap was exactly the same. He counted forty seconds between the soldier to his left and the soldier to his right passing him. And each one of those forty seconds stretched his skin a little tighter.

He thought of the dogs and their teeth, and he thought of the guns. He saw the blood and the smoke of the battles he'd been fighting for days on end. Then he thought of the other end of this marching line. When the destination was reached they'd find out who he was and he'd never get home alive. He would be killed. He thought of his mother, saw her face in his mind. He summoned the faces of his seven siblings. He whispered their names. He thought of his Joyce, the promise he'd made her. There was nothing else for it, he had to get home.

This was his chance.

Louis carried on counting, and each time, the delay between the two guards crossing seemed to be more pregnant, more weighted. He breathed deeply, waited for the guard on his right to pass him. He did. He counted ten seconds for the guard to get further down the line, glanced back to see the other guard, thirty seconds from him, and then time stopped. He jumped. He launched himself as hard as he could into the forest beside the path. Thick and green and giving after the sparsity of sea and sand and blood. He felt it take him and felt his breathing change. He began to run. And he could hear the gunshots, the barking dogs, the shouting men. He could feel the ground shake with heavy German boots but he ran with the forest not through it, ducked branches before he'd seen them, jumped dips before falling, and he kept on running, until eventually, his limbs in ribbons from thorns and brambles, his ankles twisted, his chest and throat thick with blood, he saw that it was dark, and quiet, and no one was chasing him any more.

He began his journey home. His mission was to head to Paris and then south towards Spain, for the Gibraltar Straits, where he knew he could get in a boat and sail back to Manchester.

He lived on what he could find, and the hospitality of the people in the houses he passed. Especially the children, who were usually kind to him and gave him as much food as they could sneak past their parents. He made it to Paris eventually. Living every day as Giuseppe. The way he figured it, with his complexion, he was safer an Italian on the run from Mussolini than a Jewish British soldier on the run from Hitler.

Despite the German occupation, Paris was good to him. He was given a room in a brothel where he rested for a while. He got work in a cabaret bar playing piano for the dancing girls and passed a happy few months thanking God for his life and recovering from the terrors of war. But home called him onwards, and he set out again.

Back in Manchester, the news had arrived of Louis Shogovitch's brave death on the beaches. He had fought valiantly, and held his ground proudly. He was a hero who had died fighting for the safety of his nation. His family dropped their heads and shook with grief.

When Giuseppe arrived back home at last it was raining and his boots were full of holes.

He let himself in through the back door that was always open, but found nobody there. He looked around, open-mouthed. Stuffing his face with the smells of his mother's kitchen. He marvelled at the wallpaper, freckled with damp, pale at the edges, so familiar it sent a sweet dull pain straight through his middle. He pressed his hands against every surface. Tears in his eyes. He took off his boots and left them on the mat. Walked in his socks to the front room and sat himself down in his favourite chair, pushed his face deep into the cushions and fell asleep, the first happy sleep since he'd left.

When someone dies in a Jewish family the body is buried and then a year later the gravestone is set. When Giuseppe's mother got home from the stone setting and found her son's boots on the mat, she passed out cold.

He woke from his sleep with a start to the sound of his mother's body falling to the kitchen floor. He wrenched his eyes open, expecting to see explosions, flesh, black smoke and screaming chaos, but instead he saw, to his unstoppable relief, that he was at home in his favourite chair. He sprang up and ran to the back door where he found his mother. He roused her gently, stared at her face with tears in his eyes, the first sight of land in a year lost at sea. He rocked her in his arms until she came round and saw her youngest son, back from the dead, speaking gentle words to her in the bright glow of their kitchen. Six months later he married Joyce and they stayed together for the rest of their lives.

After coming so close to death, he wanted to live a selfish life for as long as it felt like the right thing to do. Both he and Joyce worked hard. They saved money and travelled the world together. It wasn't until very late in their marriage that they had their children. Joyce was thirty-five when her eldest boy Ron was born. He was followed in the next five years by Rags and then Paula. And although by this time Louis was very much Louis again, the spirit of Giuseppe would follow the family for ever.

When Ron took over the lease of the café he knew there was only one name for it.

BECKY LOCKS UP. The high street is still busy, the market men are shouting their arias. The wind is bright and sharp. She can feel the presence of every member of her family crowding towards her, telling her to know herself and stop wasting her time.

She'd never seen her father's book before. She's sure her mum must have kept a copy somewhere, but she'd never seen one, not up close like that. Not for real. She walks down towards the station. Smiling 'alrights' at faces she's spent a lifetime passing by.

That evening Becky is in the Hanging Basket, waiting for Gloria to finish her shift. Charlotte has a load of Year 9 essays out in front of her. She is meant to have marked them by now but she hasn't looked at them for the last three hours. The pub is closed. Charlotte is smoking a spliff and playing solitaire with a pack of pornographic playing cards from the 1970s that live behind the bar.

Becky is drinking a gin and tonic. 'This guy came in the café today,' she says.

'Was it *this* guy?' Charlotte asks her, holding out the Jack of Hearts, showing two women with blonde perms and shiny red high heels fellating a man with a blond perm and shiny red cowboy boots.

'Not quite that guy. But maybe one day he could become that guy.'

'Maybe we all could, if we tried hard enough.' Charlotte looks back at her game. Waits for Becky to keep talking but she doesn't.

'Anyway,' Charlotte says. 'This guy come in the café today . . .?'

Becky leans her head into her hand, feels the back of her skull. 'No, that was it. That was all I was gonna say.' She hangs her hair down in front of her face, combs it through her fingers, plays with the ends.

Charlotte watches the cards. Speaks flatly. 'Great story. Tell it again.'

'Shut up.' Becky pushes her friend in the shoulder with a soft hand.

'No, no, it was really interesting,' Charlotte says, enthusiastically deadpan. 'It was *really* interesting.'

'Come then,' Gloria calls to them as she walks over, getting her coat and her bag from the hooks behind the till. 'I'm all finished, we're going.'

'Do we really have to go?' Charlotte asks her.

‘I don’t want to go,’ Becky says.

‘You never wanna go anywhere.’ Gloria takes Charlotte’s spliff from her, has the last couple of puffs.

‘I work hard,’ Becky tells her.

‘It’s her birthday. Course we have to go.’ Gloria stubs the roach out in the ashtray, empties the ashtray into the bin and looks at them both. ‘Come then.’

She walks to the door, opens it and holds it until they get their coats on.

‘Fuck’s sake, we’ve only been waiting for you for three hours,’ Charlotte says.

Becky finishes her drink, reaches over the bar to leave it on top of the washer, and follows them out.

It’s about one in the morning. Pete’s on the door at Mess, for a club night his mate puts on called Shitstorm, which it usually is. He’s freezing and bored.

A group of girls walk up the path to the courtyard and Neville, one of the bouncers, nudges him, rubbing his hands. ‘State of this lot, look.’

Seven or eight girls, all pissed, are walking towards them. Looking closer, Pete sees that actually it’s only one or two that are pissed; the others seem to be playing up to it a bit. Apart from three who are walking at the back of the crowd, a bit slower, talking together. He watches them. Must be a birthday or something. The one at the back is slim and dark-haired and he likes the way she’s walking, head down, hips swinging. *She looks like trouble.* He looks closer. Everything stops. Opens its mouth, screams. Starts again. *Don't be a prick.* Her body is a waterfall, her chin's down, she's talking to her friends, using the hand that holds a cigarette to punctuate her sentences. She moves across the pavement completely separate from what surrounds her. Drawing everything in. She's walking straight towards him.

Becky's standing in the courtyard outside Mess finishing her cigarette. 'We going in then?' she asks the girls. Jemma, whose birthday it is, is singing the *Home and Away* theme tune at top volume. She directs a couple of lines at Becky.

She has one hand on her heart and the other reaching towards the heavens.

Becky rolls her eyes,

'See you in there,' she says, walking towards the doors. 'Alright?' she greets the doorman. Looks in her bag for her purse. 'Can I pay for me and for that girl there?' She points towards Jemma who is sitting on the floor, rending her clothes with emotion.

'Course you can,' the doorman says.

She looks up to pay him and her hand stops in mid-air. 'You came in my caff today?'

'Yeah, that's right.' He smiles his best smile, puffs his chest up. 'How's it going?'

Her heart is hammering, the soles of her feet hurt.

'Alright, yeah. Not bad.' She looks at him, right in the face.

He tries to hold his shit together, sends an urgent message to his nose, eyes, lips, chin. *Stay put. Act natural.*

'Big night, is it?' He indicates the others with his eyes. The excitement is building in his body. She stabs a painful hope into him.

'Jemma's birthday.' She points to the one who's the most pissed; Jemma has her arms around Gloria's shoulders, dragging her down towards the pavement saying, 'I love you, Gloria, I really do.' Smoking two fags at the same time.

'Having fun?' he asks her, hands in his pockets, shoulders squared against the cold, looking down into her face.

'Think she is,' Becky says, tipping her head towards Jemma before reaching out the hand that holds the tenner again and offering it to him. He waves it away.

'No, no, you're alright,' he says. *Go on*, says his gut, *say something*. 'Save it,' he says. 'You can buy me a drink later?' But she doesn't respond. She's just looking at him, eyes flashing. He considers repeating it but she's already walking away, into the club.

Inside it's heaving. It's all so familiar. All so neon and dismal. Kids vomit discreetly in corners while they come up off their drugs. Men with old faces smile like cartoon villains at young girls with low self-esteem and terrible secrets. Gloria heads for the bar.

'Get me a thing? Drink?' Becky shouts. Gloria nods.

'We're over there.' Charlotte points to the speakers.

'Yeah,' Gloria nods, sticking her thumb up.

Charlotte grabs Becky's arm in one hand and Jemma's in the other and they push through the bodies and the noise. They take their coats off, stuff them behind the speaker stacks and stand with their faces an inch from the bass bins. The DJ's playing drum 'n' bass. Technical Itch.

Charlotte beckons her closer. 'Shock the fuck oooout, bruv,' she shouts in her ear, screwing her face up. Becky shakes her head in mock exasperation. Charlotte laughs. They start dancing.

Becky's mind calms as her body starts moving. But she can't zone out completely. *We only came in here because the other place was one in, one out.*

Pete stands there in the cold for a bit. Shivering with excitement. Pacing. Ruffling his stubbly hair and smoothing it down again.

'Neville, cover me for ten minutes, will you, mate?'

Neville nods, Pete throws him the stamp and goes inside.

There are people everywhere. Bodies and backs and hair. What colour was she wearing? She had a coat on. Pacing. Pushing people out the way. Scouring every corner. Nothing. *Maybe that girl?* He heads towards her. *No. Not her.* He's on his tiptoes, looking over everyone's heads. Hugging the walls, checking every figure. Scanning every face in the booths at the back. Nothing. Fuck it. He stands at the bar. Determined. Everything pushing.

The DJ charges off into anonymous blip core.

Becky taps Charlotte's arm. 'I'm gonna find G, help her with the drinks,' she shouts.

Charlotte nods. Becky picks her way through the bodies, stands at the bar looking for Gloria. She can't see her.

She feels a tap on her shoulder. She turns and her body plummets straight down a sudden hole that's opened in the floor. It's him. He's saying something. Leaning down towards her. She smells him. Sweat and aftershave, cigarettes, cold air. He draws his head back, looks at her for a response. She taps her ear and shakes her head. *CAN'T HEAR YOU*, she mouths. He hits his forehead with the palm of his hand. *PHONE.* She mimes it, holding out a hand as if it holds a phone and pointing to it. He gets his phone out, gives it to her. They are standing close together in a push of warm bodies. His temples are pounding. She opens a text and writes *BECKY*; they are leaning in, over the screen. Their shoulders are touching. She sees that his lips are smooth. He reaches for the phone, types in *PETE*. She smiles, takes the phone back off him. *GOOD TO MEET PEET.* They are face to face but looking down, not at each other. In her head her brain is burning, visions of a distant time, her father writing at the kitchen table, his feet bare, his battered jacket on the chair behind him, her crawling, sitting between his feet, playing with colourful bricks. The playground by their old flat, her mum there, so beautiful, smiling, her face all pink from the weather, her necklaces hanging, the climbing frame shaped like a spider, one rung at a time up the ladder legs, his arms there, his hands as big as the world.

She types her number in, gives the phone back to him. He can smell her clothes, her skin, like crushed almonds, or something. Darker though, earth after rain, smokier, like the inside of a growing plant. She looks deep into his face. He looks away, can't hold her gaze.

It's 4.18 a.m. Harry's home from another party, hours spent going through the motions, smiling at the wankers.

She's got it down to a slick operation, but some nights she finds it more taxing than others. After her long day shift of meetings with company directors in Soho, Harry and Leon took their dinner at Alberto's on Greek Street. She walked in and was greeted with cheerful kisses on her cheeks. Alberto himself came out from behind the bar to clasp their arms.

'Ciao, ciao, lovebirds!' He led them to their usual table and told them all about his latest concerns with his wayward nephew. They had the special and drank a glass of wine each with their meal. Afterwards, they sipped espresso and sucked on breath mints. They paid cash, tipped generously and headed out, back to the stash to reload. Harry only ever takes out exactly the amount she needs, and is happier to cross town three times in one day to reload than work two shifts with a big lump on her.

Tonight's shift involved a house party in a converted warehouse in Hoxton. Harry arrived, greeted her client warmly; a theatre producer called Raj. Harry set up shop in Raj's youngest child's bedroom. The child was at his mother's. After the initial sale, Harry stood around the party for some hours, drinking fizzy water, smiling when smiled at and popping back to the bedroom to sell close friends of Raj a gram or two here and there. She danced non-committally. Caught up with a couple of actors she used to sell gear to when they had roles. They told her that they were between parts, and they asked in desperate whispers if she could put in a good word for them with Raj. Harry waited around happily until the inevitable moment when Raj wanted to buy another eighth. After that, she said her goodbyes and jumped in a cab to the next party.

She sits at her kitchen table looking at commercial properties on the internet, eating Vietnamese soup. She sees a massive double-fronted place in Peckham that she likes the look of. Flats upstairs as well. Used to be a hairdresser's. Could be perfect. But Peckham's changed. It's unrecognisable now. She'd heard the rumours start five, six years before that Peckham was becoming desirable, trendy. But she didn't believe it. She thought south London would hold its own for ever. But her home town is dying, it's half-dead already. All that she knows to be true is suddenly false. Communities flattened to make room for commuters.

She closes her laptop and walks to the fridge. No beer. She gets her shoes on, keys, jogs across the road to the offie. It's cold out.

She pays for the beer, opens it and sits on someone's front-garden wall, looking up at the moon. Trying to shake off the slow-motion replay of spilling her guts out to that girl at the party that's been haunting her since she woke up. She exhales deeply. Shakes her head. Shudders.

'Idiot,' she says sadly.

A couple wander past her, hanging off each other's hips. It wrenches her to see it. She scratches the back of her head, scrunches her hair. Sighs and looks up at the street lights. Tells herself she's doing fine. She's smashing it. She's making it happen. And as she sits she feels the hum of all the endless houses she has lived amongst since she was born. She holds on to the comfort of this road, this wall, this corner. Hers. She looks around. The houses are filled with people. The people are filled with houses.

The city yawns and cracks the bones in her knuckles. Sends a few lost souls spiralling out of control; a girl is digging through a skip with cold hands, looking for copper piping, another girl is at home reading. Another girl is sleeping deeply. Another girl is laughing in her friend's flat, getting her hair done, another girl is in love with her girlfriend and lying beside her and feeling her breathing. Another girl is walking her dog round the park, tipping her head back to listen to the wind as it shouts in the trees.

Becky is dancing with Charlotte and Gloria. Pete is in the club basement studying the yellow powder Neville just took off a teenager. Leon's in bed with a girl named Delilah. Harry's drinking her beer on the wall. Everybody's looking for their tiny piece of meaning. Some fleeting, perfect thing that might make them more alive.

CHICKEN

The sun rises and nothing is left of the night. People wake up and drink water, shake off their hangovers and head for the shopping centre. It's Saturday. Dads have their children and couples are planning their weddings and old friends on a golf course talk about finance.

Pete and Harry walk beside each other up a quiet road towards their mother's new house. The grime that clings to the walls is the same grime they've lived with all their lives. They pass dirty bricks, grand old gate posts, charcoal-grey slate roofs with TV aerials sticking up like bad hair. They pass graffiti-ed lamp posts and a UKIP poster in a front window and Polish words across the shop fronts and a group of men in thobes talking outside a café.

They turn onto a residential side road that ends in a cul-de-sac. The sky is grey and muggy. It wants to rain. Skinny trees grow in cages along the pavement, litter shivers in threadbare hedges. Two girls play football in the road; their dad is washing his car. The ball sails a little too close to his windscreen and he drops his sponge and screams at them. 'YOU DO THAT AGAIN, AND I WILL SKIN YOU BOTH ALIVE!' His daughters shriek and giggle, grab their ball and run off down the road. 'NOT TOO FAR,' he shouts. 'YOU HEAR ME, GIRLS?' They slow their pace and loiter on the kerb.

'How's Dad?' Harry asks her brother.

'Fine.' Pete's voice is flat as the sky. Pete is tall and Harry's tiny, but they have the same posture, the same lolloping gait. The same bony arms swinging the same rhythm as they walk.

'Is he?' she asks. Pete kicks a stone towards the hubcap of a parked car. Scores. 'Shot.' Harry admires his skill.

'He's getting dressed again. He's going to work,' Pete says, offering a watery shrug.

'Are you taking care of him?'

'Why don't you go round and see him if you're so worried?'

'I'm busy. You know I'm busy.' Harry whines the familiar refrain.

Pete shakes his head. 'I'm busy too.'

Harry looks at him. He seems unwell. Huge bags under his eyes and dry skin and he keeps sniffing and coughing. She wants him to sort himself out. Move out of their dad's place and stand on his own feet. But if he wants to mug himself off, let him crack on. 'Couldn't you get, like, labouring work even?'

Pete's forehead tenses. He shakes her question off with a wave of his hand, as if it's beneath him to answer it. They go back to silence and listen to the girls singing together on the kerb.

Pete checks the door numbers of the houses they pass. 'Well,' Pete's smile stabs itself in the guts, 'it's good that you're making an effort today.' He cracks the bones in his neck, a jerky rolling movement.

'You think I've not made an effort?' Harry says carefully. Pete kicks at a stone again, misses it. Doesn't say anything. 'Pete?' Her voice sharpens.

Pete sighs heavily. 'Don't start. Alright?'

'No, what do you mean? I *have* made an effort, Pete. I've made—' She's cut off by him buckling under a coughing fit. His hand covers his mouth, she watches his body pumping with each rattle.

Harry sticks her hands into her pockets, listens to their footsteps.

'It's that one, there,' Pete says, getting his breath, pointing to the corner house.

The kitchen is beaming. Pleased with itself. The worktops are beech, the cupboards are teal. Recently refurbished with all the mod cons. This is David's kitchen.

He is sitting in a chair at the table watching Miriam's back as she cooks vegetables. She talks to him without looking at him.

'It'll be fine,' she says. 'Nice lunch, that's all. Nothing to worry about.'

He is chopping an onion. He's never had the knack for it. It slides across the chopping board. The kitchen is bright. The sun floods the surfaces.

'Do you think they'll like me?' He leans back in his chair, looks up from the onion.

'Of course they will. They just want me to be happy.' Her voice is melodic, gentle. With a tendency to let her words roll upwards at the ends of her sentences. The kind of speaking voice David associates with hairdressers. His favourite kind of speaking voice for a lady.

'And *are* you?' He waits for her affirmation, face tipped up to catch it all.

'Yes, David.' She looks over her shoulder at him. 'You know I am.'

He goes back to his chopping board. Satisfied. The onion, at last, gives. David blinks rapidly and opens his mouth to fight off the onion tears. Grimaces silently for a moment, waits for the sting to pass.

'Harriet's the eldest?' he asks her, rubbing his nose with the back of the hand that holds the knife.

'Don't do that, please, David, you'll have your eye out,' she tells him, without turning round. He puts his hand back down obediently. 'Yes. Harriet's the eldest,' she says.

'Which makes Peter the youngest?'

'Yes.' Her voice is level, her tone is kind.

'Pete. Right.' He stores the information in his brain. 'And Harriet works in recruitment. And Pete is looking for work?'

'That's right.'

'And Pete likes . . . reading, was it? And football? Does he like football?'

Miriam takes a deep breath, wipes her hands on her apron.

'Relax.' She turns to face him. 'Everything is going to be fine. And pass me the stock cubes from the cupboard.'

He gets up and walks to the cupboard, looks for the stock cubes. 'Do you think they'll like the house?' He can't find them. He can never find anything.

'It's a nice house.' She watches him struggle at the cupboard.

'Must be strange for them though. Mum's new house? I know I'd find it strange, if it was my mum.'

She walks over, reaches behind a jar of pasta and finds the stock cubes without looking. 'It's all arranged, and they're coming now, so we'll just have to see what happens, won't we?' Her face is set in a mask of unflinching calm, but her eyes are pale with panic.

He sits back down at his chair again, surveys the mess he's made of the onion. The sunlight through the window is dazzling; he closes his eyes and watches the patterns underneath his lids.

'BACKWARDS' IS WHAT HIS father had said. 'Backwards in coming forwards.'

When David was fifteen, his father had left and he never saw him again. Never, not once. Not even at his mother's funeral. Imagine that – you spend your whole life with a woman, you have a child with her, and then one day you go to work in the morning and you never think to come home. Not even to bury her.

After his father had been gone a week, David went out to find a job. He went to the optician's on the high street, Bright Eyes. He walked in, in his best shirt and his hair combed to the side and his glasses cleaned with his mother's silk scarf. The manager was called Susan and she had beautiful big eyes and broad shoulders and she laughed from her breasts, and it made her shake. She gave him a job. He'd never had a job before. 'No good' is what his dad had said.

No good, good for nothing, useless dumb lump. Fifteen years old and never worked a day in your life. Hard to believe you're a son of mine. I don't believe it. Must be the milkman's.

'You'll open the door for customers, and you'll sweep the floor and you'll clean the display cases,' Susan told him. And he did. He left school and worked with pride and single-mindedness, and Susan liked him.

He worked his way through that spring and into the summer, and on through the summer, and into the autumn, and then Isaiah, the optician, took him for his first pint of beer in the Horse and Groom across the street. David didn't have many friends, but Isaiah was kind to him and didn't mind how slowly he drank that first beer, or any after it. He told him that day, 'You won't like it at first, but you'll get used to it, it's better than you think.'

Every second Friday he got his pay cheque and he took it home and he gave it to his mother, and she was soft and full of pride. Watching her soaps or making their dinner or reading her crime or her romance. Always big, hardback books that she got from the library and read constantly. She'd leave the books open by her chair, with her glasses, while she dusted her ornaments or washed the clothes, and David would never touch them, but he would read the page she was on when he got home from work. Stooping over the book. Never picking it up. He was happy with the way things were. He wasn't a sociable young man. The only girlfriend he'd ever had was a nervous twenty-two-year-old called Joanne who ate her lunch on the same bench as him, outside the supermarket. She was three times David's size and she had dry, angry skin around her mouth that she was constantly applying ChapStick to. They had sex in her Honda Civic, nestled in a dark corner of the Lewisham Centre car park. Three storeys up. He can still recall climbing the stale stairwell, not saying much, walking a foot apart, staring intently at the winding ramps and low ceilings, light-headed from the petrol fumes. The hot air inside the locked car, her endless underwear, the gear stick, the steering wheel, the comforting folds of her flesh.

It had been a year. Isaiah left Bright Eyes to go to Canada with his young Canadian wife and his wife's sister and his wife's sister's fiancé. They were going to buy a house and plant a garden and start their own practice and think about children. Then it was just David and Susan, until Hong came, the new optician. Years melted away. David turned twenty.

Hong and Susan laughed in the stock room at lunchtime. David, happier than ever, meticulously polished the display cases and brought the pay cheques home to his mother.

David was promoted. He wasn't just sweeping up now; he helped the customers choose the best frames for their complexions. Watched them as they tried on the pairs he recommended. Talked about face shapes with businessmen whose eyes were failing, and showed his favourites to mothers with nervous young children who wanted colourful frames decorated with cartoon characters.

The clothes in the charity shops were getting better, more expensive. Cafés were replacing the greasy spoons, and a rash of bistros and boutiques with names David couldn't pronounce without feeling embarrassed sprang up overnight. The rent went up and Susan didn't seem to laugh so much.

It began with forgetfulness, then there were the sudden inexplicable rages. One day he came home to find his mother standing in the garden wearing his clothes, shouting at her nasturtiums. She was complaining of headaches. Mysterious blotches appeared and disappeared on her arms. She often saw things that weren't there. Miniature people sitting on top of her glasses. Two greyhounds sleeping in the corner of the bathroom.

The doctors took blood tests and samples and measured her pulse but found nothing irregular. It broke David's heart to see her in the hospital, hooked up to machines.

He took her home, made her comfortable, cooked her favourite foods, read her books out loud to her and thought she was improving, until he woke one dazzling morning and found her dead in her bed.

She looked like she was sleeping. The sunlight through the windows clogged his eyes like bright white liquid.

The post-mortem revealed a brain tumour.

David was thirty-one. Until this point in his life it had never even occurred to him that sooner or later his mother would die.

She left him money. It was strange. All these years of giving her everything he made, and here she was, giving it back. She'd never spent a penny of it. She'd been getting money from his father since the day he left. It was a strange, tumultuous realisation, to discover that his mother kept secrets from him. After a lifetime of steady, trustworthy reality, suddenly nothing was certain. He imagined the letters, the phone calls between them. Why wasn't he told? Did she write longingly to his father, beg him to come home? When did they arrange for him to give her money every month? Was it agreed between them? As far as he knew, his dad had just disappeared. The idea that they carried on talking without telling him gutted him, arsehole to jugular.

The funeral was simple. A cremation. A restrained service attended by eight staunch old ladies who were friends he never knew his mother had and the three family members that he could find phone numbers for. A cousin he'd met twice. His great-uncle who arrived with his new Filipino wife and her two teenage sons, and his mother's last surviving cousin, Irene, who came with her spaniel Samuel. Afterwards, at the wake, nobody said much to each other apart from the eight old ladies, who spoke quietly amongst themselves.

David watched these strangers in his house eating vol-au-vents and felt like it was happening on telly. He said goodbye at the end, cleaned up the glasses, put them away, took out the rubbish, boiled the kettle for a cup of tea and couldn't shake the feeling that he was in another room, watching himself from behind glass.

Weeks passed. A month. He thought he was coping. People assured him he was. One evening he walked home from work, nothing unusual had happened that day, and as he let himself into the house he heard himself shout, 'Only me, Mum,' as he shut the door.

The silence that swallowed his words was so total he dropped in the hallway and lay face down on the floor. Suddenly crying. Retching and shaking and punching the carpet, punching the walls, sitting up briefly to breathe, shaking his head and punching his thighs. He lay there for hours. Crying and calming and crying again, howling, groaning, whimpering, until he dozed off. He slept there for a moment, could have been a minute or a second or an hour, and woke up with a feeling that someone had called to him from a long way away. He found himself there in that elusive waking moment before reality catches up. He could have been anywhere, at any time in his life. Until he blinked and saw the skirting board. The dark house. The night outside. The hallway was achingly quiet, he was on the floor and his face was cramped from crying, and the carpet was wet with snot and tears.

And then it was the meeting with the accountant, and coming home to his mother's house, every corner full of her presence and full of her absence. He sat in his bedroom reminding himself that she wasn't downstairs reading her books. It was the most desolate, confusing time of his entire life.

He sold the house and rented a new place, just for him. A one-bed flat, and he walked around it, cavalier, deciding what he would put where. More alive with every minute. And feeling guilty for it.

A few months after he'd moved in, Susan called him into the office. It was hot outside, and the air was full of other people's sweat, evaporating off their skin as soon as they'd had the chance to exude it, and Susan's breasts were lower down her body than usual. Hong hadn't been in for a few days.

'David love, I'm afraid it's not good news. And you know how fond I am of you. We've worked together here the best part of two decades. Sixteen years. That's longer than some people know their own families.' David nodded, picked up some paperclips from the tray on the desk, fiddled with them. Susan's eyes were damp. 'And I really feel I've seen you grow, David. You've grown into a fine young man and it's been a pleasure being around that growth, David. But look, times are not so great, as I'm sure you've gathered. People don't have no call for going down the old high street optician's that can't, no way, compete with the successful chain stores that have got money for the advertising and the designer brands and the flash machines. And the rent is just going up and up, and as much as I'm sure that's good for someone, it ain't no good for us, is it, David?'

David was quiet, listening. He stood still, waiting for her to finish speaking. Nothing moved, he felt as if he could feel his hair growing.

'I don't understand what you mean, Susan.' His face was soft-featured and attentive. No hint of irony in him. No sarcasm, everything said as he thought it, no nuance, no hidden meanings, there was never an underlying tension, never a hint of insincerity with David. Susan cleared her throat and looked at her knee.

'Now, I don't want to have to do this as much as you don't want me to have to do this.' A pause fell on them like a duvet across a bed. She was watching him closely. He didn't flinch.

'I'm sorry, Susan, I don't understand,' he said again patiently.

'Come on, David.' Susan got up from her chair and walked over to him, and for the first time in sixteen years she put her arm around his shoulder, her cheek close to his cheek. She smelt of cocoa butter and rice pudding and sanitising hand wash. 'It's over, David,' she said sadly. 'We've got to go. Bright Eyes is closing down.'

He had all the money from the sale of the house, but nothing was stable, he recognised nothing about his life. He was learning to cook, learning to wash his own pants. He was out of the only job he'd ever had. He was giddy on terror and joy.

It was a Tuesday. He called Susan on her home phone. 'Hi, Susan, it's David, I want to buy Bright Eyes.'

The deal went through. Bright Eyes was his.

He threw himself into it. A new coat of paint on the walls. A new sign above the door. He polished the display cases, arranged the new lines of designer specs by roundness of shape.

On opening morning he'd arrived at the shop just after dawn. No one else was around but him and the road sweepers, it was too early even for the market men. He stood and felt the weight of the keys in his hand. He fitted them in to the lock. Felt them click into place. He turned the key, opened the door and walked into his shop.

His.

Shop.

Our shop, Mum, he thought to himself, enjoying the smell: the lovely cleanness, not like a chemical, impersonal cleanness – but clean, like a safe place. Like somebody cared.

David hung his coat up and took off his scarf and stood there, with his hands in his trouser pockets, staring at the racks of spectacles and thinking of his mother with infinite affection. Regretting every dish he'd left on the side, every cup of tea he hadn't thought to make her. And he began to talk to her.

'Oh I don't know, Mum,' he said. 'Silly old day, wasn't it, really, yesterday? Not much we can do though, is there? About that?'

He didn't say much that was important, he just chatted absent-mindedly to the frames as he walked the broom around the spotless floor, sweeping up nothing, over and over again.

MIRIAM'S HANDS ARE AGAINST his cheeks, they are cool and smell of cooking and soap.

'Don't worry, Dave,' she says. 'Think about the other day, how nervous you were about me meeting your Dale, but it was lovely, wasn't it? We all got on fine.'

He nods. It is true. David had been nervous about Miriam meeting his only son because Dale has a tendency to be big and rude. But Miriam is right, as she always seems to be, they had all got on fine.

'Just relax,' Miriam tells him. 'They'll love you. You'll love them.'

And she touches his face and David feels the familiar orchestra striking up in his chest.

Pete looks at his mother and sees a quietness in her that he isn't used to. No one has said anything for a few minutes. Pete looks pointedly at his sister. Harry feels his eyes but doesn't look up. David is staring out at everyone, smiling, trying to catch someone's eye, pushing his glasses up his nose.

'The chicken's great, Mum.'

Miriam looks at Pete, grateful that someone has broken the silence.

'Thanks, love, I just did it the way I always do. Just the usual.'

Pete smiles at her. Harry shudders inwardly.

David sees his moment. 'So, erm, do you do much cooking then?' He pushes his glasses up his nose.

'I wish I did more, David,' Pete says. 'Can't seem to get past beans on toast these days.'

'Oh yes? I make a good beans on toast myself!' David pushes his glasses up his nose again. He speaks all sentences as if they have an exclamation mark at the end. 'I like to sprinkle some grated cheese on top! Or sometimes underneath! You know, before you pour the beans on? Makes it melt more thoroughly!'

Harry stares at David, his thinning hair combed through with gel, silvering at the edges, face like an empty bowl, gazing dumbly, wondering what else he could say about beans. She can feel her lip crawling up into a sneer. Harry's dad is in her mind. Him and his silent, difficult ways. Him and his lofty conversation.

She feels like an impostor when she's around Pete and her mum together. She becomes aware of everything about her that she got from her dad. Shrunken and difficult next to her shining, rose-lipped brother.

'Yeah, I've done that. I've put cheese on top before. It's nice, yeah.' Pete could be saying anything, just words. As long as words are being said then it's fine, his mum will feel better.

Each nervous second pushes against the next one. David's urgent eyes seek out something to remark on. Miriam breathes quietly, wonders how she can calm him down. Her eyes find his but he can't read the gaze.

'And how's work, Harriet? Recruitment, isn't it?'

She flinches as she always does when people call her Harriet. It feels like someone else's name. A constant reminder of all she gets wrong. But her mother won't call her Harry. *I gave you a name for a reason,* she had said. *You are my daughter after all.*

'Yeah, that's right, David, it is. It's fine, thanks, trucking on. Moving up towards a more managerial role. I'm working with a good team, you know, good prospects.' She rattles off the usual.

'Oh, sounds great. That's what I did, worked my way up. Best way to do it, if you ask me.' David takes a large handkerchief out of his trouser pocket and blows his nose without breaking eye contact with Harry. Harry stares at him, unsure if this gesture is meant to be significant in a way she doesn't understand. David finishes, puts his handkerchief away and urges Harry to keep talking with an eager smile and a slight nod of the head.

'It's a good job,' Harry says, a little shaken. 'Steady. And I can't complain, you know, jobs are hard to find at the moment.'

'That's right. You're right there. That's very true. I think a lot of people are struggling these days to find anything at all, ain't that right? My boy, my Dale, he's been lucky, he works for his mother's partner's firm, been there since he was sixteen. Scaffolding, he does. He's very good at it. You're looking for work at the moment, aren't you, Pete?'

'I am, yeah. Well, I'm signing on,' Pete says.

'And what is it you'd like to do? Ideally? Your mother says you're very bright.'

'He is!' Miriam smiles at Pete. 'He's always been a keen reader. Very bright, aren't you, Pete?'

Harry glances at her mother. Her heart feels like it's squashed up underneath the table leg, keeping the surface steady.

'To be honest, Dave . . .' Pete lets his knife and fork rest in his hands. 'I don't have a clue, mate. I mean, I thought I did. But now . . .' Pete trails off, defeated.

'Oh dear. That is a shame!' David says cheerfully.

'He hasn't worked in years,' Harry explains. 'Thinks it's beneath him.'

Pete narrows his eyes at Harry, protests slowly, but with feeling. 'I don't think it's beneath me, I just can't do it, I can't do minimum wage and zero-hours contracts any more. Working all hours and still can't make the rent, still can't save a penny. I want a career like anyone else.'

'Yes! A young man must have a career!'

'I've been all sorts. Handyman in a hotel, I've worked in a shoe shop, I've cut ham at Asda's meat counter, I've couriered packages, I've poured pints. I'm hardly workshy. But I've got a *degree*, David, in international relations of all things. I thought I wanted to go into politics, but it means nothing. It means, excuse the expression, *fuck all*. I've no prospects, no security. I can't trust myself. I have no fucking future in the workplace. Look at me. I'm nearly twenty-seven, I live at home with my dad, I'm skint, I'm signing on. That's the reality for me, David, I'm afraid.' Pete breathes heavily, phlegm growls in his chest. Surprised at himself for the outburst.

'Well,' David offers, 'things might pick up!'

Pete's cutlery starts to rattle against the plate. He puts his knife and fork down and clenches his fists on the table top. 'I could study more, keep going with university, but I'd need to get sponsored, I'd need full sponsorship, and there's no way I'm bright enough or my ideas are interesting enough to get that. And for what, anyway? What's the point of learning if it can't put food on my table and a roof over my head? I mean, I've thought about teaching.'

'I'm sure you'd be a great teacher!' Did that sound sarcastic? He didn't mean it to. David listens as eagerly as he can.

'I might be one day, but right now, if I went into it, I'd be as bad as those teachers I had who I hated. You need passion for a job like that. Otherwise you'll end up one of them.'

'Perhaps you'd like to come and work at Bright Eyes with us?' It fell out of his mouth before he'd realised what he was saying and he watched it fidget on the table like a frog on a hot pavement.

THE FIRST DAY MIRIAM walked in, David had seen something in her, some longed-for hint of dignity he hadn't seen since his mother passed. She was elegant, in a straightforward kind of way. She came in smiling and looking around properly as someone should, taking in the rows of neatly stacked spectacles, the colour of the carpets, the giant pair of glasses suspended above the till, the entrance to the eye-testing room, the chairs lined up outside, the framed black-and-white poster of iconic glasses-wearers, the headed notepaper on the desk by the tills that said *Bright Eyes* and had a small sketch of a pair of glasses with the right lens twinkling.

'Hello,' she said. 'My name is Miriam Chapel and I haven't had a job in twenty years but I'm a fast learner. I'm committed, and I'll do any odd job that needs doing. I'm sociable, I enjoy people's company. I mean, I like to help people, I really do. And I've worn glasses all my life so I really understand how important it is that people choose the right frames. And I'm wondering if you need any help here?'

She was dressed in a grey pullover, a navy coat, dark trousers, flat shoes. Her hair was neat and soft and curled around her ears and her face was sparkling, just sparkling like that. He smiled deeply, from the soles of his feet, beneath them, from the carpet of his shop, and he extended his hand.

'David Fairview,' he said. 'Pleased to meet you. And let me tell you, first of all, what an absolute coincidence it is that you've come in here like this, because, look . . .' He lifted up a piece of paper that he'd been sticking Blu-tack onto the corners of as she'd walked in. It was a *Help Wanted* notice. 'Look!' he said. 'And I don't believe in coincidence, Miriam, I don't. I believe in signs.' He held up the sign in his hand.

He looked at her, right in the eyes, and held her gaze and saw something so familiar and intoxicating in the colours of her iris that he felt an electricity charging through him that made him forget himself. She was smiling.

'How strange!' she said. 'Isn't that strange?'

And David, still smiling and full of electricity and looking her right in the eyes, tore up the *Help Wanted* sign and threw it in the bin.

'You're hired, Miriam Chapel!' he said. 'I like the way you carry yourself. I feel like you'd be an asset to the shop.' He looked around, and back to her. 'Can you start tomorrow?'

Miriam adjusted her glasses. She felt a little flustered, which was strange for her. Maybe it was something to do with the way he was staring straight into her face like that, straight into her eyes. It made her feel looked at in a way she hadn't been looked at in a long time. For years, maybe.

'Yes!' she said. 'Of course!' She threw her hands up into the air, clapped them together and held them in front of her chin. 'What time do we start?'

'We start at nine thirty.' He grinned, pushing his hair back with his fingers, pulling his stomach in.

'Great!' she said. 'Wow, this is fantastic! This is the first place I've tried! Would you believe it? Thank you so much, David. I'll see you tomorrow.'

They smiled and sang out their goodbyes and, as she swung through the door, her perfume wafted in the push; David smelt the freshness of the petals, the weight of the musk.

PETE CHEWS HIS FOOD slowly.

'Thanks, David, that's very kind, but I wouldn't want to impose, and I'm sure something will come up.'

Silence falls, thick and heavy. Pete feels he is peeling thin layers of skin off the flesh of reality and peering at the pinkish texture underneath. Everything has been revealed in all its tender soreness.

Drugs.

He swallows. Shakes a gurn off.

'Harriet.' Miriam tries to sound inquisitive and friendly, but her tone is clipped with distrust. 'How are things with you?' Harry is dumb suddenly. Her mind blank. Mother and daughter eye one another warily. Harry pulls her lips into a timid half-U. 'Are you . . .?' Miriam begins to ask something but fails to think of a question. 'How's Leon?' she settles for.

'He's good, yeah. We're both fine.' Harry wonders whether she is meant to pick up this thread and sew a tapestry with it. She looks back to her plate. Moves some mash around.

Harry's brain is still catching on stills from the party the night before last; those eyes that chin those smiling lips the way she left like that and winked and left and how might it feel to have a person there. Here was someone strange and dark as she was. The things they'd told each other. Some stupid hope that spiked and hurt like nails digging in, a slapped face in the throes of it. She coughs a couple of times. Miriam passes her some water without looking at her. Harry drinks it without saying thank you.

Miriam would like to know if her daughter is OK. If she is in love or going out with friends to watch bands after work, but something stops the words from forming. There has been a wide silence between them since Harry was young and Miriam told her that two girls together was wrong. It just couldn't last, she had said. It wasn't *real* was the word she had used. Those words, although tattooed on Harry's mind, have faded from Miriam's. Harry often wonders if two people remember the same situation completely differently how either of the memories can be trusted.

'Harriet?' Miriam tries again, Harry looks up. *It's not your job to educate her*, she tells herself. *She doesn't mean to hurt you.* 'It's a nice shirt you're wearing.'

A parade of past insults marches along the promenade inside Harry's brain. Her mum sneering at her outfits as she hurried past her, out the door. 'You look like such a tramp,' she'd say. 'Do you want people to think you're a boy?' or the more frequent, 'You have such a pretty face, why do you hide yourself like this?'

Harry can't respond, not even a smile. Pete shakes his head in disapproval; he thinks she's being stubborn. At least his mum is trying.

Miriam, her head tipped to the side, waits for acknowledgement. Puzzled, as ever, by her daughter's behaviour. She looks back to her plate, eats delicately. She cuts her food up precisely and evenly so that she always has an equal amount of everything she started with at the end of her meal. 'Nothing,' she says to Pete. 'You see?' She raises her eyebrows and lets out a pantomime sign. Harry pickles in her own vinegar.

Pete's suffering. His head is pounding. Brain shrivelled, dried out, jaw aching from the pills, and it pounds in his cheekbones and his stomach is grease-foul, recalling last night, retching up nothing. But no matter how rough he feels, everything's fine because she gave him her number. He shakes the rising smile off his lips, shakes away the thought of her and looks up at the awkward scene before him: poor David, trying so hard to be liked. Harry and Miriam exchanging silences. Suddenly Pete feels like laughing, he can't help himself. He gives in to it.

'What's so funny?' Miriam asks, giggling a little.

Pete has his hand over his mouth, eyes closed, shoulders jumping around in their sockets. 'I'm sorry,' he says. 'I'm sorry.'

David smiles enthusiastically, but his smile is from a different place. He lets out a laugh like a horn honking. Just once. *HA*. It makes Pete nearly choke trying to get the breath to laugh harder. He doubles up in his chair, feet off the floor, head lowered. Laughing till his belly aches. Miriam reaches over to rub Pete's back and starts laughing too, gentle rocking, silent laughter; her cheeks go red, she's got tears in her eyes. Her whole body shaking. Pete recovers, then notices his mum laughing, which he hadn't at first because she's so quiet, and that sets him off again, her shaking there in her chair, mouth so small, the way it gets when she's cracking up, she looks like she's crying. Fanning her face. David is beaming around at them all. Harry sits still in her chair, plays with her hands. Not sure where to look. Pete and Miriam calm down. Pete finishes his mouthful. Harry reaches for her beer.

This is great, thinks David. *Couldn't be going better.*

When Pete gets back home it's growing dark, purple light draws the sky towards the pavement, and all the shapes on the street are silhouettes. He is carrying a plastic bag full of stuff from his mum. Tupperwares of leftovers and things to freeze, a loaf of bread, some cheese, a carton of juice, some toothpaste, some deodorant and two new pairs of boxers. As he approaches the house Pete sees a load of boxes hunched grumpily on the front garden wall; as he gets closer he sees that the boxes are full of books. He stops before the books and examines them, picks them up in his hands and turns them over, flicks through them and puts them back. They're Mum's books. There's her lamp. And there's her gardening gloves.

He lets himself in and finds his dad sitting on the sofa in the dark.

'Shhh,' his dad says. 'Come here. Get down, you plank. Can't you see I'm doing something?' He beckons him over to the sofa and pulls him down next to him.

Graham is a thickset, bullish man, but age and stress have shrunk him. His shoulders stand apart like two warring kingdoms, his neck the vast bridge that connects them. He walks with wide, heavy steps. Self-assured and slow-moving, but he still has the power to charge if he needs to. In the company of people he doesn't know well, he tries to make himself sound posher by rolling his Rs and smudging his vowels. It's a trait that makes his children wince in restaurants.

'What we doing?' Pete whispers.

'Shhh.' Graham holds a finger up to his lips. 'Wait and see.' He mouths it. A minute passes. Nothing happens. Pete watches his old man. He has a long, noble face, his nose straight and level, his brown eyes round and wide like cow's eyes. They are set deep and blink out from tired wrinkles. His skin is thick and tanned to the colour of leather, even in winter.

'Dad?'

'I told you!' his Dad whispers. 'Shhh.'

Pete frowns at him. 'What you doing, Dad?'

'Listen.' Graham tugs Pete's earlobe. 'Just listen.' Pete can hear footsteps on the street. They slow down. Stop outside the house.

'This is the house I was telling you about!' says a woman's voice. She sounds like she's in her thirties maybe, south London accent. 'Look!' she says, 'you could get twenty pence each for these down the car boot!'

'Ooh, I don't know about these.' Someone else. A man. A much older man, maybe her grandad. 'I'm not so sure.'

'Well, how about this one then, eh? I've heard of this one.' Pete can hear her picking up books and putting them down.

'Oh yes, I think *I've* heard of that one too.'

'*Wuthering Heights*,' says the woman.

'*The Concise Book of Eastern European Fertility Myths*,' says Grandad.

Pete looks at his dad. 'You're throwing her books out?' he whispers.

Graham's eyes blaze and his whisper is coarse as a brush. 'She doesn't want them any more. She won't come and get them. It's been a year. It's part of the healing, son. You wouldn't understand. Not till *your* wife has walked out on *you*. Which, I hope, never happens.' Pete leans his head back into the sofa, enjoying the darkness of the room. 'Sit further down, will you, they'll see the top of your head through the gap in the curtains.' Pete wriggles himself down into the sofa. Bends his head to the side.

'*War and Peace*, look!' Grandad says. 'I've always wanted to read that.'

'They're not for reading, they're for the car boot.'

'And *Call of the Wild*, look.'

'Oooh,' the woman says. '*Yoga with Pets*.' They can hear her open it and flick through. 'There's some nice pictures in this one.'

'Come on.' Graham stands up as quietly as he can, and, staying low so he can't be seen, starts to walk into the kitchen. Pete gets up slowly and follows him, also staying low. They stand either side of the kettle and listen to it boil. Strange how much you hear in an empty house. Pete watches the steam, passes his fingers through it, tickles it.

'What's he like then?'

Pete visualises David's eager grin. 'He's nice,' he says.

Nice. It tugs at Graham's small intestine. 'Who'd win in a fight though?'

'I'm not answering that, Dad.'

'You don't have to. I already know.'

'Are you drunk?' Pete asks him, but he doesn't really need to.

'I'm old. That's the problem. *This* is when you're meant to be with the woman you love. *Now*. When your face looks like this, and you've got older than you ever thought you'd get. *This* is the time for love. Not, I mean . . .' He sends his hand up into the cupboard above, finds two cups, tangles his fingers around their handles. *Her cups. She chose them.* He brings them to the counter and places them side by side. They wobble and settle. He fetches the tea bags. 'Imagine, son, five years' time, I'll be old and grey and fat and frail, and if you ever find a job I'll be all alone in this house. Do you understand me, scout?'

Graham looks at his son, misty-eyed, claps him on the back affectionately, touches his cheek. Pete stays still. Doesn't respond. Just watches him.

Graham pulls his trousers up over his paunch and rhapsodises, painting his words in the air with his hands. 'Years of marriage are *meant* to end up in wrinkles and cuddles by the telly, fish and chips on the beach, woolly hats and a Freedom pass. Who's gonna love me now? Eh?'

'We could make you an online dating profile. If you're serious.'

'Online, pah.' He spits, not actual spit, just the motion. 'Hard enough to find a girl at twenty, let alone . . .' He starts to pour the water into the cups. 'Should have loved her better when I had the chance.' He stops pouring and holds the kettle in mid-air. 'Let this be a lesson to you, Pete.' He turns to his son. 'I was too selfish.' He raises a finger to point out the importance of what he's about to impart. 'Let this be a lesson to you, OK, son? You got to work hard at it mate, OK? You got to treat them good when you got them. Coz when they leave, it's too late.' Graham's eyes burn as he stares into his son's face. 'Learn the lessons that I couldn't learn.' He points the words out. '*You* be the improvement of *me*. OK?' He rocks on his toes. 'OK?' he says, pointing. 'That's evolution, ain't it?'

'Sit down, Dad.' Pete pulls a chair out. 'You been in the pub today?'

'Maybe for a little while. I might have been,' Graham says. 'It's Saturday, isn't it?'

'Sit down here.' Pete reaches for the sugar and stirs two spoonfuls into each of their teas.

'I'll tell you what, son,' Graham says. 'All I ever wanted to be was good enough.'

GRAHAM CHAPEL HAD BEEN a solicitor all his life. He believed in the innate goodness of people, and despite the horrors he witnessed, he held on to his belief that people only went astray because of damage done to them by abuses of one kind or another. It was the unbearable violence *of* life that bred the unbearable violence *in* life.

It was like poetry to him. A soaring, difficult poetry that sought to offer all people peace. Graham knew in his guts that it was absolutely right that people should not murder, steal, torture, subjugate, defraud or deceive one another. But in an unequal society there was not enough air to breathe. Which was why he became a defence lawyer, and would find himself absorbed in the harrowing details of his cases, desperately trying to clutch on to his belief that people were good.

He rode from Brixton Prison to Wormwood Scrubs on his rickety bicycle, his casework stuffed in his threadbare rucksack. At first he worked for a dismal firm with premises above a pub in Elephant and Castle. The files were all faded and the walls shook each time a train came past. The practice was called McCallum, Diamond and Strauss. Diamond and Strauss were a long time dead. Graham's boss McCallum was a tender old man with flyaway white hair and a passion for Tchaikovsky who worked Graham to the bone because he knew that he could.

He had no weekends, took no holidays, sat coffee-high in police interview rooms in the middle of the night. He took on legal aid cases for people being tyrannised by landlords, bosses or local councils. He couldn't help but take the cases personally. Every failing was his failing and the thrumming guilt that followed a loss sent him into long nights of silence and drunkenness.

Eventually he got a job in the West End in a bigger firm with more high-profile cases. He had two small children at home, and although he kept their pictures on his desk, his mind was busy with the allegations levelled at his clients. He knew Miriam was struggling with how preoccupied he was – they fought about it constantly – but the way he saw it, this was his vocation and people's freedom was in his hands. 'What about my freedom though, Graham?' she would ask him, but he couldn't understand how it related to the conversation and told her he was not going to get dragged into an argument. He had work he had to finish and he was tired.

He'd taken to wearing shoes with thin metal plates fixed to the heels, so that as he marched down the hushed corridors of the appeal courts, with their mosaic marble floors, his footsteps banged and reverberated off the walls as if an invisible army marched behind him. When he struck down hard enough, sparks flew. The judges in their chambers would send their thin-fingered clerks to see what all the noise was, and they would return, ghostly faced, saying, 'My Lord, there is a man out there with fire at his feet, a true Daniel come to litigate.'

But all that was in his younger days. His beliefs had lost their potency some time ago, and now all he really cared about was getting home at the end of the day so that he could sit in peace. He had many projects. He was writing a play. He was inventing a synthesiser. He was building a boat in the garage, which some day he planned to sail. He had accepted the wrecked remains from a man who couldn't pay his fees; it was still mainly a rotten hull but even so, it was his project, and the joy was in the job at hand, not in the thought of finishing. These days he worked in corporate law at a big firm in St Pancras where nobody took him seriously and he got away with not doing too much.

The world in all its frenzied injustice seemed someone else's problem now. He'd fought the good fight for as long as he could. Raised two children. Buried his parents. Lost the love of his wife. Watched helplessly as his only brother fell into madness and addiction. Saw innocent people go to jail, and guilty people walk free. Felt the shudders cross his palms when murderers returned home to their girlfriends because he'd been their champion.

Even as a boy he'd had a strong sense of right and wrong and would often be called upon to settle disputes in the playground. But as a man now in late middle age, he had no burning sense of injustice left. He was worn out from carrying the hate of the world on his shoulders. He just wanted to build his boat and write his play and invent his synthesiser, and as long as his children were healthy, the world was OK by him. Other people's pain had lost its potency. The world outside his garage walls was a hideous, feverish mess, and the days of trying to make a difference were far, far behind him.

THE BEIGENESS

Pete watches the blue smoke curl like Chinese dragons towards the ceiling. In his hand his phone screen shines, more vivid than the real world; he stares into it at the text message he's been composing for an hour.

hi its Pete met u yesterday. Wanna hang out later? X

In a wave of conviction he presses send and grins firmly about it. The wave lasts about two minutes, and then breaks, churning and foam-tipped, filling him with sneering doubt. He fidgets in the dim room, stupid, one hand in his boxers, the other pushing against his closed eyes. Shuddering. Twenty minutes pass in stillness. Wrenched and hopeless, he hates himself until he feels the buzz against the mattress, the short stab that sits him up and he sends his hand blindly beneath the duvet.

Yeah. that would be good. I'm working in town till 10. Wanna meet me Soho?

He jumps to his feet and punches the air. Gets a grip. He plays it cool for as long as he can but sends his reply back in a matter of minutes.

I'll find a bar and text u. 10.15*? X*

He waits, shaking, slapping his cheeks and drumming his belly. Paces the room, distracts himself, flicking through a newspaper that's on the floor. Time is a revolving door. As it passes he feels increasingly stupid for getting in touch and he begins to hate himself again for everything he's ever done or said. Flashes of himself in her café, lurking by the counter with nothing to say, make him shake with shame.

The phone buzzes in his hand. He reads:

Very assertive. See you later.

And he is the god of all things.

Becky puts her phone back in her bag and watches the street light opposite. It's dented in the middle and it's pouring its cheap orange squash into a puddle on the pavement. A siren rolls a few streets away. A man with a huge moustache and a large fur hat walks past her and his footsteps echo wetly. There is an awning above a shop window across the street and the corner is ripped; its edges are shredded, epileptic in the wind.

She walks into the hotel lobby. It's bright and wide, the floor is shining like an ice rink, gilded luggage trolleys sit like empty birdcages. The lady at reception perches behind a vast desk, her uniform is light purple and grey. Becky passes the desk, nods at the lady, who stares at her briefly, shuffling paperwork; her nails are filed to triangle points, painted the colour of drying blood. A group is checking in, European, students maybe, they are laughing at something. One has long hair and he throws it around.

She heads for the bar and takes a seat at the furthest-left bar stool. The bar looks out onto the street. Behind the barman the bottles stand far apart on a clean shelf. Everything is symmetrical. There is no dust. All the chairs are square. Everything is light purple and white and grey. Long lines and oblongs. She picks at a loose thread on the knee of her jeans. Pulls it till it's taut.

She thinks his name to herself. Thinks his shape in the crowd, standing close. Sees his hair and his ear and his neck. It has to be a sign. She presses her palms against the bar top and studies the lines on the backs of her hands. Wonders about the client she is about to meet. Wonders where her mother is right now. Across an ocean, in some epic canyon. The red rock American hills. She wonders if her parents are in contact. Whether they send each other postcards. She can feel them, their presence is stronger today than it has been in years. They are who she is. But she doesn't even know them. Her mother used to write. Every month, but she told her to stop. She moved flats and wouldn't tell Paula the new address. She knows Linda keeps the letters. She knows they're stacked up in a file in the cupboard above the bookcase in Linda's living room. Maybe she should read them.

She stands up and heads to the bathroom to apply fresh make-up. She passes the window. She can't take her eyes from the awning. She stares as it flaps in the wind.

As Pete rides the escalator down into the depths of the underground, he feels himself growing uneasy. *Underneath the city, there are tunnels, and in those tunnels all the people sit in metal tubes and go to where they need to go.* He descends, one level at a time, deeper down, feeling the air change, feeling the heat rise in his cheeks. He takes his coat off and holds it over his arm; he shivers in his shirt, but the sweat is panting in his pores, like runners on the start line, just waiting for the gun to blast.

He boards the tube, treading carefully, and he sits amongst aliens and feels himself dying but focuses on where he is going and what he is going to do and, as he climbs out into the air of Oxford Circus, he is jubilant again. Terrified, but thankfully not bordering on losing it any more. At least, not for the minute.

He walks in and out of seven different bars trying to find the one that feels right.

Eventually he finds a place, a trendy restaurant that's got a bar in the basement. He heads down the stairs and out into a low-ceilinged room, with an old wooden bar along the wall at the end. The chairs are old cinema chairs, dark purple velvet, threadbare arms. The lighting is dim, groups of drinkers sit and talk over one another, slapping each other's backs now and then, one or two are drinking alone. Music is playing, Joy Division. He strolls to the bar for a pint.

She sees him on the other side of the room. She hasn't seen him enough times to know what he really looks like. The shape of his legs, bowed slightly. The back of his head, where his hair stops. Her eyes catch on things as she approaches the bar, the texture of the battered velvet on the chairs, looking as tired as she feels. The people drinking, the lonely-looking man trying not to watch the couple sitting at the next table kissing.

Pete turns and sees her as she walks towards him. Lean and agile, like a serpent, full of movement. She is wearing a baggy shirt and scruffy jeans, swinging her hips, and beneath her clothes he can sense the outline of her body. In that moment, she is the most beautiful woman he has ever seen. Her hair is up and longer bits fall over her face, deep dark black brown. He attempts to smile but his features are water leaving a sink. She stops beside him. He kisses her cheek.

'Drink?'

'Yeah. I'll get it though,' she says.

She commands a seriousness that Pete isn't used to. There is an intensity in the way she inhabits her body and space that cuts Pete right through the middle but they talk easily, drifting from one thing to another, without hurry or awkwardness. They drink beer then wine then whisky then gin.

They are nearly drunk when, at last, she decides it's time to find the words.

The room smudges and darkens. There are no edges to shapes. There are no edges to sounds. Everything is mulch and vacuum. Becky swims towards the point of speech. Her mouth is the funnel of a gramophone, her chest a spinning vinyl. The words are slow; they come out steeped in mud.

'The book you were reading, when you came in the caff yesterday?' She is swimming upwards from the sea bed, about to break the surface and return to life.

'Yeah?' Pete is not aware of Becky's agony.

'What was it?' she says, time returns and she is disorientated. A snap in her ears and her neck and things move as they should. The edges of objects paint themselves back on.

Pete thinks hard, everything exaggerated in the fug of drink.

'It was maybe, a book by John Darke, I think his name is. A politics book. Why?'

'Have you read it before?' she asks carefully. Her breath is a broken wing.

'No, I just got it. I've been trying to get hold of it actually for ages. Have you heard of John Darke?' They are sitting across from each other at a small table near the wall. He is leaning forwards onto his elbows; she is leaning back into her chair, her feet up on the chair opposite.

'Where did you get it?'

'Online.'

'What, did you just search for it?' Her voice is trembling slightly.

'No, it's . . . I subscribe to this website thing, it's, like, banned books, censored authors, you know. Shit like that. I get, erm, updates when things are found in print and stuff.' He watches her. She sits and thinks for a while, staring into the middle distance. He waits, drinks his gin. 'Why do you ask?'

She takes her feet off the chair and swivels so she's facing him, then studies him. He doesn't smile into her look, just sits there; her eyes cook him till he's tender. Her heart is slicked with oil. She is a Francis Bacon painting, yelling silently and staring out. His face is innocent. He has a nose, two ears, two lips just like a human, but he's bearing something mythical, carrying her dad towards her.

'John Darke?'

'Yeah?'

'Who's he then?'

Pete purses his lips, frowns. 'Well.' His tone is cheerful, he's feeling warm inside. 'He's a legend. Quite the man.'

'Why? What did he do?'

'Ah, well, now you're asking! He was a politician? I think, yep, and a writer. Teacher, too. He was, erm, a brilliant mind. Definitely. I mean, the book, it's amazing so far, he had this idea, about how to make democracy accountable, how to reinstall democracy in the West, take power back from corporations and empower people again, but . . . what happened to him? Something awful. Stitch-up. Framed for something. Murder? Something horrible. Rape? Reputation in tatters, whole nine yards. Locked him up for a long time, but his legacy lives on. His ideas, I mean. Think he's still inside somewhere.'

Her heart is pounding. She is sitting very still, mouth open slightly, clutching her glass.

Pete spreads his arms. 'Quite a guy.' He shakes his head. 'But I'm into all that, you see. You can look him up. Wikipedia or whatever.' She holds his eyes for longer than he can bear. He can't read the look. She gets up suddenly.

'I'm just gonna pop to the bathroom, Pete,' she says, her legs shaking in her jeans. She walks carefully to the Ladies, stands in front of the mirror and stares for a full minute at the features on her face.

They're out on the street, clouded with drink, smoking. Talking in friendly voices about the schools that they went to, the jobs that they've had. They are walking to the bus stop, Becky has taken Pete's arm and is holding on to his sleeve, feeling the side of his body against hers.

As the bus rolls over the bridge, back south, they both feel the same tug, the wash and blast of home.

She wants to take him to bed. He's booze-confident and he swings his arm round her shoulder and she walks close to him up the howling main road. They bundle up the stairwell, out into the fourth-floor corridor and lean over the railings of the balcony, looking out at the streets, London's bleeding gums. He follows her into her flat and stands beside her in the tiny kitchen as she opens the whisky and looks for something clean to pour it into. She leans across him for the glasses and he feels the charge of proximity, reaches out for her, and she responds. Slowly stopping, turning herself to stand a centimetre from his face, moving her nose across his skin. He is paralysed, watching her. They start to kiss, they pull each other down and undress heavily, banging their knees on the hard tiles and their heads on the kitchen units. Laughing, slipping apart, reaching out again.

In the morning she kisses him goodbye on the main road. A world-shrinking gut-smashing kiss on the mouth. She walks away, her body like machinery; he notices the perfect symmetry of every pump and thrust, skewered by the economy of her movement. She doesn't look back once. He watches her smash through the street until she's out of sight. And even then, he watches the last space she occupied until his eyeballs feel sore.

She is already thinking of other things. She's on her way to her uncle's caff. She wonders whether her uncles were kind to her mother when they were children. Whether her mother remembers the days before they moved into Uncle Ron's, when they slept in a phone box.

She thinks of a group of dancers that she studied with who have a show on in town. On the flyer they are all in black under beams of serious light. She'd laughed at the picture when she saw it online, but it comes to her now and it pains her. The thought of them meeting, rehearsing together. She had always found their ideas simplistic and their routines unsurprising. In class, they were loud, domineering characters who lacked originality. It was easier to laugh at them than acknowledge the fact that, for all the years she'd known them, she'd felt superior, but now they are doing it and she is not.

She thinks of Kemi Racine. Her dark monobrow set low like Frida Kahlo's, wanting to dance, talking about people who come to auditions wanting to be dancers more than wanting to dance. Racine is Becky's favourite living choreographer. She never gets the big commissions. She's only really known by those who seek her out. She is not famous or particularly highly regarded. Her work is often poached and passed off as the work of her more successful male peers. She teaches at an unimportant school in Copenhagen. Becky had read her newspaper article the week before. It was a call for women to stick to choreography and not be scared off by the lack of opportunity, funding or support. Build your own networks, she had said. Fuel your own engine.

Becky watches the people, the street, hears the noise and feels the pavement and dares to think of what she might like to say about it all one day, with her body, in a piece of her own.

Pete starts walking. The city lurches all around him. People push past and swear at him and he feels lost amongst it all.

Flashes of their bodies riddle him with secret glee, but he can feel the fear coming. He wards it off but feels it pushing. He never knows when it will trip him up.

He decides to knock on at Nathan and Mo's. They're two of his oldest friends and he hasn't seen them in months. They live about fifteen minutes' walk away, up towards Honor Oak Park. He turns off the main road and heads up the wide, tree-lined street with the big old houses bruised from the years, glancing up at the ornate roofs and big proud windows. He walks past the church and takes a left and strolls back out into the dirt and grit of squat brick buildings, broken window frames, road-blackened house fronts. Snarling children. Smiling dogs. He goes slowly past the chip shop, the newsagent's, the off-licence, some girls on their bikes shouting at each other, the chicken shop, the barber's, three men in prayer robes leaning against the bicycle racks outside the Co-op, the jerk shop, the Good News Bakery, the funeral parlour, the block of flats, a man moving a fridge on two skateboards, the garage with the arsehole woman who works at the counter, the carwash, the kebab shop, the houses with their whitewashed walls and gravel drives, the pub, the other pub. The nice Caribbean restaurant. Pete ducks through the iron gate and cuts across the cemetery, overgrown and rich with green. Trees everywhere. He stares up into them; they sway in sunlight, the crumbling stones, the angels and monuments, the crunch of the path under his quick feet. The smell in the air of spring.

Nathan is big-boned, heavy-set. Bearded. He's a bass player and a beat maker and he speaks like a subwoofer. Mo is gangly to the point of precarious, walks in long strides, his face is all smile. He works in an energy company call centre. They're on the sofa watching catch-up TV. They're halfway through a dating show. Pete sits down between them, stretches his legs out and starts skinning up.

'What you been up to?' Mo asks him, glancing at him, eyes red.

'Not much,' Pete says. Mo nods.

'Cool,' Nathan says, and they settle back in to the telly.

Pete stares at the colours on the widescreen plasma box in front of him. He watches the pixels unravel and merge. Everything starts going fast and he can feel a dread lurking in the corner of the room, a shadow with its mouth open, head back, unleashing maniacal laughter. He blinks. Looks back at the telly. But the world has speeded up and now everything he focuses on slows right down. He watches his hands, they are far away. He can feel things happening that he can't see. His skin starts prickling, the sweat is preparing itself behind his pores. His vision is fast, jagged, violent. *Breathe*. But his breath is pixelated, too fast. *Calm*. Hard heartbeat. Chest pains. *Calm down*. Eyes on the TV, then down to the Rizla.

'That guy's a dick,' Nathan says. 'Where do they find these people?'

'It's telly, innit,' Mo says. 'It invents these people.'

They all watch silently, faces screwed up in disdain.

'You should go on this, Mo. You'd fuckin' nail it,' Nathan tells him.

Pete smiles widely at the thought. Blinks a few times. Feels like his face is coming back to him.

'Think so?' Mo glances across him, at Nathan.

'Yeah, they'd love you,' Nathan says. 'Imagine it. You'd fucking boss it.'

The three of them look at the screen. A man wearing a waistcoat open over an oiled chest and baggy chinos slides down a pole into a TV studio where thirty women behind podiums indicate whether or not they'd go out on a date with him by turning on or off their lights. Pete looks at his hands, keeps breathing. Sitting between them, reminding himself where he is, who they are, he'd like to say something to them but the silence in his mouth is a massive apple that he can't speak around, shoved right into his throat. He's sure there's something terrible coming for them all. The dread swells from a point in his middle. Everything that could go wrong goes wrong on repeat in lurid detail. Her body keeps coming back to him. The way she turned him round and climbed across him. How she grabbed his throat like that. He sniffs, wipes his nose on his sleeve.

PETE WAS TWELVE when he got into smoking skunk. He started hanging out with the kids from round his neighbourhood who took him out painting with them.

His new mates were passionate conspiracy theorists. They would get high and talk for hours about the secret organisations that controlled the world. It all made perfect sense to Pete. There were reasons and proof, there were ancient prophecies and irrefutable evidence, and a story about the end coming. It would begin with the making of a one-world nation. United under one currency. There would be one global police force. One global justice system. One army under the beast. Once this had come to pass, we would be in the last days, and the last days would drag on until only two good people remained on Earth – the last two who refused the mark of the beast; a computer chip that the one-world government would put inside our hands. These chips, the story went, would be justified in the name of public security and convenience. A cashless economy. One chip and no more banknotes. You couldn't be robbed. It would be your ID, your credit card. It would be your new smartphone. Your travel card. What did you have to hide? It would be your passport. Without one you wouldn't be able to move between borders, buy food or pay your water bill. You wouldn't be able to survive. They'd do it slowly, so we thought it was our choice. We wouldn't see that it was forced on us, we'd see it as convenient, it would be the new must-have accessory. The solution to our fabricated fears. Why *wouldn't* you want one?

As he grew up Pete watched the growing prevalence of mobile computer chips with a bellowing, racking dread. He also watched the developments of the so-called war on terror with a choked heart; he saw it as the start of the obliteration of all nations who stood against Western global dominance.

The stories went that once these computer chips were being implanted, the one world would be divided into those who took the chip and those who wouldn't. No more racism, class war, gender inequality. Only those with the chip, and those without. All those who wouldn't take it would be deemed terrorists, enemies of progress, subjected to torture and constant surveillance, and eventually they would die. Living in bands in the wilderness, hunted by soldiers with heat-seeking bullets. And when there were only two left, the last two in the world who had refused the chip, all the souls who'd ever died would come back to Earth to fight each other, good against evil. Marked against unmarked.

Pete sat with his mates in their dark bedrooms with the posters on the wall of metal bands and hardcore rappers, in dingy flats in Catford, and he stroked their dogs while they nodded and whispered and played documentaries in the daytime with the curtains closed. And he was convinced it was true. He was sure he would be one of the last two.

As he got older, he shook himself out of it, but it never left him. Not really. He went to uni and he couldn't help it, everything he learned he learned through the filter of those heavy, scary, endless stories. It was like a secret faith he couldn't mention. He'd be reading his textbooks, or sitting in lectures, and the more he learned of the way the world worked, the more convinced he was.

He avoided getting an Oyster card for as long as he could because he didn't like the way it was made compulsory. It didn't matter that he didn't want his movements tracked. He couldn't get a bus until he did it their way. In the end though, he gave in, and every time he used it to travel or to cut a line up, he felt the tug of shame.

He knew that was the way it was going to go. The chip would come and he would fight it for about as long as he fought the Oyster, and then he'd get chipped just like everyone else, without thinking about it at all.

PETE PUFFS HIS JOINT. His head is as far back into the cushions of the sofa as it could possibly be. He smokes deeply. The TV's playing adverts, Mo turns the sound down.

Nathan shifts his body, leans his head towards Pete. 'That nice?' he asks him, nodding at the spliff, making his widest puppy-dog eyes.

'Yeah it is nice, thanks, Nathan,' says Pete.

'I bet,' Nathan says, contemplating for a moment. 'And I could just imagine what would go really lovely with that is a nice cup of tea. Wouldn't you say?'

Pete looks at him, eyes narrowed, and shakes his head firmly.

'Oh, go on, make us a cup of tea, will ya, Pete? Please?'

'I'm in *your* fucking house, you make me a tea, you prick.'

Nathan feigns shock. 'No need for that now, is there?'

They watch the adverts, sound still down.

Nathan lasts about a minute. 'Oh go on, Pete,' he says. 'No one makes tea as good as you do.' He smiles sweetly at his friend. Speaks in exaggerated awe. '*Perfect*, your tea is. Perfect. Just right. With the tea bag in just long enough, and the sugar just right. Lovely drop o' milk . . .' Nathan takes a draw on his spliff, holds it in, exhales deeply, eyes half closed. 'Shit, Pete,' he says. 'You make it an *art form*.' He holds his spliff up to Pete and nods earnestly. 'Me?' he says. 'I got no grace for it, have I? No affinity with it.' He picks a tobacco string from his lip. 'You?' he says. 'Your tea? *Wow*.'

'Ah mate, you just need to practise more, that's all. You'll get there, Nathan. I promise,' Pete says, tapping him sarcastically on the knee.

'No!' Nathan says. 'No, look, right.' He puts his spliff to his lips and gestures with his hands. 'No amount of practice could do for my tea-making what natural talent has done for yours.'

Pete rolls his eyes, shakes his head, passes his joint to Mo and stands up.

'Oh thanks, mate,' Nathan says, 'I knew I could depend on you.' Nathan grins at him, eyes shining and sleepy, exuding gratitude.

Pete heads to the other side of the carpet where the kitchen joins the living room. 'You're the best, Pete, honest,' Nathan tells him as he goes. 'I been on at Mo to do it for over an hour now.'

Mo turns the telly back up now the adverts have finished, stretches his legs out and takes a puff of Pete's joint. 'You can make your own fucking tea, you lazy cunt.'

THEY DIDN'T SEE ITS shape approaching, but it came upon them. Large and slow and full of blood. They fell towards each other.

She was hesitant. Kept telling him she wasn't up for anything serious and he agreed, of course, he wasn't up for that either. But he started popping by the café most days.

Kissing her was like opening a furnace door.

She kept telling herself it was no big deal. They were seeing how it went. No strings. No commitment. She had too much that she was committed to as it was. She didn't want a boyfriend. She made it clear that she was up for seeing other people. He told her yeah, that's what he wanted too.

The city opened up to them. Everything was theirs. They wrapped their bodies around each other's, felt the mornings rise against their naked skin in bed together, endless, dark red bright white lightning flashes, rain clouds bursting outside, while indoors the endless exploration. Close and closer still. 'Give me your mouth,' she told him, pushing her fingers in, dragging his chin towards hers with both hands.

She turned him into a man, into a woman, into a child. He'd never known anything like it. He found himself sitting on her lap at a party, looking pretty for her. Liking what her eyes did to his face. One look and it made him go all giggly and bouncy, turning it on for her. Another look would send him serious and smouldering, dark passion at the flash of her lashes. The things she put him through. She was like a foreign body in his body. Metal lodged in a vital part. Some rogue shrapnel, stuck right in there since he first clapped eyes on her and felt the blast.

A few weeks into it. Four in the morning in her flat in Deptford. Bodies all wrecked from the sex. Laid out on sweat-damp sheets. They knew it was there then, a new giddiness, dark and without any shape, but there in the room in the night in the way that he starved for her profile, the lines of her shape.

She told him who her father was. Told him how her mother made her change her name. That she'd spent fifteen years imagining she never had a dad. He couldn't believe it was true.

They held hands in cinemas, drank pints in pubs, walked beside rivers, did all the things that lovers do.

She told him who her mother was. How she'd given up her life and how she'd been miserable. Told him she could never do the same. Never sacrifice her dream for anyone. He agreed wholeheartedly that no, she must never do that. She spoke about her mother leaving without tears or sentimentality; he felt awestruck by the things she'd been through.

'Why don't you go and visit him, Becky?'

'I never want to see him.' And she said it so gently, so simply, there was nothing else to say. Pete's parents were not in jail, they hadn't absconded to convents. One was working in the optician's down the road, the other was in his office up town. All his life he'd trusted them completely. Never had to question whether feeling love was safe.

When she told him what she did for money, it was difficult for him to grasp. But against the backdrop of her past, he had to understand that her framework was different from his. He pulled his morals apart at night, questioned where they really came from. He could feel his dad in him, his dad's obsession with what governed people's moral compass. He was turning her work over and over in his head. Under her careful guidance. She explained and explained why all that he felt about it wasn't necessarily true. 'It's like my Auntie Linda says,' she told him. 'One man's flash of lightning, ripping through the air, is another's passing glare. Hardly there.'

They are in the park, the last spring wind is in the trees. Mighty. Like cymbals, like oceans crashing. All the trees together, dancing in it. Side to side like swaying drunks.

'It's really important to me, Pete, that I support myself. You're on the dole. I'm not being funny, but. You are.' Pete and Becky stare up into the shaking foliage. Unbound by it. Their hair is blowing back. Becky has a cup of tea in a polystyrene cup and the surface of it whips and curls.

'You want me to stop dancing?'

He looks at his hands. 'I'm not saying that.'

'Yes you are,' she tells him. And it cuts him open. He watches all his insides wriggling, surprised to see what he is really made of. 'If I stop giving massages, I can't afford to be a dancer.'

'But there's other things you can do, ain't there?'

She speaks slowly like he's a child, like she's explaining it for the thousandth time. 'I can work two hours giving massages and make enough to last me a week. That frees me up so that I can go to rehearsals. Go to classes. I got to work at Giuseppe's, I owe it to my uncle. But they can't pay me fuck all, Pete. You know this stuff.' He reaches for her tea, she passes it over. He takes a thoughtful sip. 'It's nothing to be jealous of.' He sits forwards on the bench, trying to listen without feeling angry. 'I don't have a problem with it, so why should you?'

'You know why I have a problem with it,' Pete says, feeling tiny.

'Whatever it is you're scared of them being, it's not like that, Pete. It's just one person touching another person's body.' The wind is drumming harder. 'Do you see, Pete? This is no threat to us. It's just my job. And I'm not going to stop doing the one thing I've ever wanted to do because you feel jealous.'

'It's not the dancing I've got a problem with.' He feels exasperated. He doesn't have a leg to stand on.

'The two things go hand in hand,' she says. 'I'm not stopping. This is how I make my living.' And she looks into his face for his eyes but she can't find them. He keeps looking down at his lap. 'I'm on my own,' she says. 'Have been since I was fifteen. No savings, can't run to my parents, can I? Can't ask my auntie for money, they've got none. It's hard enough for them trying to keep that café going. It's just me, Pete, just what *I* can make happen.' She doesn't say *not like you* but he can hear her thinking it.

He gives her back her tea.

He sits in the pub with his friends, a ghost in a hoodie. Nothing to say; he kills time. And his friends are growing bored of his dejection. He gets home and waits for her to finish her shift. It's three in the morning, He's reading. Sketching in his notebook. He's all right. He's not thinking of the hotel rooms, the men's faces, the men's bodies, their cocks in her hands. Does she smile for them when they come the way she smiles for him? He's not thinking of that. Her knocking on the hotel-room door. He's not thinking of it. Her voice in his head. *It's nothing to be jealous of.* And he knows *it's no threat*. But it's not like he can say, 'Don't work tonight, I'll cover the rent this month, you just focus on your dancing.' He's got no fucking money. *It's no threat*. He's crumpling. He gives himself a good talking-to.

An hour later she rings him to say she's outside. He opens the door and he knows where she's been and it's so good to see her face there in the street light, those eyes that he loves, that smile rising over those lips that are his favourite lips, but he knows where she's been and it hurts, he can't help it. 'Give me your mouth,' she says, and he does but he doesn't.

II

Love to faults is always blind,
Always is to joy inclined,
Lawless, wingèd, unconfined,
And breaks all chains from every mind.

The souls of men are bought and sold
In milk-fed infancy for gold,
And youth to slaughter-houses led;
And beauty, for a bit of bread.

William Blake, 'Freedom and Captivity'

HOT NIGHT COLD SPACESHIP

Harry is holding a brick of money. She's about to count it for the fourth time. Her socks are too big for her, baggy round her ankles. She hates that, but she hasn't had time to put a wash on and she uses all her best socks first. She is wearing bright red lipstick. Sometimes when she counts her money, she likes to put on lipstick and slick her hair back like a matador.

Leon is walking down the stairs and into the living room. His footsteps are soft but Harry hears him the way you hear your own legs moving. Places him in the house by feeling. Leon stands in the doorway of the kitchen.

'Alright?' Harry asks him, not taking her eyes off the money.

'All good,' he replies, sloping to the fridge, opening it and bending down to peer in. 'Want a beer?' he asks.

'Go on then,' she says, counting.

Leon pulls one out of the fridge, opens it, passes it over, gets one for himself and sits heavily down at the table, opposite Harry. 'How much we got?' he asks, not looking up from his bottle.

'Six hundred and seventy bags.' Harry blows out air through pursed lips. 'Between this and what's put away. Give it seven or eight months we'll be there, maybe sooner.'

Leon taps his heels on the lino. 'Fuck!' he says, and he makes the word last a long time.

LEON HAD GROWN UP in the block of flats by the shops at the top of Harry's road. As kids, the two had been inseparable. They played fighting games and football and hatched plans to make their millions; they were going to buy a submarine that they would live on, pulled by a fleet of sharks who would come to them like dogs when they whistled.

Leon was a quiet kid with a beautiful complexion. English mother, indigenous Venezuelan father, and a constant power surging beneath his skin. As a ten-year-old, he would spend his evenings reading up on revolutions and civil wars. He hid under the covers with library books, reading by torchlight, some nights till breakfast time. History fascinated him, maybe because he knew nothing of his own.

He never met his dad, never saw a photograph, never heard his name. Didn't know one scrap of a story about him, but the older he grew, the more he resembled him, and the more his mother seemed to shrink away.

They had met in another age, his parents. Leon's father, Alfredo, had journeyed to England at eighteen, brought over by the renowned British journalist and eco-activist James Peake, who had been living with Alfredo's people, the Wotuja, for three years, learning their ways and recording their struggle, in the Orinoco region of the Amazon rainforest.

James was a well-meaning but painfully unaware Englishman with a large amount of inherited wealth at his disposal and a hero complex. His anthropological interest was genuine, but his reverence of the indigenous people bordered on perverse. At his core, he desperately wanted to help, but he had a tendency to patronise and romanticise the tribe. He found in Alfredo an opportunity to really 'make a difference' and he seized it with all his strength.

Alfredo's spirits hardened after years of bearing witness to the destruction of everything he knew to be holy. These were the last days that the priests and the poets all sang of. He'd felt the forest shrink and scream. He'd heard the stories from his uncles of the day the men from the big American company had come with their contracts, how they had smiled at the elders as they exchanged bags of sugar and white rice and big kegs of gasoline for a mark on a piece of paper. And then, weeks later, he'd heard how they'd come back with their trucks and their machines and opened the mines. He'd seen his tribe grow sick from illnesses the shamans couldn't cure with the leaves that had always cured his people. He'd seen the miners tear the earth apart, dig the roots up from the trees and kill the gods inside them that protected the forest. He'd seen them rip the skies apart and set the clouds on fire. He'd seen the cancers come from the huge black clouds of smoke that streamed out of the mine all day and all night and he'd seen the children born with red blotches on their faces, blotches that wept and bled and meant the child would die.

Alfredo was a young man, and as with young people all over the world, he saw injustice and it hurt him and he couldn't ignore it. His rage was wild and shook in his chest like an animal. He was not yet old enough to tell himself that there was nothing he could do.

In an effort to protect his home and his people from total destruction, Alfredo, with James Peake's instruction, had learned English. He had a talent for it and read until James had no books left to bring him. Under James's diligent tutelage, he'd applied for a place at Oxford University. He was going to fight this fight in the only way that he could see working: on his enemy's terms.

He was going to speak the language, learn the laws and understand the hateful logic of his oppressor. Then, he thought, he would be better equipped to explain to them that they were murdering his people and that they couldn't last much longer. He was convinced that once they knew what was happening, once they could understand the cost of the destruction, there could be no way that whoever was responsible for what was happening to his people could choose money over human life. Not if he made them see that the choice was really that simple and that absolute.

Leon's mother, Jackie, had run away from home when she was fifteen to find an uncle she'd never met but who she'd heard stories of all her life. Alistair McAlister was her mum's twin brother. He was a famous jockey with a big house and a pop-star wife. He lived in London, where everyone was beautiful and rich. Jackie's pale spectre of a father had lost his job and couldn't find his dignity. They lived in a coastal town near Middlesbrough; there was nothing really going on for her there. Just the sea and the pubs and her dad looking for work. Her mother, into heavy drugs, had drifted slowly out of their lives. She hadn't lived at home for years. There were no tearful rows, no slamming doors. She just left one day; quietly. Her addiction was a slow and sad and silent thing. Jackie saw her sometimes sitting with the others on the high street, crumpled up and thin as rain. Jackie didn't think she missed her, but her mother's absence made her dad detached. The silence in the house was stronger even than the smell of damp.

Jackie would sit with her dad and watch the lives of others on TV. Soap stars had affairs and leather jackets. Schoolkids had dreams and adventures. Young people had romance and fashion. Jackie was a lonely teenager and didn't know what to believe. One dark winter evening, an advert exploded into the front room. Her Uncle Alistair smiled out at them from a glowing studio. He was launching a new talk show. Sports personalities laughed as he attempted to beat them at an egg and spoon race. He wore an expensive suit and shiny shoes. The colours broke all over their drab furniture like waves. The two of them, sitting there on the sofa, found themselves suddenly drenched in a fizzing multicolour brightness. Jackie's father clucked his disapproval, but Jackie knew that there was awe in it.

Jackie's mother had always hated her brother and had made no secret of it. Jackie had only met him a few times, when she was too young to remember. It was the way he had wanted something and never once thought he shouldn't have it that had bothered her mother so much, his stamina, she didn't trust it at all. But here he was. On the TV. Jackie felt her heartbeat deepen; all sub, no mid-range.

Jackie's friendships were fleeting, if not non-existent. She never had best friends or boyfriends or even invisible friends. She was the quiet one with nervous eyes and she smelt bad and was bullied because of it. At home there was no bathing, no clean clothes, her quick grey eyes had to find their own food. But one cold day in June, she woke with a heat in her temples, maybe a fever, maybe a rage. As noon came, she found herself running the wet stones of her home town to the train station. In the sky she saw a sudden flash. A siren wailed within her. She was sure the flash was disc-shaped. A bright white light. She had always believed in aliens. She knew that they were out there and they were on her side. She looked again but the sky was grey and empty. She knew it was their way of telling her she was right to be running. It spread a guilty smile across her face as she hurried through the turnstiles. Pressed up close to the woman in front, she slipped through without a ticket.

Jackie arrived in London with nothing. She had hidden in the toilet from the ticket man the entire journey. Petrified. She stepped off the train and into the vast concourse of St Pancras and suddenly felt the weight of her escape. All these strangers, tall adult strangers, bustling and meaning business. Hurrying for trains to take them to places Jackie imagined to be full of love and supermodels. She started to scold herself. Heard her father's clipped vowels in her head and pinched her arms as punishment. She tried to fight it, but she could feel it coming. She began to weep.

Lily Peake, James Peake's wife, was on her way home from visiting her mother's grave. In a reflective mood she walked the concourse of St Pancras, feeling her mother more forcibly than she'd ever felt her while she'd lived. Alive, her mother had been a source of embarrassment to Lily. A strange creature who seemed so intent on weakness that Lily could hardly bear the occasional visits, sitting with cream cakes in a London tea room. But in death, Lily saw her mother in a new light. Realised it wasn't weakness but honesty she cultivated. She walked the station and felt this unbearable desire to be near her mother one more time. To watch the way the wrinkles moved to reveal the expressions she'd looked up into since her eyes had first opened. She felt a desolate tenderness and realised she would give anything for an awkward hour listening to her mother's outdated opinions. Lily couldn't help herself; she began to cry.

And there they were, crying woman and crying child. Not ten feet apart. Jackie, half crouched but still moving through the crowd. Lily, more composed but letting the tears flow freely. And suddenly, through their tears, they saw each other. Lily was shocked by this frightened child. This dirty-faced weeping girl. Tiny-bodied and gaunt and desperate but with a calmness she hadn't seen since she'd seen her own mother's eyes. Lily Peake had always believed in signs. She dried her eyes and pulled herself together and offered Jackie a smile from the depths of her being.

Jackie took fright. She ran through the station, and tripped over bag straps and hurtled past snarling adolescents. Bony shoulders struck fleshy midriffs, people shouted at her as she ducked and made towards the exit. Lily, shocked and moving slowly, watched the child escaping. Her mind raced. She followed without knowing she was following.

'Hey!' Lily heard a voice. 'What do you think you're doing?' A pompous man, shiny-headed. Fat and outraged, the contents of his briefcase spilled. Important papers on the floor, lifted and carried on the winds of the departing trains, fluttering off in every direction. He tutted and huffed and shouted and as Lily came through the crowd, she saw he was holding the girl's shoulder.

'Look what you've done!'

The girl looked petrified, weak. Lily hurried to her aid. She shared a little of her husband's tendency to cast herself as the saviour. It was a product of their wealth, their fine education, their strong morality and their genuine, although frequently misguided, sense of liberal goodness.

'You should be ashamed of yourself,' she told the fat man. 'Handling a poor child like that.'

'With you, is she?' The man still held the shoulder. Hard. Jackie felt her bone ache beneath his thumb. She didn't move.

'Yes, she is,' Lily said, winking at the girl.

'Well, keep her under control. She's just run into me out of nowhere, knocked my case out of my hand, and look at the mess she's made.'

'Oh we're terribly sorry, aren't we, darling?' Lily put her arm around the child, and as she did so, the man let go of her shoulder. 'It's just we're running for a train.' And with that, Lily, heart beating in a way it never had before, began to run with the child. Together they sprinted clumsily out of the station and burst into the doorway of the first lit building they came to. A pub. Full of smoke and tweed and loud laughter. They caught their breath and smiled at one another.

'Well,' said Lily, wiping the tears from her face. 'As we're here, why don't we have something to eat?'

Jackie found herself going home that night with Lily Peake, and this was how, the next morning, she met Alfredo, the young friend of Lily's husband James. Alfredo was a foreign man who lived in the attic annexe of the large house by the park. The pipes were fat with water heated by the furnace in the basement. James bought the leftover olive stones from the man who owned the Greek deli at the bottom of the road and fed them to the furnace to heat the house. Jackie was so excited by everything she saw; whole days passed when she was sure she hadn't blinked once. She lay in her bed at night exhausted and confused.

Alfredo's company excited her. When she saw him, the roof of her mouth and the bottom of her tummy ached. He was quiet like she was. He stepped carefully, like she did.

Alfredo thought that Jackie was fascinating. She was as out of place as he was, as driven and as full of pain. They sat there at the dinner table with Lily and James Peake, the friendly, wealthy, childless couple who had taken them both in.

They crossed in the hall and they felt each other's bodies change in the proximity, some inside parts of them pushing out. Wanting to be near each other. Alfredo could feel her smallness and it made him want to carry her. He himself was a small man. Well, hardly man, a boy still.

This is how they fell in love. In their own soundless way. They barely spoke, but she slipped up to his room at night, unable to not be near him.

Quiet, desperate touching. His eyes like pits of wet, black earth, hers as blue and quick as wind.

Upstairs, in his annexe, Alfredo repeated phrases, committed text to memory, prepared himself for his entrance exam beneath the watchful, pacing mentorship of James. Downstairs, by the back door, Jackie – riddled with fear – slipped out into the night and ran and ran and ran.

She never found her uncle. She didn't even look. Instead, she set out on her own – just another teenage girl, pregnant and alone on London's heartless streets.

Leon grew to be a slim boy, tall as his father was short, with features like the Mayan kings he'd seen pictures of in books. He knew nothing of his parents' meeting. Nothing of his father's tribe. All he knew was Lewisham, his silent mother, his sisters with their different dads. His brown skin, the copper strands that grew amongst the black that girls loved to find with their fingers.

He had no idea that his father had put his life behind a calling or that he had struggled and fought for his people. All he knew was that his dad was a question he couldn't bring up. He didn't know the great many women and men who had carried his light from the first days, and whose light he was carrying on into the next. As far as he knew, he was all that he'd ever been.

When Leon and Harry turned thirteen, Leon, at a push, looked nine, but Harry could have passed for twenty. There was something in her face that made her seem much older than she was, and so despite her tiny frame and baby-soft skin, Harry was the only kid in the lower school that could get served cigarettes. A jackpot thing to be. It may have had something to do with the woman who worked in the shop behind the playing field. Harry walked in, awkward and angular, her clothes baggy, swaggering, her face taut with shame. The woman at the till – late twenties, smile like a bad night out, blue hair, tattooed arms – was always very kind to Harry and called her 'gorgeous', which made Harry's stomach rumble uncontrollably.

Harry and Leon started selling fags to their classmates for 50p each. They could shift two packs of ten in a good lunch break and go home a tenner richer. This was back when you could get ten Sovereign for £1.25. They kept the money in a tin in Harry's room. Locked up with a padlock that they both had a key to.

The school they went to was normal, full of sex and drugs and bullying, hysterical outbursts and dramatic confrontations. Half of Harry's schoolmates had never seen the sea, but there wasn't one among them that had never seen a joint.

By the time they finished school they'd sold enough fags to buy themselves half a bar of skunk. Once they started selling draw, people opened up to them. They found their social role. And then came parties, phone calls, busy days on bicycles, they were seventeen and popular. Life was theirs at last. They had something to live for, work with, throw themselves towards. By the time they were twenty, they'd turned those ounces of weed into ounces of coke, and took the risks that came along with it. As the money got more serious, they found themselves able to save and they began looking to the future. They weren't gonna shit this money away on new clothes and gold chains. They were going to have their own place: a bar, a restaurant, a club of their own. Something that was theirs where no one could bully them and where anyone who came in would be safe.

Harry and Leon perfected their service, got the best gear and moved it without any fuss. The love they bore each other was the kind of love that flourishes best in the dismal parts of town, between friends who want more than the cheap drugs, shit sex, casual violence and eventual dullness that all their peers seemed to be settling for. A brother–sister relationship that went deeper than blood, because it was about survival and betterment and they trusted each other completely.

They were very smart and very careful; they never bought expensive things, they only sold to those they knew, had a few different numbers they used, switched the stash every other day. They were aiming for a figure, and when they got there, they'd be out. They wanted to make a million.

Leon had always had a passion for food; when he was nineteen he got a job in a kitchen and started learning how to cook. Something about the atmosphere made him feel more like himself than he'd known how to feel before. He loved the knives, the pace, the way you started with a few things and if you did it right you ended up making something so much more than the sum of its parts.

He threw himself into it, working the hours that chefs have to work. On his days off he hit the gym and trained hard. He let Harry do the bulk of the shotting. She played it sweet when she had to. She played it smart when she had to. She understood people and how to read them, and people were disarmed by her nature. She was bubbly, conversational. They trusted her judgement. Leon was the muscle. He saw danger everywhere and knew how to stop it. He would often stay hidden until the last minute.

Leon dedicated himself to being ready for anything. He trained in three different martial arts and he practised t'ai chi for strength and grace. He lifted weights, ran circuits of the park for hours. Skipped each night for forty minutes. Fought with anyone who wanted fighting with. He soon got a reputation for being a nutcase hard man. Quiet and watchful. The scariest type. But he never went for anyone unless they went for him.

After a few years, as things got busier and busier with the business, Leon threw the apron in. It was a sad day, hanging up his chef whites, but Leon was committed to Harry and the plan. And one day, when they had their own place, Leon would keep his own kitchen.

When Leon turned thirty, he looked around and noticed how, every time he saw his friends, there would come a time of night when they would be hanging off his shoulder, rubbing their eyes, telling him how unhappy they were.

'All life is,' they would say, elegant poets after enough lines, dabs, swigs, 'is routine and bullshit. Nothing ever changes. Work, eat, sleep, fuck, drink, dance, die.'

But Leon had never seen life that way. Leon saw that life could be hideous or beautiful, often both, but never mediocre.

He knew that every tiny thing that happened had to be considered, felt, enjoyed, either fought with or fought for.

IN THE KITCHEN THEY sit in silence and drink their beers for a time.

'What's the deal then?' he asks her, fiddling with the sticker on his bottle.

'Well, apparently' – Harry looks up, raises her eyebrows – 'it's all going to be absolutely *fine*.'

Leon looks at her, sceptical. They're going to reload, but Pico, the dealer they've been working with for near enough seven years, has gone to jail, and so they're going to meet his stand-in. Leon doesn't like it.

'Same gear,' Harry tells him, 'same supplier, it's just a new link. That's all.'

'You feel OK about it?' he asks, still fiddling.

'Yeah,' Harry says. 'Don't you?'

'Seems a bit dodgy to me, mate. But then again' – Leon puts his beer down on the table and runs his hand across his head, feels the soft bumps of his hair across his palm – 'everything does if you think about it too much. Right?'

Harry agrees with him, draws her lips into a silent line.

'Funny enough, that's exactly what I thought this morning,' she says, 'just that.'

Leon hovers his hand in Harry's direction without looking at her. Harry gives him her cigarette. Leon takes a burn off it, exhales, goes for another small one, gives it back.

'You not met this guy before, have you?' he says.

'No,' says Harry, taking the cigarette.

'You don't think it's too hot? With Pico inside and that?'

'Tell you what, mate, the joke of it is' – Harry takes a loose swig of her beer, smiling as she swallows – 'feds don't have a clue who he is! He's inside for unpaid parking tickets!'

'Fuck off?' says Leon.

'I'm serious!' Harry warms to it. 'He used to just park his car wherever he wanted. He'd just say to himself, fuck it, right, £60 to park here, that's what it costs. Know what I mean? He kept all his tickets in his dash and then he'd give 'em to his accountant, end of every month or whatever, and get it all sorted. He couldn't be dealing with fannying about looking for a parking space if he had somewhere to be.'

'Well, fair enough,' says Leon.

'Anyway, turns out his accountant's gone away for a few weeks, on holiday, with the family. When he gets back, they've got much bigger fish to fry, I suppose, coz a couple months go past and everyone's forgotten about the parking tickets. Little while later, he gets a knock on the door, it's a fucking court summons!'

They both smile, shake their heads. Enjoy the irony.

'Why didn't he just pay it off?'

'I don't know for sure,' Harry tells him, 'but look.' She gets her best authoritative voice on. 'It was up in the *tens* of *grands* apparently . . .' She looks at Leon, eyes bright, nodding, lips pursed.

'Was it fuck?' says Leon, incredulous.

'I know!' Harry's voice is a squeaking trumpet.

'Tens?' Leon says, unsure.

'Apparently.' Harry lifts her palms up, shrugs.

'Fuck!' Leon makes the swear word rhyme with 'park'.

'Didn't wanna arouse suspicion by just coming up with that kind of money, did he? Far as the taxman's concerned, Pico's a self-employed interior designer. Best thing he could have done was take it on the chin, I imagine.'

'Fuck me,' Leon says, digesting it. Hands on his knees. Leaning forwards. 'Fuck me!'

'That's what I heard anyway,' Harry says, beginning to pack the money into the bag.

Leon reaches out for the last bit of her cigarette. Harry gives it to him without any reaction.

'So who is he, whoever it is holding the fort?'

'Just some guy, some relative probably,' Harry, packs the bundles carefully. One at a time.

'Not got a name?'

'Rags. Rags is his name.'

Their hearts beat the same slow pace. They've been doing this so long it's comforting. Like playing an instrument you've played all your life. But this feels different.

Leon looks at the floor, taps his feet. 'Know anything else about him?'

'Not yet. Feels weird, right?'

'S'pose we'll have to see, won't we?' Leon ponders the end of the cigarette. Looking at the butt to judge how much more life's left in it.

'The thing is, right,' Harry stops for impact, seeks out Leon's eyes, 'I never met *anyone* else from the team. *Never.* Always just Pico. Dealt with a couple of the muscle now and again, just in passing, just a quick nod or whatever, but *never* dealt with another guy. You know what I mean, Leon? Strange, innit? Don't you think?' Harry stares at him, her oldest friend, waits for the advice she knows she can trust.

Leon thinks it over. Turns it around. Weighs it up. 'You sure we can't just wait this out?' he offers. 'Till he's out, I mean.'

Harry nods deeply. 'I don't know how long he's going to be away is one thing. And, we're out of gear *and* things are booming at the minute, my phone is ringing off the fucking *hook.* I swear down, if we do this, and then we move the lot, which I think we will, I'm pretty positive, Leon – that we could be out of this whole fucking game in six months.'

They stare at each other across the kitchen table. Stare. Think about what those words mean. *Six months.*

'And I mean *out.* Then, I reckon, you know, that we could be cleaned up and ready to put some money down on a property by the end of the *year,* mate. I swear.'

They think about that. Two decades of working for a thing, and suddenly there it is, in plain sight.

Leon studies the feeling, shivers. 'We'll just have to do it then, won't we?' he says, swigging slowly. Taking his time.

'That's it,' says Harry. 'Took the words right out my mouth.'

THEME FROM BECKY

Becky tilts her chin upwards, watches the cold sun bouncing off the windows in the tops of the buildings, dripping its yolk across pale stone and glass. The leaves on the trees have crumbled, some ragged scraps still hang on. She watches the bare branches, dotted with hard, sleeping buds. The fractal sunlight dappling everything. She can't believe how beautiful it is when the seasons change.

Pete has been teaching her about her father's politics. He tells her that her dad wanted to renationalise all privatised utilities. That he believed in universal nuclear disarmament. He explains that John thought society could be run for the good of all, not the profit of a few. He believed in the importance of getting organised.

Pete reads to her, because when she reads she doesn't understand the words, but when he reads them, for some reason, they make perfect sense.

It has been strange getting to know her father's voice this way. Hearing vaguely familiar turns of phrase coming out of Pete's mouth. Sometimes, she feels herself amped up to shaking point. Inspired and furious, desperate to find him, hear him tell her how it was all a set-up. Have him explain the world and how she can save it. But these feelings are always followed with a sour scrub of shame. A cloying dirge that drags her down.

Her mother's in her mind these days. She's been looking at her photographs all morning. She feels closer to her every passing year. Her mum was twenty-six when she had her. Becky's twenty-six now. Getting older, getting closer to herself.

Marshall Law won two MTV awards for the Cool New Band video. Becky got the phone call from his PA the next day, offering three weeks' work on his next project. Unpaid rehearsals, a huge amount of effort demanded for no acclaim. It would have worked out at less than minimum wage, as usual. She had felt the old hysteria bubbling up within, the feeling that she had to take any opportunity that arose, so that one day she could be in the position to make her own decisions. She felt it pushing like water up through her body, towards her mouth, the wave about to break and say yes, of course, thanks for thinking of me. But she swallowed it.

'I can't do it,' she said. 'I'm not available.'

Marshall's PA was shocked into silence. When her voice at last returned it was devoid of its pleasantries.

'You understand that Marshall won't ask again, don't you?' she said threateningly. And that was the end of Becky's relationship with Marshall Law. After four years of working on his shoots.

She had found herself marooned, looking for work. Unable to get auditions. The classes she went to were at The Place, the home of the school she'd trained at. She attended as many as she could afford; she aimed to make three a week but she could feel her fitness slipping.

With every year that passes an out-of-work dancer is more prone to injury, less fit. No company would take her on, given the commercial stuff she'd been doing since qualifying. They would never choose to see her at an audition over an eighteen-year-old. Her CV was laughable and for every part that came up, hundreds and hundreds of women applied. There was no hope for her. And everyone she spoke to exhaled through pursed lips and lowered their eyes.

The Place was running an annual festival of new work. This was, she felt, the last push. She stepped up the classes. Started going daily. She could feel her muscles tightening, her Achilles tendons lengthening. She would have to pay her dancers, rent the studios to work in, conceive the piece and teach it without any support. But The Place would put it on stage and give her a journalist to review it.

She told her agents at the massage company that she would take work in any hotel at any time of the night. Her phone beeped and the text came and she'd have an hour and a half to get ready and get across town. She'd be sitting at her kitchen table, planning for the show, or watching TV in her pyjamas with Pete, or sitting in the pub drinking soda water and lime, and the text would come and she would have to snap herself out of her life and make the journey towards becoming someone else.

She made her money and she booked the studio and she paid her dancers and she was exhausted to the point of collapse, but much more alive than before. Her muscles on fire when she walked down the snail-grey steps of her flat; going backwards to deal with the cramps in her calves.

She conceived a piece for a cast of four women who moved in interlocking bursts and waves across the floor. Pain and poverty and struggle. Family and independence. It was well reviewed and although she received no funding off the back of it, got no parts directly, her name rang out a little louder in the audition process. It seemed to the people who glanced over her CV that although Becky had taken an unusual path, she was doing things her own way and was obviously committed.

Pete hated all the time she was spending in rehearsals, hated her being on call every night. He'd got his CSCS card and found a few weeks' work labouring. But he shrank from the banter onsite. It made him feel like an impostor in his own sex. He wanted to take Becky out with the money he made. But she was never around. The work dried up after three weeks, and he was back on the dole.

Every time they have a row it makes him cry. He doesn't know how it happens, but as soon as her tone hardens, he feels this heat behind his face like being punched from the inside, and tears come and his throat swells and he gets all snotty and stupid. She freezes when she sees him sob, ices over in an instant. She never cries in front of people, she thinks that it's manipulative.

Pete is ashamed of his behaviour, but he doesn't really recognise it. When she's not around he feels chirpy and fine and reasonable. But as soon as they're together he can't think straight and he behaves like a madman.

When she asks him about it, it just makes him angry and embarrassed and he gets silent and visualises shooting himself in the face. Over and over. Shooting himself in the mouth, in the temple, in the eye. Over and over.

Bang.

He's been going through her things. She knows because the most recent batch of letters to her parents that she keeps in the box in her wardrobe are all in the wrong order and the pile of business cards she printed for her massage work is half the size it should be. But something keeps her coming back.

They kiss in the supermarket and smoke spliffs in bubble baths, but his moods are getting worse and worse, and she begins to keep her distance. When he feels her pulling away from him, he panics, pushes harder. Turns up unannounced outside her flat. Too embarrassed to ring the bell in case he has to talk to her flatmate, he waits on the dark balcony, smoking. Imagining her moving through hotel rooms, hearing the squelch of other men's parts in her hands. Red-eyed from the weed with a hacking cough that bends him double.

When she's at work he punches walls until his knuckles bleed and later, in the pub, his wounds seeping and hardening, he hates her for what she's done to him but still can't wait to see her, can't wait to hold her in his arms.

The jobcentre's killing him. Becky's love is killing him. Coming home to his childhood bedroom is killing him. Everything is killing him, and yet his life just keeps on dragging; the morning comes and here he is, awake again. Alive.

After her piece went on at The Place, Becky attended some open auditions: a hundred girls in a room, picked off one by one and told to go home. The day split into three sections, a ballet class in the morning to check for correct training. Then, the teaching and performance of a routine to check body and temperament. And finally an improvisation, to check whether the dancers were knowledgeable or creative enough. The whole day racked with pressure. Body like a catapult, pulled right back. Some of the auditions she had to pay to attend. Becky had been out of this world for three years, but was so desperate to shine that she worked harder than the others. No matter the effort though, she was still too old. Three months later, even after attending open auditions every single day, Becky couldn't get an audition for a part in a company. But she had made herself visible, and she was a dancer again.

As autumn reared its golden mane and shook the leaves down from the branches, Becky got a call from a rehearsal director who had a show about to open at Sadler's Wells. They needed a swing.

She had to sit in rehearsals and learn every part from just watching. The choreographer had no time to teach her the phrases. Her arms and her legs were alone in the room. Along with two other swings, she had to learn every single part in the piece, with no support and for even less money than everyone else. The other dancers in the company ignored them, because they weren't worth their time, and because they knew that at some level they would be hoping for falls, sickness, injuries. But even so, Becky was happier than she'd been in years.

When Nima got sick, Becky stepped in. There was something nasty going round. She had one day to prepare for the part. Nima was too ill to teach her, so she was entirely alone with the transition. Ryan and Mahesh got sick the next night. All three swings had to be ready. Half-sick themselves from stress and fatigue, but burning up. Elated.

Becky stands outside Sadler's Wells Theatre finishing her cigarette. She drops the butt, stubs it out with her toe and heads back through the stage door, down into the depths of the building.

In the corridor outside the dressing rooms, she paces for a while, then sits down heavily on the floor, pulls her knees up to her chest, rests her head on her knees and closes her eyes. She tries to calm her nerves but she can't stop tapping her feet, which means she keeps kneeing herself in the forehead.

The other two swings walk into the corridor. Becky looks up, stands. 'Hi, guys,' she says, brushing the backs of her legs off.

Patrice has calm brown eyes, smooth skin. His neat, short hair curls up and clings to his head. His legs are long, his hips are high, his chest is broad; he has a small mouth that is often pouting in disapproval. He walks like a supermodel. Marina, beside him, is small and muscular, solidly built, but all her edges are soft. Her red hair spills out in a perfect circle when she lets it. She hates nobody, has complicated relationships with everyone she sleeps with and writes furiously in her diary at night, secretly imagining that one day, after she is dead, it will be published.

'Hi, Becky!' Marina squeals all her greetings.

'You OK?' Patrice asks Becky, holding her arms at the wrists, shaking them, loosening her up. 'You're nervous?' He puts his chin down, pouts at her.

'No. I'm OK,' Becky says.

They stand in a line between the two walls of the corridor. Becky stretches her hands high above her head, links them together and points to the ceiling with the flat of her palms. Up onto her toes. As tall as she can make herself, breathing into her belly, she bends at the waist, touching the floor, pushing her palms down, breathing out slowly. Eyes closed. Counting the seconds. On the other side of the frosted glass doors that line the corridor, the dancers from the company are getting ready. Becky and Marina and Patrice can hear voices rising and falling, waves of laughter rolling in and out.

'Someone's having fun in their *dressing room*,' says Patrice.

'One day,' says Marina, 'we will have dressing rooms, and then *we* will have fun.'

Becky checks the clock. Marina sees her doing it. 'Twenty minutes,' she says, eyes shining.

'It's been twenty minutes for ages.' Becky shakes her hands gently, rolls her neck from side to side, bends at the waist to lay her hands flat against the floor.

Marina rotates her shoulders, making circles with her arms while jogging gently on the spot with soft feet. Patrice lowers himself to sit on the floor with his legs out to either side of him; he holds the sole of his left foot with both hands, forehead touching his knee like a prayer.

When Becky steps out onto the stage, the blackness beyond the lights is total. Everything is reduced to tiny, precise movements. Her muscles. The music. The bodies on stage. Time is irrelevant.

The applause brings her back to the world. She stands breathing, looking out, re-entering life, sweating like a human. Looking for Pete as the house lights come up.

The three dancers get changed and head down together. Arm in arm. Pete is standing at the bar, facing out, shoulders hunched, staring into space. His hair is getting long; he's grown it past the stage where it mushrooms outwards and now it falls downwards into his eyes. Becky watches him, tries to work out what kind of mood he's in. He looks stoned.

'Hi!' she says, reaching up to kiss him.

'Alright,' he says, his kiss dry.

'These are my friends, Patrice and Marina. This is Pete, my boyfriend.' Marina smiles, Pete looks at the floor and back at Becky. 'Are you OK if we have a drink here with these guys?' she asks him.

Pete shrugs. 'Course,' he says, 'whatever you want.'

Patrice extends his hand. 'Pleased to meet you.'

'Hiya, mate. Alright.' Pete shakes his hand. Patrice looks over his shoulder at Marina and pouts.

'Very firm,' he says to Pete. Pete stares at him, doesn't respond in any visible way. Just stares. 'OK,' Patrice says slowly.

'And I'm Marina.' Marina reaches her face up for a kiss on the cheek, Pete bends down clumsily, hesitates, and offers his hand instead. Marina pulls back, laughing. 'Oops!' she says. 'How awkward.' She shakes his hand.

'Sorry,' says Pete. 'I'm not from round here.'

'What did you think of the show?' Becky asks him, her whole face opening up into a hopeful smile.

Pete looks over her head at the wall beyond and doesn't make eye contact. He rocks back onto his heels. 'It was good,' he says.

Becky takes some lip balm out of her pocket, applies some to her lips, rubs them together, waits for him to say more. He doesn't. 'OK. Well, thanks.' Her sarcasm is faint but unmistakable.

Pete says nothing. Puts his hands in his pockets.

'Drinks?' Patrice says.

Even here in the bar, the dancers group themselves according to status. The leads are in the middle, sitting with the choreographer and the director, making a literal inner circle; the lesser dancers ripple out around them. Becky, Pete, Patrice and Marina, not even in the company, take a table tucked away in the corner, by the toilets. They are offered small kisses or shoulder squeezes as dancers and tech crew walk in and out of the cubicles.

The bar is crowded. It's a light, spacious room with high ceilings; long velvet curtains hang over arched windows. Becky, Patrice and Marina huddle together, chairs pulled in tight to the table, leaning towards each other. Pete sits with his chair further out from the table and watches them speak to each other, drinking from his pint in big gulps, wiping his mouth after each gulp with his thumb and forefingers.

'That was an insane amount of work,' Becky says, her voice giddy with excitement. 'I can't believe we did it.' They smile at each other, proud and swooning from the effort.

'I mucked up, like, three times and I think certain people are angry with me,' Marina says, sticking her bottom lip out.

'*I'm* angry with you.' Patrice pours Prosecco into their glasses. 'But it's only because I've never learned to truly love myself.'

'No one's angry with you. Don't be silly,' Becky says.

Marina leans in closer, looks towards the lead dancers in the centre of the room, dropping her voice. 'Those lot are angry with everyone, *all* the time. Especially me. They think I'm clumsy and today I *was* clumsy and now they'll never want to sleep with me.'

Becky laughs.

'They think everyone's clumsy. It's because everyone is clumsy compared to them. And I don't think they sleep with anyone except each other.'

'It's not fair,' Marina says. 'They literally have genetic superiority over me. It's not an equal playing field.'

'Honey, you have *different* blessings.' Patrice raises his glass for a toast. 'You have a great personality.' He flashes his teeth at her.

'You can be so mean.' Marina picks up her glass.

'It's only because I love you. You know that. Now, cheers me.'

They raise their glasses. Becky looks at Pete, urges him to participate. He smiles with his lips closed, the smile sinking into his face. He raises his glass.

'Cheers, everyone,' Becky says. 'Well done.' And they all drink.

'I just couldn't get low enough today. I don't know what else I can do. I've practised for five, six hours today, yesterday, every day, for ever, and it just comes to it, and I can't do it.' Patrice fiddles with his hair as he talks.

'You'll get it. You just have to relax,' Marina says. Becky nods.

A pause descends as they sip from their glasses. They listen to the room.

Marina, the most uncomfortable with silence, breaks it, as she always does. 'What about you, Pete?' she asks. 'What do you do?'

Pete looks at her. He shrugs. 'Not much.'

Another silence falls. Nobody minds but Marina.

'Smoothies!' she screams. 'I nearly forgot to tell you, guys. My mum got me a machine thing for my birthday. OMG, guys, GUYS, I'm doing, like, a little bit of turmeric root, big handful of kale, some pineapple, a few almonds, not too many. One of those *every* day, and I'm feeling great. Honestly.'

'It's a fad,' Patrice says.

'You're a fad,' Marina shoots back at him.

'*I'm* a fad?' Patrice lowers his eyebrows, strokes his chin, pantomimes trying to work out the insult.

Pete is silent, sitting back, watching. Knees as far apart as they can go. His jacket's done up to the chin and he's holding the top of his zip in his mouth, only moving to flick his hair out of his eyes now and again, and gripping his pint like it's a tree root at the edge of a cliff. Becky is laughing along with her friends but distracted by him. She has her hand on his thigh; she squeezes it, catches his eye.

'Are you OK?' She leans back towards him and says it quietly. She knows he's not. He nods. 'What's going on?' she whispers. He looks away from her, to the others at the table. She watches the side of his face. He doesn't respond. She squeezes his leg again. 'Pete?'

He turns his head and, smiling at her, he speaks slowly, his eyes burning with embarrassment. 'I'm fine.'

'Do you want to go?' she asks him quietly.

He looks at her blankly. 'Me?' he says, leaning towards her. 'It's your night.'

Marina pours the last of the bottle out. 'Another bottle?' she asks the table. 'And don't even think about saying *I shouldn't,* Rebecca Shogovitch, because *I've* already had two bars of chocolate and an apple Danish today. To balance out the kale.'

'Well, actually, I think we're gonna go,' Becky says, looking at Pete, reaching for his hand. His hand stays limp on his lap. She holds it.

'Oh come on, we've just got started,' Patrice says.

'No.' Becky's face is drawn, apologetic. 'I think. Me and Pete had plans. So, maybe we should—'

'Don't mind me.' Pete says, 'I'm alright.' He smiles sweetly at her. It's an empty smile, but no one knows except Becky.

'Well, OK,' she says. 'If you're OK?'

'Stay,' Marina says. 'He doesn't mind, do you, Pete?'

'I don't mind.' Pete sends his eyebrows high up into his forehead. His voice is syrup. 'I'm easy, hon,' he says. 'Let's stay.'

They get off the tube and change for the Overground. They haven't said anything to each other since they left the venue. At the top of the escalators Becky walks to the exit to smoke a cigarette. Pete follows a couple of steps behind, head down. Outside, she leans against the wall, lights one up. He stands in front of her, staring at her cigarette.

'Do you want one?' Becky asks.

'Yeah,' he says. 'I ran out this morning.'

'Why didn't you get some more?'

'Got no money, have I.'

'Course you haven't.' She gives him a cigarette. He takes it, lights it. They smoke. Becky heaves a deep sigh, Pete leans back against the wall.

'Have I done something wrong?' she asks him.

'No.' He hardly opens his mouth to talk. They stand side by side and don't touch. Don't look at each other.

'What's happening?' she asks him.

'I'm fine.' His voice is a low monotone.

They smoke in silence. They watch the taxis at the taxi rank, the buses turning off their engines.

His voice is a trap door opening beneath her. He speaks slowly. 'We were meant to go out just the two of us.'

Becky throws her hands up in disbelief. 'I knew it!' A spurt of scornful laughter escapes from her lips.

Pete plays innocent. 'Knew what?'

'I knew you wouldn't want to go for drinks with my friends.' She has tears in her eyes already.

'They're not your friends.' Pete is stone-faced.

'I like them a lot, Pete.' Her voice is shaking.

'I could tell.' His tone is spiteful.

'What does that mean?'

'You were talking differently. You were trying to talk like them.' He squares his shoulders and smokes and looks away from her. 'And I saw what you were like with that guy, letting him hug you so much at the end. Making me feel like a right prick.'

'I don't know what you mean.' She shakes her head, blinks. She's not going to cry. 'And if you're talking about Patrice, he's *gay* for fuck's sake.' She breathes in through her nose. Out through her mouth. He sneers at her. Looks away. 'If you didn't want to be there why didn't you say something? Why didn't you say when I *asked* you if you wanted to have a drink there that you'd rather we go somewhere else, together?' She waits for him to answer.

He tips his head back, exasperated. Rubs his forehead. Rubs the back of his neck, speaks slowly at last, trying to keep his voice level, but behind every syllable is the threat of shouting. 'You should have *known* I wouldn't want to be there. Fucking place like that, people like that.'

'People like what, Pete? It was a really important night for me. I wanted to make the best impression that I could.'

'It was bullshit.'

'What was bullshit?'

'The SHOW. It was a load of pretentious fucking bullshit.' He breathes heavily. She stares at him, disbelieving. His chest rises and falls. 'All you done for the last month is talk about this fucking thing. I've hardly *seen* you. You never have no time for me. For *us*. You always have time for rehearsals, for fucking drinks with your posh dancer mates.' His voice is rising. His eyes are wide. 'You're getting paid a pittance for it, so you're swanning off to hotels in the middle of the night to wank off strangers, just so you can prance around at the back of the stage. I could hardly fucking *see* you up there, you had like two things to do in the whole fucking thing, and you're telling yourself you're living your dream.' He pokes his fingers against his temples, glares at her. 'And fucking all of you, sat there with your fucking fizzy wine talking about fucking smoothies. It's not *real*. None of it's real. And it does my fucking head in.'

Becky stares at him. Doesn't move. Her arms are crossed against the wind. He looks at her, calm suddenly, blows smoke out in a thin stream. She shakes her head. A minute passes.

At last, Becky finds the words. 'I'm going to go home now, Pete,' she says. 'And I don't think you should come with me.'

'Fine.' He shrugs.

She stares at him again. Waiting. Tilts her head to one side, chews her lip. He doesn't respond, just keeps smoking, looking past her. She nods to herself and walks off, back into the station to change for the southbound Overground. She looks back before she goes through the turnstiles; she can just about make out his shape. He hasn't moved.

She rides the train and feels numb. Her brain flickers with images, shadows and stage lights, the audience, her legs like tissues crumpling beneath her in the moments before she walked out there, and then like lion's legs as soon as she felt the stage. The train is packed with happy revellers returning home from nights out. She watches a couple as they kiss each other's noses.

Pete watches the sky; the moon is fat and hungry. Glowing yellow at its edges. He is lost and he can't feel anything. He would like to see some friends, but he can't remember how to do it.

He is stranded. Bitter afternoons, spoiled occasions, unsaid things. She is desperate for so much. Independence, acclaim and she doesn't need support and she can take it or leave it with love. She is on such high alert. *Don't you make me exist for what you want, Pete. Don't you fucking dare think that I am going to cut my dreams in half to try and make you happy.* Hard words in bed instead of love words. Hard looks, hard sulks. He's so tired but she is electricity, fire, snake-muscled, angry, intense woman who haunts him. All that weed you smoke, and you have no perspective on your behaviour, you're like a child, she tells him. And then she fucks him and he can't breathe because her body. Her body. And he is losing everything. His friends are boring. His sister. His interests are all so grey compared to her stark flashing colours. He hasn't enjoyed anything for months. Everything apart from her is happening on another channel. But they're there, with them, each night, in the bedroom, standing around, kissing each other, all the men from all the hotel rooms, dicks out, waiting for Pete to fuck up. He wants to talk to her about the way he's feeling, but what words for all this? It's just noise inside his brain, it's so loud in here, can't speak this stuff, it's too noisy and every time he tries, he starts wrong and it ends up like this.

She never gave a fuck what people thought of it before. The way she sees it, bar work's more degrading. Or some dogsbody office job.

Life, for some people, is just a dry-cleaned suit and boardrooms and shit hotels in faceless towns with deadlines to meet and sleeping pills to fall off the edge of the tedious days. Months at a time living in transit. Going for targets. Sales and accounts.

She was eighteen when she learned the value of her body, a tequila girl in awful bars in town where men, wearing shoes they cherished in the absence of real friendships, wound down after work by pretending they were much happier than they really were. She wore skimpy clothes and learned how to slap drunken hands away when they mistook her professional flirtations for genuine sexual interest. She hated that job. It gave her no power. Playing up to a role to sell shots that she barely made anything out of. *That* felt dirty. This work, she thinks, doesn't feel dirty at all.

If Pete had the same job, she wouldn't have a problem with it.

It's a few hours before dawn. Becky sits on the night bus, forehead against the dark glass watching memories play out on the streets she passes. Younger Beckys, laughing, kissing, drinking, crying. Back then, the best people she knew were full of love. Gooey-eyed on acid, playing with their fingers, giggling like toddlers at the shape of household objects. But now those same kids are grown-ups, parents with kids of their own, supervising the moving of boxes round factories, or getting chubby in a travel agent's, answering phones and hunting for deals, biting into cheese-and-meatball melts every lunchtime and taking two sugars with every weak tea.

What makes what I do any different from what they do? Or what he does? Fifty pounds a week or whatever he gets, it's a pack of fags and a loaf of bread and a shitload of worry about anything else. At least I'm providing. It's not like he doesn't spend the money I make. She stops thinking about it. None of it matters.

She wakes up just after midday. Alone at last. But not for long. She rolls over, pulls the covers right up to her chin and closes her eyes. At two o'clock she is supposed to go and meet Pete's family. She can't think of anything she'd like to do less. Last night drifts past, everything he said when they were outside the station. She seethes.

Every cell of her body is heavy. Her eyes close and she sinks through the mattress, floating towards sleep.

The doorbell goes. Three times in a row.

Pete is on the doorstep, nervous as she opens it. He gives her some flowers that he's picked from her neighbour's garden. Her neighbour is an old lady, a widow, whose garden is the most important thing in her life. Becky imagines her standing at her window, hiding behind her nets, watching the tall scruffy man stepping in her beds and snapping her roses off the bushes.

Miriam answers the door smiling and drying her hands on a tea towel. She beams at Becky.

'Hi,' she says, 'you must be Becky!'

Becky smiles. 'Hi,' she says. Wanting to run.

Miriam has a soft, open face, delicate wrinkles tiptoe around the edges. Becky kisses her cheek and follows Miriam into the dining room.

'Sit yourself down.'

Becky sits on the far side of the table, back to the wall, facing in. *They have a dining room.* David is standing at the end of the room, holding a bottle of wine and rifling through a drawer for a corkscrew. Pete sits down next to Becky, Miriam stands by the dresser and, once she sees Pete and Becky settled, she joins them, sitting opposite. David opens the wine, sets it on the table, opens another, sets it beside the first one, turns them round so that their labels are facing the same way, smiles and sits down at the head of the table, jiggling on his seat at the excitement of having visitors.

'And what do you do then, Becky?' Miriam leans forwards, hands on the table, one on top of the other.

'I'm a dancer.' Becky notices how graceful Miriam is, how elegantly she holds herself. 'I'm a waitress, but dancing is my passion.' Becky's voice is edged with exhaustion. This is the last place she wants to be.

'That's exciting.' Miriam's face lights up. 'Dancing! What style? Is it much like *Strictly*?'

'No, not so much,' Becky says, smiling shyly. 'Do you watch *Strictly*?'

'Oh yes, David and I love it, don't we, David?'

'Yes!' David says gleefully. 'We do.'

'I'm in a show actually, at the moment. A very small part, but it's still exciting to be involved.' Becky speaks carefully, quietly.

'A show! In town?' Miriam's face is a Catherine wheel. She looks at Pete, Pete nods.

'Yes,' Becky says. 'It's very exciting.' And she looks at Pete pointedly, but he's looking at his fingernails.

'My goodness me!' Miriam takes her hands away from each other and lays them flat on the table, parallel. They are slender and gentle-looking, her nails are neat, no wedding ring, but a thin gold band holding two dark green, opaque stones on her middle finger. She leans in towards Becky. 'I'd love to come and see it!' David is watching her, smiling to himself. 'I used to love the ballet.' Miriam holds her arms above her head, fingertips touching. Laughing.

'Oh yeah?' Becky smiles. 'I haven't been for years. I went once . . .' Her voice cracks into shards. She breathes, swallows the sharp points. 'With my mum.' She doesn't want to invite discussion of what her mum does or where she might be in the world, but she's said it now. She carries on. 'When I was very young but never since.'

'Oh, we'll have to go.' Miriam is sure of it. 'My mother loved the ballerinas too.'

Miriam hadn't noticed Becky's discomfort. Becky relaxes. 'I'd like that,' she says softly.

'Pete, have you seen the show?' David asks him.

'Yeah.' Pete looks up from his fingernails, sniffs, nods.

'And . . .?' David presses him.

Pete flicks his hair out of his eyes, taps his toes on the floor. 'Yeah, it was good.'

'He didn't like it much,' Becky explains to David.

'Wasn't his thing, no?' Miriam folds her arms and looks disapprovingly at Pete for a moment. 'I shouldn't take it personally, Becky, he's very chalk and cheese about things. He gets it from his father. Some might call it . . .' She pauses, stage whispers, '*closed-minded*.'

Pete leans back in his chair. 'What's for lunch then, Mum?'

'You'll see,' Miriam tells him, looking at him carefully for a hint of the meanness his father was prone to. 'So, you work as a waitress by day, and then you go off and dance in the theatre by night?' Miriam asks warmly. 'You're putting us all to shame, Becky!'

Becky smiles self-consciously. Wants to disappear into the tablecloth.

'Well said.' David slaps the table top. Miriam jumps. Pete stares at him, confused. 'Smart lady,' he says to Pete. Pete doesn't respond. Keeps staring at him. David tries to match the stare but can't. He picks up his fork and looks at the prongs carefully.

'So, what do you get up to on your days off?'

'Normal stuff,' Becky tells her. 'Money's tight so we don't go out much or things like that, do we?' She turns her body towards Pete.

He shakes his head sadly. 'Not so much.'

'But we go out with friends and that, don't we?'

'We do.' Pete puts his arm around the back of her chair, squeezes her shoulder gently. Becky touches his hand. Miriam's never seen her son show affection to anyone. She melts, pools and evaporates.

'We go to the pub, and we go to parties and things. If Pete's up for it.'

'Oh good.' Miriam's eyes grow wider and wider. 'Does he take you out to the clubs, show you off?'

'That's exactly what I do,' Pete says, straight-faced.

'What else? Tell me more. It's nice to hear about young people's lives, isn't it, David?'

'We're not quite at the knacker's yard yet, sweetheart,' David huffs cheerfully.

'Yes, but you know, we're not in our twenties, are we, *dancing* and going out to parties with all our friends. I remember those days. Good times, they were. Enjoy every minute, won't you, my darlings?'

'We try,' Pete says.

'So, do you take classes?'

'Yes. I take a couple a week, but it all adds up, so sometimes more, sometimes less, depending on what I can afford.'

'Waitressing is tough, isn't it? It's all tips. And rude people.' Miriam leans forwards, enjoying the presence of a young lady in her house. Her daughter is so boyish that she's more like another son.

Becky laughs. 'Yeah, tell me about it. But it's my uncle and auntie's place, so I like to help out.'

'Oh that's good. If it's a family business.' Becky glances at Pete.

'And I do massage as well. So it's just about enough. We survive.' Pete grows rigid in his seat.

'Oh how nice. Lucky you, eh, Pete?' Miriam winks at him.

Pete detonates the bomb strapped to his chest and his body explodes and splatters the room with his insides. 'Very lucky,' he says. Squeezing her shoulder again.

'I love all those holistic therapies,' Miriam tells her. 'I get Reiki every other Thursday. *And* I've had past-life regression.' Miriam grins at Becky, looking for understanding. 'David thinks I'm barmy for it, but I love it. I've had it a few times now.'

'What did you see?' Becky asks her.

'The first time, I was in ancient Egypt.'

Pete closes his eyes, sighs, leaves them closed for a full second before looking back at his mother.

Becky nods. 'Right.'

'I was a boy. I was a noble boy, but I was running in the slums, being chased. I had stolen something and I knew that I'd done wrong and I knew that I was done for.'

'Scary,' says David. 'I once had to run from a gang of thugs when I was a lad.' No one responds.

'I don't know what I had stolen, or why, but I ran, through dirty yellow alleyways, past workmen, women carrying babies on their backs and fronts, market stalls, wagons.'

'Just like on TV,' Pete says.

'Shut up, you.' Miriam wags a finger at him. 'I'm talking to Becky.' She gives her a knowing look. Becky moves her hair behind her ears. 'It was hot. The middle of the day. Blazing heat. A group of young people threw a ball in the shade, and beyond, I saw the building site, a pyramid! Unfinished! Thousands of bodies, everywhere, I kept ducking through gaps, into doorways and around corners, but they caught up with me, I felt a hand grab my hair and pull me backwards.

And that must have been the end of that life.' She sits back in her chair. Nodding slowly, eyebrows raised.

'It's like I've always said.' David spreads his palms, implores the room. 'We contain multitudes.'

Pete and Miriam stare straight ahead. Becky looks at him and smiles appreciatively at his wisdom.

The doorbell goes.

'I'll go,' Pete says, scraping his chair on the tiled floor.

'How many times, Peter?' Miriam calls after him. 'Don't scrape your chair like that.'

Pete opens the door and Becky hears voices. She looks around the dining room. Pete walks back in followed by his sister. Becky looks up and the house falls in on her.

'Harry, this is Becky,' Pete says, standing between them. Harry stands in the doorway. 'Becky, this is my sister, Harry.'

Harry feels her guts lurch. Her body is a dry sponge. Becky feels her lungs expand, each pocket fills with air. She is suddenly aware of every organ in her body, working at the same time.

'Hi,' she says quietly. Her hair falls in front of her face. She sweeps it across. 'Nice to meet you.'

Harry leans down and kisses her cheek gently. 'Hi.' Her smile is kind and quiet. Becky is grateful for it. Miriam shifts in her seat to see it. Harry sits down next to her mother and offers a guarded smile. Pete chews his thumbnail. Harry can't breathe.

'Well,' says David, 'here we all are.' And he claps his hands together, jubilant.

'OK then,' Miriam says, getting up and leaving the room. She returns wearing oven gloves and holding five plates. 'Nice and warm,' she says happily.

She heated the plates. Becky's never had a family meal, not like this. She sits back in her chair, her body poised, always. She sneaks a look at Harry. Her tiny frame leant back on her chair, she's rubbing her cheeks with both hands. Their eyes meet briefly, a current courses between them, leaves a trail of ashes in its path. Harry looks away, her restless hands grip the edge of the table as she tucks herself in and examines her cutlery.

Miriam leaves again and comes back with a big pot and puts it in the middle of the table on a serving mat. 'I just made a stew, so. Nothing fancy. Pete assured me you weren't a veggie. That's right, isn't it?'

'Yep. No. I eat everything,' Becky says.

'Good, that's what I like to hear,' Miriam says. 'Although I hardly believe it with a figure like that,' Miriam says on her way out again. Becky squirms, blushes. Looks into her wine. Miriam returns. 'And mash here,' she says, 'and veg too'. She brings two dishes to the table and places them on matching serving mats that also match the serviettes beside each knife and fork. Becky notices all these details. 'And, here's some salad too. Just a little salad.' Miriam puts a big bowl of colourful salad on the other side of the stew. 'Oh almost forgot.' She jogs out, they all listen to her footsteps making the short walk to the kitchen and then returning. She comes back through the door. 'Aaannd the dressing here.' She's carrying a jug that matches the plates on the table, she sets it down, and then, before sitting, she removes the lid from the stew and the steam rises up like it's an advert for a happy home.

Pete leans over and puts his nose above the pot. 'It smells so good, Mum.'

'Well, it's getting colder out there.' She looks at him fondly. 'And we need to keep our strength up.'

'It looks well nice, Miriam, thank you,' Becky says. Struggling with a ticking grit inside, trying to hold down an anger swelling for every meal she never ate with her own parents.

'Oh it's just a little lunch,' Miriam says, obviously pleased with the compliments. 'And David helped me. Didn't you, love?'

'Oh no, I must confess, I was no help whatsoever. I am useless in the kitchen.' He pauses, takes a sip of wine. 'In other rooms, however, I am extremely adept.'

Pete chokes a little on his wine. Becky leans over to rub his back and starts laughing silently into her hand. Feeling better. Harry looks mortified. Doesn't know where to look. Miriam blushes deeply.

David is unaware of anyone's discomfort. 'Have some water, Pete.' Pete stares at him in dismay. David sees the look, cogs tick in his well-meaning brain. Nobody speaks. 'Oh God, no!' he says suddenly. 'No, I meant the living room. The lounge. I meant I'm very good at putting my feet up and watching the telly. Goodness. No. I would never. Although, you know. We are all adults.'

Nobody speaks. Becky stifles laughter. Pushes her hand into her mouth. Pete drinks water, shakes his head.

'Right. OK,' David says. 'Who wants stew? Pass your plates.' He dishes out the lunch and once everyone has their food and more wine, he serves himself.

They sit in silence. Listen to the sound of wet mouths chewing wet meat. The second hand ticks.

MIRIAM WAS BORN A butcher's daughter. Her whole life had been lived among carcass and flesh; the thump of the steaks as they were cut from the flanks of the beasts. Her brothers and uncles wrapping up slabs in white paper, her dad in his apron. The first shop in Leyton. Her father was Raymond. Her mother was Annabelle. Her mother worked as a nursery teacher and loved her husband and children above all else. They'd met during the war. Ray was a pilot, and Annabelle waved the planes down, held up the bright flags that would guide the descending aircrafts back to solid ground. They were married on the aircraft carrier where they were deployed, somewhere in the middle of the Indian Ocean. Miriam was the last-born, youngest sister of a proud bunch. Many years younger than her three elder brothers. Annabelle had almost given up hoping for a girl.

When Miriam arrived, she was her mother's pride and joy, and Annabelle did her best to keep her daughter far from the shriek of the abattoirs and the swish of her father's cleaver.

She went to a nice school, her friends were clean, polite children. They lived in a green suburb in east London in a simple, homely house with a sweet-smelling garden. But Miriam was drawn to the floor of the butcher's shop. She found herself lingering there, begging her brothers to not tell their mother they'd seen her.

At bedtime, Annabelle would sit at the head of her daughter's bed, showing her postcards of ballerinas that she kept in a special envelope that lived in a drawer in her dressing table. She would whisper the names of the ballerinas, and which ballets they were dancing in in the pictures.

'To be a woman, you must struggle, like the ballerina struggles. You have to work hard. It is painful work. And when you do it right, it will look effortless. But where we're different from the dancers, my sweet, is that we will never be applauded for getting it right.'

Miriam listened quietly, as she always did, but she couldn't make sense of a word of it. Her heart pumped red with butcher's blood.

While her brothers were free to work and study and take girls out and smoke cigarettes, she was expected to follow her mother's example and be careful and quiet and kind. She hit puberty and learned to feel shame. Began to wish that she was different. Came to hate the noise and stench of her father's shops. She came to see that life was not what you made of it, but what you persevered with. She felt she wasn't quite enough. Not a proper girl somehow.

She turned seventeen and moved away from her parents' home. She crossed the river and found a room above a pub in Camberwell. She took a job licking stamps and stuffing envelopes at an accountant's firm. She hated every minute but she made the rent with cash to spare. She found another job in the evenings as a waitress in the bingo hall and started saving diligently so that when she turned eighteen she could buy herself a motorbike. Her mother hated the room above the pub, the motorbike, the jobs. She couldn't understand what had happened to her precious daughter. She wanted her Miriam to meet a nice man and get settled.

Miriam read voraciously at night, listened to albums by her favourite bands – the Jam and the Clash and the Buzzcocks and Patti Smith. She wore tight black jeans and boots and men's jackets. She studied movies, she studied poetry. She studied people in the bingo hall. She revved her engine and drove the bike down to Brighton at weekends. She slept with men she liked but didn't want the hassle of a boyfriend. She had a group of friends she loved who worked as nurses and receptionists and life models. They went out dancing at night and walked each other home when the morning came.

When she turned twenty-two she was living in a cold-water squat in King's Cross with two Marxist postmen, a tube driver and a lab technician. They imagined it to be a commune, but Miriam found herself doing the majority of the housework, the cooking and the killing of the mice. She was working on the front desk of the library at King's College, doing the late shift. She was saving up to travel. She wanted to see the mountains of Afghanistan. She spent her days nannying for well-to-do families in Hampstead and her evenings at the front desk of the library, reading textbooks.

Graham was studying law at King's. In the evenings he pored over books in a hash cloud, memorising cases. At first they nodded at each other, and soon the nods turned into smiles. When it was closing time, Miriam began to look forward to waking Graham up and telling him he had to go. The third time it happened, she asked him out for a drink. They found a late-night seedy King's Cross bar and giggled easily.

He was clumsy and charming and they lingered in the corridors when she was making her rounds, delivering the books back to their shelves. She found herself staring at pages and not being able to take in a word, just waiting for his shape to loom through the turnstiles.

She took Graham out on her motorbike one evening. He fell off before they'd even started and seeing him there, fragile and awkward, sprawled in the road, laughing like a baby, she felt something happening in her guts that hadn't happened before.

She went away travelling, he finished his studies. They wrote each other long letters. Graham was frustrated by the distance. He wanted them to move in together, start a life, the kind of life that couples are supposed to have. But she had a world she wanted to see. He didn't know if she would come back to him or not. But she did. And the minute she settled, he forgot to love her in the same way.

For the next twenty-two years Miriam threw herself into being a housewife and a mother and it flooded her with a happiness she'd never known. But the girl she used to be crept around inside her in her quietest moments.

Her only daughter, Harriet, had always been a tomboy. She wanted her hair cut short and didn't play with girls' toys or wear girls' clothes. Her boyishness, harmless at eight, seemed stranger as she got older. At twelve she was getting into trouble all the time; violence followed her around in a way that shocked Miriam. Harriet would come home bloody and bruised and not say a word, just stagger into the kitchen for the frozen peas and then go quietly up to her room. She grew into a very private and independent teenager. Miriam didn't know how to reach her. Harriet hated going shopping; she couldn't bear even setting foot inside a clothes store. She was too embarrassed to walk over to the boys' section where they sold the shirts she liked, and standing in the girls' section made her feel like an alien. Nothing ever fitted, and she'd think it was her fault. She hated the hairdresser's too; in fact, Miriam noticed, she found most public places difficult.

Miriam was sure it was just a matter of time before Harriet met the right man, in the way she'd met Graham, and then she would settle down and become a wife and a mother and realise that was where true happiness lived. It wasn't that she didn't believe that her daughter thought she was gay. It was more that she didn't believe that women could be, really, deep down.

Miriam gradually became stuffy with age and blinkered by comfort, and told herself that nothing was drastically wrong and things would work out OK in the end.

'SO, WHAT HAVE YOU been up to then, Pete? Any developments on the work front?' David looks at him over the top of his glasses, a piece of spinach sticking out of his mouth, chewing.

'I had two weeks moving office furniture. That was good. And then I set up an eBay account for a friend's nan and helped her sell off some of her late husband's suits. She gave me fifty quid. So, that was good.' He talks to the piece of spinach.

'And are you any closer to working out what you want to do, in the, erm, long run?' David wipes his face with his serviette. The spinach comes out of his mouth. Sticks to his chin.

'Erm. No,' Pete says. 'Nope.' His family watch him, waiting. He looks at them. 'There is nothing for me out there.' He raises his palms, lifts them, speaking in an Italian–American accent. 'But heyyyyy, wa ya gonna do?' The family cat. Pete finishes his wine. Pours another glass. 'You have some spinach on your face, David,' he says.

'Oh,' says David. Miriam looks at him.

'So you do,' she says and wipes it off with her serviette.

Harry finishes the last mouthful on her plate and sets her knife and fork down.

'Been to the pictures lately anyone?' David pipes up. No one responds. David looks at each of them, waiting patiently.

'No. I haven't.' Harry says. 'Have you, guys?' She points the question at Pete and Becky.

Becky looks at Pete. 'No. We haven't,' Becky says. 'What about you, David, have you?'

'No,' David says thoughtfully. 'I haven't either.'

Becky finishes eating and rests her knife and fork on her plate. Wipes her mouth with her serviette. Notices that it matches the frieze around the walls. Miriam puts her knife and fork down too.

'Just wondered if any of you young people had seen anything good recently,' David says. 'That was all.'

Pete puts his cutlery down. 'Is there any more wine, Mum?'

David stands and walks to the side. 'Yes, there's another one here. Have we finished two bottles already? How naughty.' Pete winces at the expression. David opens the wine and pours everyone another glass. Everyone drinks. 'Well,' he says. 'That. Was. Delicious.' Everyone agrees.

'All finished?' Miriam asks. Everyone nods. She stands to clear the plates.

Becky jumps up. 'No, no,' she says. 'Let me.'

'Oh don't be silly, love, you're our guest, you don't have to do that.'

Becky shakes her head. 'No,' she says. 'I wouldn't offer if I didn't want to.'

Miriam, touched, sits down again. 'But you don't know where anything goes,' she says.

'I'm sure I can work it out,' Becky says, piling up the plates and heading for the kitchen.

Miriam looks sternly from David to Pete to Harry. Pete takes a leisurely swill of his wine. Knocks it back. Leaves barely a sip in the bowl of the glass.

Harry springs up to help. 'I'll give her a hand,' she says.

'Cheers, Harriet!' David smiles.

'More wine, darling?' Miriam tops up Pete's glass. Gazing at him softly.

'Thanks, Mum,' he says. Nearly pissed.

'How's your dad doing?' she asks him, in the careful tone she uses every time she asks that question.

'He's OK. He's volunteering at the hospice.' It's a lie but Pete believes it as he says it.

'Good for him.' Miriam seems almost hurt with surprise. 'What a kind thing for him to be doing.'

Becky moves towards the kitchen, letting her face relax at last, hyper-aware of herself, her beginnings. The kitchen is new and everything's shining, eager. *This room*, Becky thinks, *looks quite a lot like David*. She puts the dishes down beside the sink, and runs some water. Two rectangular windows along the wall behind the sink give out to a small, neat back garden, fruit trees in pots, a gnome fishing by the back fence.

Harry walks in and puts a load more dirties down on the side and takes a tea towel from its hook, slings it over her shoulder. 'You wash, I'll dry?' she asks her. The air between them prickles and roars with dense pressure.

'Yeah. Great,' Becky says. Squeezing some washing-up liquid into the sink that's still filling up.

Harry takes the plates and scrapes them into the bin. Everything is slow and edged with static. She puts them back on the side. Turns to head out of the room.

'Nice to see you again,' she says quietly before going to the dining room to get the big pot and the serving dishes. Becky smiles to herself and turns off the taps. Harry comes back, puts the dirties down and moves past her to stand beside her. 'I'll do the pots though.'

'Sadist,' Becky says, without looking up from the sink.

Harry can't help sneaking stills out of the corner of her eye. Becky's body washed gold in the late-afternoon sun, her open mouth, smiling, the light across her lips, the occasional glimpse of her dimples. Her nose-piercing. Harry's heart is cooked.

'I did wonder if I was ever going to bump into you again,' Becky tells her and the pressure wails between them and pushes down on them.

'Mental, eh?' They both laugh. 'Fucking mental.' Becky looks around the sink for a sponge or a cloth. Finds what she needs.

'So, how've you been?' Harry asks. Speaking quietly.

'I don't know. Pretty good. I think.'

'How's the dancing?'

Harry seems more confident than before. Lighter. 'Yeah, it's good. How's yours?'

'My dancing?'

'Mmm-hmm.'

'Well, I'm still excellent at the bogle.' Becky lets a snort of laughter out, surprised. Harry concentrates on the plate in her hands. The tea towel. The stoic gnome outside. 'Can't believe it's you, here,' she says.

Becky shakes her head, smiling.

Harry points out the window. Her face disappears in a mask of confusion. 'The gnome, though,' she whispers. 'The gnome!' And the absurdity of the whole afternoon strikes them like a mallet and they begin to ring like gongs; the two of them break into unbearable laughter that winds upwards through them, unfurling new depths as each wave dies away. Weakened, clutching the worktop until the laughter ebbs. They sigh like old women after a good joke.

Harry wipes her eyes, and turns to Becky, suddenly grave. 'Look, look, Becky,' she says quietly.

Becky laughs again, the severity of her expression striking her as part of the joke. But Harry's face doesn't change, and Becky's laughter stutters to a stop. 'Sorry, yes. Serious talk.' Becky puts down the sponge she's holding and concentrates.

'Them things I told you? When we met?'

'Uh huh?'

'About what I *do*.' Harry knots her eyebrows desperately, panic in her eyes. 'For a *living*?' she whispers.

'Yeah, I remember.' Becky fishes for the cutlery in the soapy water. 'What about it?'

Pete keeps glancing at the doorway, trying to see down the hall into the kitchen. He hears a peal of laughter build and break and ebb away. It pulls him down.

'You OK, son?' David asks him. Pete looks at him. Stares at his face thinking cruel thoughts. David pushes his glasses up his doughy nose.

Pete stands up without speaking or showing any kind of emotion and walks slowly out of the room.

David looks at Miriam, shrugs his shoulders. 'Beats me,' he says.

Miriam folds her hands in her lap, drops her head and breathes deeply.

'He's a complicated sort of young man,' he tells her. 'Too many books probably.'

She looks into his eyes despairingly. '"Son"?' she hisses.

David throws his hands up and covers his face. 'Oh my God, I didn't even think. Oh my God. I hope I haven't upset him?'

Pete creeps along the hallway, not thinking about why he's doing it, just doing it. He tiptoes, back against the wall, until he arrives at the kitchen door and peeks through the crack to see Harry close to Becky, her lips leaning down towards her ears, her eyes glistening.

'Have you told Pete?' Harry's voice is too familiar.

'No.' She shakes her head. 'Of course not.'

'Well, don't.' Harry is urgent, pleading. 'Don't say a word. No one can know. Please, Becky. This is really important.'

'It's fine,' Becky reassures her, looks at her kindly. 'Don't worry. We shouldn't even be talking about it here.'

Sudden heat roars in his torso and limbs. His wrists get fizzy with tension and his chest and neck and jaw grow rigid, like static is pumping through his veins instead of blood. His breath is not breath, it is a picture of breath, an idea of breath, but not air, not breathing. His mouth is gulping and drawing in air but it's not going into his blood. His head is hard inside. He watches the room, hidden from view, feeling like a stalker or something, some shaky weirdo, peering through the crack in the door, and Harry is close and relieved and smiling, and Becky is breathing fast, her lips are parted, she's smiling deeply, head inclined, laughing now, the soapy water sparkling in the sunlight, she steps towards it, plunges plates and Harry's there, saying something, her voice too low to hear, and Becky's laughing over shoulders, hair drops down, she tucks it back. Blinking. It feels to Pete that Becky hasn't laughed like that with him for months. She never enjoys the things he has to say. What can Harry have to say that makes her laugh like that? How has Harry managed to get her on her own? He looks at his sister and sees her body carved from alabaster. Knows that Becky sleeps with girls and boys.

Maybe Becky wants his sister. He's sure his sister must want Becky. Nothing is safe when Becky is near him. Every single person in the world is a threat. He would burn the whole world to have her to himself. But even if he did, she'd be more interested in staring at the embers than looking lovingly at him. But still. She doesn't like him. She doesn't like what he's becoming. He doesn't know how to stop it happening. He stares at them and wants to do something terrible. He breathes into it, the panic rising in his throat, gripping his ears. Everything is loud inside him. He turns from the door and walks in fast awkward stamping guilty steps down the hallway and out of the front door. Slamming it behind him. *They can have each other*. He holds his heart with a damp hand. *Fuck 'em*. He holds his throat.

The cold air feels hot and too thick to be air, it feels like he's breathing porridge. He can't take a proper breath, it's like a hand has its thumb over the top of his windpipe. He used to care about things. He wanted to improve things. Challenge things. Understand things. Now it's too much to hold anything in his head beyond the immediate. He can't think of why he's got no money, got no work. All he knows is that he's got no money, got no work. Got no hope for a fulfilling life. He can't see anything but Becky in his brain. He struggles, panics that he isn't taking enough oxygen, he can feel his throat constricting. He walks fast, tries to forget the panic. Tells himself that he's breathing already. He doesn't have to think about it. He's doing it. He's breathing.

The slamming door brings Harry and Becky out of the kitchen, and Miriam and David out of the dining room. They stand in the hallway looking at each other.

'What happened?' Harry asks Miriam.

'Has he gone?' Miriam asks Harry. Neither acknowledges the other's question.

'Pete?' Becky calls up the stairs but nothing comes down them.

'Was that Pete that just went out the door?' Harry asks no one.

'Oh David.' Miriam turns away from him.

'I'm so sorry, love.' David turns with her, talking to her back.

'What happened?' Becky asks them both.

'We were talking, and I called him "son". You know, a turn of phrase. And I think it upset him.'

'It obviously upset him! Poor Pete.' Miriam has one hand on her hip, the other holding her forehead.

'Maybe he just went for a bit of air,' Becky says. 'He'll probably be back in a second.'

They nod. Miriam looks heartbroken. Harry stands listlessly, feeling awkward without her brother there, the buffer between her and her mum.

'Shall I put the kettle on, Mum?' Harry asks her. 'Cup of tea?'

'Yes.' Miriam agrees on tea, but doesn't smile at her daughter. She turns to Becky, 'I made afters. If anyone still wants?'

'I, for one, would love a spot of crumble!' says David, trying to cheer things up between them.

'Doesn't feel right though,' Miriam says, heading to the kitchen to heat up the custard. 'Him upset, and us eating crumble. Sweet boy.' David walks after her, head hanging. Becky says nothing, just opens the front door and looks out at the empty cul-de-sac.

Harry wanders slowly into the kitchen behind David. 'Have you made any plans for his birthday?' she asks.

'Oh yes, I've got a couple of ideas for gifts, but I'm not sure what he's doing. Have you spoken to him?'

'I've been thinking it might be nice to throw him a party.' Harry leans against the worktop, waits for the kettle to boil. Miriam is by the fridge getting the custard. If they don't look at each other, they can keep a conversation going much longer. 'But, you know, he hates his birthday.'

'Course he doesn't, no one hates their birthday. People just worry no one will make a fuss. That's all,' Miriam explains patiently.

'So you think it's a nice idea?' Harry throws a tea bag in the air and catches it. Throws it up again.

'Yes of course. It's about time he had a party.' Miriam glances over her shoulder. 'Don't handle the tea bag like that.'

Harry puts the tea bag in a cup. 'It's alright, I'll have that one.'

'What kind of thing are you thinking?'

'Well, knowing him.' Harry pours the water, David makes a big show of fetching her the milk, bringing it over, even unscrewing the cap before passing it. Harry shouts towards the hallway, 'WANT A TEA, BECKY?' Waits for a reply but doesn't hear one. She carries on. 'It would have to be a surprise thing.'

'Lovely idea.'

'Yes.' David lifts himself over the worktop and sits with his back against the wall, his feet swinging. 'I LOVE surprise parties. SO much fun! Is it a big one this year?'

'No, not particularly,' Miriam tells him. 'Twenty-seven,' she says. Harry hands her a cup of tea, Miriam looks at it. 'It's a little strong for me actually.' She turns to David. 'Can I have a drop more milk, please, David?'

David jumps off the worktop and hurries over to the milk, which is still beside Harry, lifts it up and splashes a little more in Miriam's cup. They smile at each other.

Harry feels a wave of anger. She breathes into it until it passes. She hands David his tea.

'Perfect,' David says. Harry nods her thanks.

Outside the front door Becky looks up and down the street but can't see him. She calls him again. He doesn't answer. She tries him one last time but it goes to voicemail. She walks back into the house and leans against the hallway wall. She can hear Miriam clucking about crumble.

Harry comes out of the kitchen. Nods at the phone in Becky's hand. 'Did he answer?'

'No.' Becky chews the inside of her lip. Looks at her phone.

Harry gets her coat from where it's hanging over the banister. 'Well,' she says, 'I'm heading home if you wanna go station?' Harry is standing in her usual awkward stance, her shoulders like two pegs the rest of her hangs from.

'I'll just say goodbye to Miriam and David.' Becky walks past her, touches her arm at the elbow.

In the kitchen Miriam and David are debating custard or ice cream. Miriam has put her apron on and is holding a dish of apple crumble.

'Thanks for dinner,' Becky says from the doorway. 'I'm not gonna stay, actually, for pudding.'

'Are you getting off then, love?' Miriam puts the crumble down.

'If Pete comes back here, tell him to call me, would you?'

'Course I will. Likewise if you hear from him first.' They smile at each other. 'Such a pleasure to meet you.' Miriam walks towards her, arms out, and takes her into a hug. Becky notices the apron she's wearing matches the serviettes and hugs Miriam a little tighter. David, leaning against the fridge holding a tub of ice cream, pushes his glasses up his nose, smiling.

Harry walks beside Becky. They keep in step and watch the paving stones. Neither of them feels the need to speak. Becky pushes her hair out of her face, gathers her collar up round her neck. Everything about the day feels close. They hear every passing car and gurgling bird. Harry swings her arms at her sides, walks on lazy legs. Becky's hands are in her jacket pockets. They turn left at the end of the road. Harry points.

'That's the station, just down there.' They keep walking, cross the road and through the doors, they look at the train times.

'Where do you live?' Becky asks.

'Off Lewisham Way. Tanner's Hill. You know it?'

'Yeah, I live round the corner. In the block behind the high street,' Becky says, smiling in surprise.

'Deptford?' Harry's voice jumps up in excitement.

'Yeah.' Becky nods.

'I would have thought I'd seen you 'round?'

'Well, maybe you will now you know that I'm there.' Becky studies the screen. Her hair ruffles in a passing wind that drills through the station; it touches her neck and she shivers. 'There's one in nine minutes.'

'Come then.'

They walk down the steps, and up the other side. Becky blows on her hands and leans against the station wall. They watch the clock ticking over; one of the panels is broken and the 3 shows up like an 8.

'They're so nice, your family.' Becky's voice is soft, hushed on the empty platform.

Harry looks down at her feet, embarrassed. 'We have our moments.'

'It's lovely. You all get on so well.' Harry lets out a little laugh. 'Why's that funny?'

'We never used to.' She glances up into Becky's eyes. Falls in, flounders. Clambers out.

'What d'you mean?' Becky feels the wind picking up around them, watches Harry's outline.

'Long story.'

'Well' – Becky looks up at the clock – 'we got seven minutes.' She closes her jacket around herself, her face is calm and cool.

Harry hunches inwards without realising, then slowly straightens. Her posture has never been good. She begins to speak, one word at a time, like feet treading a narrow path. 'I didn't speak to my mum for, like, ten years.' Becky's eyebrows climb. Harry shrugs. 'She couldn't deal with my . . .' She breaks off into a quietness. She looks for the words but can't find them. 'The way I am.'

'The way you are what?' Becky leans against the wall and watches her new friend closely. Her fingers scrape the mortar between the bricks behind her, rubbing the red crumbs and pushing them down into the groove.

'Me.' Harry leans back too and places the flat of her shoe against the wall, bouncing a little against it.

'You can't bring yourself to say it?' Becky leans in towards her, eyes wide and round as a greyhound's. Harry flinches in the face, a little pinch across the cheeks. A subtle tic she can't control that betrays the force of her feelings.

'No, what? It's not that. I'm fine with it. It's cool.' Becky watches Harry's profile; her cheekbones catch the winter sun.

She's blushing. She looks away, down the empty tracks, searches her pocket for her tobacco. Absorbs herself in rolling a cigarette. Speaks to the distance. 'I went to live with my uncle when I was fifteen.' Harry's voice crackles at the base of her vowels. She speaks quietly, rich as music, a rattling sonata. The sloping toughness of the south London accent. 'He was good to me. But he wasn't well, though. He was an addict, he got sick. He passed away a few years ago. It was at his funeral that I reconnected with my mum. We speak now, yeah. We're on OK terms.'

Becky turns her body so that she is facing Harry. The last light of the evening is being drawn out of the sky. Her skin is deepening in the coming darkness. 'I'm sorry to hear that.'

'Oh no. It's OK.' Harry takes her foot off the wall, turns to face Becky, leaning on her shoulder; the side of her head kisses the bricks. 'Family, innit, things happen in families.' Becky nods her agreement, folds her arms and runs a hand over her head, through her hair. 'Surprised Pete didn't fill you in,' Harry says, and Pete's name opens a well in the ground, a dark sucking wind screams from its depths and pulls the station down towards it.

'He doesn't talk about you guys that much.' Becky doesn't take her eyes off Harry's face. Her body is ashes and mud and clay. Everything is shaking with relevance. She is about to reach out a hand and touch Harry's cheek when the train pulls in. The crack and the rattle smack all the quiet out of the platform. The hiss of electric and steel. Becky watches the train slowing. Yellow and blue lines stagger into shapes, doors, people's faces.

'Wanna wait for the next one?' Becky asks.

Harry blinks in the wind from the train, looks sideways at Becky, catches her smile. 'OK,' she says quietly.

They watch the people get off the train, three young boys dressed in black tracksuits shout slang words. A drunk woman clutches a burger in both hands and brings it tentatively to and from her mouth, dropping shredded lettuce and splodges of ketchup onto the floor. A man in a suit with a fold-away bicycle stops to tie his shoelace. The train leaves, the people roll away and the platform returns to silence. They succumb to it, each in their own for a moment. Harry pushes herself off the wall and stares down the tracks. The wind bashes at her forehead, she closes her eyes and squints into it, shaking her head in joy. Becky laughs.

'It's nice,' Harry tells her. 'You try.' So Becky stands beside Harry and faces the wind with her eyes closed, leaning into it, feeling it whipping around her ears, and she smiles. 'See?'

'Yeah, it's nice,' she agrees, but the wind dies down then.

'What about your family?' Harry asks.

'What about them?'

'What are they like? You get on well?' Becky reaches a hand out for Harry's roll-up, Harry gives it to her. Becky lights it. Watches the tracks curving into the distance.

'My dad's in jail. And my mum's in a convent. She's Jewish, but she's born-again now. They're both nuts. I don't speak to either of them.' She flicks her words like lit matches. They drop delicately, burning.

'Not even letters?'

'My mum writes letters, yeah.' Her hair falls in front of her forehead, longer on one side; it swings across her eyes and down towards her neck. She pushes it away with the back of her hand. It looks so soft to Harry.

'But you don't write back?'

'I haven't, no. Not yet.' She passes the cigarette back. Two pigeons land in front of them, peck each other's feathers. Search the ground for chicken bones. Settle for the dropped lettuce.

'That must be hard.'

'Is what it is.' Becky shrugs.

'Do you visit him?'

'No.' Becky shakes her head. 'Never been.'

Harry is absorbed. Listening intently. The slats on the clock judder, stuck. 'Do you want to?' The wind picks up again, takes dead leaves up in its arms and spins them around. Harry's heart like an open hand, reaching.

'Sometimes I want to. But I don't know where he is.' Becky's voice comes from a place very deep down in her stomach.

'You can find out, you know.' Harry speaks kindly.

'Yeah, I know.' The sky is rolling inwards, dark pink to purple. Sinking to darkness.

'But you don't want to?'

'Don't think so, no. Not right now.' Becky smiles at Harry, feeling exposed.

'Who raised you?' Harry's questions are considered. She keeps her eyes on Becky's face the whole time. Blows her smoke out to the side.

'Myself. My friends. My auntie.' Harry turns each word Becky says over in her mind. Divining. Becky reaches for the roll-up again, smokes some, retreating back to lean against the wall.

A can crawls across the platform in a sudden gust. Rings like church bells. They watch the trees rising over the corrugated-iron sheds that line the tracks, the dusk settles over the backs of people's houses. The rotting fence posts and barbed wire and piles of old tyres.

'So was it always girls?'

Becky's face is smooth in the dimly lit night. Her skin sings the dusks and dawns of her grandmother's country. Harry feels Becky's beauty in her mouth like thirst.

'Pretty much.' Harry mulls it over.

'No boys?'

'Couple. But nothing serious, no,' Harry explains.

'Who was the first girl you fell for then, Harry?'

Harry lets out the same little laugh as before. Drops her chin. Furrowing her brow. Taken aback. She looks up at Becky, Becky's eyes are calm and steady.

'Ellie O'Dowd from the year above.' She speaks slow; each word drags out as she relishes the thought, watches the ghost of Ellie swaying through the platform. 'I thought about her every minute of the day, man. Used to walk out of my way before every lesson just to catch a glimpse of her. Then I couldn't speak when she walked past.' She shakes her head happily. 'She used to, like, sit on my lap when no one was around and play with the chain I used to wear round my neck.' She looks up laughing at Becky, shy but not embarrassed.

'So you always knew you was gay?' Becky's voice is a missile. Straight to Harry's core. Exploding on impact.

'Yeah, think so.'

'How did you know?'

Harry thinks about it. Rocks on her toes. Shuffling. 'Well, how did you know you were straight?'

'I'm not.'

'You're not?' Harry's voice comes out higher than she means it to.

Becky kicks at something on the station floor. 'I like people, that's all. I think it's silly to limit yourself.' Harry stuffs her hands into her pocket, leans backwards into her body. Stretching. Looking at a point in the sky. Smiling gently. 'How old were you? With Ellie?'

'I don't know, thirteen maybe?'

Becky walks up and stands beside her. The crisp packets on the floor begin to spin and flutter. The Tannoy squirts a few muffled words. 'I bet you were cute,' she says. The train slams towards them. They watch the graffiti crystallising on the side panels as it slows.

When Becky gets home it's dark and Pete is sitting on the step outside her flat.

'I knocked. I don't think no one's in.'

'How long you been out here?'

'Not long. You took your time getting back.'

'Why did you leave me at your mum's like that?' The moon is nearly full, tangled in thin clouds, high up in the sky. He doesn't answer. 'Pete?'

'I just had to get out of there. It was doing my head in.'

'You wanna come in?'

'Can I?'

'S'pose you better.' She sighs. 'Come on.' She reaches her hand out, he takes it. She walks him into the house, he drags along behind her. His head hangs low, he's all shoulders.

STINK

A rolling wind sprang up in the night and lifted the roofs of the garden sheds and pushed the heavy boughs of the trees around.

Leon stares out at the new morning. Something prickles in his body. He can smell fires burning in the cool new air, onions, curry paste, jerk ovens, motor oil, incense. The sirens scream their usual song, get louder, wilder, pass, grow faint again. He stares up at the sky. He can only access a little patch of it from the small brick courtyard, tall walls either side create a cuboid funnel upwards. He is shaken by the desire to see it stretching out, uninterrupted. To see it arching over sea waves, nothing stopping it at all.

Harry walks in, hair still wet from the shower, and finds Leon leaning against the door frame, craning his neck.

'Morning,' Harry says, flicking the kettle.

Leon turns his head and looks over his shoulder but his body stays facing the garden. 'Let's go to the beach,' he says.

Harry joins him at the door. 'What beach?' She drapes an arm around his neck.

He points to the sky. 'Yeah. Nice bit of sea air, settle us down.'

They stand and watch the pigeons on the barbed wire that scowls down from the top of their walls, separating them from the train tracks. Little round clouds puff like gunshots in the blue.

Harry lets her arm drop back to her side. Plays with the back-door handle. 'You still feeling shaky? About tonight?' she asks him without looking at him, noticing him massaging the muscles in his forearms, a thing he does when he's nervous.

Leon turns, smiling, heads back into the kitchen. 'Come on, let's go have a walk by the sea, eat some fish and chips.'

Harry stands where she is, looking up at the sky, trying to see what Leon had just been seeing. The idea illuminates her. The pleasure of it washing out the dread that's been churning her all night. 'Alright then, yeah,' she says. The kettle wobbles on its cradle, boiling madly.

They're just turning onto Deptford Broadway, past the junction of the High Street where the anchor used to stand, when Harry sits forwards. 'Stop,' she says. 'Pull over.' Leon takes the next left and tucks in behind a Vauxhall outside the Kingdom Hall, the Jehovah's Witness meeting room. 'Stay here for a sec.' Harry jumps out and runs back to the main road.

Becky is coming out of a shop on the high street, with a packet of tobacco and some Rizlas in her hand. She looks tired and sad in the way that people look when they don't know that anyone is watching. The anonymity of a city street makes it a safe place to let your guard down. 'Becky!' Harry calls as she jogs up. Becky turns, sees Harry and drops her Rizlas.

She bends to pick it up. 'Shocked me.' She laughs.

They stand in front of one another, not sure how to greet. Becky leans in and kisses Harry's cheek. Harry puts her hand on her waist lightly as she does it.

'What you doing now?'

'Was just on my way to the caff but they don't need me today, so I don't know, actually, what I'm doing.'

'Ah brilliant!' Harry's face is a lottery win. She throws her hands up, open arms.

'What's brilliant?'

'You should come to the beach!' she says, as if it's obvious.

'What beach?'

'Me and Leon going now, to the seaside. Sheerness maybe, Camber Sands.' Harry's words come out like a racing commentary. Becky laughs at her enthusiasm.

'Who's Leon?'

'He's my mate. You'll love him.'

'What, now?'

Mothers sway past them with bulging carrier bags, stuffed like the last bus home. Their arms are like tree trunks as they carry yams, meat, sacks of rice and tins of beans. They walk three abreast, laughing, towards the market. Kids late for school drag their feet, their ties undone, showing each other things on their phones. The men outside the greengrocer talk in Arabic, French, Punjabi, thick patois, Tamil. The men selling duvet covers from the patch on the corner talk in sing-song south London marketese – *Come and getcha covers eeyah, look, any pillahcayse a pand*. Students rifle through the old stereos, novelty cutlery and ancient brass ornaments that sit in boxes on the pavement. Looking for things for their art projects. Women test the fabric of the cheap shirts with expert fingers.

'Yeah. Come on, let's go? Leon's just down there in the car.' She points.

Becky imagines sunlight on the freezing sea. Fresh wind. 'Pete's got a job on today. He's working at some event doing catering in west London.'

Harry nods. Raises her eyebrows. 'That's good,' she says. 'But you could still come, couldn't you? Without him. If you fancied it?' The words say more than Harry means them to.

'Yeah.' Becky nods heartily, speaks slowly through a blooming smile. 'Why not.' They walk together past the shouting market, past the drunks and schoolkids, past the mural on the wall, ducking out the way of old ladies with their shopping carts, and they find Leon watching the people in their suits and hats and smart shoes talking outside Kingdom Hall.

He shines his golden smile at Becky, surprised to see Harry returning with a stranger. 'Hello!' he says. 'Seaside?' And they climb in the car and they head for the beach. Becky in the front, Harry in the back. Becky fidgets with excitement, dances in her seat.

‘Seaside!’ She opens her window to feel the cold city wind. Smiling into it as it blows her hair back. She watches the road fall away beneath the car as they turn onto the motorway. House FM plays loud; the bassline is warm and the sunlight is golden. ‘This is nice,’ she says to Leon.

‘Yeah,’ he says. ‘The open road, eh?’ He drums his hands on the wheel. ‘Can’t beat it.’

The sun swells on its way down. They sit on the stones with their fish and chips, drinking bottles of beer. People walk dogs and hold hands. Harry stares at the waves, grey and green and breaking gently on the groynes. The cold English sea, rolling beneath its reflection. The sky is the sea is the sea is the sky for ever.

Leon finds a triangular stone and uses the point to dig down through the pebbles into the sand, hacking at the space beside his feet. They listen to the puck and glint of stone on stone. The wind whipping the tops of the fishing boats parked up the beach. The giddy cackle of the gulls. Harry lets her head lean on Becky’s shoulder as she eats her chips and Becky turns her face and feels her hair against her cheeks. Harry’s hair smells clean and warm and sweet. Becky breathes in deeply, eyes quenched by the endless sea.

She moves her hand along the stones, feeling the hardy blades of grass that sprout up through the sand. She picks up pebbles and holds them and lets them fall, enjoying their smoothness.

Waves greet the beach like giddy puppies. Becky's hand comes to rest on Harry's knee. It fills her with a silent heat. Harry lifts her knee and they push briefly towards each other. Harry looks sideways at Becky. Squints in the setting sun. Becky's hair all messy in the breeze, her baggy shirt billows, her little feet in all-black Air Max 95s. Leon is making a pile of good skimmers. Engrossed. He gathers up the best ones and jogs towards the surf. Harry's hand finds Becky's, Becky turns hers round and they push each other's fingertips. Stroke each other's wrists. Burning up. All sound drowns in the bass of the touch. Harry sits back suddenly, quick as a swerving car. Puts her hands behind her and leans into them. Pushing them into the stones where they'll be safe. Becky's hand lies open, still resting on Harry's knee.

Harry looks out at the water pounding the shore. She watches Leon, skimmer's stance, his body tensed and tall, and feels a gnawing dread about the night they have ahead of them.

'How's Pete doing?' she asks. Keeping her voice light.

Becky breathes deeply, shakes her head. Doesn't know what to say. A day passes in the silence.

'We're fighting all the time.'

Harry looks over, making a pantomime of her concern. 'How come?'

Becky finishes her chips, scrunches the paper up, enjoying the smell of sea air and chip grease and vinegar. She takes her time to answer, speaking without emphasis or sentimentality.

'I'm pretty sure he only wants us to be together because he's scared of what will happen to his life if I leave.'

The mood grows heavy as a fallen scaffold. Determined not to be trapped beneath it, Harry climbs to her feet, adjusting her clothes, pulling her jumper down, pulling her trousers up. She bends to pick up her chips and her beer. 'You know how to skim stones?' she asks.

'Yeah,' Becky nods, squinting up at her.

'Can you teach me, please? Leon hates teaching me things.'

Becky gets to her feet in a graceful surge of travel, all movement a dance, even scrambling up from the shingle. 'Help me find some good ones then,' she says. 'Just gotta be flat really, that's all.' They head towards the water, eyes low, looking for stones.

They drop Becky off in Streatham, she's going to see a friend who's been working in a recording studio there. Leon stares out the windscreen, watching the crowded street, waiting for the crossing to clear. Harry leans her head back into the seat, lets her eyes glaze on all the people moving. Arm in arm and on their own and holding kids and shopping.

A woman on crutches in a white RUN DMC jumper. An old man with a small face in battered leather trousers and a red cowboy hat. A girl in a massive duffel coat trying to get her lighter going. Harry watches all the people. Two young women in veils dance and push each other behind the counter of the empty coffee shop. A thousand different sudden colours sing through the window of the fabric store. A man holding a small bird in his fist brings it up to his lips and whispers to it as he passes the car.

'Well?' Leon says, pushing the accelerator gently and easing off.

'Well what?' Harry asks him, more defensively than she realises. Leon waits quietly. 'What?' Harry asks again.

'She was nice,' Leon says pointedly, not taking his eyes off the street.

Harry glances at him, looks back at the road. 'What you trying to say?' she asks him.

'Nothing,' Leon says simply. 'She was nice.'

'She's going out with Pete,' Harry tells him.

'I know,' Leon says.

They say no more until they reach New Cross.

'Was a good day though, weren't it?' Harry leans her head back, watching the dark wet gloom of the night outside.

'Yeah, lovely day.'

'You feeling ready? To do this?'

'Think so. You?' Leon grips the wheel tighter. His hands begin to throb.

'Yeah. Sure it'll be fine.' Harry blows breath onto the window and draws patterns in it with her fingertips. 'I think she's lovely, Leon,' she says slowly.

'I know you do, mate.'

'What am I gonna do about it?'

'Nothing,' Leon says, reversing into a space outside their flat and turning the motor off. They sit there in the quiet car. 'Right.' Leon checks his watch. 'Let's chill for a couple hours and then head out.'

THE HEIST

It's midnight in the metropolis. Harry's driving. Leon's in the back seat, as if he's in a cab. They listen to the radio. Everything's dreary and insubstantial. Generic rock, generic indie, generic indie rock, generic dance, generic rap pop. They wince afresh with each turn of the dial. Magic FM's dishing out the power ballads. There's a posh woman on Talk FM laughing at her own jokes. Harry switches it off, opens the window, listens to the engine. They pull up a street or two from their destination. They can see the bar they're heading for out of the back window.

'This it then, is it?' Leon whispers into the car. He barely moves his head but Harry knows he's just scoped out every entrance, exit, window. It's a two-storey corner bar, run down, but with memories of better times clinging to its doorways, like a threadbare mink round the neck of an elderly showgirl. A sign above the door says *Paradise*. The *P* is a palm tree.

'Must be.' Harry turns the engine off. They sit and watch the entrance in the rear-view mirror.

'What d'you make of it?' Leon asks her. 'Bit isolated, innit?'

Harry hears him, agrees. 'Busy though,' she counters. 'Does seem busy.'

'True.'

They watch for a moment. In the large courtyard, groups of people stand around by the picnic benches smoking. The girls are dressed in short skirts and long coats and the guys are in jeans and smart shoes.

'Lot of muscle about,' Leon says, pointing with his eyelashes towards the bigger men, standing slightly away from the others, watching the punters with their hands in their pockets.

'Usual, then?' Harry asks him, taking a deep breath in.

'Yeah, mate.' Leon passes his hand through the gap in the seats, palm up. Harry leans over and slaps him a soft five.

'I'm right behind you, bruv,' Leon says.

Harry gets out the car, leaving the keys in the ignition. She's wearing dark trousers and jacket and a pale shirt, creased at the cuffs from rolling them up. A long dark navy trench coat, open, collar turned up. Her hair pulled back. She holds a briefcase in her left hand and smokes with her right. She strolls down towards Paradise as if on the way from the station, comes to a gentle stop at the courtyard and looks around. She asks one of the bouncers what kind of thing's going on in there tonight. The bouncer smiles at her; he's pushing sixty, skinhead, built like a building.

'Oh you know, there's a DJ playing, bit of a dance floor, cheap drinks. Bit of soul, bit of house, bit of, you know, groovy stuff. It's a giggle in there, sweetheart.'

'Gotta pay to get in?' Harry asks.

'Nah, not tonight, free all night on a week night.'

'Thanks.' Harry nods at him and goes to stroll in.

'Ah, just check your bag there, darlin'?' The bouncer touches her gently on the shoulder, hardly a touch at all, but still, enough.

'Course you can!' Harry smiles, sweet as a flower, opens her briefcase and stares at the bouncer, holding his eyes. 'Just paperwork. I'm straight out the office.'

'Right you are,' says the bouncer, not even looking in the briefcase. 'Have a good one now.' He turns his gaze back to the group of girls jogging on the spot to keep warm while they share cigarettes.

Inside, there's a long bar. Two barmaids move behind it, the same purpose and poise as wolves. On the other side, groups of just-legal boys slap each other on the back and swear loudly while older, more fashionable young men with beards and retro shirts stand nonchalantly with their arms round their girlfriends, looking around for something better going on somewhere else. Beyond them a couple of women, well into their thirties and long overdue a night out, giggle hysterically and talk in gestures, standing at the bar while the others in their group dance together, self-conscious and fake-laughing, waiting for the drinks.

The room is lit with strip-neons and cheap disco lights. There are tables in the corners and along the back wall, and a dance floor edged with bodies standing still, not drunk enough yet to forget how fat they feel in their new dresses. A group of five or six young kids, off their faces on pills and acid, stroke each other's cheeks and grind innocently. At the tables, two women talk earnestly. Neither can really hear what the other's saying, but it doesn't really matter. The DJ is wearing sunglasses and playing soulless dance music, chart-friendly vocoder pap, beats-by-number dubstep with high-pitched synths cutting through. People throw their hands in the air. *I know this one! YEAH, this is my TUNE.*

Harry sits at the bar, nodding to the music, briefcase on the floor between her feet. She can feel it against the side of her shoe. She undoes a button on her shirt, gives her neck a bit of air, and leans on the bar with her elbows, catching the barmaid's eye. She waits, looks around, eyes drawn back to the barmaid. She checks her body out, watches her shoulders, her waist. The barmaid holds her eyes, looks her up and down, sends a dark smile her way before turning to serve someone else.

Leon waits a while in the back of the car, sitting low, watching the club in the rear-view. After a few minutes, six, maybe eight, he lets himself out of the car and gets into the driver's seat, drives down the road and parks up. He flattens his shirt and his hair and checks his blade; it hangs flat beneath his armpit in its sheath, sharp enough to cut through wood. He goes to the door, pretending to be on his phone. Every now and then he says, 'Oh come on, I know but . . . Wait. Wait a minute now . . .' which gives him an excuse to walk distractedly in circles, while really he's studying the courtyard from all angles, noticing the weaker panels in the fence, the loose chain on the back door, the bloodstained paving stone beneath the far-right window.

He smiles wearily at the bouncers, holds his phone between his ear and his shoulder, keeping his armpit clamped down on the handle of his blade, gesturing with his hands. He cloaks himself in an air of frustration and dejection, exchanging sympathetic nods with the bouncers.

'Can't live with 'em, eh?' he offers as they pat his flanks down, nod, smile, roll their eyes.

'No, baby, I wasn't talking to you, I wasn't, look . . . please . . . I didn't mean . . .' The bouncers chuckle, Leon strolls in.

The dance floor is starting to fill up with vague patches of clumsily moving girls doing fake sexy and ironic sexy, but secretly hoping that they look actual sexy. Sarcastic, overblown expressions are exchanged while they dance how they've seen other people dance in other, cooler clubs all their lives. Loneliness looms large in the room despite all the couples kissing and all the groups of women with their arms around each other's shoulders.

Leon notices a man approach the bar stool next to Harry's. He glances a little longer than necessary at the side of

Harry's face, Harry notices. Leon keeps his eyes exactly where they need to be, aware of every inch of his best friend's body. In the space between the slow strobes, all the years they've had each other's backs play out in stop-motion. He sees the small rooms full of weed smoke and teenage giggling, talking in slang. Afternoons like eternities in the rain at the bus stop, freestyling four lines at a time about fuck all. When his mum threw him out coz her new boyfriend didn't like him, threw him across the kitchen, bruised his ribs and split his lip in half and Harry put her arm around his shoulder and said nothing, walked next to him. Brought him home and made a bed on her bedroom floor and they went up the park and smoked hash. In Talia's car with the windows down playing 'It's a London Thing' on the way to the rave at the Lighthouse. Fresh fade and a gold bracelet. Pair of fucking dickheads. Leon watches, as he's always done. Ready.

The man next to Harry is slim-limbed but with a sloppy paunch pushing against his shirt buttons, dark hair, long and greasy at the sides of his scalp. He wears a blue suit with a shine running through it, his shoulders slope away like cats after a kill. Leon doesn't like the look of him at all.

'Harry?' asks the man. His voice cuts through the music and sends a chill through the veins in Harry's neck.

'Yeah.' Harry sips her beer and doesn't turn round.

'I'm Joey. I'm a friend of Pico's.'

Harry says nothing for a while, watches the barmaid moving at the other end of the bar, gathers herself, turns slightly and smiles at the guy, hardly moving her lips, but still, a smile.

'I'll be acting on behalf of Rags tonight. Now, if you wanna follow me, Harry?' Joey's voice is dull and monotonous but with a shriek running through it. He begins to move away without waiting for Harry to reply. Harry finishes her beer and places the bottle carefully on the bar before moving through the crowds, following Joey, watching the people who all seem a little drunker now than when she came in, pushing their bodies together.

Without being seen, Leon is standing now too, holding the wall. He sees the man opening a door he hadn't noticed on the other side of the bar. He moves through the crowd and finds the door with his toe just in time to stop it closing. He holds it, breathes, checks for the muscle, three by the fire escape, two by the bar, another by the dance floor talking to a girl. Three more to his left. He walks through the door and presses his back against the wall, so cold it feels damp. Stairs going down; there's a basement room beneath him. He hears their footsteps, Harry's voice saying, 'OK, no problem.'

The other guy's voice. 'Now, Pico's gonna be away for a little while, as you know. It's good to make acquaintance face to face. I hear you've been a loyal customer, and I respect that, but, the thing is, we don't know each other, do we? Not met you, have I? So, I suppose it's only natural that we start from the beginning.'

Harry steps off the last stair and onto the tiled floor of the basement. There is a large, low fish tank stretching out across the room, lit up brightly inside, with purple-neon underlighting. A baby shark swims amongst plastic shipwrecks, pieces of coral and various tropical fish. Either side of the tank are two long white-leather sofas and a couple of smaller black-leather armchairs. *Pico would hate this place.*

Pico was an extremely stylish, flamboyant Peruvian man with impeccable taste, a charismatic wife named Angela, four beautiful kids, and a penchant for butterfly collecting. He and Ange had a good name for themselves in interior design; he was freelance, and she worked as a consultant at the biggest company in London. Together, they had collaborated on half the renovated stores on New Bond Street. He was subtle about his dealing – he sourced the best gear and sold only to a few trusted people. *Pico wouldn't be seen dead in a place like this.* The hairs on the back of her neck stand up.

There's a massive pile of powder on top of the fish tank, a rolled-up fifty, a small razor blade for cutting lines. Harry looks around, a poster on the wall of Marilyn Monroe in her underwear listening to a song on a record player. No light apart from the light coming from the fish tank. There's a desk, a safe, an empty shelving unit and a chest in the corner.

'Please.' Joey indicates the sofa. 'Be my guest, sit yourself down, make yourself comfy.'

Harry feels a prickling sensation in the back of her legs. *Who the fuck* is *this guy? With this trashy club and all that muscle out there and a fucking baby shark in a fish tank?* She sits down, feeling uncomfortable, keeping her face absolutely still.

'So, I heard that you move a good deal of gear?'

Harry says nothing, waits for the next part of the sentence; Joey finds the silence a little intimidating. Can't help but break it.

'But, thing is, mate, I been asking around, and no one I've spoke to seems to have even heard of you. Eh?' He waits again, but Harry doesn't speak. Harry watches him, legs crossed on the white-leather sofa. Not moving. Joey clears his throat, looks away from Harry's eyes, continues. 'No one seems to know a thing about you. They can't tell me nothing.' Harry stares at him, the shark moves through the water of the tank. 'So, I want to know more. Basically.' Joey puts his hands on his kneecaps, leans forwards. 'Who the fuck is Harry and how are you moving all that gear and nobody knows who you are? Are you a policewoman, Harry?' Harry says nothing. 'Are you working for the Russians, Harry?' Still Harry says nothing. Joey raises his arms, shows his palms, shakes his head. Brings his hands back down to his knees, leans even further off his seat. 'Are you a deaf mute, Harry?' Harry stays quiet. She watches the water. The light. The skin on the smaller fish. 'OK, mate, OK. Poker face. I've heard the fucking song.' Joey lights a cigarette. 'You're a private person, I can see that, like to keep yourself to yourself, do you? That's all well and good, I can respect that.' He smokes, leans back into the sofa, shiny suit squeaking on the leather as he slips down. His eyes jump to

Harry's. 'That weren't a fart,' he says, 'it was the leather.' Harry says nothing, keeps watching, but offers a smile of understanding. Joey gathers himself. 'Don't get me wrong, I just wanted to know a little about you before we start doing business, you know what I mean? And it's looking like Pico might be away for a year or so, so we better get used to one another, wouldn't you say? Mate?' Harry waits. *What is he trying to say to me?* 'Would you like a drink, Harry?' Joey stands up, suit trousers riding up between his thighs. He walks to the desk. On top are a few bottles, beneath is a little beer fridge. 'I got vodka, bourbon, beers, what you gonna have? I'm drinking brandy.'

Harry tells herself to snap out of it. That really what's happening is that this flashy guy who works in a shitty bar, which he obviously imagines to be some classy fucking joint because he's got no taste, is some kind of relative of Pico's, some husband of some niece or whatever, some mate of a mate with great expectations, who is desperate to be a big shot, so Pico's let him handle things for a couple of months till he gets out, thinking what harm can he do. And he doesn't mean to be putting the creeps on her, he's just a weird, washed-up little man with a chip on his shoulder. Harry breathes deep. But she can't shake the feeling, the discomfort, the tension in her ankles, the movement of the shark through that fucking tank.

'Yeah, go on then, mate,' she says, 'I'll have the same.'

Joey grins, pleased. 'She talks!' He turns to the desk and makes a great show of pouring two glasses of brandy, two cubes of ice in each, an inch of soda. A dash of bitters. Laborious display. Like a child putting a show on for his parents.

The bass from upstairs is troubling the foundations of the building. Harry gets the feeling any minute now the dance floor will come crashing through the ceiling and all the young pilled-up kids and hen-party work friends will come falling down on top of her. She sees it in her mind's eye, hears their screams. Sees the shark gorging itself on mouthfuls of love handles while it suffocates. Joey hands her the glass, smiling like a paedo in a playground, and sits down opposite her again.

Harry nods her thanks, sips her drink. 'You got the same gear?' she asks Joey.

'Oh yeah, lovely stuff. Premium quality. Better even.'

'So, not the same then?' Harry asks him, frowning.

'Well . . .' Joey rubs his thumbnail with his middle finger. 'A different batch, but yeah, essentially the same stuff, it's the same supplier.'

Harry nods. 'And you have enough for me to take the usual? Did Pico tell you?'

'Yep, no worries. That's not gonna be a problem at all.' Joey tries to cross his legs, can't quite manage it in his tight suit. He takes a cigarette packet from his breast pocket, puts it on the tank between them. 'Want one?' he says.

Harry declines, takes one from her own packet, but does accept the lighter Joey offers. They sit and smoke.

Joey stands, walks over to the chest in the corner, opens it. Even in the dim room Harry can see that inside the chest is a massive amount of coke. *Why did he just show me where his stash is?*

'You see, mate,' Joey says. 'No problem. One key, two, five, whatever you fucking fancy, not gonna be a problem at all.'

Joey waits for Harry to register how impressive his stash is. Harry says nothing. Does nothing. Joey feels a little hurt. He shakes it off.

He's either a complete fucking idiot or he's going to rob me and kill me. Harry hopes Leon is not too far away.

'Wanna taste then?' Joey says. 'Little taste?' He hauls a heavy package from the chest, the size of a sleeping toddler. 'Just to prove it's the same stuff, know what I mean, taste from the package you're gonna walk away with, right? Try before you buy, if you're not fully satisfied blah blah blah.'

Joey smiles and he looks like a stroke victim, the smile grates against his face. Harry stays neutral, waiting for him to say something definite, to direct a clear question at her. Joey drops the package, heavily, on top of the tank, Harry worries that it's going to break the glass and fall in and kill the fish. Nothing happens. It just sits there between them for a while.

Joey sniffs loudly, wipes his nose with the back of his hand. Shifts around in his seat. The leather squeaks. 'There it goes again!'

'Yep,' Harry agrees.

'Look, mate. Thing is,' Joey says, 'with Pico away, things have changed slightly.' Harry finishes her cigarette, lets the ash fall on the floor, waits. 'The price has doubled.'

Harry watches Joey smile at her. She sees it clearly now, at least. He wants to rob her. *Cheeky bastard.*

'The gear's much better quality than Pico's ever was. It's had to come down different routes. I'm an honest man, trying to make an honest living.' He flashes his gravestone teeth, runs his fingers through his greasy hair, wipes his hand on his suit jacket. 'You're free to leave here and not take it, sweetheart, by all means, leave right now, I ain't gonna stop you. It's just you and me down here.'

Joey looks around, sniffs loudly again, holds a cigarette between his fingers but doesn't light it. Looks at Harry, closely, leans towards her, shoulders squaring. 'But you won't find anything better out there, darlin', and you know it and all.' He pauses, serious now, twirling the unlit cigarette between the fingers of his right hand. '*This* stuff' – he uses the cigarette to point to the sack of coke on the fish tank – 'fresh off the boat this morning. No one ain't laid a fucking finger on that cocaine since Bolivia.' He waits for that to sink in. Pushes his crotch out a little, shifts his thighs on the leather. 'The one thing I did hear when I was asking around is that you like to sell to the discerning user, the bigwigs, yeah? Happy to pay premium prices for premium gear? That's right, ain't it? In fact, men like them, the more expensive it is, the more they fucking enjoy it. Ain't that how it goes with the CEOs?'

Joey smiles again, with his lips closed this time. He sticks his little finger in his ear, wiggles it around. Discovers a little kernel of wax, digs for it, reaches it, pulls it out. 'Excuse me,' he says, looking at it, wiping it on his suit jacket.

Harry keeps her silence, sips her brandy soda. *This is actually the best brandy soda I've ever had in my life, I'll give you that, you creepy fuck.*

Joey's features are thick and cumbersome, his lips are like Cumberland sausages. His face is marked with deep acne scars. He wears crocodile-skin boots, he's got fat thighs and skinny calves. He's sweating at his temples, his crotch is pushed out towards Harry, his head is nodding slightly, balanced like a toffee apple on top of his weird, thin neck.

'What d'you reckon then?' he's saying. 'Coz I've been thinking all day about this, sweets, and the only way I can see us moving forward together, as I've already said, is by starting afresh. Me and you. Whole new game. Whole new pitch. New rules. New fucking balls, please. You know what I mean? Whole new arrangement.'

Harry watches, sips her drink. She swallows hard. Joey keeps talking.

'Look,' he says. 'Cut to the chase – I'll continue sourcing you the best coke money can buy, and you'll pay me for my work. Simple as that. All it is, is it's double what you paid Pico. Double bubble. Toil and trouble. And that's non-negotiable.' He takes a pen from his pocket and writes a figure on a scrap of paper, slides it across the top of the tank, raising his eyebrows as he does it. 'Welcome to sample if you like, as I mentioned.'

He points to the pile of coke beside the figure. Harry doesn't pick up the paper, she reaches for another cigarette. Lights it, smokes deeply. She watches Joey, the shark, the coke on the table, notices Leon's presence against the wall behind the sofa Joey's sitting on, hidden, breathing with the bass from upstairs. *Man's a fucking joker. Got to give him that.*

'Look, Joey,' Harry says, calmly, like she's tired of all this. 'The price is fixed as far as I'm concerned. If you want to make your sale, we'll make it now, at the price I've been paying since I began dealing with Pico, seven years ago. If you don't want to make the sale at that price, I'm not interested.'

Joey's eyes are bulging slightly; there is something, some shift, taking place in his face. He lets out a laugh, and it sounds like a car skidding. It goes on for a long time. Harry grits her teeth against it.

'I like you!' Joey says. 'I like you, Harry. You're a funny bitch.' He laughs again. Stops abruptly. 'OK,' he says. 'So here's how we're gonna do it, OK?' His smile spreads like a rash across his face. 'You're gonna give me all the money you have on you, and then I'm gonna give you *half* a key. OK?' Joey waits, thinks, bites his fingernails for a moment. '*Or*, what we could do is, you give me that suitcase, and I let you go without breaking all your bones.' He shrugs, turns a bit of fingernail around in his mouth, spits it out. 'We could do that if you want, you stupid little cunt.' Joey looks her up and down. 'When was the last time you went with a man, Harry?'

he says, his tone dropping deep into the back of his throat. 'Funny that you work on your own, don't you think? Being what you are.'

It hits Harry then, like a punch in the face from a passing stranger. *This* isn't *the guy. This isn't the guy I'm meant to be meeting. This is some fucking chancer. Could be fucking anyone.* Harry sits still and feels her stomach move. Wishes that they hadn't come. *Now there's only one fucking way left for this weird fucking night to go.* She closes her eyes briefly. She can feel a headache coming, a strain in the back of her eyeballs. She should be wearing her glasses, but she can't get used to her face in them, and the idea of contact lenses freaks her out. *Wonder if Becky wears contact lenses.*

In the time it takes for these thoughts to go through her mind, for her cigarette to burn down a fraction of a millimetre, for her hand to move an inch closer to the briefcase by her feet, Leon has stepped from the wall, grabbed Joey in a choke-hold and is wrestling him to the floor.

Real-time returns, the echoes of slow-motion roar in Harry's head. She snaps herself out of it. Sees Joey and Leon fighting on the floor, too close to each other to land a blow. Leon untangles himself, stands and hauls Joey up with him and kicks him hard in the hip, the waist, and punches him four times, fast, in the face and then again in the chest. Joey is dazed, doesn't know where to fall, his eyes are rolling, the punch to the chest was so hard there's blood on his shirt. Leon keeps pummelling him. Harry watches, fascinated. Joey's body drops. He thrashes limply, rolls over, moaning like a distant train. Leon kicks him in the shoulder, in the legs, goes to swing one at his head.

'Don't,' Harry says.

Leon looks back at Harry, who's still sitting, motionless, on the sofa. 'What?' he says. 'It ain't worth doing nothing half-hearted.'

Harry sighs, gets up and moves without thinking; she heads to the stash, takes one of the massive packages and squeezes it into her briefcase. She leaves the rest, goes for the money. She stuffs bundles into the waistband of her trousers, the lining of her jacket. She packs money inside her shirt, under her fucking armpits. Joey is moaning on the floor. Face a mess, looking like a pattern in the carpet. Harry watches him, feeling sympathy for him, almost. Joey looks up at her, empty eyes searching for meaning.

Harry puts a cigarette between his lips, lights it for him, slaps him gently on the cheeks. 'You'll be OK,' she says. 'You'll be fine, mate.'

She does her coat up, picks up her briefcase. Leon shakes his head at her, puts a finger to his lips and leads her towards the fire escape he'd seen earlier.

The cold of the night shocks them back to feeling. They say nothing, walk as fast as they can without running. Then it's keys, car door, the squeak as it opens, the squeak as it closes. Leon's in the front, Harry's in the back. They pull away without turning the lights on, watching out for the bullies. They get to the end of the road. Lights on, they cross the junction, left at the roundabout; they slide away into the night.

Leon's eyes shine in the rear-view. He turns his head. Harry, body rigid, feels Leon turning, looks towards him, their eyes meet briefly. The hint of a smile. Leon looks back to the road. Both take a deep breath in, before crumpling under an all-consuming, childlike laughter that lays Harry flat on the back seat.

'FUUUUUCCCCCKKKKK!' Leon hits the steering wheel with the heel of his hands.

'You're a fucking nutcase, Leon.' Harry lies across the seats, one leg up, knee bent, the other in the footwell. Catching her breath. She pulls herself back up. It's a struggle; the remnants of laughter in her muscles make her weak.

'He *was* trying to do us over, mate. Or hadn't you fucking noticed?'

Harry rubs her face. After the laughter the reality hits her; nausea and adrenalin butt heads in her gut like raging bulls.

'I shouldn't have taken the money.' Harry's voice is low and haunted, full of dread. She hits the back of the seats with open palms.

Leon shakes his head. Speaks calmly. 'You did what you had to do.'

'This is gonna be trouble, Leon.' A tightness in her throat, her tone rising. Anger coming in at the edges.

'What do you wanna do? Go back? Put it all back?' Leon watches her briefly in the rear-view.

The city swims out the windows, unchanged.

'Fuck,' Harry says, full of new fear. 'Fuck fuck fuck fuck.' But her excitement is washing and dressing, preparing itself to step out into the world; the cash packed tight inside her shirt, her jacket lining, down her waistband, these bundles of cash are real. She bends her head, closes her eyes. Counts to ten. Opens, smiling a strange smile.

'FUCK OFF!' she shouts, grabbing the back of Leon's seat. 'What we gonna do now, Leon?' Her voice is cracking with emotion.

'I don't know, Harry,' Leon replies, his voice steadier, but higher than usual. 'I don't have a fucking clue.'

TO THE VICTOR THE SPOILS

It's five in the morning. The lights are on in Giuseppe's. The blinds are drawn but the glow from the bulbs is creeping through the slats, slanting like jazzmen in zoot suits across the dark street.

Ron is sitting in a chair in the corner of the room, furthest from the door. Big head leant back against the wall, legs stretched out straight, crossed at the ankles. His hands are covering his face. One elbow leans on the table and keeps sliding away from him. He looks shaken by something, solid frame hollowed, even his usually perky belly is sinking towards the floor. Ron's brown hair is messed up, sticking out from his head, parted awkwardly. He keeps running his hands through it and now it stands up tall like a breaking wave.

His brother, Rags, is sitting on the other side of the room, one foot up on the chair in front of him, making them both another drink. They are silent for a minute. Two.

'Will I lose this place?' Ron asks his brother. Voice thick with drink.

'I don't think so,' Rags tells him gently.

Rags is taller than his brother and better-looking. Broad brow, straight nose, shining dark-green eyes. The stubble of a hard night starting to bristle, badger-like, across his jaw. His chin juts pleasantly. He watches his brother with the same harrowing love he has always watched him with. He has always felt the desperation to improve Ron's life, and the misery that comes from not being able to protect anyone from themselves.

'I *will* lose it.' Ron is on the brink of tears, voice rising to a whine. 'Pico will come down like a ton of bricks on everyone, and I'm going to lose this place. My lifeline. He's going to take it from me.' His voice collapses. His face falls further into his hands.

'Not going to happen, mate,' Rags says. 'If you'd just let me tell you what went on, then you'd see.'

'I DON'T WANT TO KNOW,' Ron shouts, words wet in his mouth. 'I don't want to know what happened. I can see the end and it's coming and it's now, and I don't want to fucking KNOW. So don't fucking even think about telling me.'

'Fair enough,' Rags says simply, fully aware that it's not about trying to calm his brother down. Better to just wait for him to calm himself. He gets up and walks to the sink where a bag of ice sits in cold water. He puts two cubes in each glass and returns to his seat. Ron is breathing loudly with his nose crushed against his hands. Rags pours two large gins, enjoys the way the ice crackles.

'Got any gear on you, Rags?' Ron says from beneath his hands.

'Not for you, you don't do it any more.' Rags speaks to the gins.

'I'm drunk,' Ron proclaims tragically. His elbow slips away, he brings it back to where he wants it.

'So what?' Rags begins juicing a lemon into a glass with a fork.

'I can't stay awake any more unless I have a line,' Ron says, explaining it carefully, like an important clue in a puzzling mystery. 'If I don't have a line I'm going to fall asleep.'

'You're all talk.' Rags holds the lemon-juice glass up to his face and searches for pips with a narrowed eye.

'You won't be saying that when I vomit all over the floor and you have to clear it up because I've passed out.' Ron's elbow slips away from him again, his armpit falls flat against the table. He leaves it there, defeated.

'You really want one?' Rags finds two pips, and levers them out with his fork.

'Don't make me fucking beg.'

Rags looks at him. 'Alright,' he says, 'here y'are then.' He takes a hard wrap out of his jeans pocket and goes to throw it at Ron.

'Don't throw it,' Ron says from behind his hands, without looking. 'Stand up and bring it over.'

'You stand up and come and get it,' Rags says to him, turning his attention to the bag of brown sugar beside the glasses.

'I can't,' Ron says. 'Don't make me do that.' Ron is still hiding his face, pushing the comforting darkness of his hands against his spinning eyes. 'I'm your little brother,' he slurs delicately. 'Protect me.'

'There you go, invoking blood, only when you need a favour.' Rags measures an exact teaspoonful of sugar and adds it to the cocktail.

'When else should you invoke it?' Ron asks him.

'Every day of your miserable life, Ronald Shogovitch. Either that, or never at all,' he tells him, stirring furiously. Smiling at the effort.

Ron takes a deep breath and pulls his hands away from his face and sits there, exposed suddenly, blinking. He closes his eyes, opens them slowly, testing the waters. Gradually, moaning, he gets to his feet and walks over to sit opposite his brother. With clumsy, heavy hands he goes about cutting the gack into thick, messy lines. Rags says nothing, keeps his attention fixed firmly on the gin fizzes.

At last, Ron sniffs his line and coughs and sits back and waits for his vision to sharpen up. He thinks he sees a shadow cross the threshold of the window. 'Is the door locked, yeah?' he asks.

Rags nods. Adds the soda water. Looks at the finished drinks, studies them. Happy, he nods at his brother to take his glass, takes his silver sniffing straw from his inside pocket, and leans over the table to have his line.

Ron blinks and swallows. Shakes his head a few times. Can feel the edges coming back to his vision. He smiles. 'Here I am,' he says.

'Back in the room?' Rags dabs the crumbs with the pad of his thumb and rubs them into his gums.

'Yes, after a short hiatus, I am officially back in the room,' Ron says. He keeps his hands on his thighs and jumps his knees up and down in a furious tremor.

'Good,' Rags says, raising his glass. 'Welcome. You were missed.' He sips theatrically.

'Rags?' Ron stops his knees.

'Yes.' Rags looks at him.

'Tell me what happened?' Ron keeps his eyes levelled at his brother.

His brother looks into them. 'You're sure you want to know?'

'I feel ready.' Ron nods.

'OK, mate.' Rags takes another sip and winces, pleasured by the lemon. 'OK. Well.' He waits. Leans back and looks up at the ceiling. Purses his lips. 'Well,' he says again. 'We got robbed.'

Ron looks at him, waiting for more. Rags looks back at him. Shrugs without moving his shoulders, shrugs with his eyes.

'I know that,' Ron says, leaning towards him. 'I've known that for the last four hours since you got me out of my bed and dragged me down here. But what I'm saying is . . .' Ron leans back again into his chair, rolls his neck from side to side, wonders about what exactly it is he's saying, remembers. 'I'm ready to know what happened. I'm ready for you to tell me exactly what happened. I'm ready to listen. My anxieties are under control.'

Ron reaches for the cigarettes by Rags' elbow. Rags pushes them towards him, passes him the lighter with his other hand.

'OK,' he says. He rubs his face with the palm of his hand. Wipes his nose. Nods. 'So. I'm there, at this fucking club in the unwashed armpit of south London. As you know. This Paradise, it's called. And I'm waiting to meet this Harry that Pico's told me is coming down.'

'Why were you there, Rags, and not somewhere you knew?' Ron asks quietly.

Rags is annoyed at the interjection, he was just getting into it. 'I don't know, Ron. Because that's where I was told to go.'

'I'm being serious. Why there?' Ron turns it over in his head. He can't work it out. Rags reaches for Ron's cigarette, takes it off him, smokes it, doesn't give it back. 'Whose club is it?' Ron asks him.

'Mate of mine,' Rags says.

'Trust him?' Ron pushes him.

'Trust *her* unequivocally.'

'You're sure?' Ron pushes his forehead towards him.

'Yes,' Rags replies. 'Her name's Lucy. We go back.'

'Lucy what?'

'Trust me.' Rags holds up an extended finger, points at his brother. 'She had nothing to do with this.'

Ron points at Rags' pointing finger. 'Why did she let you use her bar, though? I'm just thinking out loud here.'

'Look.' Rags takes hold of his brother's hand and pushes it slowly down until it lies flat on the table. 'She's got loads of security there, she runs this illegal fighting thing out the back.'

'What kind of fighting thing?'

'All kinds,' he says. 'Animals, kids, men, women. Sometimes all four.'

'Jesus.' Ron narrows his eyes.

'It's a weird fucking place, I can tell you. But it's safe. You know, one thing about it is, it's fucking safe.' Rags draws his lips into a line, shrugs.

'Not that safe though, was it, Rags? Tonight, I mean, for us.' Ron looks at him disapprovingly.

Rags bristles. 'Do you want me to tell you what happened, or what?'

'I'm not saying anything.' Ron spreads his arms. Innocent.

'You are, you keep interrupting.'

'I don't.'

'You just did.' Rags stares at his brother, indignant.

'Alright, from now on, I'm saying nothing,' Ron offers, smiling sweetly. Rags eyes him warily. 'I want to know, I'm ready to hear. What the fuck went on?'

Rags stares at him. Looking for something. Satisfied, he pushes his legs down into the seat, rubs the back of his neck. Begins again. 'So,' he says, 'I'm there, at the bar, it's packed.'

'On a Tuesday? Packed?'

'What did we *just* say you were going to do?' Rags throws one hand towards his brother, palm upwards.

'What?' Ron hunches his shoulders up, rocks back in his chair and crosses his arms. 'Packed on a *Tuesday*?'

'Ron.' Rags unknowingly mimics his brother's pose, leans back in his chair, crosses his arms. 'Bars like this are packed *every* night. Cheap booze, cheap drugs, cheap music, cheap sex. People aren't in bed at ten p.m. these days, mate. There is no early nights no more, there's only the drudgery of work and the fleeting fucking joy of a gobful of dancing powder and a stranger's sweaty genitals.' Rags stares hard at his brother. Angry.

Ron holds a finger up to his lips. 'Not another word from me. Sorry.'

Rags hesitates, searches for his place in the story. 'OK,' he says. 'There's this guy that works there, Joey he's called.' He pauses, waits for the interjection, receives none, continues. 'He's got a right chip on his shoulder. He works for Lucy but he gets treated like an arsehole by everyone, because, by all accounts, he is an absolute arsehole. Full of himself, but with nothing going for him. Now, early in the day, around three or four in the afternoon, I've got a fucking shitload of gear to transport, so Lucy's sent one of her kids over, school uniform and that, and I've put him in the car and we've driven round to Paradise. School run, you know? Very low key. So we get there, all fine, and I load the gear into the club. And I've got a *lot* on me. The plan was, we were going to proposition this girl, this Harry, she comes vouched for by Pico, right? So I was going to say, like, look, love, take *all* this, we don't know how long Pico's away for, just take this on tick, it's got to be a few keys, and then settle up with Pico incrementally. Through Ange.'

'Who's Ange?' The interruption is spontaneous, genuine.

Rags angers, but relents. 'You know Ange.'

'Pico's wife?' Ron asks him.

'Yeah.' Rags nods.

'I thought her name was Cherub?'

'*He* calls her "cherub", but her name's Ange.' Rags watches his brother open his mouth wide and hold his cheeks. 'What's the matter?'

'Are you fucking joking?' Ron says. Burying his head.

'What?' Rags asks him.

'*I've* been calling her Cherub. Ever since I met her, I thought that's what her fucking name was.' Ron hits himself on the back of the head.

'Well, you're an idiot, Ronny,' Rags tells him.

Ron starts laughing. 'I've called her Cherub about three hundred times. I've never once called her Ange.'

Rags waits for him to stop laughing. 'You quite finished?' he asks.

Ron nods, stops laughing.

'So, this little weasel-bollocks, Joey, lets me into the basement. Lucy's asked him to show me around kind of thing. He's got the keys, that's about all he's trusted with. Dogsbody type, right? Opens up the venue and sets up the chairs, things like that. So, he's taken me down to this basement they've got there, weird fucking room. Shark in a tank. The lot.'

'Right.' Ron nods.

'Lucy's into all sorts,' Rags explains.

'Fishing?'

'Probably,' Rags says. 'So this Joey guy's let me in the basement.'

'With the shark?'

'That's right, and I think he's left me to it, but he's obviously hidden somewhere and watched me dump the stash. I've left a load of money down there too, just what I had on me from the day, just to get it somewhere safe. There's a fucking ton of security everywhere. I'm thinking, stupidly, this is all *fine*. Anyway, I've got a couple of bits to take care of. I tell Lucy I'm off for a couple hours, she puts a guy on the door of the basement. I head off, run a couple of errands, have dinner. Come back about eleven. You with me?'

'Fine. I'm with you.'

'OK. So, Joey lets me into the basement, I see everything's all present and correct, just where I left it. He's asked me what time I'm expecting this Harry to show up and if I know what she looks like. I say after midnight sometime, half past, she's going to be on her own, and that's all I know. Then he's escorted me to this booth above the dance floor and he's told me to wait there and that he'll bring her over to me. So I've waited an hour or so. More maybe. I'm alright, I'm having a drink. People-watching.'

'You like that,' Ron says, enjoying the story.

'I do,' Rags agrees.

'What next?'

'Well.' Rags takes a sip. 'Eventually I think fuck this, what the fuck's going on? I go and have a look for Joey and I can't find him, he's not at the bar, not on the dance floor, and the basement door's locked.'

'Can't get in.'

'Can't get in. Exactly. So, I ask one of the Arnies moping around if he can get me another key because the guy who's meant to be looking after me has gone AWOL. *Fine*, says the guy, *no worries, come with me*. So we faff around for half an hour getting the key off someone, then we faff around getting lost in all these weird basement corridors, and then *eventually* we get to the actual room we wanna be in. Open the door.'

Rags pauses for effect. Ron leans forwards.

'And there's Joey, looking like a fucking Picasso painting, all his bits are in the wrong place, like, lying on the floor murmuring to himself. All the cash has gone, along with about a key and a half of uncut gear.'

He stops dead. The silence swallows them both. Ron shakes his head. Stands up and paces the café floor. Rags watches him. 'Sit down,' he says, 'you're making me nervous.'

'I can pace if I want to,' Ron tells him without looking at him, strolling up and down the aisle between the tables. He stops suddenly. His face a green snarl. 'How could you be so FUCKING STUPID?' he roars at his brother.

'What?' Rags' voice jumps up two octaves. 'Me?' He points at his chest, outraged. 'I trust this Lucy with my *life*, right? I thought it was OK to leave the shit there.'

'When, in all the days of this wretched planet, has it EVER been OK to leave that much money ANYWHERE? You PLANK. You fucking IDIOT. You . . . Urgh . . .' Seething, waving his hands in front of his face as if to wave the night away, shaking his head, Ron paces towards his brother, stands over him, about to draw his fist back.

'IF YOU HIT ME, RON, WE ARE GOING TO HAVE A FIGHT. IS THAT WHAT YOU WANT?' Rags shouts at his brother, levelling with him.

Ron lets a bark of laughter out. Eyes like two smashed cymbals, ringing. 'Yes! That's what I want, you fucking idiot. You fucking stupid—'

Rags stands quickly, his chair falls back, he grips Ron's arms, pins them to his side. Holds him still.

'You're angry, so you're lashing out.' Their noses an inch apart.

Ron breathes heavy like a panicked horse. 'Course I'm lashing out. We're in the fucking shit here,' he whines.

'It wasn't my fault,' Rags explains, patient as he can be holding his struggling brother.

'Whose fault was it then?'

Rags doesn't answer, just stares knowingly into Ron's face, taking deep breaths in and out, indicating that Ron should do the same. Ron begins to breathe with him, and Rags holds his eyes until he sees the madness has gone out of them. They stand, saying nothing, breathing, for a good few minutes. Staring at each other. Eventually satisfied, Rags pats Ron's shoulders and lets go. He walks back over to his chair, picks it up, and sits delicately back down. Crossing his legs and leaning his head back into his hands. Ron goes back to pacing. Slower this time.

'Look, mate,' Rags begins apologetically. 'I'm still adjusting to all this, you know. I never *asked* for this responsibility. I never said to Pico, you know, look, why don't you pop off to jail for eight months and give me a chance to get my blood pressure up. Did I?'

'No matter if you asked for it or not, just, what I'm saying is, what the fuck were you *thinking*?' Ron has his face in his hands, rubbing his eyes.

'I wasn't really thinking anything. OK?'

Ron is victorious, throws his arms out to the sides. 'See?' he says. 'My point exactly.'

'Things have been, you know . . . since Amy left. I've not been . . . You know what I'm saying.'

'My God, Rags! You're not bringing THAT into this, are you?'

'What?' Rags takes a sip. 'I was just saying.' He swallows as he speaks, his words come out a damp gurgle.

Ron glares at him for a moment, bemused, before retrieving his glass from the table and holding it in the air grandly, like a trophy, thrusting it about. 'It's this Harry that's done it then? No?' He stops and turns to Rags, shows him his most questioning eyebrows.

'Well . . .' Rags uncrosses his legs and crosses them again, stretches his back in his chair. 'It came out, eventually, after a particularly tedious Q and A, that this miserable little drywank, Joey, tried to rob *Harry*, is the thing.' Rags spreads his arms, incredulous. 'That's what happened.' He lets his hands hang in the air, shakes his head and brings them back to his lap. 'He thought he'd charge this girl Harry double the price and keep the difference. Or keep it all if he could get away with it. When Harry didn't go for it, he panicked, and said OK, gimme all your money then. At which point—'

Ron cuts in, clicking his finger as the penny drops. 'Harry beat him up, robbed him, and left.'

'Exactly.' Rags breathes deeply. Strokes the stubble on his cheeks.

'Harry, who is a *girl*?'

'Yes.'

'Beat the fuck out of this guy, *alone*?'

'Yes.'

'Who the fuck is this Harry character?'

'Superwoman, by all accounts.'

'And given the nature of Pico's friendship with Harry, which we know is extremely amicable' – Ron goes back to strolling – 'we think he's going to be pretty understanding about what went on.' Ron takes a measured swig, holds it in his mouth and swills it round before swallowing it.

'Yes. That's about the size of it,' Rags tells him, satisfied.

'Fucking hell.' Ron looks at him. 'Do us another line then, will you?'

Rags nods, begins the process. 'Joey got disciplined, there and then.' He opens the wrap, takes out a rock, crushes it beneath the flat of his credit card, smooths the little boulders down to powder. 'Told us everything. Described this Harry. She was slim, five foot nothing, you know, tiny frame, geezer bird. Hard as nails apparently. Joey says she came out of nowhere. They were talking one minute, next minute she'd beat the fucking shit out of him and was giving him a cigarette to smoke while she walked out the room. Trained in martial arts, the lot. Brown hair, shortish. Unusual face. Funny nose, or something. Was it funny mouth? Might be alright, apparently, if she tried a bit harder. But yeah, absolute nutter.'

Ron nods as he listens, *nutter, funny-looking, comes out of nowhere*. 'So we're going after her then?'

'Well . . .' Rags looks up from the lines he's cutting, wiggles his nose around, a strangely cute gesture in such a brutish face. 'No.'

'WHAT?' Ron shouts the word like it's the name of a sleeping god. The walls shout the word back at him.

Rags flinches, runs his hand across the top of his head. 'It seems like, word from Pico is, let's just take this on the chin for now. Wait for things to settle down, wait for him to get out of jail, and pick it up again then.' Ron stares at his brother, unmoving. One hand holding his throat. Rags ignores him. Carries on talking. 'The way Pico sees it—'

'You've spoken to Pico?' Ron interrupts him.

'I rang him as soon as it happened.' Rags lowers himself for his line. 'He knows Harry. He reckons that this is a . . .' He pauses, sniffs the line in a short hard blast, leans his head back, wrinkles his nostrils, wipes at the edge of his nose with his knuckle, 'a *misunderstanding* that he can iron out, but he doesn't want *us* dealing with anything. He's pretty angry with us, actually.'

'With *you*? Not *us*, surely?'

'Everyone. He's effing and blinding, you know, I'm gone five minutes and you can't fucking blah blah blah. He left us in charge, and we, you know . . .'

'You,' Ron says forcefully.

'Well, the way he sees it, *we* fucked up.'

'So am I gonna lose this place then or what?' Ron's voice rises, climbs up his throat and throws itself out of his mouth.

'No. If you keep your payments up, I don't see why he would want to kick you out. It's good business, this place.'

'What else did he say?'

'He said OK, we lost a chunk of cash. But it's not the end of the world.' Rags looks at his brother calmly.

'Not the end of the world?' Ron is outraged.

'Not the end of the world.' Rags doesn't rise to it.

'So what about this Harry?'

'Well, we don't know who she is, where she's from. Even Pico can't really tell us much. Obviously, he wants her found. I mean, there can't be too many girls out there selling big lumps of gear called Harry, now can there?'

'No.'

'And obviously he wants his cash back, but it's not on *us* is the thing. It's on this Joey character, it's *him* who's gotta pay.'

'How the fuck is he gonna make that kind of money?' Ron sits down again, opposite Rags.

Rags shrugs. 'Lucy's guaranteed he'll get Pico what he owes him.' They consider what that means, shudder briefly. 'Obviously, *if* she's found . . .' Rags tails off, lets Ron fill the blank in.

'It's hardly gonna be frowned upon?'

Rags nods. 'Exactly.'

They mull it over. Ron finishes his drink. 'Nice, that,' he says.

'I know. Gin fizz. Can't beat it.'

'Shall we have another one?' Ron asks him.

'Probably.' Rags drops his head and exhales deeply. Rubs the back of his neck. Holds his shoulders.

Ron looks at him. 'You've had me pacing this fucking floor. I've been going out of my MIND. He left us in charge, Rags, he left *us* in charge, and now this has happened. It don't sit right with me.'

Rags stands up and walks over to his brother.

Ron watches him, perplexed. 'What you doing?' he asks him.

'Giving you a cuddle,' Rags tells him.

'I don't want a cuddle,' Ron says.

'Course you do. You always want a cuddle.' And he leans down over his brother and wraps him in an uncomfortable embrace, cricking his neck at an awkward angle and slapping his back too hard.

Ron winces. 'Get off me.' Rags ignores him. 'You're hurting me.' Ron struggles. Pushing him off.

Rags laughs, puts up his fists. 'Come on then,' he says, 'spar with me?' and he starts dancing around Ron's chair.

Ron waves him away. 'I'm not in the mood.'

'Everything's fine,' Rags tells him. 'You need to lighten up a bit.'

'Lighten up? You fucking prick. You call me up, I was sleeping soundly, get me down here, tell me it's all gone to shit, my fucking *life* flashed before my eyes. I thought we were in serious trouble. It's gonna take me a little while to be all fucking peace, love and bell-bottoms again, I'm afraid.' Ron spits while he talks, too excited. Beads of white foam gather at the corner of his mouth.

Rags walks over to the sink behind the counter, splashes his face. 'We're getting too old for all this,' he says to his brother in a kind voice.

'I pay that fucking Pico rat good money every month,' Ron says, congested with cocaine residue. 'If he can afford to let this go, why can't he let *me* go, Rags?'

Rags walks back over to him, rests his elbow on his brother's shoulder. Leans down. 'Because you made a deal, and you're an honourable businessman. You stick to your word and that's a good thing. This Harry kid will get what's coming to her. If you hear anything, you know, do what you need to do, of course. But in the meantime, it's late.' Ron nods to the lightening sky outside. 'You should go back home, make Linda a nice cup of tea, tickle her toes and get into bed.'

Ron looks at his brother's face, leaning down close to him, and fights the urge to scream at it. His brain feels condensed and hard and overexcited.

'OK?' Rags asks him.

'OK,' Ron spits back. Agitated.

'Good man.' Rags ruffles his hair, a gesture Ron has hated ever since he can remember.

The morning comes up fast. As cold and blank as a stranger in rush hour. Baggy-faced. Eyes shrinking in their lids, Leon and Harry stare at each other across the table of a twenty-four-hour American diner in a part of town they've never been to before. They are on the edge of a sprawling park seamed with monuments and sculpture. The shops sell floaty dresses and designer pestles and mortars. They feel this is probably as good a place as any to stop for breakfast.

Despite having spent their entire lives together, and a lot of that time just them, alone, it seems to Harry that she's never looked Leon directly in the face before. She doesn't know where to focus. They look away from each other, stare out the window at the car in the car park. The cash like a corpse in the boot.

Harry checks her phone for the tenth time that minute. Leon raises an eyebrow over his milkshake. He leans over, takes the phone off Harry, who extends her arm to give it to him, but clings a little too tightly to it, and so they sit there with it held between them like a Christmas cracker. 'Harry,' Leon says gently, and she drops her hand, a little surprised. Leon takes the battery off the back and removes the SIM card. He drops the SIM and the battery in his glass of water. Harry nods her thanks. They watch the SIM float towards the bottom of the glass.

Plates of food sit untouched before them. Leon ordered pancakes and fruit and syrup. Harry ordered eggs and bacon. Harry drinks black coffee, thickened with sugar. Leon drinks a strawberry milkshake. All night they have driven around, pulling over to kill time in various bars. They spent a good two hours browsing the electronics aisle in an all-night outskirts superstore. Walked away with a new TV and a top-of-the-range pressure cooker. Now they are far west and regretting not being closer to home. It's just after dawn and the pale sky is streaked with yellow. The sun's on its way, sending its first colours ahead of it to let the people know it's coming. Harry watches the colours. *Must be nearly eight.*

'Do you think they're going to kill me?' she asks Leon quietly.

'Us,' he corrects her.

'No one knows you exist.'

'Well, maybe so, but they'd have to kill me first.'

'We fucked up, Leon.'

'Come on, mate. Snap out of it.' Leon's voice is firm.

Harry drinks her coffee and listens to the music barely playing through the speakers. Just too quiet to hear. She hates it when music's played at that volume. She tries to ignore it but can't drag her ears away. She turns to her bacon and eggs. Eats tentatively, feeling the food with her teeth as she chews it. Life is on autopilot – too busy getting things done to really think about what's happening. She stares out, past the car, at the road edging the park, the closed Turkish cafés, the buses packed with workers, even this early. The first joggers pumping their legs around the park's freezing perimeter, neon and grey bodies, pushing forwards, committed to the idea of a better self.

She finishes her mouthful, wipes the edges of her lips with her napkin. Her stomach waking up to hunger now she's started feeding it.

'We'll have to leave.'

Harry's voice is gentle and soft. So quiet Leon can hear other people at other tables more easily than he can hear Harry. Leon's heart pangs for Harry's panic. He wishes he could think of something. 'They set *us* up,' he tells her. 'If you can get word to Pico—'

Harry interrupts. 'Yeah but I can't though. I don't know what number he's on till he contacts me.'

'Fine, but, if you *could*. He might be sympathetic.'

They push mouthfuls down towards their gullets. Grind egg and bread and fruit with heavy molars.

'We got a lot of money in that car. We could go anywhere.'

'Where should we go?' Leon scoops blueberries up with his fork. They fall off on the way to his mouth. He tries again. They fall again.

'We'd have to go careful, with all that cash.'

'We can sort it out. Change it up slowly. I've got a mate in Barcelona could help us out.'

Harry reaches over, takes Leon's fork and stabs a few blueberries with the prongs and delivers the fork back. 'It don't feel right, man. I don't feel good.' Harry is dizzy, she feels far away. 'We took a lot of money,' Harry whispers, her voice scratching through the hush of the diner. Her eyes wide. Forehead deeply lined. 'And what we gonna do with all that gear?'

'Sell it. One time.'

'To *who*?'

'They don't know who our clients are.' Leon's voice is a low rumble.

The day at the beach is shouting at her. Sat there on the stones. And what about her family? What's she gonna tell them? Will they be safe if she leaves town?

'I should have been more careful,' she whimpers. 'That's all I'm saying.' Her voice is sonorous with sadness. 'Coz now we'll have to leave, Leon. We'll have to fucking leave, mate.'

The thought speeds past them and they sit there in its wake, bobbing away.

'Come on, dickhead, sort it out,' Leon tuts. 'Not so bad, is it? We could have an adventure. Go fucking anywhere.'

Harry eyes him warily, not sure.

Even at this hour of the morning, other people are dotted around the diner. A man, alone, in workman's clothes, is eating steak and eggs. A group of three eager tourists are looking at photos on their cameras and drinking cups of coffee. A woman and a small boy are eating a giant ice-cream sundae. He has a hospital wristband and Batman pyjamas on. Harry sees all this and feels herself collapsing inwards like a bouncy castle at the end of a fair. *To be a person with a normal life.*

'OK, so let's just think carefully now, right? What do they know about us?' Leon's face is drawn in concentration.

'Hopefully, nothing?' Harry answers his questions like it's a quiz show. Trying to get it right.

'Does Pico know where you live?'

'No,' Harry says.

'No. That's right.'

'He's never been round.'

'Course not.'

'They'll be looking for us though. Right?'

'We'll be OK. We just need to keep calm.' Leon stretches up, holding his hands above him, and brings them back down. 'We've been very careful. No one knows who you are. No one's seen the car. Everyone we know thinks you work in recruitment.' Harry looks at the table top, listening hard. 'Everyone we sell to, all they know is your name and your numbers.' Leon taps the glass of water with the SIM card and the battery in it. 'And,' it occurs to him, 'to be honest, a lot of the people we deal with think you're a bloke anyway.' Harry shrinks visibly. 'Not being funny,' Leon backtracks, 'but they do.' Harry is flying with tiredness, cruising at great height. 'Look.' Leon has found his thinking pace. 'We fought our way out of a set-up, essentially. You took that money for recompense.'

Harry lets Leon's cool words soothe her panic. She laps them up like milk. 'Yeah. Yeah, that's right.' She knocks back a gulp of coffee. Looks up, startled. 'Think his goons are gonna see it that way though?'

Leon is not flustered. 'That's what happened,' he says flatly.

'They've got *guns*, Leon, they're not playing. This is proper dark stuff, man. Some of those boys are fucking ex-military and all sorts.' She pauses, her thoughts are cold in her head and she shivers. 'We could die over this.' Harry's voice is a broken window, letting the rain in.

Leon holds his friend's arm across the table. Stares at her intensely. 'Fairy tales, sis, don't worry. No one is going to die.' He looks at her with patience and love. Harry searches his face for a flicker of fear. Finds none. 'Eat your eggs,' he tells her.

'How can you be so calm, you fucking android?'

'One of us has to be.' He lets go of her arm and leans back in his chair. His brain feels too big for his skull. His stomach feels strange and he can hear a high-pitched ringing in his left ear.

'What, am I freaking out?' Harry asks shyly.

Leon smiles. 'Little bit, yeah.'

She nods, gets her shit together, eats a mouthful of eggs. Hard to digest. The idea of eggs suddenly occurs to her as monstrous, she puts her fork down.

'Sorry,' she says. 'Sorry, mate.'

He waves it off. He looks up, watches the ceiling, which Harry knows is what he does when he's thinking. She scrapes the egg off the toast and eats the toast. 'Pico's a successful interior designer with a good link in Peru. He's no gangster. He's no killer. He's an opportunist. A clever man. He loves his wife and his home. I don't think you need to worry about getting bodied or anything like that.' Harry looks up from her toast and watches Leon's face with dubious eyes. 'What?' Leon asks her defensively. His tone a little edgy.

'They'll want this money back.'

'So what? You think we should give it to them? Pop round, give it all back and carry on like before?'

Harry looks sheepish. Reaches over for Leon's milkshake and takes a thoughtful slurp. 'No, course not,' she mumbles.

Leon's getting frustrated. What's happened has happened and now they need to think pragmatically. Harry's always been too much of a worrier in a crisis. 'So what do you wanna do then?' he asks her.

Tired, Harry considers her options. 'I wanna keep the money.'

Leon nods heartily. Relieved. 'Thank you,' he says.

'Yeah,' she says seriously, her eyes dry from tiredness. Strained. 'I want to get out of all this. Stop shotting. Live life.'

'Well, there you go. That's what we're gonna have to do.' Leon lays his hand on the table for Harry to take. She does. They shake. Grip each other's hands for a long moment. Leon takes his hand back, wipes his mouth with it. The night before is dragging on, sitting with its arms around them, resting its bleeding head on their shoulders. Leon drinks his milkshake, his eyes closed.

'We need to sleep,' she says. Leon agrees, nodding his head, opening his eyes fast. Harry necks the last of her coffee. Cold now. 'Do I look alright to drive?' she asks him. Leon looks at her. Harry shows him *sober, composed*.

'Yeah, fine.' Leon digs in his pocket for some notes. Leaves thirty quid on the table. They stand, walk delicately out to the car, smiling at the waiter as they go.

By the time they get to their flat it's well and truly morning. Leon nods at the neighbours as Harry looks for her key. *It's just a briefcase.* Every braking car is the coming of a killer. Every distant footstep is police. Harry's heart is racing like a fox who smells the hunt.

The day is up, the high street's becoming clogged with early-rising working people. Ron and Rags are behind the closed blinds of Giuseppe's wishing it wasn't morning yet.

'Look,' Rags says. Having abandoned his elaborate gin fizz ritual, he is now drinking his gin straight, with a dash of tap water. 'I think we should call it a night.'

'Why? Where are you going?'

'Well, I've got to get myself spruced up, haven't I? I'm off to a matinee with a nice girl I met last week. And after that, if all goes to plan, I imagine I'll be drinking some wine in a posh restaurant and hopefully cracking into an oyster or two.' Rags looks like his face has been assembled by a drunk child. Nothing fits right. The booze, the stress, the lack of sleep, the lines of coke have all contributed to a bulging, vacant edginess lingering behind every movement. He stands and stretches and strolls purposefully to the counter, walks behind it and watches himself in the mirror above the worktop. 'Nothing a shower won't put right.'

Ron is racking another line. Getting stuck in to the gear as if it hasn't been a minute since he last indulged. *Old habits die hard*, he thinks to himself.

Rags steps back out from behind the counter, walks over to the table he was sitting at, gets his coat from the back of the chair and swings it over his shoulders.

Ron bends down and takes the line up his nose. Everything behind his face is concrete. Most of the line falls back out onto the table. Exasperated, he wiggles his nose vigorously with his thumb and forefinger. 'Fucking nose,' he says.

'Mate, clear up in here, and get yourself home to Linda.'

Ron looks up at his brother. 'Linda? I can't let her see me like this.'

'Why not?' Rags asks him, confused. 'You look fine to me.'

Ron shakes his head. 'No,' he says, 'I still got some stuff to work out.'

'There's nothing to work out. Go home, sleep.'

Rags roots around in the inside pocket of his coat. Retrieves a plastic pill sheet, pops a small blue pill out and places it tenderly in front of his brother. 'Valium,' he says. 'No worries.'

Ron has both hands on the table top, his shoulders are tensed, his head down, his chest tight, his body like a bombed-out building. 'Thanks.'

'Have a nice day, won't you? Don't stay in here with the blinds shut. You'll get the bullies knocking on. Go home. Get some kip.' Rags pulls black-leather gloves from his pocket, stretches them over his hands. 'We'll find her. She can't be too hard to find.'

The brothers stare at each other, considering the statement.

'Go on then, fuck off,' Ron says tenderly.

'Thanks for the drinks.' Rags unlocks the door.

'Don't mention it.' Ron stands and stretches, surveys the damage to the café.

Rags opens the door and steps through it. 'Don't do anything on your own, OK? Call me if you find something?'

Ron locks the door behind Rags and sits down at the table by the window, peering out onto the high street through a crack in the closed blinds. In a couple of hours it will be well and truly daytime.

He gets up, breathing deeply, and takes the glasses to the sink. Puts the radio on while he washes up. 'China In Your Hands'.

CIRCLES

Harry is holding her head in the bathroom, leaning over the sink. Cold water hurls itself against her cheeks and breaks against her closed eyes. She lifts her face; the water falls off her nose and eyebrows, T-shirt wet at the neck. Her body hurts. Every muscle aches. She stares at her reflection and doesn't look away. A wet face, pale and blotched with stress, stares out. The cheeks are hollowed. Wisps of hair stagger upwards from the head. A thin-lipped mouth is hanging open. She looks inside it. Opens it as wide as it will go until it hurts her jaw and then she clenches her fists and she holds them up by her face and she closes her eyes and she convulses wildly for a short burst and her open mouth shouts without sound. It's not like she hasn't heard what Pico is capable of. All her life she's been so careful.

She has no girlfriend, no children, she sells drugs for a living to people she can't stand. She can feel the city caving in on itself. She wakes up in the morning and stares at Facebook profiles of people she never liked and sees photographs of their wedding days and their charity runs and their children's birthday parties and their wild nights out.

If they came for her, today. If they'd followed them, or something. If they found out who she was and they came for her today and they came into the house and grabbed her body in their hands and took her out into their car and drove away with petrol in the boot, what would it all have been for?

She takes her T-shirt off. Stares at her body in her bra. Watches awkwardly and sees herself. As if she wasn't there before she looked. She unhooks the bra, lets it drop. Watches. Always surprised to see what lives in the mirror. It seems so far away from who she feels she is.

She remembers being twelve or so. Staring like this. Topless, lifting her arms above her head and clasping her wrists and pulling as hard as she could to try and make her new breasts disappear.

She is still that child.

She feels the presence of danger. She sees head-on collisions in her mind's eye.

Images spark and flare in her brain. Her most shameful moments. All of her lovers. Piles of cocaine. Leon's eyes. The day she bought the Ford Cortina. The seaside wind and Becky's earrings dangling when she laughed, those holy dimples rising. She's worked like this for what? She's just been going round in circles. She's nowhere closer really. Not really.

The loneliness that's always known her is curled around her ankles, getting comfy.

It moved through her like lightning when girls walked past and the shame of it threw her against the walls of her school buildings, head hanging. The hard bones in her body showed black against her skin after fighting again. *What are you?* they asked her, laughing. Ran across the street to say, *Excuse me, what are you?* Not even laughing sometimes. She grew with it a part of her, a secret part. And while the others she knew started to investigate each other, she couldn't bear the thought of undressing. Secret things she did with boys from her street. Let them touch her body. Hump her, fully dressed. The older boys caught on and she let them do whatever they wanted. She'd never tell a soul. She didn't know what else she could be for. She thought that when she grew up she would grow up to be male.

There were things she wanted to know. What happened underneath girls' clothes? Were there other people like her?

She was fourteen. Their weaving limbs in little tops in summer on the darkening heath. The girls, their interest spiked, would lead her into foliage and sit down with her. Pull her T-shirt off her shoulders. Let her kiss them, kiss them harder till their breathing became heavy, lips like storm clouds, opening.

What she had with Leon she could trust. They shared a bed when they were growing. Fought each other. Kept each other safe. Leon was a bullied kid before he learned his own strength.

His mum's boyfriends would too often slap him hard across the floor. He was taunted by the tough lads who waited round outside the sweetshop on the main square of his block. He preferred the company of books. What Harry offered him, what Leon offered Harry was a kinship that allowed them both to grow into much stronger people than they could have been without each other.

She loved to feel them buck beneath her, their eyes widening in desperation, staring at her, disbelieving. Shaking with the power of it. But they were only ever hers for moments. They all went back to real life eventually. She'd see them on the bus weeks later, holding hands with their boyfriends and flicking their hair.

Her name was Talia. She was taller than Harry by an inch or two. Her breasts were moons, they governed Harry, pulled her around and affected her moods. And the curve of her hips, the curve of her hips. The Curve Of Her Hips was an altar. Her hair was thick black shiny oil and it fell long long down her back and around her shoulders. Her skinny arms were scarred from cuts. She worked behind the counter in the bong shop. She had a birthmark on her neck that looked like a skull and crossbones. She was a local myth. They said her sister was a prostitute. They said her dad was a killer. None of it was true. Her legs were flowing lava when she walked. She stopped Harry in her tracks and knew it and she started smiling over her shoulder in the street when they walked past each other, and one night at a party Harry found the courage, walked up close and they danced and she had never danced like that with a girl before. Talia hung off Harry's shoulders, traced her fingertips across her back, leant in close and giggled. Deep dark pull a total opiate. Talia. There was no other human in the world. Five years it lasted.

After heartbreak, loneliness. After loneliness, a new conviction, an all-consuming work ethic. A new recklessness with women.

She never went to gay bars. She never said the words out loud. Some girls just seemed to know and they approached and threw their kisses down like swords. But the loneliness of it was unbearable. Smiling at a stranger, thinking maybe, maybe them? All her friends were blokes and she would sit and listen to them bullshit about girls and it hurt her what they said and how they said it.

There were other women. Baking-hot summer days with nothing moving but their bodies. Lying impossibly close, learning how to feel how the other wanted it and voices rising, shouting wet loud screams of joy. But she never fell in love again. She concentrated on her dream. She put everything she had into buying splitting selling. Life was good. She laughed at things and snorted lines of powder off the edge of the pub pool table. Impressing girls who felt her strangeness and wanted it for theirs.

All of this she sees. Naked in the mirror.

She wants to be more than she's been. She wants to hold Becky's hand and run around the city smashed on pills and dance in raves again like she used to, or eat mushrooms in the woods beneath the sky the clouds the sun the rain and fuck the afternoons away. She wants to stop this endless circling. She wants to be an adult with a life. She wants to be in love and travel and eat food in the evenings. She feels screwed up so tight and small. She wants to stretch out underneath somebody's hands.

Becky's in her brain like wasps trapped in a sticky classroom. It's just like her to want someone impossible. She thinks they understand each other, but they hardly know each other.

Maybe they might get away with it? Maybe Pico will understand; they've done business together a long time and Pico always seemed to like her, they were friends, or something similar. The thought of leaving south London, her family, Honeyjar, the Caribbean takeaway where she gets her steam fish on a Friday, the wall outside her house where all the old men gather in their robes and hats every evening and talk in melodious Arabic. Her friends. Her streets and roads and alleyways. Her little brother. As annoying as he is. *Poor Pete.* Her mind is ripped apart by guilt and terror.

She watches as the skin around her nipples puckers in the cold bathroom. She tenses the muscles in her abdomen. Punches herself in the stomach weakly. If they came in now. Right now. Smashed through this door, there'd be nothing she could do.

Maybe she should call her mum and tell her that she loves her.

A HAMMER

Dale is massive; his features are twice the size of Pete's. When they are introduced, Pete feels he is in the presence of some ancient behemoth, trapped in a pair of designer jeans. Graceless, slack-jawed, unsmiling, loud. His skin dirtied with pockmarks and scars. But Pete has spent a lifetime playing sidekick to boys like this and he knows that they are sweet deep down. Pete can't understand how this man could have sprung from David.

'Nice to meet you, mate,' Pete says as they shake hands in the hallway, Dale looks him up and down. He looks to Pete like he could lift the whole house up with his hands. It's meant to be a relaxed evening, but it feels to Pete like a chaperoned blind date. Miriam clasps her hands in front of her stomach and walks busily out from the kitchen, smiling at them.

Dale eats fast and without chewing his food. He doesn't listen and speaks constantly. Pete eats slowly and watches the room with the same derisory attentiveness as always. David seems happy, as usual. But behind those calm and eager eyes Pete can see a deep-seated panic, a dread that, at any minute now, it's all going to go horribly wrong. This makes him warm to David. He can trust eyes like that.

The dinner is long and full of dead ends and Pete can't work out what's expected from him and Dale. Are they meant to be forming a brotherly bond?

'Pete likes bands, don't you, Pete?' Miriam tells the table.

'Yeah, I like bands,' Pete says.

'Dale likes bands too,' David says, more to Miriam than to anyone else.

'Oh right, what kind of bands do you like, Dale?' Pete asks, bored of his question before he's finished asking it.

Dale looks up from his steak. 'Once I went to an all-you-can-eat steak buffet.'

'Steak buffet? I like them too.' Pete speaks to his knife and fork.

'Mate of mine told me about it,' Dale continues, shifting his weight in his chair. The chair creaks beneath him.

'Right?' Pete signifies he is listening, although he doesn't need to, Dale doesn't need his participation to feel that what he's saying is interesting.

'Imagine that,' Dale says, wide-eyed. 'All-you-can-eat *steak* buffet.' He leaves a pause. Looks at the steak on his plate for effect. Looks back to the table. 'Cooked fresh, you know! You go in, and the waiter comes over, and you order *whatever* you want. But the only thing is, if you don't finish it, you have to pay for what you don't eat. If you *do* finish though, it's only £12 and you can have like, £100 worth of meat.' He nods, eyebrows raised. 'I ate about four steaks just sat there, and took the rest home in my pockets! I was eating ribeye out a tissue for the next three days!' He points at them all, nodding.

'Ha. That was very clever of you, Dale.' David chews his steak thoughtfully. 'Very economic.'

Silence approaches the table like an overeager waiter. Hovers around making everyone feel looked at.

'You know, my father was a butcher. I always liked watching him cutting steaks.' Miriam's eyes seem to glaze slightly as she journeys back towards that bustling shop. Her brothers on their tea breaks. The smell of fresh meat and soap. 'But even with that in my family, we still fell into the habit, didn't we, David, of buying from Tesco's like everyone else.' She smiles at him.

David catches her smile and pins it to his chest like a Year 6 swimming badge. 'Yes,' he says, 'but after all that horse meat stuff, we thought better to buy locally, you know, off someone we can trust.' His voice sounds like it's being funnelled through a decaying log; there's a phlegmy, damp quality to it. 'And, it's actually worked out cheaper this way' – Pete shudders as David's voice ascends the nasal cavity – 'because we only buy what we need.' Everybody nods.

Miriam places her knife and fork on the edge of her plate, looks wistfully towards the window, punctuating her sentence by floating her hands towards the ceiling. 'It seems such a shame. I remember when you could go into a shop, and you knew the person who owned it, and you wanted whatever it was you wanted, and you knew it would be of a certain quality, you could *trust* that it was what you thought it was. Those days are gone now, when you could trust anything to be what it purported to be. It's just plastic packets on shelves now. They could have anything inside.'

David reaches for her hand and strokes her knuckles.

Dale looks up from his plate, picks something out of his teeth with his knife. 'I don't see what all the fuss is for,' he says, shrugging. 'Horse is a delicacy, ain't it? Some places? Two for the price of one, if you ask me.' Miriam nods, smiles at Dale. 'Paying for beef,' he tells her, 'and you end up with beef, *and* horse.'

She nods. 'I hadn't thought of it that way.'

'Would anyone like another beer?' Pete asks the table, getting up to go to the fridge.

'There was no room in there,' David pipes up. 'They're in a bucket outside the front door keeping cold.' Pete looks wearily at David, and heads down the hall to the front door.

Miriam leans in and whispers urgently. 'It's his birthday next week.' David leans in too, excited. 'His sister's organised a party. Dale, will you come? You must come? We're going, and all the family. And friends too. But it's a *surprise* though, so not a peep, OK?'

'Sure, yeah, I'll come,' Dale says loudly. 'I love a good party.'

'Do either of you boys fancy watching a movie or something?' David says. 'We could see what's on the telly, couldn't we? Watch a bit of telly together?'

Pete can feel it in the room. Maybe Dale doesn't have any mates, or maybe Miriam is worried about him not having any mates. Or whatever it is, he can feel it. Something urgent and hopeful and sticky in the air.

'I tell you what,' Pete says. 'It's getting late, and I'm sure you guys will be thinking about getting to bed soon. Why don't I take Dale out for a pint on our way home and let you guys relax?'

Miriam's eyes light up. 'That's a lovely idea, son.'

'I'm up for that, Pete.' Dale slaps his hands down on the table and pushes himself to standing. 'Come on then, no strippers though, eh? Not on the first date!' Chuckle chuckle all round. *Happy families*.

At the door, David shakes Pete's hand and clasps him warmly by the shoulder. *Is this a hug coming?* Pete stands awkwardly receiving David's affection. *Can't be . . . no, wait . . . Shit . . . It is*. Standing there, in the nervous arms of David, Pete feels suddenly close to his father. As much as he can't stand his old man, at least he doesn't swaddle him in steaky embraces at the door.

They find a pub near the station. Neither of them have drunk in here before. They push through the doors and Dale nods at the barman. He wears long shorts with pockets in the side and a polo shirt with a sports club logo on it. He jokes with the regulars, the barmaid rolls her eyes. They busily own their space. Pete looks around, *Live music! Tonight! Mitch!* says the blackboard above the bar. To the left, in the corner of the room, a man in his late fifties, wearing a Jack Daniels T-shirt and black jeans, is playing electric guitar. He triggers a backing track from a tiny laptop taped to a music stand and plays to a bedroom recording of drums, bass and his own voice doing backing vocals. He's playing a medley of Beach Boys songs. Two old men stand in the corner watching him, singing along under their breath. A younger man, long-haired and leather-jacketed, is swaying out of time at the bar. Beside him his two mates, in brightly coloured shirts and short-back-and-sides haircuts, tell each other stories they've already heard. Four middle-aged women sit on high bar stools tapping their feet, clapping on the one. Their hair is perfectly cloudlike and their earrings are sparkling. At a table by the back door that leads out to a smoking yard, a group of younger women in pretty tops and tight jeans gossip and drink red wine.

Mitch finishes the medley and speaks into the mic. 'Well, that was some songs about surfing, and if the lovely lady at the bar wants to surf some beer up this way that would be much appreciated!' He grins into feedback and silence. 'Let's get some more surf action from the bar, shall we, ladies and gents?' he says enthusiastically.

The peril of a microphone. Pete is fascinated. *Why does it make people say such strange things?* Mitch is ignored by the punters and the barmaid looks at him, confused.

'Are you asking for a beer, Mitch?' she says.

'Oh, that look she's giving me!' says Mitch, speaking to the room, although the room's ignoring him. 'I get that look at home.'

He is desperate for applause, laughter, justification. He has been singing these same songs in these same pubs for thirty long years. The silence is not enough to deter him. He pulls his trousers up over his belly, smooths his hair down on both sides and enters into a psychedelic, vaguely tango version of 'Black Magic Woman'. On the wall behind him is a close-up picture of a frowning gorilla with the caption *SOD OFF*. On the other wall is a picture of a sentence written in broken nails. *WHEN ALL YOU'VE GOT IS A HAMMER, EVERYTHING LOOKS LIKE NAILS.*

The barmaid has a kind face, massive dangly earrings and a piercing in her lip. She's wearing jogging bottoms and a short vest that stops before her belly button. She has tattoos across the inside of her arms and a word in Celtic script on either hip.

Mitch finishes his song. No one claps. Suddenly everyone's conversations are too loud and everyone stops talking.

'Thank you, ladies and gentlemen!' A couple of the older people clap politely.

Dale and Pete sit opposite each other with pints of lager and double whiskies, and begin the challenge of keeping a conversation going. They start with the usual preliminaries – football, Dale's work, weather. Work in general. Football. Pete's lack of work.

'Oh yeah,' Dale agrees with him. 'I'll tell you what it is, mate – it's a fucking trap is what it is. Get on the dole to keep you going, but then you can't afford to get off it. You take a job, part-time or whatever – you're worse off than you are getting your JSA.' Dale speaks loudly, fast.

'Tell me about it.' Pete stares into his pint. Shaking his head. 'It's fucking outrageous.'

'They just want to keep everybody down.' Dale knocks his whisky back, maintaining eye contact. He doesn't flinch as he swallows it. Slams the glass down. 'That's the thing. Better for the government, innit, if we're all skint and miserable and feeling like we can't even get a day's work. If we can't feel good about the work of our own fucking hands, how we gonna rise up, make trouble?'

'True. When you put it like that.' Pete has his elbows on the table, leaning over them, head down.

'You heard about the toothpaste?' Dale asks him, sitting upright, square in his chair.

'What do you mean?' Pete looks up at him, right hand round his beer glass, swirling his pint a little.

'The fluoride. In the toothpaste?' Dale's hands are on his thighs, elbows poking out.

'What about the fluoride?' Pete picks himself up so that he's not so low down any more. Straightens his back. Frowns as he listens.

'Well, it's been scientifically proven that there's no *use* for fluoride at all. Fluoride *has no benefit to cleaning teeth.*' Dale leans forwards, nodding.

'So why's it in all the toothpaste? And the tap water?' Pete asks him.

Dale looks at him, raises a finger, points at him. 'Keep us passive.'

'Does fluoride make you passive?' Pete drinks his whisky, winces.

'Yep.' Dale scratches the nape of his neck, runs his hand over his head. 'Fucked up, eh? You know about the pineal gland?' he asks, speaking low.

'No,' says Pete, dropping his eyebrows. 'What is it?'

'It's your Third Eye,' Dale whispers, tapping the space in the middle of his forehead. 'A gland in the brain, in exactly the spot the Third Eye is in. It's the part where visions and higher understanding are stored. It's how you access higher truth.' Dale nods, his fingertip paused at his forehead.

'Right,' says Pete, nodding.

'Fluoride . . .' Dale pauses for effect, 'calcifies the pineal gland. Blocks it.' His eyes are wide, his voice a desperate whisper. 'Stops it from being able to see beyond the here and now, to access the deeper worlds.' Dale closes his eyes and takes a deep breath in. His forehead creased and troubled. He calms himself, opens his eyes and stares at Pete. 'You need to smoke DMT or something, man. You need to access.' He taps his forehead again.

Pete nods slowly. A pause settles as they mull it over. They each take deep swigs, the beer clings to their chops. They wipe their faces with the backs of their hands. Dale looks at him right in the eyes. 'Do you toot?'

'What?' Pete puts his pint down.

'Fancy a line?'

'Yeah, go on then.'

They place beer mats on top of their glasses, leave their pints on the table, and Pete follows Dale into the toilets while Mitch presses play on his laptop.

'This one's by Neil Young, and here we go.'

Straight in, Pete notices. *True showman.*

The cubicle's small and Dale is massive. Pete stands drunkenly against the tiled wall and nods along with interest as Dale talks and digs around for his wrap.

'There was this guy, right, I saw it on *Vice*, I think – he drank controlled doses of snake venom every day of his life for like twenty-five years or something.'

'Oh yeah?'

'Yeah. He has all these pet snakes, fucking beasts, you know, hundred foot long or whatever, fucking three foot wide. I'm exaggerating, but, you know what I'm getting at?'

'Yeah. What? How did he take the venom? He let them bite him?'

'No no, he would just kind of squeeze their heads so that venom come shooting out by their fangs, and collect it in test tubes, and then just, like, neck it.'

'Drink it?'

'Yeah – that might have been more for the cameras, like – but what he would do, right, is . . .' He finds the wrap and opens it out on the closed toilet lid. Hunches over. *Huge man.* Pete watches him. *Foetal like that.* He wipes his nose in anticipation.

'He would take measured amounts of this snake venom, and, like, cook it up with some kind of solution, I forget now what it was, and he would, erm, inject it. You know. Mainline. In the video he's, like, "Fucking hell – it BURNS, you know, it BURNS," but he went to the doctor's, and turns out . . .' Dale chops up two fat lines on the lid of the toilet seat. Thick as your middle finger. Long as a cigarette. *Fuck*, thinks Pete. 'Turns out he's got the respiratory system of an eighteen-year-old. Fit as you like, all his insides, tip-top. And he's an average guy – doesn't smoke or anything, but he drinks, and he don't do that much exercise. So he reckons it's the venom that's done it.' Dale looks over his shoulder at Pete. Pete nods, impressed. 'Put thirty years on his heart.'

They sniff it up. One after the other, crouched down, knees an inch from the toilet floor. Sniff and hold.

Back at the table things seem much brighter already. Dale gets the next round. Whiskies first. Then the lager.

'Want a dab of MDMA?' Dale asks.

'Why not?' Pete says. 'It's Wednesday.'

Dale glances around, satisfied that no one is looking, he cradles a wrap of MDMA in the palm of his hand. They lick their little fingers, each scoop a glistening beige clump of dirt into their mouths, rub the crystals into their gums. Pete shudders, sticks his tongue out in disgust, grabs his drink and swills it around his mouth, frowning, trying to escape the taste. Dale doesn't register any response.

'You got a missus then, have you?' Dale asks him.

'Yep.' Pete smashes a gulp of beer down. 'I do, yep.'

'Wedding bells yet?'

'Fuck me, no.'

'Why not? If I had a girlfriend I'd marry her straight away.' Dale has a habit of pointing aggressively, even when he's saying something essentially quite sweet. 'Don't you love her?' Dale has not yet managed to meet a girl he can trust enough to fall in love with. It's the one thing about his life that bothers him.

'Course I do,' Pete says, a little drunk, the coke loosening his lips. Dale is sitting, legs miles apart, one hand on his knee, the other hand palm down on the table. Taking up as much space as he possibly can. Pete is more contained. Skinny and tall and hunched down, slouching against the wall. Knees touching the underside of the table top. 'I do,' he says, 'I do. I do love her.'

'Course you do, mate.' Dale nods. Kindly. Understanding.

'I just, things are just . . .' Pete picks a beer mat up. Rips it into shreds, places the shreds neatly in a pile. Dale waits for him to continue, studying him. 'Not good. You know what I mean? Not cool.' This is the first time Pete has spoken to anyone apart from Becky about his troubles with her. He doesn't know how to put it into words that aren't hers. He struggles to find his own take on it.

Mitch is still singing away. Dale crosses his legs so his ankle rests on his knee, examines his bootlace. Satisfied, he drops his massive foot back to the floor.

'We're fighting all the time. We fight *all* the fucking time,' Pete says angrily. Exasperated.

'What about?'

'I don't know.' Pete waves his hand in front of his face, shrugs it off like it's nothing really.

Back in the cubicle, fast and slow at the same time. More present than before, and further away, Pete shrinks into the corner while Dale takes up the rest of the space.

'It's her job,' he says. 'Her job causes a lot of beef.'

'Got a lot of work stress, has she?' Dale asks, crouching and flattening the wrap out, cutting a piece off the main clump with the edge of his card. Dragging it off the wrap and onto the toilet lid. 'Not switching off properly?' he asks.

'No. Not that.' Pete puts his hands in his pockets, leans his head back against the cubicle wall. 'It's not her. It's *me*. I can't stand her fucking job.'

Dale looks at him, registers the remark. Looks back at the coke, reaches round with his note like an aardvark. Sniff. And hold. Head back. *That's the ticket.*

'Why?' Dale asks, holding his breath, head tilted back, not wanting to drop a crumb, looking searchingly at Pete.

Pete crouches. He reaches the note to the end of the line, scans the ceramic surface for anything missed. Sniff. And hold. And up. He blinks, brushing down his trousers. He stands in front of Dale, an inch apart in the cubicle. He doesn't know how to say it. Dale watches him patiently. Pete looks at his shoes. 'She's a masseuse.'

Dale sticks his bottom lip out in surprise. Scratches his head. 'A masseuse?'

'Yeah, you know,' Pete says, raising his eyebrows. 'A *masseuse*.'

'Oh right,' Dale says nodding. 'A prostitute?'

Pete buries his head in his hands. 'No,' he says. 'No. No. No.' Dale raises a finger, points at him, eyebrows raised, questioning him. 'No,' Pete says again. 'It's different. She doesn't sleep with them. At least, she says she doesn't.'

'What does she do with them then?'

'Like, a massage, full body or whatever, I don't know the exact fucking technique. Swedish or shiatsu or whatever. All I know is it all ends happily, know what I mean?'

'But no more than that?'

'No. And they can't touch her. There's all kinds of rules. She rubs them down and then, you know, wanks them off.'

Dale puts his hands on his hips, looks up towards the flickering light bulb. 'Tough one, mate,' he says. 'Tough one, that.'

Sweat prickles at his temples, shivers skate across the back of his neck, Pete sits down at the table, tells himself to act natural.

'I can't help it, mate,' he says. 'I'm worried.'

'Of course you're worried.' Dale's large mouth opens and swallows half a pint.

'Well, she tells me it's not a big deal, says I can trust her, and she loves me and that.'

'Do you trust her?' Dale wriggles his nose about, opens and closes his mouth.

'Yeah,' Pete says, flicking his hair out of his eyes. Sitting up straight.

'Well, not being funny, mate,' Dale says, 'but obviously you don't.'

It smacks Pete in the face, brings him down like a breaking wave. 'How is that obvious?' he asks timidly.

'Because, mate, if you trusted her, it wouldn't be a problem, would it?' Dale opens the hole in his face and the rest of his pint disappears down it. He shrugs at Pete as he swallows. Beer froth clings to his top lip. Shining. 'You think she's fucking them?' Dale whispers it; a conspiracy.

Pete's head rests in his hands, elbows on the table top. He rubs the back of his head, looks up. 'Do you?' His jealousy is staggering towards them, thumbs in its belt loops, screaming.

Back at the bar now, they're ordering rums.

'And a couple black sambucas. And two more pints, please.'

They stand close, down the sambuca shots. Wince happily.

They sit down at their table and look out at the people.

'I like it in here,' Dale says.

Mitch is singing Chuck Berry.

The old men at the bar are jiggling their hips and the women with the purple wine smiles are throwing their arms around and shaking their knees. Dale nods his head to the beat, Pete watches him.

'I'VE GOT IT!' he shouts over the music. Everything feels louder than it felt an hour ago.

'WHAT?' Dale shouts back.

'CAN I TRUST YOU, DALE?' Pete's voice is urgent, his eyes are shining.

'YEAH. COURSE YOU CAN, MATE.' Dale grins at his new friend, nodding.

'I FEEL LIKE I CAN,' Pete tells him.

Dale points at him. Winks. 'GOOD!' he shouts. 'YOU CAN TRUST ME.'

'IT'S PERFECT.' Pete sees it play out in the space between their pints. Watches the table top, excited.

'WHAT IS IT?' Dale leans in like a dog leaning out a car window, tongue to the wind.

'*YOU* COULD BOOK IN WITH HER, COULDN'T YOU?' Pete shouts.

The music stops, the people applaud. Mitch beams. Pushes his belly out. Hands on the small of his back, letting his guitar hang by its strap.

'ME?' Dale's voice is suddenly huge in the quiet room. Awkward, they look around and huddle closer. 'What do you mean?' Dale is entranced.

'It's perfect!' Pete is overwhelmed. 'She don't know you,' he says, eyes darting left and right. 'She knows all my other mates. And I can't trust them anyway.' He looks at Dale, who is grinning madly.

'What would I have to do?' Their eyes burn brightly together.

'I'll pay,' Pete says. 'I'll give you some money, so you can get a room somewhere. Book in with her, she comes to you.' Dale nods. Smiling, wet-mouthed. 'She gives you a massage and that, and then you tell me what happens. OK?'

'You want me to try it on with her?' Dale asks, voice low, serious. 'Try and get, like, a full service?'

Pete thinks about it, considers it, looks at his friend, his caring confidant. 'Yeah,' he says gravely.

'You sure?' Dale asks him. 'I mean, I will do that, if you want me to.'

Pete is stunned by this man's generosity, his comradeship. 'Just to put my mind at ease.' He is serious and thoughtful. 'I know she won't do it. I know I can trust her. I just need to be sure. That's all.'

They nod at each other. Pete flicks his hair out of his eyes.

'Yeah,' Dale says. 'Wow. Alright. Yeah.'

'Look, here's her card, OK? Take it.' Pete has a business card of Becky's he stole from her room. He keeps it in his wallet, a little vicious reminder that he looks at when he hates himself. On the card is a close-up photo of her naked back and hips and in the bottom-right corner the name *Jade* and a phone number.

Dale takes it. 'I'll do it, mate, I'll help you out. We'll put your mind at rest.' They both look at the card in Dale's enormous hand. Dale tucks it into his top pocket, taps it a couple of times.

'Can you get these, mate? I'm out of cash.' Pete can't look up from the floor.

Dale swings his hefty arm around Pete's shoulder. 'Don't worry about that, mate,' he says, going into his pocket and slipping a twenty off a folded wedge and handing it to the barman.

They take their drinks and their change and Dale winks at a woman he'd been talking to as they head back to the toilet to rack up another line.

'Think you're in there, mate,' Pete tells him.

'You think so?' Dale asks, looking back over his shoulder to catch her watching him.

'She likes you.' Pete digs him in the ribs with his elbow.

'I always had a thing for the older ladies,' Dale says.

'I think she used to be a dinner lady at my school.' Pete turns and pushes the toilet doors open with his shoulder.

'Sexy.' Dale takes one more look back at the bar before following Pete into the cubicle. 'Wonder if she's still got her hairnet.'

Mitch is on his last number. 'Sweet Caroline'. He holds the mic out for the crowd to do the chorus. Dale and Pete are arm in arm, giving it all they've got.

'"SWWEEET CARRROLLLIIINE."' Wild applause follows the end of the song.

'Thank you very much, ladies and gentlemen, you've been a wonderful crowd,' Mitch says, deadpan. The couples are starting to leave. A big man waves goodbye to his pals and walks ahead of his girlfriend to the door.

She's wearing a lovely bright blue coat and stops to kiss Mitch goodbye. 'Well done, darling, it was great,' she says.

'Thanks very much, Michelle.'

She gets to the door where her boyfriend's waiting for her. He opens it, is about to go through it but then steps out the way to let her go first, holding it open for her.

There's a comedy bicycle horn taped up behind the bar. The barman honks it twice.

'Waheyy, well done, Terry,' he says. Honk Honk. Terry raises his eyebrows and dips his head at the barman and leaves, smiling, after his girlfriend.

'See you later, boys!' the barman shouts to all the old men getting up from their stools. He honks his horn a few more times as they put their hats on and head off into the night.

Dale and Pete stumble towards the main road. Concentrate at the bus stop, working out routes home.

'That was banging,' Dale says.

'Smashed it, yeah.' Pete shakes his hand. Sniffing, desperate to swallow, mouth too dry. Feels like he's got a pip in his throat. A few pips. When he was young, a boy at school told him if you eat an apple core an apple tree grows in your belly and branches stick out of your ears.

'I'll see you again soon, mate,' he says, flagging the bus down. It pulls up in front of them.

'Oh yeah. Go safely now,' Dale says as Pete climbs into the bus.

'Easy then mate.' The doors close and the bus pulls away. Pete gives Dale a little wave out the bus window. More like a salute, then he sits down, head moving forwards, body moving backwards. He stares out into the night and counts the lamp posts to keep himself from vomiting.

He gets off the bus in New Cross, walks towards Lewisham Way, turns left, under the railway bridge and down through the park by the flats and up the hill. He sees his house at the end of the road. He lets himself in using the same keys he's had for ten years. His dad's asleep upstairs. The lights are on in the front room and an empty wine bottle mopes on the coffee table next to a pile of papers and two boxes of half-eaten cold curry and rice. He picks the rubbish up, turns the lights off and heads to the kitchen. He hears the mice scatter as he approaches. He throws the food and the bottle away, takes a beer from the fridge and goes upstairs to his room.

He sits down on the chair by his desk, takes out his sketch-book and starts drawing. Just lines and shapes; the same cartoonish character always appears when he puts pen to paper. A long, haunted face, hood up over a wrinkled brow, troubled, wonky eyes staring out. He writes his tag a few times, bores and lets his pen go. He sees it fall and settle into stillness. It strikes him as very beautiful. He drops his forehead onto the desk in tribute but it doesn't feel as good as he thought it might.

He sits on the floor and wrenches his socks off. Wriggles out of his jeans at last. Stands again and gets his beer and looks at the pictures on his wall. Photographs of mates he hasn't seen all year. Sitting at a rave together, grinning out from their hoods. Skinny, dark-eyed boys and girls, faces full of bass. The girls in lurid neon, the boys in baggy black and blue. The cocaine is charging around in the space behind his forehead. A sudden pain stabs itself across his chest. He holds his heart and breathes until it passes. *Would I be happier without her?* He finishes his beer, lies down under his covers without brushing his teeth. Closes his eyes and watches the changing shapes of his brain.

At some point he must have fallen asleep, because he wakes up the next day. He stands on shaky legs and heads to the tap for water – last night already faded. All he remembers is Mitch playing his guitar and the white tiles of the toilet cubicle.

In seven days he turns twenty-seven. That's the age that rock stars die at. If he died at twenty-seven, he would leave nothing behind him. No legacy. Nothing of note. Nothing to separate him in any way from the countless other bodies that he's spent his life amongst. A man in the mass. Part of the crowd.

He sits at his kitchen table and sips water. This is the same kitchen table that he ate his dinners at when he was four. He sees his younger selves, occupying all the chairs and slouching in the corners. The passionate ten-year-old with answers for everything. The bullied twelve-year-old, getting trouble from the neighbourhood gangs, the fourteen-year-old graffiti writer who lived for his outcast friends. The desolate eighteen-year-old, black-eyed from the ketamine. The cynical twenty-year-old, miserable at uni.

All the years of hopes and drugs and shit jobs and big ideas, the dole, the booze, the weed, the heartbreak. The funerals he'd attended. The promises he'd broken to girls he never cared about. The boy he'd been, smart and careful. Book club, karate club. Playing guitar at lunchtime.

He puts the coffee on the stove.

'It's time,' he says. 'It's time to sort this out.' He enters into slow-motion montage footage of himself running laps around the park and getting fitter. Lifting weights in the gym. Wearing a suit in an office. Laughing with the boys in the bar. His head in his hands, he's listening to the coffee as it begins to percolate. He looks out the window; it's raining. The rain is hard and fat. He watches it for a while. *Fuck it*. He pours the coffee and walks into the front room, turns the telly on. It's a daytime chat show. He watches four smug women sat behind a desk in front of a studio audience.

'How can we trust our partners,' one says, extending her hands out to encompass her audience, 'when we can't even trust our*selves*?'

Dale waits in his room at the Hotel Hacienda. He called the number on the business card a few hours ago and arranged for a masseuse called Jade to come and visit him. He has spent the last hour tidying up a spotless room, showering and putting on his lucky pants. He checks the time, walks around the room and stares out of the window at the busy street below. He picks up all the tea bags and the sachets of sugar and examines them carefully before putting them back in their little pots. He takes his lucky pants off. Folds them. Puts on the dressing gown that's hanging on the bathroom hooks. He's not really one for wearing dressing gowns. He stares at himself in the mirror, breathing in the nerves and panic. He walks away from the mirror, stroking his belly, holding on to himself. He feels like he might be having heart palpitations.

Becky steps off the tube and walks against the flow of bodies towards the Hotel Hacienda. A buttery mansion, all spa-baths and dead pleasure. Opulent bedspreads. Inside, a degenerate businessman flashes his credit card and his tooth-enamel at the young father behind the bar before heading up to his room, gripping wine in a cold bucket, to peel his cashmere socks off and let his belly slump. Becky hates this place. She prepares herself for the switch in reality. She leaves Becky on the street outside, and enters the hotel as Jade. She walks confidently past the receptionist, straight to the lift. Hoping this isn't the kind of lift you need a key card to operate. There've been times where she's had to wait in the closed lift for someone to call it or enter with a room key, which she always finds embarrassing.

She checks the information on her phone: *James,* 316. It's been a long mission, crossing town in the rain. The grime of the tube still clings to her skin and the mood of the crush and the flickering adverts and the checking of Twitter still quicken her thoughts. She hopes that when she knocks on the door she's got the right room. A shiver of nerves flutters and pinches her stomach as usual. She doesn't fight the feeling, but checks her make-up in the mirrored wall at the back of the lift and breathes deeply.

Dale hears the knock on the door at last. He opens it carefully. She's tall, her hair is nearly black but with a deep red shining through it. Strands hang over her face and swing down towards her shoulders behind her ears. She has dark brown endless eyes, her eyelashes leap and fall like the legs of a chorus line. Her lips are full and explode in the middle, her cheekbones are high. He smiles, his mouth is dry. He can't feel his feet.

Becky sees a stocky man with bulging eyes and a gormless face in a white fluffy robe; his thick legs stick strangely out the bottom. He's heavily built. Broad-chested, but cowed by nerves. He stares at her shyly.

'James?' she asks. He nods. 'Hi,' she smiles. 'I'm Jade.'

He steps back as she walks in and she closes the door behind her. He doesn't know whether to kiss her cheek or shake her hand. He stands still. His brain as empty as a broken bucket. Becky moves softly, her job is to relax him, to put them both in a calm space. He swallows hard and laughs at nothing. She eyes him kindly.

'What brings you to London, James?' she asks.

'I live here,' Dale tells her. Stumped. Wondering if he should have prepared some lie.

'In the hotel?' Becky smiles at him.

'No, it's a work thing. In town.' He's panicking. His ankles are cold.

'Have you had this kind of massage before?' she asks. Her voice as soft as she can make it. He shakes his head. Looks at his hands. 'OK,' she tells him. 'Don't worry,' and she smiles a little smile that bites his heart to bits.

'That's for you,' he says, pointing to a pile of cash on the bedside table.

'Thank you,' she says, picking it up and holding it, folded, in her hand. 'I'll just tell you what's going to happen, OK?' She holds his eyes. Everything gentle.

'Do you . . .' He looks for the words. 'Any extras?' he asks her. 'Do you do any extras?' He offers a shrug, attempts as much of a smile as his dry mouth can find.

'No,' she tells him. 'No extras.' And he nods.

'OK, cool,' he says. Feeling vulnerable. She has all the power. He is standing awkwardly, a few paces from the door.

'I'm going to dim the lights, and light some candles, and then I'm going to go into the bathroom and get ready.' She walks past him into the bathroom and gets a towel from the rail, comes back out into the room and lays it across the bed. 'If you can just take your gown off and lie down?' she asks him. He nods, watching her. She takes three tea lights from her bag and lights them, places one on the bedside table, one on the desk, and one by the minibar. She turns off the lights and goes into the bathroom.

Dale takes his dressing gown off and lies down on the towel. His heart hammering, sweat prickling in his pores. He can hear his blood in his ears. He smiles to himself. Giddy with excitement. All thoughts of Pete are gone. He is stunned by this woman and the way she moves.

In the bathroom Becky texts her agency, tells them she's arrived safely and everything's OK. She counts the money, finds it all there and puts it away in her bag.

She runs the shower. Looks around at the things in the bathroom and has the moment that she always has when she looks at a stranger's things, all neat and laid out. A pang of excitement at being allowed into someone's privacy. She washes methodically. Avoiding her make-up, not wetting her hair. She uses a sweet-smelling shower gel that she finds on the side. This is her last moment to prepare herself. To get rid of the night bus and the traffic and the phone calls from Pete. It's like being backstage. Mentally shifting gear.

She gets out of the shower and puts on the robe she always wears. She walks back out into the room and Dale is lying, naked, on his front. His left bum cheek twitching. He wonders if she's noticed. 'OK, James,' she says. 'Now, all you have to do is relax.'

'OK,' he mumbles into the mattress.

'I'd appreciate it if you don't touch me, just let me take care of you, OK?' she says. And he nods with his face pressed into the bed and the mattress absorbs the nod but she sees it. Satisfied, she takes a bottle of oil out of her bag and starts with his feet. He lets out a high-pitched burst of air. And laughs, embarrassed.

'It's OK,' she tells him, 'just relax.' Her voice is a whisper.

She lifts his legs and massages slowly; everything she does is more gentle than he'd expected it would be. Becky thinks of giving these kinds of massages as being very much like dancing. She uses a lot of physical strength to be as delicate as she needs to be to make it feel right. She has to move like water on top of them, and so she has to be able to hold herself. She wants them to be unaware of her performance.

She rubs her body up against the backs of his legs. Massages his back with her breasts. Thinking carefully of which part of her should touch his skin at which point. The dance of it. He is stunned by her agility and tenderness. He's never been touched like this. His eyes are closed, he feels each part of their bodies connecting.

After half an hour, she asks him, voice as low and soft as oil, to turn over. He shifts his weight, his belly drags, he turns and she brushes his face with her breasts and sits her naked body across him. He's breathless, he can't believe what he's seeing. He stares at her, his eyes starving pits in his face. He reaches a desperate hand and clutches her thigh. She stops moving. Takes his hand off her and places it on the bed. She stares at his face, stern. He does not reach for her again.

She moves over him. Everything is gentle, she is building a feeling between them, and naturally, she leads him to the inevitable point. When eventually she touches his cock, he comes quickly. She smiles at him. He breathes in short shuddering gasps. Gazing at her.

'Stay there,' she tells him, and he does.

She gets him a hand towel from the bathroom, walks back over. He watches her body, all the parts moving. She places the towel over his bits and leaves him to clean himself up while she gathers her things. He lies in silence, looking for his voice. It comes out soft and high-pitched, stuttering away at the ends of his words.

'That was the most amazing thing ever,' he tells her.

'I'm going to get dressed now,' she says. He nods. His head sinks back into the bed.

She showers again and dresses in the bathroom. She comes out to find him lying still, not nervous any more. His eyes sparkling and weak.

'Can I see you again?' he asks her.

'If you call the agency and it's my shift, then maybe.' She sweeps the room again to check for all her things. Looks through her bag just to be sure. 'Have a nice evening, James,' she says as she closes the door behind her.

Back out on the street, the cars are loud, blaring horns and radios, shouting voices bleed into each other, shoulders push and hustle, swerve and square themselves, music plays and everything is lit; neon signs blaze white and blue and the yellow glow of late-night bars fuzzes the rain-damp pavement. She lights a cigarette, rubbing her temples.

HAPPY END

Pete stares at the light cracking the blinds. He can taste rot in his gums. He turns and watches Becky sleep. He wants her to wake up without him having to wake her. He feels sorry for himself. Tells himself that if she really loved him she'd have woken up before him, made him a coffee and bought it up to bed. His throat is sore and his mouth tastes bad and he'd love a nice hot cup of coffee. He reaches for her, holds her sides and she hurts him everywhere. He pulls at her shape, desperate and dying for her until she blinks in the new day, stretches like a leopard and grins through sleep-squidged eyes. 'It's your birthday!' she squeals and climbs across him to kiss his face.

Harry wakes up, sweat-drenched, the wrong way round in the sheets, and lies still, clutching her head, breathing deeply. She swings her legs off the edge of the bed, feels the cold against her shins. She shakes herself, heart pounding, blinking. The nightmares retreating as she walks to the chest of drawers by the window and pulls a shirt on, running a shaking palm over her stomach, hips, breasts, taking deep breaths. She opens the wardrobe and checks for the suitcase. It's still there. She crouches. Opens it carefully and looks at the money. Feels her body respond, the electricity of this much cash. A giddy, guilty jubilation. It's been a week. No one's come after them yet. She hasn't taken a step without the suitcase by her side. The thought that maybe they won't have to leave runs full pelt across her mind before she can stop it.

In the kitchen, she flicks the kettle on and hides behind the blind to peek out at the street, noticing every car. Today is her little brother's birthday, and this fucking surprise party she's been organising for him is suddenly a terrifying prospect. She's been freaking out, afraid to close her eyes in the shower in case she opens them and there's a killer in her bathroom, brandishing sharks. The idea of smiling along with her entire family is gruesome. She'd tried to track down all his old mates, but the wind had gone out of her sails, and she'd had to settle for the three she could find numbers for and ask them to bring some people.

Harry hears footsteps up the path and holds her breath, listening to keys scraping the lock. The lock clicks and gives and she watches the door swing inwards. She only breathes out when she sees Leon's face pushing through into the hallway. 'Only me.'

'How was the run?'

'Well.' Leon walks heavily to the kitchen tap for water. 'I'm still breathing,' he says, turning the tap on and ducking his face underneath it.

The Hanging Basket is a pub on an old Roman road overlooking a roundabout. A strong, grand structure, four storeys high, it keeps watch over Deptford. Its bricks are dark and crumbling. Pot plants, broken furniture, window boxes and fag-burnt armchairs are scattered across the flat rooftop, their outlines squint down at the road. What this pub offers is a calming of the blood. The warmth and fear of booze. Friendship. A flirtation or two. Music.

There is a railing that keeps the smokers from the road. They lean their backs against it in the wind and throw stories around like punctured footballs. The doors are heavy, they demand a push with the shoulder and, like the best of us, they swing both ways. Greetings are yelled across the room, then repeated in close-up; soft cheeks and hot stubble. The laughing lady at the bar kisses her favourites on the mouth. Her hair is thick and dark as rum. Rough-nailed hands clasp their glasses, smash their rasping laughter out. The bar staff are heroes, the regulars are legends and the drunks are poets.

This is the Basket. People shelter here. People who wear colourful clothes and have half-shaved heads and leather jackets and live in squats or on old boats or in vans. Or grey-haired, square-shouldered men who work all day and sit with paint-flecked jeans, tip the Guinness and talk it over. Or sensitive young artists reading alone with pints of ale. Or wreck heads ready for anything, they scan the room as they eat their dinner, caps and trainers, nods and nudges, prone to a little naughtiness. Modern punks and ancient drunks and new-school rude-girls escaping the drudgery. If you need love, you can come here. You can find it where it hangs.

Today Gloria is queen of this ship. There's not too many in yet. She is behind the bar, staring at Miriam, who is crouching down behind the bar while David, who is standing in the doorway, watches, on tiptoes.

'No good,' he says. Miriam moves slightly to her left.

'Is this better?' she shouts from her crouch.

'Bit better. But I can see the top of your head,' David tells her.

Gloria's boyfriend Tommy is sitting at the bar drawing in his sketchbook. She goes over and stands next to him, leaning on his shoulder.

'You alright?' he asks her.

'Yeah. Fine. Just watching.' She fiddles with the hair at the nape of his neck.

'You need a haircut,' she says. He doesn't look up from his drawings.

'I don't tell you that you need a haircut,' he says, 'so why would you tell me?'

She leans down and kisses the back of his neck. 'You do though.'

He reaches round his back and holds her waist. She puts her arms around his shoulders, leans her weight against him. He swivels round on his stool so he's facing her, puts his knees either side of her hips. She pushes her face against his neck and presses her cheek into the side of his face, shuts her eyes and opens her mouth and catches his earlobe in between her lips.

'What are you doing?' he asks her.

'Nothing,' she says. He extricates himself from her. Holds her ears and kisses her mouth.

Miriam is still crouching behind the bar in various shapes.

Gloria watches her, bemused.

'Just getting prepared,' she sings out, excited. 'Just checking my knees are up to it!' She huddles down under the bar and shouts to David. 'How's this, love?'

David walks two paces in, looks at the bar from different angles. 'It's great!' he shouts. She rises from her crouch, he gives her a double thumbs-up. 'Right there is perfect, love! I couldn't see a thing.'

'We can get at least fifteen down here, all in a line,' Miriam says, 'don't you think, Gloria? Or is there some kind of health and safety thingy that means we can't have any fun?'

Tommy sketches quickly, draws the people in the pub without looking at the page. Miriam, Gloria, the old man doing his word-search opposite. He is covering his sketch-book with faces, hands and a close-up of a pair of crossed ankles.

Charlotte pushes through the doors.

'Alright, trouble,' Gloria says as she collapses dramatically against the bar.

'Oh my God,' Charlotte says. 'I want to quit my job.'

'No you don't,' Gloria says.

'No, I don't.' Charlotte reaches out to land a kiss on Gloria's cheek, hugs her awkwardly with the bar between them.

'What you drinking?' Gloria holds on to the bar and leans backwards.

'White wine, please.' Charlotte stretches up and lets out a moan as she reaches for the ceiling. 'And a tequila.' Tommy tries to sketch her fingers stretched up like that, but he misses them. 'Hi, Tommy,' she says.

'Alright, Charlotte.' He smiles at her before looking back to David and Miriam.

Charlotte nods, looks around. 'What's been going on here?' she asks as Gloria leans down to get the wine out of the fridge.

'Nothing really, why you wanna quit your job?' Gloria puts the wine in front of her.

'I just had a shit day and I've got this student and she's a nightmare and I don't know what to do about it.'

'You were a nightmare once.'

Charlotte looks around at the decorations. 'Really gone to town with the decor.'

Gloria rolls her eyes. 'Tell me about it.'

'Bunting?'

‘I know.’ They look at the bunting and the sad paper chains and the banner that says *BIRTHDAY!!!* in gold capitals.

‘We lost the *HAPPY*,’ Gloria says.

‘Oh well. Less pressure this way.’ Charlotte drinks her wine, leans back against the bar. ‘Less of a command. More of a statement.’

Ron and Rags are walking up towards the pub. ‘You sure she wants us here, Ron?’

‘She called me three times this week to check we were coming.’

‘Strange, innit?’

‘She’s worried that no one’s gonna show, I think.’

‘Poor kid.’

‘He’s a nice enough lad.’ They stop outside, finish their cigarettes. ‘Not got a lot of social skills though, has he?’

‘I like him,’ Rags says.

‘I was only saying.’

They push through the doors and greet Gloria.

‘Here for the party,’ Ron tells her, leaning against the bar, flashing his friendliest grin.

‘Cool. What you having?’ Gloria asks them both.

Harry stands at the table by the fireplace. Drinking a bottle of beer, listening to Danny, Charlotte’s boyfriend, talk about his band. He’s been saying the same things about new demos and new managers for a long ten minutes but Harry's not really listening. Harry's wondering what will happen when Becky arrives. Wondering how she will greet her. Wondering if she's OK. Her body is tense with the prospect of seeing her walk through the doors any minute. She stamps the feeling down. Focuses on Danny's moving mouth.

Ron and Rags clutch their pints and head past the fire-place, towards the pool table.

Miriam stands beside David and Dale, assessing the *BIRTHDAY!!!* sign.

'I quite like it,' David says. 'Very cheerful.'

Miriam's not so sure. But the bunting's nice. She fidgets from foot to foot, rubbing her hands together, gripping them and letting go and gripping them again. Tonight will be the first time she's seen Graham in eight months. She's not sure that he's going to be able to behave himself. As she thinks his name, he arrives.

'Hi.' He stops still and smiles. He's wearing new jeans. They are tighter than she would have advised him to wear when they were together.

'Hi!' She grins uncomfortably, then leans in and kisses him on the cheek. *Be nice*, she thinks. *Please, Graham.*

David sticks out his hand, smile like a windscreen. 'I'm David,' he says. 'It's good to meet at last.'

Graham wishes he was strapped full of explosives so he could blow them both up. 'Hi,' he says. 'Great to meet you, David.'

Dale is standing still, staring over the head of his father at Charlotte and Gloria standing at the bar. He drools a little baggy grin like dirty underwear left on the floor of his face. He doesn't look away when they frown at him.

Gloria gets the text from Becky. 'Everybody down!' she shouts. 'He'll be here in a second!'

Everyone runs behind the bar.

Miriam and Graham are crouched down in the middle, suddenly side by side and breathing excitedly. 'Our little boy!' Graham leans over and says into Miriam's ear. 'Twenty-seven years old! We were parents at that age, weren't we, doll?'

Miriam's smile is strained. 'Yes,' she says. 'Funny that.'

David, slower at getting round the bar, is crouched next to Rags, craning his neck to try and hear what it is Graham and Miriam are saying to each other. Rags is chuckling away, Ron leans an arm on his brother's back, chuckling too. Harry is bent double, next to them, pushed up against Rags' epic shoulders. She has to move to get comfortable and nearly falls over. She reaches out to steady herself and ends up with her hand on Rags' knee.

'All very intimate, isn't it?' she says smiling.

Rags claps her on the back. 'Don't you worry,' he says.

'We're Becky's uncles,' Ron tells her, whispering.

'Pete's sister,' says Harry.

'Oh, right.' They nod and kiss cheeks from their awkward crouches, laughing about it. 'Nice to meet you.'

Leon runs through the door, blowing the last bit of smoke out. The suitcase in his hand. 'Am I too late?' he asks no one in particular.

'Get behind the bar, quick,' Gloria tells him, jumping out the way for him to crouch down.

He finds himself next to Nathan, one of Pete's friends. 'Alright, mate?' he says, smiling excitedly.

Nathan nods hello. 'Does your fucking legs in after a while.'

Becky's cousin Ted and his girlfriend Sally are crouched at the end of the line, smiling at each other, holding hands.

'Do you think he suspects anything?' Sally asks him.

'No. I shouldn't think so,' he says.

Danny and Charlotte, Dale and Pete's mate Mo are behind the first row, crouching down on their heels. Everyone holds their breath.

Outside the pub, Becky is being patient. Pete smokes morosely and pulls his hair around. 'I like the pub and everything,' he's been moaning for the past two hours, checking his phone and finding no messages, 'but it's hardly a special thing, is it?' He drops his cigarette butt and kicks it out with the toe of his trainer.

'Let's have a drink, Pete.' She takes his hand and leads him towards the doors. He drags behind.

Pete trudges towards the bar, looking around at the empty pub. Feeling like he's never had a friend in his life. He stops just before the bar and rocks back on his heels, surveying the beer taps, even though he knows which beers they serve in this pub off by heart.

'What can I get you?' Gloria asks him.

He thinks about it. 'Erm . . .'

'HAPPY BIRTHDAY, PETE!!!!' The crowd erupts from behind the bar. Arms in the air.

Pete's mouth drops open. He cracks a grin. For the first time in ages Becky sees him properly smiling.

'Ahh shit!' he says. 'No way!!' His eyes sparkle as he looks at all the faces.

'FUUUUCK!' he says, and he lifts Becky up and gives her a kiss. Harry's heart stabs itself in the stomach with a blunt sword. 'Was this you?' Pete asks her. 'Was this you done this?!' Everyone runs round from behind the bar and waits for their turn to hug him.

'Hi, Dad,' Pete says, slapping his dad on the shoulder. Graham grips his son's face in two large hands and kisses him hard on the head.

'You look smashing, son.'

'Well, you too, Dad, you look very well.'

'I put my smart shirt on,' Graham says, 'for the occasion.'

Miriam and David stand close by and smile into the conversation from the edges.

Pete has his arm around Becky. 'This is great! This is really great. You're all here . . .' He grins round the room. 'Just look at you all!'

Gloria's boyfriend Tommy and Becky's cousin Ted, who knows Pete from school, are opening a bottle of Prosecco and organising glasses.

'How many are we?' Tommy asks.

'Fuck knows. Hold on.' Ted stands on his tiptoes and counts the heads. 'We'll need another bottle, I think.'

'How many glasses though?' Tommy stares at the glasses on the bar, lost.

'Just start pouring, mate, we'll work it out,' Ted tells him.

Charlotte and Becky help them pass the glasses out. When everyone's got a glass in their hands, they raise them up to Pete. Pete is leaning on Becky's shoulder. Becky is smiling beneath the point of his elbow, but she looks tired, far away.

Rags is having a great time. 'SPEECH, SPEECH, SPEECH!' he shouts, laughing. Leon and Harry join in.

Pete clears his throat, acts all tearful. 'Oh it's all too much,' he says. 'I don't know what to say . . .' He breaks off, mimes being overwhelmed, one hand on his heart, frowning with emotion. 'I'd just like to thank my mum and my dad for making me . . .' Everyone laughs.

'Come on, say something proper,' Nathan tells him, slapping him on the back.

Pete thinks about it, nods, raises his glass. 'OK.' He clears his throat. 'I'd just like to say . . .' He pauses for effect, looks around the faces in the room. 'Let's get fucking shitfaced!'

Everybody yawls and stamps, displaying their best affection. They raise their glasses. Their smiles are wide enough to fall in.

Danny puts his arm around Charlotte. 'Lovely, innit?'

'Yeah,' she says. But she's not sure. She watches Becky floating in the background, not saying much, just fiddling with her glass and keeping a foot away from conversations.

Harry walks up from the other side of the room, and joins the circle round Pete, puts her arm around her little brother. 'Happy Birthday, kid,' she says, gripping him tight.

'Oh. Thank you,' Pete says, slapping her on the back. The drinks are flowing and spirits are high. 'I'm sorry we've not seen so much of each other recently,' he says quietly.

Harry looks at the ground, nodding. 'Yeah, me too,' she says, still holding on to her brother's waist. 'Just the way it goes, I suppose. You like the party then?'

'Was it you? You did this?' Pete grins, gobsmacked.

'I just thought, you know, might be nice for you, see all your friends and family in one place.' Harry kisses her brother's cheek and strokes his head a few times, messing his hair up and smoothing it down.

Pete brushes her off, laughing. 'Soppy twit,' he tells her, voice heavy with booze and camaraderie.

Graham grins at Harry and clasps her in a fierce hug. 'Hello, love,' he says. 'When you coming round to see me then, eh?'

Harry slaps her dad on the back a few times. 'Soon, Dad. I'll be over soon, I promise.'

'How you keeping?' Graham asks her, studying her. Brushing his daughter's shoulders, rubbing her arms, holding on to her wrists, admiring his eldest.

'I'm well, Dad,' Harry tells him. 'I'm good.'

Ron wanders up to the circle, puts his arms around Pete. 'Happy birthday, mate,' he proclaims. 'All grown up, eh? Far cry from that little wretch mooning around my café all day staring at my niece. Eh?'

Pete is tipsy already and wobbling from all the affection. 'This is Ron,' he explains to the circle, 'Becky's uncle, and Ron, this is Graham, my dad, and Harry, my sister.'

Ron smiles and shakes hands with Graham. 'Hello, Graham, good to meet you.' He turns to Harry. 'Hello,' he says, looking her dead in the face before leaning in and kissing both of her cheeks deliberately, his stubble coarse as sunburn. 'Harry?' Ron asks her.

'That's right, yeah,' Harry tells him. Something about the intensity of his gaze rattles her. He is staring into her face, eyes shining like blades in the sun.

Ron can feel his veins growing heavy with rage. 'Good to meet you too,' he says, attempting a charming tone but speaking in gruff, dissonant sing-song. On the other side of the room, by the jukebox, Leon can feel his shoulders tensing.

Dale is looming cheerfully around. He watches Pete and Becky as they stand at the bar. Becky looks up and sees him staring. She recognises him but she can't place him. She smiles vaguely and looks back to the Prosecco she's pouring but she can feel his eyes lingering on her body and it's making her uncomfortable.

'Who's that over there?'

Pete turns, drunk, happy. 'Oh, that's Dale,' he says. 'Believe it or not, that's David's son.'

Becky looks over at him, surprised, Dale's face lacking even a trace of David's eager veneer.

Pete beckons him over, grinning amiably. 'Dale!' he shouts. 'Come over here, mate.' Pete watches Dale walk over, grinning intensely. Nose fidgeting on his face like a kid bursting for a wee. He admires the expanse of his chest. 'This is Dale,' Pete tells Becky. 'Dale, this is Becky, the love of my life.'

Becky winces and sends an elbow towards Pete's ribs. 'Cheesy bastard,' she says.

'What?' Pete plays crestfallen before sneaking a kiss of her neck, then another.

Suddenly, publicly, Pete is in love with her. But an hour before, he couldn't even hold her hand. Becky finds herself looking behind her, checking to see if Harry has noticed the kisses.

'Nice to meet you, Dale,' she says, looking back at them.

'Actually, we've met before,' Dale says. His voice is hoarse. His heart is butter. Thick and shivering in his chest.

Becky stares blankly at his strange, solid face.

'Thanks for coming along, mate,' Pete says warmly. 'I didn't expect a thing. Honest, I thought we was just going for a drink, me and her, and then, look at all this. What a treat. Eh? What a treat.'

'You was at work,' he tells her, ignoring Pete.

'At the caff?' she suggests.

'No, it wasn't the caff. Your other job.'

She feels the gradient of the floor increase. She's being pushed up a hill into a vacuum. There is an unwritten rule between people involved in a professionally intimate exchange: if they meet out in the real world, they respect each other enough not to mention it. Becky stares at the man, daggers in her eyes.

Pete's stomach rips itself apart as it all comes screaming back.

'Let's not do this here,' she says quietly but with violence behind the words.

'You remember, don't you, Pete?' Dale asks him. The drunken mist blown clear.

'What?' Pete's voice tremolos, in its highest register. He shakes his head at Dale, but Dale isn't looking at him. Dale is looking at Becky, front on, bearing down.

'Yeah, you remember,' Dale says. 'I met you in the Hotel Hacienda.' Pete pushes Dale, but Dale doesn't stop, doesn't flinch. Pete's push is absorbed by Dale's mass. 'You said your name was Jade and I said my name was James.'

Becky is silent. She looks at Pete who's covering his mouth with his hand, stepping from one foot to the other. Around them, people are drinking, singing at each other, swearing fondly. Low bursts of laughter rip through the room like accordion solos.

Pete snaps out of his stupor. 'Come on, Becky,' he says. 'Fuck this.' And he starts to usher Becky away from Dale but Becky roots herself, leans away from Pete's arms.

Dale leans round Pete's bony shoulders. Pete stands between them both but neither acknowledges him, only each other. Becky forces her mind back through last week's clients. Unless something particularly interesting happens, she forgets them as soon as she leaves the hotel room. She watches his paddle-shaped head, his anonymous doughy features. She glimpses a memory, his awkward body and predatory eyes. He'd asked her for extras.

'Pete was worried,' Dale says. 'About how you'd been carrying on and that, with the clients? So he asked me to go undercover, if you like, check it out for him.' He nods, winks at Becky. Slaps Pete on the back from behind, grips Pete's shoulder. Pete sinks. 'Eh, Petey?' Dale leans in closer to Becky.

Her body is on fire. She stands in her bones, but her tissues, her organs, her guts have burnt to a crisp. 'Pete?' Her voice is not her voice. Her voice is her mother's voice that night when they left the flat and the paparazzi bulbs made the street into a nightclub.

Ron is outside the toilets, drying his face with his handkerchief. Harry breezes out of the door to the Ladies, covering her nose with the fingers of her right hand. She snorts, loud and long. A sniff that starts in the mouth and ends in the back of the brain. Ron takes the handkerchief from his face and Harry sees him standing there as she lets the door swing closed behind her. 'Oh hello,' she says, big smile.

'Alright, Harry.' Ron dips his head, speaks low, pushes a hoarse whisper out through a conspirator's smile. 'Haven't got a spare one, have you?' He taps the side of his nose. 'I'm flagging here.'

Harry grins. 'Oh yeah. No sweat,' she says, digging the wrap out of her pocket and passing it on. 'Help yourself,' she says. 'I'm going for a fag.' Ron nods, holds the wrap in his fist, still damp from the taps. 'See you at the bar in a sec?' Harry squeezes his arm briefly.

'Yeah, lovely,' Ron says. 'I'll get 'em in.'

'Nice one.'

'What you having?' Ron asks her.

'Mine's a pint of Sea View,' Harry tells him, smiling.

Ron heads into the Gents, closes the door of the cubicle, opens the wrap. He studies the coke. So dense it looks beige. Clumped into wet rocks, stinking. The smell so strong his belly responds before his nose knows it's smelt it. The lurch of his gut is the telltale sign. He splits a few granules off with his little fingernail, watches the spread of the powder as he pushes his nail down into it. He takes a small pinch to his nose and inhales it. He fucking knew it. He'd know this gear anywhere.

David leans against the bar, top button of his shirt undone, drinking his pint slowly.

Graham is slaughtered and leaning in close. 'Look,' he says, 'all I'm saying is you better take care of her, you. I've seen your type before, with your . . .' He stops talking and makes gestures David doesn't recognise. Curling his hands around in the air, waving his palms and swinging his head from side to side. 'Hair.' He spits. 'And your—'

'Look, it's OK, Graham,' David interrupts him.

'What's OK?'

'I owe you an apology,' David says calmly.

Graham stops gesturing. Watches David suspiciously. 'An apology, eh? A likely story.' In his mind he is debonair and cavalier. In reality he is swaying, eyebrows scrunched up, face red and blotchy, pointing vaguely like a weathervane on a windless afternoon.

'I didn't know she was married when I met her,' David tells him. 'When I found out she was married, I very respectfully kept my distance. But I loved her very much, and when it became apparent that things were not going so well with you, and that she might be having similar feelings for me, well, I told her how I felt.'

Graham is expanding slowly. Becoming tight with air.

'The thing is, Graham, I want only the best for her. And it would mean the world to her if we were able to be civil.

She cares very much for you. And I would like it if we could one day be, well . . . Friends is probably a bit steep, but you see what I'm getting at?' David finishes speaking, lays his eyebrows down.

Graham filters David's words through a complicated lens of suspicion and booze. He thinks for a minute. 'I don't trust you, David,' he says, swaying. 'You're not to be trusted. That's all I have to say on the matter.' He walks away to find Miriam and throw himself at her feet.

Outside, the wind blows hard and cold and the sky is angry. Harry smokes her cigarette and leans her head against the bricks. Thinks that Becky looks so lovely this evening. Nice to see Pete smiling too.

Ron steps through the doors carefully. Feeling the floor through the soles of his shoes. Concrete. Steady now. He walks up very close to Harry before Harry notices him coming. He stands beside her.

Harry smiles at him. 'All good?' she asks. Ron says nothing. Harry feels uncomfortable but waits it out. Stares straight ahead.

Ron looks up at the clouds, rolls on his heels and then back onto the balls of his feet, leans against the wall, speaks in a slow growl. 'I know what you did, darlin'.'

His voice is as dark as the sky. Harry's fingertips start tingling; the onset of simultaneous pins and needles attacks every digit. Her pulse picks up its feet and starts to run.

'What you talking about?' Harry looks at him out of the corner of her eye.

Ron turns to face her, places a hand on her arm, above the elbow, and stares at her with eyes like dirty water. Thick and oily. Full of dead things. 'I know who you *are*.'

'Leave it out,' Harry tells him, her arm rotting beneath his touch. She tries to shake herself free but he clings on.

'No more bullshit, missy.'

'What is this?' Harry asks him, speaking calmly. Gently. Ron stares into her face, looking for something, Harry meets his stare for as long as she can, but can feel herself weakening.

'I work for Pico,' Ron tells her, matching her tone.

Harry's body is propelled through the air at great speed and lands in a heap at the bottom of a cliff. She can feel every bone as it breaks into a million splinters. His hand still on her arm, she waits out the initial shock and tries to engage her brain with what this means. She looks up into this man's face. She can't work out how *this* could be happening *here*. Her entire family are metres away. The care she's taken all her life to keep things separate . . . The weird basement room looms before her. The shark swims in Ron's eyes.

'Pico?' Her voice is strong as she pulls her arm out of Ron's hand. Ron lets her go. She speaks Pico's name like it means nothing.

'Yeah.'

'I ain't seen Pico in a long time.' Harry puts her hands on her hips, stares off into the middle distance, acts as casual as she can. Frowning slightly as she mimes trying to recall the last time she'd seen him.

'Stop it, Harry.' Ron holds up a finger. 'I know what's happened here, OK? We don't need to fuck around.' Harry straightens her back, looks about. Is Leon in the shadows? She can't be sure. Ron carries on. 'I know you came to have a party. So, no trouble right now, OK? But hear me, listen up good.'

Harry doesn't move. She stares at Ron, his bulk held together in a perfect stillness, like an elephant on its tiptoes. Something around the cheeks, the chin, something there does remind her of Becky a little. Something. The prospect of a swinging blow that lays her body down, beneath a speeding car; it's all very close now, the end. She feels it. Woozy as booze. Is he going to smash her face in? He is close enough for her to smell the cocaine in his nose. The beer on his lips. His aftershave. The money's in the suitcase. The suitcase is in Leon's hand.

'You owe me, Harry. What you stole was mine. OK? And so we are going to need to talk about that.' He leans down, his voice a quiet croak, his face as taut and pained as a chess master losing. Veins stand out all over his neck and head. He offers a smile but it dies on his lips and its corpse is too heavy to lift.

Harry says nothing, studies his face in enthralled disgust. *Is he going to take all my money? Is he going to break my bones and take all the money I've saved and we'll have to start again, with nothing?* She looks at him, feeling very small. He looks pretty serious. *Is he going to kill me?* She feels light with excitement. Like something is actually happening and the prospect of danger makes her sure that she's breathing. Alive at last. She runs her hand through her hair and scratches her scalp. Levels her gaze at Ron, her legs shaking.

Becky feels nothing but rage. She looks at Pete and doesn't recognise him. Can't see him. All she can see is disgust and guilt and blame and months of silent, moody control.

Pete is shrivelled up in his clothes, his body racked with guilt. He stares at his girlfriend, his eyes like open graves, and gesticulates his innocence wildly. Shaking his head, throwing his arms towards her as she backs away. 'It's not like that,' he tells her. 'It wasn't like that, Becky,' and his voice is so high it's hardly there. A desperate scratch. The yell of ten stubbed toes.

'You little fucking shit,' she says, and her voice isn't loud but her body is loud; her body is shouting. The party pretends not to notice as she rears up like a charging horse, stares down her nose at his simpering mess, and then walks away from him, taller with every stride.

'Becky, wait?' Pete tries to put his arms out for her, for her waist. He just had her in his arms, just five minutes ago. 'Come back!'

She stops walking, turns, raises a finger and points at him. 'You fucking *liar.* You set me up.' She is shaking all over. She drops her finger. Balls her fists. 'I've been SO HONEST with you. You fucking . . .' Her voice dies. She feels dizzy. 'I can't,' she says, moving away from him as he moves towards her. 'I don't.'

Dale watches her shape, fascinated. Excited to be near her again.

'Don't you dare fucking touch me, Pete,' she shouts as he reaches out for her. Chaka Khan is on the jukebox. *I feel for you* . . . 'I can't look at you,' she tells him. Shaking, holding her head.

'Becky, look. Wait . . . Please.' His arms are flailing, his forehead creased. She scowls at him. He feels himself becoming what she sees. 'I love you, Becky,' he says, but it sounds hollow. Hopeless. 'PLEASE?' he shouts.

She walks off. Fuming. Gloria runs out from the bar, follows her, but Becky shakes her head. 'I need to be on my own,' she tells her. Gloria stops following, Charlotte is behind them both.

Pete heads for the door, but hesitates. He turns, for Harry, for someone. Sees Dale, massive and still and grinning at him. Pete throws himself towards Dale. All of his strength shakes in his hands. 'I'll kill him!' he shouts. 'I'll fucking—'

They collide, like a rock thrown at a bottle, and smash. Pete grabs Dale's neck, but Dale is the bigger man and elbows Pete in the crown of his head and kicks him off him. Pete is skinny but drunk and full of indignant rage and charges at Dale again and throws two quick hard punches at Dale's nose. Dale sits back into thin air and falls, dragging Pete with him.

Graham, seeing his son switch, runs drunkenly to help and falls into the mess. He knocks over a row of glasses and drenches himself with beer. He slips on the beer he spilled and knocks a bottle off the bar. As he falls, the bottle lands on his head and he sits, stunned, where he lands, shouting drowsy encouragement at his son until he finds the strength to stand and launch himself at Dale.

David is outraged to see Graham trying to get involved. He throws himself towards the falling Graham and stands over him feeling his heart beating hard in his chest.

'Go on!!' Graham says. 'Hit me!! You can't hurt me!' He staggers to his feet and swings a blow that knocks David against the jukebox and makes Chaka Khan start again from the top.

Graham moves over towards him and is ready to kick his head in when he sees Miriam, horrified, emerging from the toilet.

Ron is firm and focused. Harry can see the curve of his eyeballs, two bloodshot moons.

'So, go on back inside and raise a glass with your old man and celebrate your baby brother getting another year older.

But . . .' He stares at Harry, hard. 'But, Harry, you need to lay your hands on that cash you took and that gear you took, and you need to bring that cash to Giuseppe's – and leave it with me. That's what you need to do.' Ron holds one massive hand up in front of Harry's face, index finger extended, pointing upwards. 'I know who you are, Harry. I know where your dad lives, I know your little brother's National fucking Insurance number. OK? I'm not fucking around, you with me?' His other hand reaches for Harry's neck. Ron holds Harry's throat for a brief moment, squeezes it. A slight smile curling around his lip.

Harry's getting dizzy, shooting pains are wrenching her insides. 'Fuck off, mate, you're all talk,' she croaks. Her head is pounding with the lack of oxygen. Her throat hurts from his grip. She stares him out, trying to keep calm, holding her breath.

Ron squeezes harder, enjoying himself. Looking at Harry like a cat with a wounded bird. He loosens his grip on her throat, lets her get a breath, takes her shoulder in his other hand and grips it hard. Pushes his fingers down into her muscle, pinching the bone. Smiling.

Becky runs out of the pub, falling towards the road. Sees Harry talking to Ron. Sees the face on her uncle, the menace at the edges of his mouth. Harry is holding herself together, or at least trying to. She hurries over, threads her arm through Harry's and smiles at Ron.

'What's this?' she says. 'Mothers' meeting?' She walks Harry off. 'Sorry, Ron,' she calls back over her shoulder. 'I need her for a sec.'

Harry says nothing. *Where's Leon?* Ron stands merciless and still like an iceberg.

Becky's breath is tearing in and out of her lungs. They turn the corner, slow the pace.

'Are you OK?' Harry asks. Becky shakes her head. 'What's happened?'

'I don't want to talk about it.' She holds Harry's arm tighter, leads her across the road and on to the high street. After a hundred yards or so Harry stops walking, ducking under the awning of a closed greengrocer's, pulling Becky to a stop beside her. Rubbing her throat.

'Why've you stopped?'

'I need to tell you something,' Harry says, looking around for Ron, for Leon. Staring back behind her over her shoulders, looking down the street the way they've just come and then swivelling to stare ahead at every figure, shrinking from every face that passes. Her eyes as wide and crazed as a panicked factory calf.

'What's wrong?' Becky watches Harry's screwed-up face. Harry stares dumbly at the sky, tears prickling. 'You got yourself in trouble with my uncle?' she offers.

'Yeah,' she says, reaching for a cigarette, putting it into her mouth the wrong way round. Becky stops her hand before she can strike the lighter. Harry looks at her, confused, and Becky takes the cigarette out of her mouth and turns it the right way round. Harry nods her thanks, looking worried, grateful. 'I think he's going to kill me,' she says as she lights up.

'What have you done?'

Harry can feel herself sweating despite the cold wind. The cigarette churns her stomach. She wobbles a little. 'I need to get out of here,' she whispers. Becky leans close so that she can hear her above the street sounds. 'I need to leave town.' Becky narrows her eyes. 'Tonight.' She tries not to be too dramatic about it. Becky stands with her, watching the trouble on her face. Harry pushes her knuckles into her forehead, holds the back of her skull.

'It's OK,' Becky tells her and Harry nods grimly. Stares around the street for looming silhouettes, aware of every dark doorway.

She looks back at Becky and feels the punch to the throat she always feels when she looks into Becky's face. She fights for breath, clambers off imaginary ropes and claws her folded body back to standing. Her heart rattles her ribs. The storm's coming; she can smell it rising up from the tarmac.

'Will you come with me?' She tries to say it quiet but it comes out fast and loud. It's been a long time coming but now there's no more time. She holds her breath, and waits. Everything is very slow. She watches Becky's chin, Becky's ears, Becky's left shoulder. She can feel Becky's eyes on her like cameras. Time is passing cruelly, every second bringing greater danger.

Becky notices the little curves beside Harry's nostrils, the smile lines, scared eyes as bright as wet stones. The sharpness of her cheekbones, the roundness of her cheeks. The little open face, small and tough and pretty. Stood there biting her bottom lip, back straight, holding her fag, knuckles pressing into her forehead. Becky walks towards her slowly. She gets up as close as she can and stands an inch from Harry's body, breathing, looking at her neck, her cheek, her eyebrows. They hug for a thundering minute, holding tightly to each other, like they'd fall down if they let go. Harry pulls away. Stares around her. No one's coming. She looks back, breathless, at Becky's lips, and everything evaporates. She sees Becky's kiss before she feels it. Slowly at first. A searching kiss, hot small tonguefuls of each other's mouths. Becky's hands on Harry's collar like Harry always dreamed of, fingertips across her neck, finding her ears, the tops of her small cheeks. They stand there kissing in the glow of the shopfronts and street lights, not blinking, the two of them breathing like animals.

The clouds open. The rain falls out all over the street.

Becky laughs then, and it takes Harry by surprise and she wants to kiss more, but before she can try Becky grabs her hand and they are running, up towards the roundabout. They take a breathless left and there's Leon, sitting in the car with the motor running. The money in the case on the back seat.

She lets go of Harry's hand, walks round to the passenger side, smiling a quick, dark smile that shakes Harry's blood before she gets in the car and closes the door behind her.

Harry tries to make sense of it, feels the clouds throwing their darts at her back. She glances over her shoulder towards the shouting voices outside the pub. She holds her forehead, taps her fingers against the drum of her skull. To run? Or stay and try and sort this out? Either way, they risk losing everything. Even if they give it all back, it's not safe here any more. She looks at Becky in the car. Thinks of her brother. Her arm pounds from where Ron had gripped it. She can still see his eyes burning down, feel his thumb on her windpipe. What will he do to them? She can't think. She opens the door and gets in the back, next to the suitcase.

They pull up outside Becky's flat. She lets herself in and runs to her room, looks at all the things that she has that she doesn't need or want or understand the use for any more. *Passport. Underwear. Phone charger. Wash stuff. How many clothes? These jeans? Phone charger. Passport. Where's that blue jumper? Which coat? Underwear.* She gets a bag and fills it quickly, moving round her room, seeing everything as if for the first time; all the things that are Pete's things, and all the things that are her things, that were either from him or about him or hold some spiteful memory. The phantom Pete follows her around while she packs; she can sense him there, sobbing in her knicker drawer as she digs around for socks. She's getting out. She's leaving.

Outside in the car, Harry grips her knees. Rocking from the panic. Every muscle tensed and sore. Her body diced to mincemeat, her mouth a mess of bullet holes from Becky's burning kisses.

RETURNING

a year later

Becky gets off the plane at Gatwick and walks through the arrivals gate without breathing.

London.

She moves, zombie-like, towards a faceless coffee counter, orders and sits at a table in a shiny armchair. In the bleached fake light of the airport arrivals lounge she is reminded of the ferry they crossed the Channel on together.

They were eight hours into France when she had phoned her uncle Ron.

'I've left town,' she told him. 'I'm OK.' She wouldn't tell him where she was. He shouted at her, called her irresponsible. Spoilt. As mad as her mother. 'Please don't hurt Pete or Pete's parents,' she asked him. She'd never got involved in her uncle's affairs before. She knew they were into some back-alley stuff. When she was young, things would turn up at the house; three hundred scented candles or fifteen massive boxes of Fairy Liquid or a crate of universal TV remotes. She didn't know where they came from. They were in and out usually within a week. He had supported her and her mother, and Becky was eternally grateful. She would never think to challenge what had put food in her mouth when she had no other means of feeding herself.

But this was different. She leant against the metal ledge in the phone booth; it was freezing cold against her back and she could feel it through her coat. They were deep in the French countryside, a village somewhere in the north-east. It was winter and there was ice on the ground. Harry paced at a respectful distance. Staring at the woods beyond, shrunken in the cold. 'I don't know what's gone on,' she said, 'but please, Ron, for me, leave Harry and Pete and their family alone.' Ron turned the phone blue with swear words. Screamed and shouted. Called her things she'd never been called. But she knew this to be a good sign. His silence was much more dangerous. This noise meant he was hearing her. 'I don't know when I'm coming back,' she told him. 'Tell Auntie Linda that I love her.' And she hung up and his screaming stopped abruptly and the birds sang in the cold quiet.

They'd spent eight months on the road. They kept away from borders. Neither of them had ever had nothing to do before. They couldn't stop touching: unbearable, electric, fanatical touching.

People tutted and huffed to see them kissing against petrol pumps. People frowned and shouted in Flemish or German or French as they paid for dry sandwiches and watery service-station soup and killed more hours, going nowhere together. The Pyrenees, Toulouse. Amsterdam and Utrecht. Hamburg, Berlin, Cologne. Places passed beneath them. Touching and holding and kissing and staring at each other's bodies and shouting with pleasure. They felt safe. Leon had journeyed to Barcelona with three quarters of the cash and left Harry with the rest, which she kept in her battered suitcase. They swapped it for euros in 500 bundles in various bureaux de change and made regular deposits into the bank account Leon had set up. Becky went to dance classes, Harry read biographics of notable club owners and sat peacefully in cinemas.

They entered a dream state. A time that would be recalled in future misery as the happiest they had known, and it was heavy, it made them both dizzy to carry it.

They found themselves in Belgium, where they went to seedy nightclubs and laughed with thin men who nodded to slow techno behind elaborate moustaches, and they stayed in rooms in old buildings with balconies that opened out onto car parks or busy market squares or the red light district. They spent days in bed and lay across each other, watching the world outside the balcony doors. Weeks and weeks and weeks of fucking and sleeping and sitting in bathtubs and fucking and smoking and fucking and waking up hungry and watching each other and thinking of breakfast, the light through the blinds, the light on the water as they walked beside the canal not saying much and then on to the next place, driving, hands on each other, the most boring song in the world on the radio and it didn't matter, it sounded quite good actually. They stood and drank coffee at high tables on the pavements in little towns with pretty names where the women carried shopping bags and babies and wore work clothes and the men got pissed all day.

They cruised down the Autobahn listening to Kraftwerk. They ate sausages and drank black beer in high-altitude Bavarian bars where the air smelt of bread and snow and they wrapped themselves around each other at night and fell asleep.

They crossed the Alps. Harry couldn't help herself, she burst into tears the first time she saw those mountains rising up into the sky and plunging down at the same time, reflected for ever in the perfect mirror of those Italian lakes.

Leon was back in London, keeping his eye on things. There was an email account that was checked every other day.

Summer began and everything was becoming increasingly intense.

Harry retreated into herself. Started biting her nails. Becky wondered where her life had gone. Itching to dance. The years she'd put into her training. For this? To run away like this?

She began to write a long letter to her mother and in the back of her mind was the thought that if she ever finished it, this one she would send.

The news came in June. They were in an internet café in Montepulciano. Harry's face went green as glass as she read it.

Pico was out of jail. He had requested that they meet. She felt like all the days that had passed since they left had just been treading water. Her body was a mess of panic. A walking ulcer. She drank constantly the rest of that day and passed out in the hotel lobby. Becky found her at nine in the evening, useless, frowning like a newborn baby, and carried her up in the lift.

Harry was to travel to a hotel in Fribourg the following Tuesday where she would find Leon.

The morning came up bright and warm. Becky spent the day thinking hard. She went walking round the old town, stumbled on a small gallery and she made her decision staring at stained-glass depictions of illuminated saints. She felt peeled. Shuddery and not herself. Harry's arms were like a vice these days, tightening, squeezing her into an impossible flatness. She stood, staring at these saints, these broken women, in attitudes of servitude and beatification, and they horrified her. She couldn't see them at all, only the idea of them. She felt like that. Not herself. Just whatever Harry saw. She gazed and saw time passing. Somebody's legacy. Not the women depicted but the person who had laid the lead and placed them there. Someone had made something beautiful and terrifying and left it for her to see. She walked slowly round the room. Her mouth hung open before vast images of sacrifice and contrition that seemed to chant the word 'purpose'.

That night Becky lay on top of her love and held her face and kissed her eyes and told her she was going to go back home.

They drove to the Italian coast and said their goodbyes to the roll of the ocean. Drank wine and ate pasta and smoked cigarettes and didn't speak much about what was going to happen next.

Becky told her it was better that they enjoyed their last night together rather than cry and fight. 'Let's just have this time and then let each other go.'

Harry was floundering. Nothing was clear. Her mouth was a trapped animal. And everywhere she looked, Pico stalked the background; his moustache, his bright white teeth. Pico, Pete. Ron and Pico. Pete and Ron and Becky. Leon. Pete. Pico. Becky. Becky. Pico. The eternal carousel within. Her bones felt ground to spice. *Don't leave*, she thought. But she said nothing.

They went to bed and didn't touch.

Becky stares at all the faces in the plastic airport light, all the families and loved ones reunited in the arrivals lounge, and she wipes her face with rough hands and bites back tears. Hard as she ever was. But coming home.

PETE WAKES IN A sun-bright bed. The broken slats are letting the morning flood the room in uneven waves. Bare floorboards stretch towards an open door, a threadbare red Moroccan rug. There is singing through the walls. The sound of people talking cheerful morning talk and laughter. In the room he lies in is a stuffed bookcase. A table by the window, a wooden chair before it. A framed Kandinsky print. A portrait of Haile Selassie. Ribbons and strips of cloth hang on hooks and are draped across a mirror. The words of the Desiderata are written in fluid lines across the ceiling. There are clothes all over the floor. And sheets of paper. Charcoal drawings. It is freezing. He listens to heavy boots on the stairs pummelling the bones of the rickety building. He is in a grandiose townhouse, falling apart. Recently squatted, inhabited by Spanish anarchists and trainee welders. They'd seemed alright to Pete the night before.

What was her name? He lies still, investigating his belly button.

She's standing in the doorway, naked beneath a long shirt, two buttons done up. She's having a conversation with someone Pete can't see. They're talking in a language he can't place. Turkish maybe. Berber. She has geometric patterns tattooed in white ink across her hips and they wind around her legs. She laughs. French reggae is playing from a distant speaker. There is the sound of frying and banging doors and the smell of toast and coffee. Pete hasn't been around noise like this in a long while.

Smiling, she shuts the door behind her. The noise is muffled now. She stalks the bare floorboards and places a cup of hot coffee on his chest. He wraps his palms around the cup to warm them. 'Coffee?' she says. 'No milk here. Vegan.'

'No,' he says. 'Fine.'

She sits on the bed and crosses her legs and leans so she can see out of the broken blinds. She holds her cup into her body. Pete watches the steam and her naked stomach. He gets up, scans the floor for his boxers. She watches him. He crouches, searches, aware of his body beneath her gaze. He finds his pants at last, pulls them up clumsily and stands tall in the cold room. They judge one another calmly in the milky morning light.

He has found himself flitting between two states recently. The first is his usual state: strung-out, stalking the streets of his youth, skunk-strange, coke-vexed, wanting to staple himself to strangers and push his body through the shuddering windscreens of accelerating buses. But the second state is newer, one that creeps up on him when he least expects it. He will notice himself pacing peacefully, weightless, enjoying the neon through the chicken-shop windows, aware of how pleasantly it illuminates the pallid faces of the lifesick children that patrol the strip. He's caught somewhere between raging self-pitying blame and a new softness, a sweet and settled feeling. Relief. To be alone at last.

The best thing is how good it is not feeling useless. He likes his friends again.

He's been getting out more. He's not afraid of everyone he meets.

Her shadow haunts every corner. She's in every woman he speaks to. His sister's hateful face makes him smash things up when he's drunk.

He misses her. It's like a rat's mouth eating him slowly. But he's starting to realise how funny and good people are. He's remembering the sound of his laughter.

He works now. Two jobs. Five days a week. Night porter in a cheap hotel. He reads all night. He's got new glasses. They make him feel like someone else.

He starts his shift at eleven at night, finishes at seven in the morning, sleeps till three in the afternoon then heads off to work a miserable shift in a pub kitchen washing pots. He finishes there and goes straight to the hotel. He's never had energy like this before. He likes the tiredness. It gives him something to do. He's still got no money. The council tax, the electric, the phone bill.

There are women everywhere. Now he knows how to talk to them. Maybe he's getting older. He seems to know what they are telling him before they've even spoken.

He understands her more with every passing day. He sees her much more clearly now she's gone. Sometimes, when he's with women, he feels like he's becoming her. It happens when he least expects it; he'll take his clothes off and move towards a woman taking her clothes off, and suddenly he'll feel so much like Becky that he'll forget how his body moves and he'll have to relearn what it is to kiss.

PICO GREETS HARRY LIKE an old friend. Grips her arms above the elbow gently and pulls her in to kiss both cheeks. He indicates that she should sit beside him. The restaurant is grand, everything brilliant white. A huge domed glass ceiling, mirrors line the walls. The waiters wear waistcoats and smart shoes. Harry sits down beside Pico and gazes around. She wonders what the other people in the restaurant think their relationship might be.

Pico orders for them both. He tips his face towards the waiter and speaks his demands without please or thank you, like a man too used to service. He orders seafood and salad and expensive white wine. Harry sits silently, not smiling. Watching the edge of the waiter's collar. The perfect slick of his parting. Pico stretches his arms around the back of the banquette they are sharing. Time passes like it's wounded, dragging itself across the restaurant.

Pico begins to speak quietly in Harry's ear. 'I know what happened, so don't worry for saying it, OK? It's easy now.' His breath is warm and smells clean, like cardamom and liquorice. 'I'm out now, so we start from scratch.' His accent is round and ripe as fruit. 'No worry no more.' Harry swallows, hot and shy. Her throat feels like it is crawling with insects. 'The man . . . Joey?' Pico's J's are Y's. 'Joey. He try rob you, no? I heard.' He watches the side of her face carefully. Breathes gently for a long moment, like an optician leaning in with a blazing torch, before he pulls his arm away and reaches across the table for bread, olive oil and the glass bottle of balsamic vinegar, sculpted like an upturned teardrop. His white shirt, his thin moustache. His cufflinks gold-rimmed St George's flags.

'Believe or don't believe, it's you to choose. But . . .' He widens his eyes, traces his moustache to its end, smiles kindly at Harry. 'I was going ask you take over, while I was inside.' He clears his throat, the olive oil held in still hands. Harry feels a wave of heat and sickness passing through her head. A plate of cracked oysters arrives on a tray of ice and they shudder in their shells like her stomach. 'But now, we see, there is debt.' Pico surveys the room, leans back into the padded seat and watches the blazing white world of spotless china and napkins and rich women discussing their business while subservient waiters bring them plates of red meat.

Harry looks at her knees and gathers her thoughts before looking up at the opposite wall and speaking in a panicked churn of sound, her voice too high in her chest. 'I don't want to owe you anything, Pico. I don't want to be in your debt.'

A silence stalks the table like a hungry wolf. Pico frowns. Carefully pools yellow olive oil and black balsamic vinegar in a small white plate, making a yin-yang which he admires and grinds pepper into. He wipes soft bread across the pool and folds it, dripping, into his neat mouth. He chews, swallows and wipes the corners of his lips.

'OK,' he tells her. 'Now. Here.' He taps the table with his thumb and forefinger. 'You have to pay your debts in life, Harry,' he says sadly. 'You work for me now, is what I say. I'm looking for a person who can help me, more direct. It's hard to trust when there's, you know, this . . . the money like this. It make people lose their centre. This money.' He sighs deeply.

Harry watches the serrated edge of the knife on her napkin, the uneaten oysters, cold and snotty. 'You come back, you work for me.'

Her heart is broken and she can't move and she wishes Becky was here to tell her what to do. Her body begins to shake. Pico can feel it. He is surprised.

'Your man tried to set me up, Pico,' she says, her tone a snarl. 'I trusted you and our arrangements, but that's what happened.' Her voice gets louder, the room swims. She speaks towards his ears. 'That money I took was my recompense, for the danger you put me in. If I hadn't been prepared to fight, he could have killed me.' She spits the words out, her body shaking. 'This money is my life insurance. I don't want to work for anyone. I want out. I want out of this.' Her voice is heavy now and thick and beaded with growls. She's been chain-smoking for weeks and her throat hurts and she's too scared to drink the posh water. She looks at him with dark ferocious eyes and Pico lets out a good-natured chortle. He leans his head down to rest on Harry's shoulder. He taps her arm, friendly as a man with his pet. He stays leaning there and the moment is paused in a strained still image. Harry is as awkward as always. Pico is chortling and patting her arm. He sits up, smiling heartily, to lean a pale kiss onto the top of her head and ruffle her hair.

'A good one,' he tells her. 'A good one such as you.' He giggles a little. 'People die for less. But you no scared of me that way.' He breathes deeply and raises his glass to his lips, sips thoughtfully. 'So what we gonna do then, Harriety?' he asks softly. Placing his glass back down on the spotless tablecloth and reaching across her for an oyster.

'Just let me go, Pico. I'll give you half the money back. But let this be the end of it. I want to come home. I want to draw a line under all this.' She blinks slowly. Waits.

'Home?' He leans towards her.

'Yeah.' She reaches for a glass, pours the cold clear water into her mouth. Holds it at the point of swallowing, lets it soothe her burning throat.

'You come home, you work for me,' Pico says, smiling. 'You stay out here, fine. But you get back to London, you work for me.'

Harry shifts in her chair, massages her jaw. 'No,' she says. 'I don't want to work for you, Pico.'

Pico's attitude changes. Something hardens in his eyes, some switch is flicked in his circuitry and he seems to take up twice the space he had a moment earlier.

'I understand you say it was a set-up and this Joey has been punish, you can trust. He pays the debt for you, he pays.' Pico cracks the knuckles in his thumbs and little fingers. 'But you refuse me? When I offer the work? When I say you come work for me? In friendship I offer this, and you say no?' His voice is quiet and monotonous. Harry is chilled. 'You think I'm not a serious man?'

Harry waits it out. Knows better than to speak before she absolutely has to. Pico waits too. The wolfish silence comes again. Hunting. A waiter appears but Pico waves him away with a flick of his hand. The gesture feels so rude to Harry that it makes her stomach ache. Pico sips wine. Eats a forkful of chopped bright leaves. Chews like a farm animal, which seems strange to Harry, given his delicate disposition.

Harry holds on to the table leg. Becky in her brain. Her heart an empty boot since the morning that she left. She has nothing to protect; it makes her stronger than she's been. Without Becky, what's the money worth? Without London, what's the dream? She shrugs. 'You can do what you like to me, Pico.' She levels her gaze. 'I'm finished with this work.' She stares at the side of his face until her eyes are sore. 'No more,' she tells him. Burning up.

HER LONDON HAS CHANGED.

Becky looks around for all the things that she has missed so much, but nothing is the same. The snooker hall has gone; its foundations are wrapped in construction hoardings and it stands four storeys taller than it used to, rapidly becoming another block of luxury apartments. The half-derelict bridal store and beauty bar where she used to get her nails done and pick up weed – the one that had the mournful mannequin in the window, dressed in the same peacock-blue sequin gown for years – is now a glass-fronted café with exposed brickwork and low-hanging lamps. She wonders what's happened to Naima, the woman who used to run the shop.

She'd been a friend of Becky's mum and she knew Becky's name before Becky did.

The swimming baths have been bulldozed, along with the old town hall where she used to go to playgroup. The old police station. Everything has been or is being turned into flats. The actual flats stand empty and black-eyed. Their windows smashed, their fronts ripped off. Their insides on display. Wallpaper and old sofas and kitchen units shivering in the rain. The area secured. Cameras like crows on the tops of the fencing. She stands and stares up. She feels like stopping someone and shaking them and screaming, *What's happened here?*

Becky watches all the strangers that she passes with increasing panic. Is it just her imagination or are these people really fuller in their faces? Glossier? Healthier? More robust? What's different? The streets are as busy as ever, but it feels empty.

She steps into Sunshine, holding down panic. They used to come here for breakfast every Saturday when they were hungover and she couldn't face seeing her auntie and uncle. She feels a hopeless sense of longing for that time and looks around tentatively, glad to see that at least the caff is still the same. Pictures of dogs dressed as aristocrats hang on the brown-tiled walls. Articles from the local paper are faded in their frames. Plastic chairs are nailed to the tables. People eat food from huge plates that are twice the size of plates. The chef has burned some toast and he is standing at the door flapping it open and closed, but the door gets stuck and scrapes on the lino each time it closes so he has to push it closed and then wrench it back open and the whole thing is proving quite dramatic. She sits at the table by the window and listens to what people are saying, only realising now that for all the long months she'd been away, she'd been unable to listen to strangers speaking. She sinks into it.

'Here y'are, love, dropped this.'

'Oh did I? It's not mine.'

'Well I don't want it. I got too much in my bag as it is.' The waitress takes the pen and walks off.

'They wrote me a letter, said the rent's going up at the end of March. I thought, what's the point?'

'Oh dear.'

'This is what I was thinking. I was thinking this is what I'm going to say – I'll say – it's ridiculous. They can't expect—'

'No.'

'It's just ridiculous.'

'You want a mushroom?'

'I'm not too keen on them.'

The chef opens and closes the door. His face is pouring with sweat. The girl whose toast is burnt eats her beans with a teaspoon.

'Well I've got the letter here anyway.'

'He's even saying that they're so bad they wanna do the two together. But they don't know if I'm strong enough.'

'No?'

'Over twenty-six years I've lived there and I've never had anyone talk to me like that.'

'So I looked at him, right in the eye and I said have you looked at my medical? I've got severe colic for one thing.'

'My Girl' plays on the radio. Memories of weeping at the cinema, Macaulay Culkin and the bees.

'He's a big guy, supposed to be a professor. He's a professor.'

'I thought – yeah, but are you in my shoes, mate?'

'I've got two titanium hips, I got nuts and bolts in me.'

She sits into it, like a bath. Drinks her tea. A man in a wide-brimmed hat and a fleece with a logo on the chest that says *Kent Park Equestrian Centre* has a tabloid paper spread flat on the table and his hands are pressed down against it, neatly pushing each crease out to the edge of the page. Reading the sports.

'What you doing over the holidays? Got anything?'

'Do you know, I'm dreading it myself.'

Two older women, one in a lime-green hoodie, the other in a brown-and-cream woollen jacket, are talking about the offers in Sainsbury's.

Becky could weep. Shakespeare's Sister on the radio. The smell of burnt toast is dying down.

'Lord Almighty, will you SHUT THAT DOOR.' A man with one high-soled shoe – medical correction rather than fashion statement – and lank ginger hair, bald at the top, small ponytail out the back, reads a council pamphlet about tax. His daughter is beautiful and has a red patent Alice band pushing her hair back, a pile of burnt toast beside her on the table top. The chef, a Turkish man with a beleaguered look, is being shouted at by everyone. He brings the girl with the Alice band a new plate of toast. She thanks him. Becky realises it's not the high-shoe man's daughter at all. She's got to be twenty at least. He's touching her legs. She looks just like the Ukrainian girl that used to massage with Becky a few years ago. Stunning in a troubling way. A packet of fruit pastilles sits open beside her fry-up, she eats a mouthful of beans and then a fruit pastille. The man she eats with reads the pamphlet. She smiles at him. She asks the waitress for a box, for the toast. She puts the burnt pieces away for later.

Becky watches the passing people and she could swear she sees herself, younger, arm in arm with Gloria and Charlotte, walking past, smoking fags, but it isn't them. It's some other teenagers, with too much confidence, singing along to X-rated American pop-rap blaring out their mobile phone speakers.

Becky finishes her tea, pays and smiles deeply at the woman. She feels her heart skip to be called 'babes' like that.

Becky approaches the Hanging Basket and stands outside it. She leans against the railings, smokes a cigarette and doesn't look at anyone that walks past. Last time she was here was the night she left.

It's three in the afternoon and there's a gathering of good drinkers singing Van Morrison on the benches out the front. One guy has a guitar and he's standing, strumming it, throwing his head back, one foot on the bench. The others sing with him, smiling. Shot through with life and pain, and lonely, lonely days, they hold hearts and glasses and sing their battered souls out. Their haggard faces are deeply lined. Becky glances at the shaven-headed woman, the pretty teenage boy, the square-faced strong-man, hard as nails, the peaceful quiet drunk whose grey dreadlocks brush his ankles, the pot bellies, skinny shoulders, bright eyes, closed eyes, red eyes, missing teeth, gold teeth, crooked teeth, the sharp suits and old clothes and battered shoes she's always known. The pretty young drunks with their dogs and their hoods, tattoos and piercings, heavy old boots, sexy as new love, looking like an advert for a life you never had the guts to live. The curly-haired women with the swear words and the sharp tongues. Their hands on their hips, cleavage and perfume, and their lives stretch into the distance like railway tracks behind them. Always laughing. They blow kisses Becky's way; she returns the gesture. Holds their arms at the elbows as she passes. They swing their bodies to the song. Today they will drink to the point of delirium, cheerful and drug-racked. This place is the jewel in south London's shackles.

She pushes through the doors. Her bag gets caught on the handle and she has to twist awkwardly to free it. The doors hit her legs as they swing back. She steps inside, tucking her hair behind her ears. She pulls at her clothes, aware of herself, touches her hair again. Nothing's changed but the flyers on the wall. She stares around wondering how it's supposed to feel. And then, there she is.

Gloria is talking to a woman in her fifties who is leaning backwards against the bar. The woman shakes her head, throws her hands up. Gloria laughs and goes to pour the woman another glass of wine. As she does she sees Becky and almost drops the bottle, but she has been a barmaid too long for that.

'Hi,' Becky says, waving like a tourist posing for a picture.

'You idiot. Just standing there,' Gloria says, taking the money for the wine and coming out from behind the bar to embrace her.

'Oh my God,' Becky moans, collapsing into her arms.

'Becky Becky Becky Becky.' They hold each other at arm's length and look at each other, then hug each other again. Becky's face is pressed against Gloria's hairclip or something and it hurts but it doesn't matter because they need to hug like this. But it does hurt. Gloria squeezes her tighter and tighter saying, 'Oh my God oh my God oh my God,' and Becky doesn't know what to do with her hands. She holds them together in front of her belly while Gloria takes a step back.

'Let me have a look at you then,' she says. 'Where've you fucking been for one thing?'

Becky shakes her head. 'Not yet, G. Just give me a minute, yet, is that OK?' Becky holds a hand to her head, Gloria wraps an arm around her shoulder and squeezes her close, kissing her head before moving back behind her bar.

Becky stands in front of the bar, Gloria stands behind it. They look at each other. Becky feels nervous suddenly, silly.

'What you having then?' Gloria asks her.

'Dunno. Are we drinking?'

'Probably should be, shouldn't we?'

'Vodka, lime and soda then,' Becky says, tapping on the bar with her fingers while Gloria turns to fix the drinks. There's a rail that runs round the bar a couple of inches off the floor. Becky stands with one foot on it, leaning her elbows on the bar, looking around. The cars go past outside, the TV is on and Gloria puts the drink down in front of Becky, standing opposite her with her arms crossed. One hand on her earlobe, spinning her hoop around.

'What you been up to then?' Becky asks Gloria.

Gloria takes her time to answer; it feels like gravity has tripled. 'I've been here, doing this, haven't I? Working. Same old.' Gloria gets a packet of cheese-and-onion crisps out the box and throws them at Becky. 'Still your favourite?' Becky nods. Opens the crisps. Starts eating them. Two, three at a time. Drinking her drink in small, staccato sips. 'What about you?' Gloria asks. 'What've *you* been up to?'

Becky shakes her head. Eats crisps. Gloria raises her eyebrows. 'I worked a bit, we drove around. Then we had a little flat we lived in.'

'You and Harry?' Gloria spins her hoop.

'Yeah.' Becky nods again.

'And you just got back?' Gloria asks her.

'Yeah.' Gloria thinks that her friend looks thin and tired and far away.

Becky slumps a little over the bar. All these months have passed and she can't work out where to start or whether she even needs to start. 'You look really well,' she says. 'Healthy.'

'I been going boxing,' Gloria tells her.

'Boxing?' Becky says.

'I had some trouble.' Gloria breathes out loudly, blinks fast a couple of times.

'What kind of trouble?' Becky asks her.

'Nothing really. Couple of guys one night.' She shrugs.

'In here?' Becky looks around at the pub, the regulars.

'Another pub, down the road.'

Becky watches Gloria. Her wide eyes sweep the room for drinkers getting to their last swigs. Her body, as sure as stone, all the edges neat and compact. Tall and strong and golden brown. Broad, open face, like an ancient goddess. *Gloria.* Becky feels her pulse pick up its speed and go hurtling through her at the thought of her friend in danger.

'What happened?' she asks her. 'What did they do?' Her voice is heavy and fast.

'Nothing,' Gloria says calmly. 'I fought them off.' She speaks matter-of-factly, no big deal. She spins her hoop, stands with her weight on her right hip.

'You fought them off?'

'Yeah.'

'Jesus.' Becky shakes her head. They stand in silence for a moment.

'With a bottle,' she says, smoothing her hair down.

'A fucking *bottle*?' Becky is horrified. Her face screwed up.

'Yeah.' Gloria sighs.

Becky's panic constricts her words, they come out strangled and strangely pitched. 'Were you alright?'

'In the end, yeah, I was fine.' Gloria smiles at Becky, her voice level as always. Becky winces, shakes her head. 'I was alright. And I like the boxing. Tommy keeps saying he'll come with me, but he never does. He's getting fat as well, don't tell him I told you.'

Becky watches Gloria's hands, gold rings on three fingers, the thin tattoo that bracelets the wrist.

She turns to serve a customer. 'Yes, darlin', what'll it be?'

ACKNOWLEDGEMENTS

My producer, Dan Carey, who was the first person to hear any of these ideas and who encouraged me to make it a story.

My agent, Becky Thomas.

My editor, Alexa von Hirschberg.

Alexandra Pringle at Bloomsbury.

My US editor, Rachel Mannheimer.

I spent a month writing at 57a in Whitstable, thank you Katie Gordon for allowing me the space.

I wrote the bulk of the final draft in the back of the tour van driving through Europe and the United States. I have to acknowledge the patience and support of my bandmates and crew; Alex Gent, Anth Clarke, Archie Marsh, Caragh Campbell, Clare Uchima, Dan Carey, Ed Feilden, Francesco Caccamo, Gareth Routledge, Georgia Barnes, Hannah Tee-Dub, Kwake Bass, Liam Hutton, Raisa Khan, Sebastian

Renaud and Toby Donnelly, who've been with me touring for the last eighteen months. Love you lot, my Welfare Unit.

Elaine Williams, thanks for chatting Paul Gilroy, the Lewisham Riots and knife crime with me. You're a G. And I'm blessed to call you mate.

Lucy McGeowen for the invaluable blow-by-blow description of years spent working in cafés. Thank you sis.

I had huge help from three dancers: Daisy Smith, Jennifer Leung and Julie Cunningham. Big, big thanks to you all for your generosity and time. I want to acknowledge that some of Becky's thoughts about dancing and choreography come directly from conversations I had with these three. Especially Daisy Smith.

The staff, drinkers and friends of The Birds Nest pub.

I began to tell the stories which would lead to this story in my first play *Wasted*. I want to acknowledge Paines Plough, who commissioned that play, and especially James Grieve and Stef O'Driscoll, who directed it and who supported me through that time. Also, the cast of *Wasted* – Alex Cobb, Alice Haig, Ashley George, Bradley Taylor, Cary Crankson and Lizzie Watts – who bought my characters to life. And the tech team and crew who put it on.

Brand New Ancients was the next step. I want to acknowledge the support of the Battersea Arts Centre, especially David Jubb and Sophie Bradey, in the writing and staging of that piece. I need to acknowledge the musicians and crew who played that show with me over the course of the tour:

Alex Gent, Ben Burns, Christina Hardinge, Emma Smith, George Bird, Ian Rickson, India Banks, Joanne Gibson, Kwake Bass, Matt O'Leary, Natasha Zielazinski, Nell Catchpole, Raven Bush, Sarah O'Connor and Tara Franks.

I need to acknowledge the love and support I have had from my family: my parents, Gill and Nigel Calvert. My sisters, Laura, Sita, Ruth and Claudia. My brothers, Jack, Matt and Martin. And little Bess and Zig. All my brilliant cousins. All my uncles and aunties. My grandparents, who I love and miss.

Need to acknowledge my brother Jimmy Davey and my good good friends that haven't been mentioned above: Adam Bloomfield. Billy Carabine. Callum Locke. Dawna King. Evie Manning. Freddy Vernon. George Latham. Kieran Barry. Kitty Zinovieff. Luke Eastop. Maisy Siggurdson. Niaomh Convery. Sophie McGeevor. Sam Soan. Mica Levi. Thank you guys so much.

Want to acknowledge south-east London; even though you're changing, you're still my engine and my anchor.

Want to acknowledge Murphy; my wolf.

Charissa Gregson, Emma Brook, Rebecca Danicic; thank you for your time and attention, your patience and encouragement.

Assia Ghendir, thank you for your love.

Finally, I want to acknowledge the help I have received from India Banks – in this novel and in all the things I've written. But especially for the guidance in understanding Becky better and for the support in writing 'A Hammer'.

A NOTE ON THE AUTHOR

Kate Tempest was born in London in 1985. She has published two plays, *Wasted* and *Hopelessly Devoted,* and two collections of poetry, *Everything Speaks in its Own Way* and the acclaimed *Hold Your Own*. Her epic poem, *Brand New Ancients,* won the 2012 Ted Hughes Award for New Work in Poetry. Her album *Everybody Down* was nominated for the 2014 Mercury Music Prize. She is a Next Generation Poet. *The Bricks that Built the Houses* is her first novel.

A NOTE ON THE TYPE

The text of this book is set in Bembo, which was first used in 1495 by the Venetian printer Aldus Manutius for Cardinal Bembo's *De Aetna*. The original types were cut for Manutius by Francesco Griffo. Bembo was one of the types used by Claude Garamond (1480–1561) as a model for his Romain de l'Université, and so it was a forerunner of what became the standard European type for the following two centuries. Its modern form follows the original types and was designed for Monotype in 1929.